THE LIES THAT BIND

Ed Protzel

TouchPoint
Press

THE LIES THAT BIND by Ed Protzel
Published by TouchPoint Press
4737 Wildwood Lane
Jonesboro, AR 72401
www.touchpointpress.com

ISBN-10: 0692591885
ISBN-13: 978-0-69259-188-8

Editor: Tamara Trudeau
Cover Design: Colbie Myles, colbiemyles.com

Visit the author's website at www.edprotzel.com

First Edition

Printed in the United States of America.

To Janet, my muse, wife, friend.

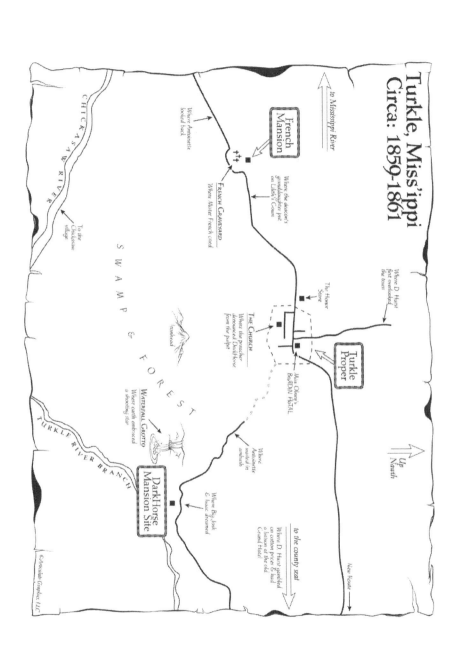

Turkle, Miss'ippi
Circa: 1859-1861

to Mississippi River

French Mansion

Where Antoinette looked back

Where the doctor's granddaughter put on Lilith's Gown

FRENCH GRAVEYARD
Where Mister French died

To the Chickasaw village

CHICKASAW RIVER

SWAMP & FOREST

Ironhead

WATERFALL GROTTO
Where earth embraced a shooting star

TURKLE RIVER BRANCH

DarkHorse Mansion Site

The House Store

THE CHURCH
Where the preacher denounced deathknow from the pulpit

Miss Olean's BoARDIN' HoTEL

Where Antoinette waited in ambush

Where Big Josh & Isaac dreamed

Where D. Hurst first overlooked the town

Turkle Proper

Up North

to the county seat
Where D. Hurst gambled on cotton prices & had a liaison at the old Grand Hotel

New Route

©Arcidale Graphics, LLC

Section I

Elysian Scrubland

Chapter One

1859, Turkle, Mississippi

The setting sun recoiled from the shadows descending upon the Mississippi swamp. Glancing desperately over his shoulder, Durksen Hurst urged his roan mare on through a foreboding stand of weeping willow draped with Spanish moss. Nearby, a barred owl cried out and flapped away, its wings echoing through silent slough and backwash, through tangled vine and creeper. Day creatures slunk to hidden dens; hungry night creatures began their prowl.

If the mob chasing Hurst captured him in this desolate place, the fact that he was innocent would do him no good. His former friends and business partners might be convinced to give him a hearing. But they'd been joined by a host of ragged scum with no stake in the outcome, whose sole purpose was to humiliate him in the most savage manner their twisted imaginations could devise, to gloat and taunt him as he writhed and cried out in his death throes.

In the pervading dusk, Hurst drew rein to give the roan a badly needed blow. After three days of ramshackle escape, Hurst's Memphis-bought suit was now mud-splattered and torn, his body and mind past exhaustion. He took a deep breath in the chill evening, trying to relax away the painful knot his scrambling flight had worried into his empty stomach. When he exhaled, a cloud hung in the air like lazy fog over the nearby bayou.

I must sleep.

By a sympathetic stretch of a lonely woman's imagination, Durksen Hurst could be considered handsome. Forty years old, hungry slim, and of above average height, he had a square jaw, a strong face. Yet the feeling that he was different was always with him. Part Seminole on his mother's side, he had her high cheekbones, thick black hair, and brown, sparkling eyes. Looking neither Indian nor white, his quick glances often caught people staring at him, trying to figure out "what" he was. Even the Chickasaws who raised him from the age of ten never fully accepted him. No matter how hard he tried to act like the locals in any given town across the South, he always had to overcome people's sense that he was foreign, as if there was some disharmonious odor about him.

He dismounted, noting the twisted lay of nearby swamp. A Tupelo gum tree, hollowed out by termites, obscured an elevated patch of dry land just ahead of the dead end where he stood. To Hurst, the thought of a clear spot of grass-covered earth promised more comfort than a boarding house pillow.

Must sleep.

He led the roan through ankle-deep water onto solid ground. Continuing on, he passed a fallen black gum, not stopping until he and the roan were concealed in the dappled shadows of a mature cypress.

Sleep.

He paused to listen. In the distance, over two hundred yards away, his trained ear detected urgent shouts. Horses and mules crashed through the brier and scrub behind him and up ahead; he was surrounded. His only hope was that his pursuers would not accidently stumble upon him.

Two hours earlier he'd plunged into this familiar stretch of Chickasaw wilderness like a fish diving for safety into deep waters. Night, and the Indian Territory could—again—provide refuge. There might even be old acquaintances at the Chickasaw village a few miles further south who still remembered him. If he made it that far.

Sleep. Must.

***

"He on foot now. Over by the big cypress, straight ahead," a frantic, wilds-wise Isaac whispered, shrinking back into the shadows where the eleven other black faces crouched among the foliage, fear suffocating them like quicksand.

"What we gonna do?" Bammer whispered.

"We gots to bury him in the swamp," Isaac said, "befo' he turn us in for that reward money they give for 'scaped slaves."

"Bury him... You mean, kill a white man?" Long Lou asked, horrified.

"W-we ain't gonna do nothing of the sort," Big Josh said authoritatively, his natural stutter becoming pronounced. "Ain't we already in it b-bad enough?"

"Maybe we should turn ourself over to him and get us out of this swamp, away from that killer Chickasaw, anyhow," Little Turby suggested.

"And get ourself hung?" Long Lou objected. There were many grunts of approval for that sentiment.

"Sh-h-h," ragged Isaac cautioned. He put a hand to his ear, listening hard. "They's more comin'! All over the swamp, ahead, behind, on all sides. Must be chasin' the man."

"Wh-where can we hide?" Big Josh asked, hot blood rising in his ears.

9

He turned to Isaac for the answer, but Isaac had already disappeared into the tangle.

"He gone," Bammer said. "Nobody gonna see that swamp rat till he want."

"Then w-we on our own," Big Josh concluded. "Just hide down all night. Lay over in that brush yonder. And be quiet. We s-see what we do in the morning, if we ain't caught tonight."

***

By chance or fate, Hurst knew he was just a half day's ride from Turkle, Mississippi, and too weary to resist its pull. A patchwork of frame houses, white-columned mansions, and outlying cropper shacks, the town rose like a specter in his mind, fearsome yet somehow comforting. Of all the forgotten places he'd run across, this crossroad hamlet was the only one with a name, the last place he'd had any semblance of a family. The place from which, as a ten-year-old boy, he had sought refuge in these very woods, enabling him to evade another deadly mob, its appetite whetted by Hurst blood on its hands.

In a moment of fatigued clarity, it seemed to Hurst that since the day he'd left the kindly Chickasaw tribe, a budding man seeking to begin his random travels, he'd been unconsciously circling Turkle in an ever-decreasing arc, like an insect being pulled into a swirling whirlpool.

Sleep...

All at once, Hurst was overwhelmed by a profound sense of loss. Old enough to be wiser and still hitching his hopes to another threadbare illusion. Now he had fallen into the pit where all his sky-high dreams and clever plans, his fine-figuring and fast-talking inevitably left him—broke, desperate, and alone.

He'd called his latest scheme Everybody's Company, and it was his best yet. With an agreement signed by the county bank to lean on, he'd gathered enough petty investors to make small loans to hard-pressed farmers, even to wives and widows. With a few dollars in their hands, ordinary people could start a little business or replace a broken farm implement and prosper. And it was working better than anyone had imagined—even him! He had come to believe Everybody's Company would spell the end of his vagabond existence, of his decades-long chain of overly ambitious busts. Everybody's Company would help dirt-poor families condemned to breaking bad soil throughout the South. And make him rich.

Or maybe not. He'd been wrong before, carried away by his wild imagination and overweening vanity.

A bitter lump formed in Hurst's throat as he thought of the folks who'd put their trust in him. *These people did kindnesses for me. Had me to supper.*

It was so unfair, and utterly irrevocable. She had their money—and his, too. The raw young woman he'd partnered with, so tender in the night, had stolen their company money and was undoubtedly halfway to Texas, the standard destination for thieves and cutthroats. He chided himself for being too trusting again.

An ugly, fat cottonmouth slithered through a water-filled ditch, causing the nervous roan to spook and back away wild-eyed. Too spent to chase the animal, Hurst jammed a boot onto the exposed roots of a fallen swamp ash, resisting the tug from the rein with all his strength, while speaking soothingly to the panicked beast. The rawhide burned his palms, but he held on, pulling and twisting. The animal was powerful in its panic, but he couldn't let go. Finally the roan settled, leaving Hurst's hands stinging and bleeding.

Hurst clenched and unclenched his fists trying to get feeling back in them. It irked him that his survival was dependent on a beast moodier than a circuit preacher's wife. These he knew well; he'd shared hurried grappling in the weeds back of churches and Chautauqua tents with more than one, unbeknownst to their fire-eyed spouses saving souls inside.

Finally.

He tied the roan where she could nibble the sparse grass. Then he spread his blanket on a mound and fell face first into the soothing aroma of fecund earth.

***

As the rising sun peeked above the mist and trees, something struck the sole of Hurst's boot, startling him awake. He resisted the intrusion, mumbling a protest, but no matter which way he rolled, the irritating blows kept coming. Then he remembered his predicament and attempted to wake up. Glancing through the haze of slumber, trying to focus, he saw what appeared to be a great bear hovering above him. Heart racing, Hurst scrambled back, scuttling crablike on elbows and heels to get away from the creature.

"Wh-what you d-doing here?" the figure stuttered.

Hurst rubbed his eyes. Standing there was a mountain of a black man. Hurst appraised the ebony Goliath, a man with arms as big around as tree trunks, a broad chest and shoulders to match. He looked capable of lifting a wagon. The man's clothes were shabby, like a field hand's, creek-clean, but

11

in bad need of repair.

The man, who appeared to be in his late forties, glared at Hurst, face muscles set in warning, but the pose couldn't hide the natural smile lines around his eyes.

Hurst caught his breath. He had slept at the edge of a stand of pine, through which he could see a wide, gently sloping clearing beyond. Not fifty yards down the hill, beside a creek, there sat more than a half-dozen skillfully-built, roughhewn lean-tos, of saplings and wire. The setup was too solid for a mere encampment and not of Chickasaw design. This giant was not alone.

An eerie quiet descended, as Hurst sensed eyes upon him. He had a pistol hanging from the roan's pommel, unloaded, but when he located the animal it was grazing twenty yards away. Clearly, any thought of a bluff would be useless against the number of men needed to occupy a camp this large. Besides, Hurst didn't believe in threatening strangers, especially with an empty weapon. It was bad for business—and could be fatal. He rose shakily to his feet.

Time to make the situation a common one. "I'm Durksen Hurst, Durk," he said in his friendliest manner, offering his hand and doing his best to conceal the fear gripping him.

The big man merely studied Hurst. He noted the interloper's suit was a poor imitation of their late master's go-to-gathering duds, wrinkled, mucked up, and worn, as if he'd been traveling hard, and fast. His hollow face told the whole story.

"Th-they calls me B-big Josh," the man said.

Hurst appraised him, head to foot. The man had simple looks, and his tongue stumbled. Add in black skin, and a hasty person might brand him a fool. But Hurst could sense the man was accustomed to giving orders, not taking them. Like he was a plantation field boss or a steamboat gang boss.

"How many of you are there?" Hurst asked. "Six? Nine? A dozen?" Big Josh refused to answer. "What are you folks doing on Chickasaw land?"

"Ain't none of your b-business," Big Josh replied, unaware that he'd made a fist.

Without warning, a skinny, ragged black man strutted from the pines to confront Hurst. The wild-eyed scarecrow wore a patchwork of rough-cut animal pelts, which hung in layers over a shirt many sizes too large. His hair dangled in long, unkempt flows. Likely a swamp fugitive, Hurst concluded.

"What you want here, white folks?" the wild man challenged.

Hurst could hear voices chattering in the surrounding woods, as if the man's bravado had broken a spell of silence.

"This h-here's Isaac," Big Josh said, still watchful.

"Durk Hurst, Isaac," Hurst smiled, hand extended. "Some folks call me 'Dark Horse.' A while back the Chickasaws got their American mixed up, and it stuck."

While he waited for the handshake that never came, ten more men brandishing farm tools filtered in from the brush and wordlessly surrounded him. A shovel on the back of the head was all it would take. Everyone knew it. He looked from face to face, but everyone was inscrutable, Sphinx-like.

He was relieved to see the ten were clothed like Big Josh, indicating they, too, were displaced field hands. Hurst figured Isaac must be a local runaway living in the woods who hitched on with the rest; meaning the rest came a distance to be there.

He wanted to ask, where's the white man with you? But he saw the fearful looks they gave each other, the questioning glances toward Big Josh, the desperate way they gripped their tools. They had no white man to cover for them!

That explained their terror; there were rewards for turning in free-booting slaves. If he reported them, they faced beatings—or worse. Unfortunately, they might believe it's their life against his.

Escape would require delicacy and patience. Hurst couldn't let on that he had deduced their predicament, but he was burning to know how they'd become trapped here, and he was never a man to control his curiosity.

"Y'all ain't staying on this dusty rock, are you?" he asked. No one replied. "A hidden field is fine to grow corn for squeezings. Maybe even feed Isaac here. But as many as you got, you'll starve."

Suddenly, Hurst was gripped by a vision. As had happened with his most profitable—and his most disastrous—schemes, an entire plan, fully formed, flashed like a sunburst in his skull. He was struck by the magnitude of what he saw as their mutual good fortune. They would be like explorers in a book, making first landfall in a New World with its great, untamed forests and rich soil.

"Why, I've got a beautiful piece of land not a day from here, laid out like it had plans drawn on it reaching to the sky. Fresh water, fields, timber! It only needs us to fill in the lines with crops and barns and such.

"My *plantation*," he added, emphasizing the word so they wouldn't think he wanted them to be outlaws. But, in truth, that's what they could be considered, himself included.

"Plantation!" Isaac exclaimed, waving a finger in Hurst's face. "Look at him!"

Two of the group narrowed their eyes, brandishing their tools. The rest stirred, exchanging glances.

"H-he look like a charlatan man," Big Josh said.

"Yes, I've had to play the charlatan," Hurst admitted with a wry grin, "though always an honest one."

"He a ricochet-talker," Isaac said. "Don't believe nothing he say."

"Listen, my friend," Hurst replied, "I never told a lie I didn't believe in myself."

Big Josh eased Isaac back to a polite distance. This stranger wasn't much, but he was the only straw they had to grasp.

"Why sh-should we go wit' you, Mister Hurst?" he said, testing the waters. "You ain't got no papers."

"Papers?" Hurst responded, startled. Then he realized Big Josh was talking about their being his slaves—that's all they'd ever known.

"No, no, there ain't gonna be no slaves on our place, on our plantation. Your manumission is the only paper I'll sign, which will make you free men. *Legal*. I promise you." He watched his words register on the men's faces. Big Josh's scowl returned, but Hurst could see he'd made his point.

Slavery! As a boy, Hurst had barely listened to his father's ongoing rants against the South's so-called peculiar institution. Through a child's eyes, Hurst had seen dark people wearing ragged clothes, working in the field as part of the natural order, just as he'd seen squirrels living in trees, fish in the water. He didn't know any better, except for what his father had told him. But when he left the Chickasaws at seventeen for the wider world, he saw clearly the violence inherent in maintaining that order, and it frightened and repelled him. In retrospect, his father had been right.

Why, as Hurst had blown around the South, clutching onto dirt-work when he was desperate, he'd often felt like a slave, even compared himself to a slave. He'd slept on a pallet in a one-room shack and ate food unfit for livestock.

But Hurst knew a slave couldn't pack his goods in a handkerchief and leave his troubles behind like a white man. For a time, Hurst had spoken forthrightly against slavery, not in drunken diatribes like his father, yet still condemning the practice. But he soon learned what his father had failed to learn: there was no talking to people on the subject. Even trying to defend individual black men led to beatings. Now, though, he saw a way around this disease infecting the land—to their mutual benefit.

But Isaac was having none of it. "Ain't no lawyer-paper in Miss'ippi gone make us free. Who gonna sign it? You?"

"But what…what if y'all become partners with me? Working alongside me? The plantation will be ours, all of ours!" Hurst said loudly, dropping the other boot. "Do you understand? Partners?" He could see the big man's mind working. "We'll split the money even, share everything. What's hard on you, will be hard on me."

That was the deal he'd always offered, the old Chickasaw way. Not that some white partners hadn't robbed him blind in the past, even after shaking his hand.

"Now if you're waiting for a better offer than that," he said emphatically, "I wish you luck."

"Man could talk a rabbit into a trap," bone-skinny Isaac said disdainfully.

"But our plantation will belong to all of us, Isaac," Hurst countered, offering his hand with his warmest we-got-a-deal smile. "Partner."

"Partner, ha!" Isaac spit. "Even if you ain't lying—which I knows you is even if these fools don't—you think them white folks in town gonna throw us a Sunday church social? Le's make a pie to welcome our new black plantation owners," he mocked. "We gots to get us north, Josh."

"Tha's right, we gots to get north," two men chimed in.

"We got to get somewhere," Big Josh said.

"From Miss'ippi?" Hurst said. "How?"

Big Josh placed his hands on his hips. This tormented vigil on Indian land offered no solution to their suspended and vulnerable state. And venturing back to the white world was a bed of vipers, especially considering their master's fate. When your best hopes amount to either starving in the woods or risking a rope, it seemed hard times would only get worse.

But Hurst's wild words about an even wilder offer was disorienting, as if a ghost had appeared to invite them to the moon! "Partners"? The whole notion was crazy. This man was no rich planter, so what would they be stepping into?

Maybe they'd be stepping into honest work, and cover. Josh had been General's big boss, knew everything about running a plantation. That's all he wanted, work and a home again, all any of them wanted, except maybe Isaac, of course.

On the other hand, he wouldn't put it past this trickster to convince them to walk into a trap and get a reward for their capture.

"If we goes back, we just more run-off slaves," tall Long Lou said.

"Maybe they think we kill General," towheaded Bammer suggested.

"We gots to bury him in the swamp or we be wearing hemp round our neck," Isaac said, squeezing his own for effect.

Hurst looked Isaac over. *This man is more like me than any of the others,* he thought. *Not believing in anyone or anything; as torn loose from the world as I am.*

Isaac saw the subtle change in Hurst's face and, not sure what to make of it, let up on his anger and fear—for the moment.

"Back off, Isaac," Big Josh said, jerking the swamper away like a rag doll. It was time to test this stranger.

"All right, Mister Hurst," Big Josh ventured. "We was brought here by a Chickasaw chief. We had no choice."

"That doesn't sound like any Chickasaw I've ever known," Hurst replied, growing suspicious. *Why would they lie?*

"He k-kill General," Big Josh added.

Hurst mulled over this claim, then an explanation dawned on him. He ran a finger down his cheek. "This chief, does he have a scar, a knife scar?" No one answered, but Hurst saw their faces. Waves of fear gripped him as his punctured plan poured into the dirt.

"That's bad," Hurst said. "He fits his name; the man's got the conscience of a wounded wolf, and twice the appetite."

Wounded Wolf! Hurst thought. *No wonder these men are terrified; so am I. They must be desperate to get away.*

But Hurst knew the uncertainty inherent in their dilemma. Further delay could spoil the deal, could even lead to tragedy. He needed to force their decision now!

Fearing a fatal blow, he pushed his way through the wall of men surrounding him, toward the roan, his ears attuned to every potentially deadly *clank* and *rattle* of their tools.

"Y'all just stay here," he announced. "At least until Wounded Wolf finds some white men who'll trade horses without papers for slaves without papers. I'm sure they'll be kindly folks, looking to serve you with a bow and scrape."

As he reached his horse, he heard a babble of whispers behind him.

"Wait," Big Josh called after him.

Hurst stopped in his tracks, a smile spreading across his lips.

"Now I ain't promise nothing yet," Big Josh continued, rubbing his chin in thought. "But if we go, *if* we go, s'pose we pretend to be your slaves when folks come around? We could do that. Least we be some place besides here."

"That would work! Sure!" Hurst exclaimed, leading the roan back to the group. "We could keep our deal a secret. And you'd still have your manumission papers to fall back on." Hurst liked the way the man's thoughts were blowing. He felt like he was playing for his life, and the first two cards dealt to him were kings.

Then Big Josh fixed him eye-to-eye. "They catch on to us, we be in jail trouble, prob'bly gets a wh-whipping. But *you*, bein' the white man, you be in hangin' trouble."

Chapter Two

"Mother, it's dug, the grave is dug," Devereau French gasped, his throat tightening. Devereau abruptly entered his mother's great master suite on the second floor of the mansion, wearing his finest black satin suit. His slim, pale figure advanced up the irregular pathway formed between his mother's priceless relics, his boots clicking against the hardwood floor. Although Devereau was thirty-one, the rosy softness of his naked cheeks and his slight stature gave one the sense of an adolescent boy, not a mature man. Lightly freckled and frail, with cropped auburn hair, this morning he appeared a trembling, emaciated stick figure, with eyes bloodshot and swollen.

"Then go down and stick him in the ground," his mother, Missus Marie Brussard French, demanded, clearly not about to budge from where she sat at the ornate chessboard that dominated her room.

"You're not attending your grandson's burial!" Devereau exclaimed, dry voice cracking.

He stared at his mother, waiting for a response, but Missus French obstinately clenched her jaws. Her eyes scanned her elaborate chessboard in jerks and starts, refusing to look up from the game she was studying.

"Are you spotting God a pawn like you sacrificed me?" Devereau cried sardonically, his voice rising. Again he was ignored. "You'd go down to sign papers for the bank, but not to attend my child's funeral?" He dabbed his eyes with a handkerchief.

Missus French exhaled and slumped in her chair, cradling her forehead in her palm. Reluctantly, she fixed her eyes on him. "Do you think I have the slightest intention of going down there where those fools can gawk at me? Me, the village villain?"

A shaft of light from the opened door spilled across her, revealing a colorful, child-sized chair positioned beside her desk. A local furniture maker had adorned the tiny seat with brightly painted bluebirds, grapes, and wildflowers. Now it sat empty.

"And send someone to remove this chair," Missus French added. "I've seen enough of these damn bluebirds."

***

Dust motes drifted and settled from the scarlet velvet curtains, which Missus French's servants kept tightly pinned to cover her formidable banks of windows. This morning, the ponderous drapery blocked out any dregs of sunlight filtering through the early haze and drizzle outdoors.

With her days and nights virtually indistinguishable, the reclusive widow spent most of her waking hours tucked back in a shadowy, confined clearing in the deep recesses of her bedroom, overall a chamber more than twice the size of any other in the house. This living area, about a third of her quarters, contained simply her bed, working desk, a guest chair, her bath, and her chess table. A padlocked chest, the object of overwrought servant speculation, completed her appointments.

On the rare occasions that Missus French ventured downstairs, the house servants would hurry in to clean her constricted habitation and be done before she returned, thus avoiding any unpleasant encounter with her. They had long ago given up even thinking about polishing or dusting the estate's most precious fine furnishings, all crammed haphazardly into the remaining two-thirds of the room. Stuffed among these artifacts, collected from capital cities across the South, languished rare paintings and statuary; chests filled with forgotten caches; rich, rolled tapestries; and sets of artisan-worked gold, silver, and jewels.

This morning, a single candle flickered, casting faint glimmers that revealed the grotesque heaps and piles in the room's cluttered expanses. It was as if Missus French were a ghost inhabiting an unspoiled island in a sea of tarnished treasures. Beyond her haunt, the layers of dust rested in triumph from the tops of the highboys to the indiscriminately-stacked, gilt-framed ancestral portraiture, upon which generations of spiders had left their own epic ruins in frantic wisp-strands.

Although Missus French was in her early sixties, time had not greatly diminished the legendary beauty that had been both her boon and her curse. She never painted her face unless planning to meet with outsiders; hadn't for many years. Nevertheless, only fools and youth imagine classic beauty will diminish over time. In good light, a glimpse of her would still take a stranger's breath, like seeing a rude charcoal sketch of a despairing Cleopatra.

This morning, Missus French sat in fierce delirium, wearing the black she'd worn every day for the thirty-odd years of her widowhood. Her gray-streaked raven hair cascaded down her back, uncombed, like a river at flood crest. Her hands, their gnarled state concealed in white gloves, rested in her lap.

"Cheat!" Missus French started in horror and anger, her voice breaking unnaturally to speech as if from a nightmare, seemingly protesting the travesties of a capricious and malevolent God.

She tried to avoid unwelcome, intruding thoughts of the child's demise, to ignore Devereau's disturbing presence, by concentrating on her precious chess table, her favored preoccupation, but found it impossible to adequately divert her attention. Without warning, she began to rearrange the pieces on the inlaid squares of ebony and ivory. In short order, her deformed fingers placed the set's intricately-carved gold-leafed horsemen, aristocratic churchmen, elephant-borne towers, and foot soldiers back to the exact position of mortal combat they had occupied when she and Devereau quit in mid-game over a month before, an act of a prodigious memory that was, also, her boon and curse.

The only anomaly among the two miniature baronies were the kings of her armies. She had replaced these with stylized porcelain female statuettes, pieces inconsistent with the set's design and, of course, of the wrong gender. She even named one of these monarchs "Devereau," her most frequent, but not favorite, opponent.

On the rare occasion someone was lured to *French Acres* to play against her, she would meet them downstairs in the study, where a less elaborate chess set awaited her victims—visitors were never permitted upstairs, the sole province of the two surviving Frenches. Most of these unsatisfying contests were against antagonists dependent upon her good will—her lawyer or one of the cotton traders from the county seat at Lethe Creek. These men politely endured defeat, sacrificing modest monetary stakes to keep on her good side. She had long ago found it impossible to attract challenging, high-stakes gamesmen to a backwater nowhere like Turkle for worthwhile matches, which would require a journey by steamboat to an improvised river dock and, from there, by French carriage on dirt roads. Certainly not to play against a woman, even one of her means and reputation. It didn't help that no bragging tales about wagers won against her ever crowed forth; only bitter cautions against Caissa's deftness on the sixty-four squares.

Satisfied that the pieces' arrangement duplicated her suspended game with Devereau, Missus French tapped the board with her forefinger repeatedly. "Move, it's your move!" she ordered, hoping, inexplicably, to entice Devereau to complete the long-abandoned contest.

"Do you think I'd let you spring your trap on me today?" Devereau shouted in fury, turning over his king. "If that's what you need, Mother, I fall upon my sword. End of game. Forever!"

But Missus French merely returned her attention to the game, as if by an act of will she had made Devereau and his hysterics disappear.

"Rest assured, Mother, I will not be there when they drop *you* in the ground either," Devereau spit angrily, sharp as an arrow meant to penetrate the heart no one believed inhabited his mother's ribs.

"Just seal me up in my room here with my chessboard and all these worldly goods," Missus French replied with a hurt smirk.

"Of course, Mother," Devereau said angrily. "Don't give that little boy another thought."

"Listen," Missus French said, "I took a terrible chance bringing Louis Edward here for you! His death hurts me as much as it hurts you. You'd best learn to lose a child without all these maudlin theatrics. The sooner the better."

"What do you know about losing a child?" Devereau asked, a parry and thrust meant to maim, but his mother's stare made him lose his breath.

"I know," Missus French said, then waited for the remark to sink in. "You must gather all your strength or this will drive you insane. You'll be useless to us."

Growing dizzy, Devereau settled into the chair across the board from her. "What are you hiding?" Devereau demanded.

***

As Missus French's son and surrogate, Devereau brought her business correspondence and carried her edicts to the region's merchants, freeholders, and slaves. At times she would descend the stairs to seek the advice of a select few of her business associates, the region's elite bankers and cotton brokers, then send them away to carry out her secret instructions. Otherwise, her orders were relayed by hired messenger or by slave, depending on the sensitivity of the missive. On rare occasion, when she wished to foist some confounding decision on her harried son, she would send him an invitation to meet for supper in the first floor dining room. She had to send these summons well in advance because receiving one would invariably set off one of Devereau's incapacitating headaches.

Actually, Devereau had received clear title to the plantation upon reaching his majority of eighteen-years-old. Until that day, his bedroom had been adjacent to his mother's, a proximity he blamed for his melancholy nature. He had grown up suspecting that his mother's hearing was so acute she could detect his rustlings in bed at night, even his breathing, and that she knew from his footsteps where he had been and what he had done. Even now, he never felt free from the eyes and ears of her network of spies.

That special birthday morning, Devereau awoke singing, the first time the startled servants could remember him doing such a thing. Without taking breakfast, he had Missus French transported to the suite she now occupied at the opposite end of the otherwise deserted mansion. Devereau had already seen to knocking down the wall between two of the mansion's largest bedrooms, which accounted for the chamber's vastness. This way, he told his mother, she would not be distracted by stirrings in the kitchen downstairs, nor by his comings and goings.

French then ordered the cream of his mother's priceless collectibles to be stuffed into the greater part of her solitary boudoir, which the frightened servants, hurrying to be done and retreat, performed randomly with no plan or order, thus accounting for the room's warehouse-like quality, for its sole irregular path exposed by a break through the random jumble. In effect, Missus French's new habitation became a virtual wealth-and-mother storage chamber. To everyone's surprise, Missus French seemed pleased by her newfound isolation.

But Devereau did not celebrate this move as an act of personal liberation. How could he? In the years leading up to his majority, his mother had liquidated practically every chattel of any value upon the estate. Methodically selling the livestock and equipment, she single-mindedly funneled the proceeds into her account at the Turkle Bank, in which she held a majority stake. The astonished Devereau soon discovered his legacy encompassed merely the land and whatever buildings sat upon it, plus a few trusted house servants. To grow a crop on the denuded and depopulated plantation, the helplessly strapped son had no recourse but to contract with his mother at usurious rates. This arrangement created an ongoing dependence, leaving Devereau with as little freedom of action as in his youth.

People still whisper about the day, a month before her transplantation, that Missus French sold her field slaves downriver. As the astonished citizens watched, the pitiful hands came wailing and crying in a barefoot mass the twelve miles down the dusty road to the river wharf, to be loaded like cattle onto a steamboat she'd hired. Unbeknownst to anyone, she had actually sold the field hands to a straw party that she owned. Devereau was forced to sign a long-term bond to purchase them back, a burdensome obligation he had only recently paid off.

His predicament was impossible to hide. People believed that Missus French still controlled Devereau, moving him about like one of her chess pieces. Devereau had, in fact, become an erratic substitute patriarch for his mother, who directed him through her dupes and hirelings as best she could.

He resisted her manipulations, but in vain. He had long ago learned that if he fired or sold, in the case of a slave, anyone he believed was reporting his activities to his mother, she'd only replace the poor wretch.

Instead, he learned to distrust everyone with whom he came into contact, an education well-funded by his mother, who monopolized his attentions through any means she could devise, the most successful of her enterprises. The whole of Lethe Creek County was terrified of the unpredictable and often vindictive Missus French, and, as a result, her son Devereau's encounters with the county's denizens were invariably brief and cold, businesslike and done.

Folks were always careful to call him "Mister French" to his face; no one ever called him "Devereau" or any endearing nickname which might make him want to tarry, lest a careless remark reach his mother's ear. Behind his back, Devereau was referred to as "French", at best, or scorned using vulgar terms that suggested he was odd, "not right" or worse.

Highly educated by personal tutors from New Orleans, Devereau had nothing in common with a citizenry without much, if any, schooling, with a rural community who used pronouns and such by social convention and self-interest, not by book learning.

***

"It was a brilliant gambit," Missus French remarked, "but the child's dying spoiled my entire combination. Well, the damn epidemics take hordes of them, so what can you expect?"

"That little boy was one of your chess maneuvers?"

"Don't be a fool. Didn't he sit in my lap and call me Maw-Maw? Didn't I wrap my arms around him? But yes, Louis Edward could have fulfilled us both in so many ways—so many ways. Hell, he could have brought you a wife."

"A wife!" Devereau screamed. "Now I know you are insane."

"At least there'd be papers and a ceremony, if not conjugal affection. A grown man of twenty-eight is expected…"

"Thirty-one, Mother, I'm thirty-one."

"*Thirty-one*, with no wife, no sweetheart. A man rich enough to marry into some favorable alliance, much less barnyard any farm girl. It's unseemly."

"But a wife?" Devereau whispered, horrified.

"Yes, a wife, to dispel the rumors. People do wonder, if you haven't noticed."

Devereau rose, trembling. Face drained of blood, he sent a chest

23

crashing, spilling its silver goblets across the floorboards with a hollow clatter. He stumbled back the way he'd come, down the long twisted path between his mother's hoard. When he reached the door, he turned.

"I hope you are prepared to run *French Acres* by yourself, Mother," he cried threateningly. "Because I am going to New Orleans or Memphis or somewhere civilized. I warn you."

"I'll take the plantation back. The lawyer says I can do it!"

The inevitability of the trap in which Devereau lived overwhelmed him. He stormed out, slamming the door.

"You hate me more than anyone. I can't blame you," Missus French said, a tear catching in her throat.

Without warning, she was blinded in an ocean of milky white. Fire shot through her head, her temples, her forehead, and the room began to swirl. She stumbled to her bed and fell upon it, groaning and cursing.

"Damn, Devereau," she cried, "if only you'd act like a man!"

***

Shaken, Devereau French hurried through the hallways, each a line of closed doors concealing abandoned bedrooms once occupied by the prolific French clan. He pulled first one glove, then the other over his small, delicate hands and straightened his jacket.

"Sits in that dusty old mausoleum," he grumbled under his breath.

A fresh handkerchief was silently handed to him by a servant as he passed.

Without warning, his knees began to tremble, and he stumbled, almost collapsing. His shoulders began to shake, his whole body erupting in painful sobs; he couldn't catch his breath. Couldn't breathe.

Never to hold my little boy again. Never to feel his tender softness, his moth-wing-breath on my neck, on my breast, gone forever.

"Here's rue for your grave," he muttered softly, a rhyme he had chanted when he was little and sadness overtook him. He envisioned the tiny alabaster face he would never see again, sealed in the coffin outside.

He tried to go on, sing-songing softly with the weakness of a dying child.

"Rue, rue, rue, rue. Here's rue for your grave, rue for mine too
Rue for your grave…"

Tears consumed him again, threatening to tear apart his insides. Devereau covered his face with his handkerchief and, weeping uncontrollably, settled weakly onto the floor. He had often suffered black, black melancholy. But this one was darker, blacker than any. He couldn't endure any more. *Only a pistol can relieve me,* he anguished. *I'd trade French Acres for one…*

The pair of mourners at the graveside, the preacher and the sheriff, would just have to stand waiting in the rain.

Chapter Three

"It was the strangest thing," the old woman said. "She been watching our house, from over there in the woods, is what I think. Then around suppertime, when she saw that it was only us, only this old couple making do out here by ourself, she come to the door begging, but most polite-like, like she's not really begging, you see."

"Tied her horse behind the cabin," her husband, Earl, added, "out sight of the road. Piece of horseflesh like I never seen, not in these parts."

"And where was she runnin' to," the old woman asked, "a-way up here in the middle of nowhere? A city woman liken that? Oh, she was something, all right, long, pretty black hair tied up under that beat-up old hat. Awful tight-lip, you see, but when she did speak, talking fancy-like, with manners just so. Her fingers sholy ain't done no hoeing, I will tell you that. And very awkward-like with asking for seconds, like she was accustomed to servants at hand and didn't know how to be around just folks, if you see what I mean. Oh, she was running from something."

"Or to somewhere," Earl interjected.

"Wore some kind of fancy riding clothes," the old woman noted. "I sewed up her sleeve, and it was softer than a baby's bottom. Imagine wearing Sunday church material liken that to ride a horse. With britches, like she wanted to be taken for a man. Well, I guess, a woman like that on the run through country like this…"

"A body'd sholy have to be a fer piece to mistake her for anything but a woman," her husband interjected.

"Hush, now, Earl. No, she weren't no man. The Lord given her more than anybody's fair share of lovely, I will say. Though you could see in them big dark eyes that, as if payment for that beautiful face, He'd given her more than her share of trials. And so tired, poor thing! Fell asleep 'fore I pulled the blanket to her shoulder, bless her heart."

"Who or what do you think she was runnin' from?" her husband asked.

"And where to?" his wife added.

***

The rain fell lightly like restrained tears. Beneath the threatening skies, two burly men looking like masses of white dough dressed in black stood near the open grave beside the miniature coffin. Reverend Jedediah L. K. Cain wore a hangdog expression tailored by his wife's skilled needle to fit like his burial suit. Bake Gowan, the rotund sheriff, a bachelor, practically burst out of his Sunday suit, as if it had shrunk or been made for a smaller man. His pants grasped for dear life to his thighs below the massive overhang of his belly.

The pair was dependent on Missus French's largesse, like most folks in Turkle either were or hoped to be, and so could not refuse her request to be there. Completing the meager group of summoned mourners, a handful of black field hands waited at a respectful distance, quiet and watchful. In one hand they held their battered hats, in the other the digging shovels.

The neglected French family graveyard in back of the mansion had long ago gone to scrub. With a number of toppled and shattered stones lying fallen among wild vines and weeds, it was surrounded by a knee-high fence, slats broken and absent like missing teeth. The weeping willows gave the thirty-foot square an ominous, gruesome feel; empty, like death itself. Children didn't play here.

At the head of the freshly-dug grave stood a black headstone, smooth except for the eight words carved onto its surface:

Suffer the Little Children to Come Unto Me.

Nothing else. No name, dates, or words of endearment.

The men shuffled from foot to foot. It had been a long wait in the dampness and chill, and they had begun to wonder if Mister French had changed his mind and failed to send word.

"Most pitiful buryin' I ever seen," Bake whispered, scratching under his belt.

The preacher hushed him. The door to the mansion opened and a pale Devereau French stepped out, his movements slow, unsteady, as if he were lost. French was followed by Annie, his personal maid, holding an umbrella over him, more to stand beside him for courage than to shield him from the drizzle. Annie, an aging black woman, was reputed to be the only person in whom French confided.

The preacher glanced at Bake, a signal that they had both guessed right. *She* didn't even have the decency to come down, not because the child in the box meant anything to her; people believed that woman valued no one. But apparently her son had invested some affection in the child.

No one had seen the boy until five weeks before, when Devereau French showed up at church leading the child by the hand. Rumors about the boy spread like wildfire, but even the most active gossip knew nothing of the youngster's origin or purpose.

French stopped five feet from the open grave, as if the spot was a port in a blinding storm. There he stood, hunched, brushing his eyes with his sleeve, trying desperately to hold in the tears. If he let go, he knew he'd open a floodgate, and he couldn't allow people to see that display. He stared silently at the coffin, drawing upon his faded will to remain stone-like, his slowly contorting face belying his efforts. Annie remained behind him, holding the umbrella, the rain falling on her as it did the rest of the bareheaded gathering.

The preacher waited for a signal, but seeing there wasn't going to be any, opened the Book and started mumbling words in a monotonous undertone. Meanwhile, Bake and the field hands stared at the ground, pretending they didn't know or see.

After the preacher closed the Book and said a few final words, two of the field hands effortlessly lowered the lightweight coffin. And then it was done. Annie wiped tears away with her palm.

Dreamlike, French floated to the graveside, seemingly blind and deaf. He dropped to his knees and stared into the chasm for what felt like hours, as if he wanted to join that little coffin. Then, shoulders shaking violently, he covered his face with his handkerchief, rose, and ran awkwardly back to the house.

Bake waited until French and Annie disappeared inside the mansion, then signaled the rest of the field hands over to finish.

"That's the loneliest man on the earth," Bake whispered.

The preacher nodded knowingly.

***

"Agreed, partners?" Hurst said, offering his hand.

Ignoring the gesture, Big Josh grasped Hurst's wrist and pulled him close, wrapping his giant left hand around Hurst's neck. "Just remember, *p-partner*," he said, "if partner you is, I can snap your neck with either hand. If you thinking 'bout any reward, think 'bout th-that."

Big Josh released Hurst and turned to his group. "You want to see if the land this man be talkin' about is any good?" There were no objections.

Everything seemed to pause, momentarily frozen. Hurst looked the men over, as if seeing them for the first time, and they stared back at him. The realization washed over everyone that their hopes were now wrapped up with each other, as dubious as their prospects seemed. The air seemed alive and liquid, menacing, yet somehow hopeful.

Elated, Hurst pulled his pistol from the bag hanging on his saddle. The group flinched, but Hurst aimed it in the air.

"By the power vested in me by our partnership," Hurst pontificated, "I hereby dub our empire *DarkHorse*, my Indian name." Seeing no objection, Hurst shouted, "Your honors, to *DarkHorse!*" and pulled the trigger.

Click. The empty chamber released the tension. One after another, smiles appeared. Then they began to laugh, hard, holding their stomachs, till they were howling and falling on the ground.

Empty pistol has sealed more deals than all the numbers in my head, Hurst thought. *We're going to need every trick in my bag, and some I haven't thought of yet.*

Big Josh began to introduce everyone: young Little Turby, who had an intelligent, quizzical expression; Old Moses, an elderly man in soiled house servant's livery, the only one not a field hand; tall Long Lou; strong Bammer; the rest.

Muscled Bammer ventured, "What if that Indian come after us?"

"Don't worry," Hurst replied. "I'll make a deal with him." How, if a deal was even possible, was another matter.

"Can we take the mules and wagon?" Long Lou ventured. "They belong to General. Or did."

"He won't need them," Hurst replied.

"Load up," Big Josh ordered loudly.

Old Moses, the white-haired former house servant, worked himself slowly to his feet. "I gone run the Big House like I run General's place back home. Get me away from here, white folks."

***

Big Josh worked to rearrange his thinking, preparing to lead everyone to the new land, but his line of thought was tangled. A dazzling light had only recently entered his life. She was a field hand on the French place. The first time he saw her, she had reawakened feelings he'd assumed would never return after his wife died.

Ceeba was a big woman, like he was big, but as tender of face as he'd ever imagined a woman could be. Only a week before he'd managed to sneak over to visit her in the French slave quarters, a long trek each way, just to talk in the moonlight and hold her hand. He knew from the look in her warm brown eyes that she wanted to be with him, too.

Now they were going to accompany this stranger to somewhere he claimed was across town. Big Josh had promised he'd come to see Ceeba Sunday, and now he didn't know when, or if, he would ever see her again. Would she think he'd forgotten her? Would she fear for him? He felt his chest twist.

But this Hurst deal was their chance, and everyone was depending on him. He had to put her out of his mind, to not picture her face feeling deserted, hurt that he didn't show.

So was the life of a black man. You clutch a glowing hope to your chest, then it is torn away—along with a bleeding hunk of your heart. You suck in your breath and go on.

Chapter Four

Growing up, Devereau French prided himself on never crying—nowhere anyone but his handservant Annie could see him, anyway. Throughout his childhood, he endured whatever hurts his mother laid upon him and never showed fear or remorse. Even when she beat him, he stood rigid and took it, staring angrily into space until his punishment was over. If he wanted to cry, he waited until his mother was away. But lately, perhaps the last five years—seven years?—there were days when, without warning, he could barely hold back tears. Often he found himself drowning in an all-encompassing despair that wouldn't go away no matter how much he wished to make its oppressive presence pass.

Returning the feathered pen into its inkwell, French pushed away his papers. He couldn't add one more column of sums to his wealth, or write one more check to a supplicant supplier, or sign one more agreement to conspire with brokers against the cotton markets.

French could tell tonight was going to be a bad one. Outside his bedroom window, the sky was overwhelmingly black; no stars or any moon visible through the dense, omnipresent clouds. Fierce downpours had battered his walls with ever-increasing anger, punctuated by violent lightning, drenching the world outside with savage fury. Periodically, it would pause briefly, only to resume its assault with increased force.

His heavy smoking jacket buttoned against the chill, French stared out the second story window at the spot where the tall cedar once stood within reaching distance. When he was small, the cedar had been his gateway to the high-walled, enclosed gardens below, and beyond to the mansion's back quarter.

Wiping his eyes and blowing his nose, French remembered the day he had vowed never again to cry…

He was five. He'd already done it four times in the last two weeks without his mother catching him. He guessed she'd gone away somewhere on business, as she still occasionally did in those days to manage her investments: her regular rounds to the banker, the cotton broker, and the lawyer.

She never announced her departure. Before she left, he would hear her feet approach his door, then the key fumbling at the lock until it clicked. He was expected to study or amuse himself in his room until she returned.

Being in the rear of the mansion, he couldn't hear the servants bring her carriage to the front, nor could he hear it depart.

When she returned it was always the same in reverse. He'd hear her rapid footsteps, her always-gloved hands fumbling to place the key into the lock, the key turning. Then her footsteps would fade away, without ceremony or acknowledgment.

So that day, he thought she was gone. When the key turned and the lock clicked, he tiptoed to the door as he had been doing in earnest the last two weeks. With racing heart, he placed his ear against the oak door; not that he expected to hear her leave, but that he might hear any unusual movements if servants were still around. The entire wing sounded deserted.

But still he waited, listening for what seemed forever, holding himself there long after he was sure.

Gathering his courage, he tiptoed back across his room and opened his window, then climbed down the cedar slowly, clinging onto one branch with his arms while his feet felt below for the next, always careful not to tear or soil his velveteen suit. When he was on the bottom branch, he dropped to the ground, rose and brushed himself off meticulously, making certain he got every flake of bark off his outfit, lest his mother notice.

Within a few minutes he found his two friends outside the back gate and followed them around, trying to learn their games.

This day, he let them into the garden: Caleb, the nine-year-old white boy whose rheumy-eyed father did odd jobs around the mansion, and Doody, the smallish seven-year-old son of one of the French kitchen slaves. Even though frail Doody was two years older than Devereau, the boy was the smaller of the two.

Caleb ran to the large oak, unbuttoned his pants. "I gonna water this tree," he giggled.

Doody ran up beside him, untied the rope around his waist, dropping his ragged pants. "Me, too. Come on, Devereau. Ain't you gonna help?"

"My-my mother says I can't," was little Devereau's shaken answer as he stood in awe and horror, watching the two boys' pee arch downward onto the oak's great roots.

"That witch!" Doody laughed.

Then, terror. His mother came rushing from the study. She was dressed as he'd never seen her before, wearing a low-cut satin gown that revealed the roundness of her breasts. Her lips, eyes and face were made up to accentuate her breathtaking natural beauty, and her smell was different. But belying that inviting facade, her face was contorted with anger.

He turned to run, but his mother's hand hooked the back of his collar and pulled him roughly to the ground, knocking the wind out of him. Had she been hiding, watching for him? Only in retrospect would he conclude that she had had a visitor to the house that day, one she wanted to conceal from him; she hadn't gone anywhere. But why would she dress like that? Only as he neared adulthood would French imagine the kind of visitor she had invited, and why the man had come.

"What are you boys doing? Get the hell out of here. If I ever see you two again, I'll cut them off, and you know I will."

Caleb ran off through the garden and out its gate in absolute terror, trying to hold his bladder but dribbling down his pants. Doody followed, holding his pants about him as he hopped and stumbled away.

She slapped Devereau once, hard on the bottom.

"How come I can't ever have any friends, Mother?" the boy cried, tears running down his cheeks. "Not even one!"

"Because you're a French," she growled, half-screaming at him. "Do you want to live in a 'cropper shack? Or in the quarters?"

Oh, *he thought,* imagine if I could stay with Caleb's family or with Doody's; hearing their talk and laughter, smelling their food cooking, and luxuriating in the intimate atmosphere of their homes.

"Yes! Could I, Mother? Please," he pleaded, his shoulders shaking as he tried to sniffle back tears.

The wrong answer. Infuriated, his mother began to beat him in earnest, savagely, out of control, raining blows as he lay on the ground trying to cover himself, his tears flowing.

"Live in the … I'll teach you, fool!" she shouted, the blows increasing in ferocity. "You aren't like other children, you hear! They'll rip your skin off with a big knife and burn you alive!"

She pulled him to his feet and half-dragged him into the house, down the hall and up the stairs to his door, where, in her agitation, she had more difficulty than usual inserting the key with her gloved hands. After opening his door, she pulled him to his bed and threw him down on it. While he watched wide-eyed, trembling with fear, she ripped the cord free from the curtains and used them to tie him to the headboard. That done, she stormed out of the room as he cried after her, begging to be set free, to be forgiven.

She slammed the door and locked it. Within an hour, bound to his bed, he could hear men below his window cutting down the grand cedar, then methodically chopping it up and hauling it away. Finally, their voices and the work sounds ceased. Later, as dusk crept into his room, he could hear men working farther off, nailing up the garden gate from the outside.

Then silence, a silence unbroken for the rest of the night, save for his cries for Annie or his mother to come and untie him, pleadings which became desperate shouts when he had to empty his bladder and his bowels. But no one came, not even Annie. After resisting for what seemed forever, with no relief, he wetted and dirtied himself and laid in his filth all night, miserable and afraid of the consequences. As darkness descended over him, minute by excruciating minute, hour by endless hour, he became terrified that he had been abandoned there to starve.

That's when the father-dream started, a fantasy that would give him some modicum of refuge as years went by. Sometimes he escaped into it even now, although less often, his adult daydream more troubled than his childhood imaginings. In the dream, his father was his protector, a dignified, benevolent figure who loved and held him. A man who protected him from his mother.

No, he didn't know how to play; he'd never learned. But in the father-dream, his father played with him out in the garden. But the games weren't very good, and he quickly outgrew them. But one part of the dream he did not outgrow, the part where he nestled in his father's arms beneath the shade of the absent cedar. Just the two of them talking quietly together, young French telling the man about his troubles. That was French's favorite part of the dream, the warmth, confidences, safety, resting in his arms. But that, too, was fading.

The next morning it was light when he awoke to the sound of his mother and Annie in his room. His mother ordered Annie to clean him up and change him for breakfast; then she disappeared. He didn't see her again that day. It was then that he vowed never to let his mother make him cry, a vow he had failed to keep an uncountable number of times.

The wall-enclosed garden with the boarded-up gate began going to ruin that day. Under Missus French's orders, no one ever entered it again. The seeds of wild weeds and trees blew over its walls and grew helter-skelter, obscuring its paths and overtaking its original plants and flowerbeds. Most of the domesticated flowers, left untended, died off, choked by the hardier roots of briars, vines, and saplings, as the plot metamorphosed into rugged overgrowth and wild offshoots. Now, after almost thirty years, the entire area was nothing but a mad tangle, a lost garden never restored, not even by Devereau himself.

He never again saw Caleb or Doody, nor Caleb's father nor Doody's mother. It was as if they'd vanished, like he'd dreamed them. Probably fired and sold off by his mother, he surmised long ago. Throughout the remainder of his childhood, Devereau had never made another friend; his mother saw to that. Even today, he doubted he'd know what to do with a friend if he had one. And his prospects of that changing, never good, were dimming.

But French did not see this as the primary tragedy in his life. He'd had a lover once, unknown to Turkle, but the reality of living intimately with someone not dependent on his largess—someone unwilling to be commanded—startled him with its ferocity. He had returned home in tears, his face bruised and lip bleeding.

The real tragedy was that the only thing French really longed for—a child of his own—he would never touch, never hold. The new headstone in the family plot supplied haunting proof of that. And so French's life remained void, meaningless.

The rain outside resumed, at first fitful, then becoming a torrential downpour that crashed against the window like a child begging to be granted entrance to another world. But that child was lost long ago, and the world no longer had any window worth escaping from. Nor would there ever again be any garden of magic delight upon which to descend.

***

She was in a hurry, furious, passing through the labyrinthine mansion without glancing aside. She turned the corner to face the long hallway leading to her son's suite, a corridor lined by rooms empty for decades, by doors long closed. She carried a candle to navigate this hated stretch on the second floor, windowless and, therefore, lightless, even on the brightest day. She took a deep breath, then continued.

As she made her way down this final hall, her mind was flooded with visions of the time when her husband had been alive and these rooms peopled by Frenches. She passed a door only loosely attached to its shattered frame.

They were both naked, she and the young French cousin from Alabama. As she went to kiss him, in one motion he gripped her hair, then picked her up and threw her onto the bed, following hard, his stinking breath fast, almost choking...

The next day, her leering husband dragged her to the room. He forced her to watch as he shot down the boy right before her eyes...

She passed a nailed-up door.

They surrounded her, her husband's red-faced brother reeking of alcohol and tobacco, and two of their drunken uncles. At a word, the brother grabbed her wrist and then the three of them were on her, tearing at her dress…

Dispelling the thoughts as best she could, she burst into her son's bedroom. The room was lit by four candles, its curtains open, but it took only a moment for her eyes to adjust. Devereau was packing a trunk.

Startled by the intrusion, French stopped and turned. Seeing his mother, he nodded grimly, a sarcastic smirk spreading across his face. *Of course! When they brought the trunk up, one of the servants must have told her to gain some minuscule reward, no doubt.* But that wasn't going to stop him; he resumed packing.

"Where do you think you're going?" his mother demanded.

He threw two pairs of shoes into the trunk, one hard, one colorful. "I'm moving to New Orleans for a year, Mother. Maybe longer. Just like father went there and found you! Remember? Don't try to stop me."

Missus French let herself down heavily into the nearest chair. "You? New Orleans? What nonsense. I'll take *French Acres*. You know I'll do it."

French bent over, expelling his breath as if hit in the stomach, touching his forehead to the trunk. Then he straightened up to face her.

"I don't care, Mother," he pleaded, "I-I want a child. A child of my own."

"That boy's mother is coming to Turkle. Perhaps to kill me."

French rubbed the throbbing in the back of his neck, a precursor to another of his dreaded, severe headaches.

"I can't blame her, Mother. But don't worry, I've hired practically an army of riffraff to protect you," he said wearily. "Hell, you can hardly avoid stepping on one."

He tried rubbing his temples, but his left eye and eyebrow had already begun to pound and scorch. This headache was going to be a screamer, with fire shooting through his skull and eyes. He was always afraid that one of them would be so excruciating he'd kill himself to relieve the agony. In fact, he'd contemplated suicide so often while writhing in pain that his mother had had to ban firearms from the house.

"You're mad! Do you think those idiots can stop a woman like her? *You* must see to capturing her. You, personally." She lowered her voice to a sympathetic tone. "Then you may attend your *grand romantic adventure.* Won't that be a fiasco!"

She had him; he was defeated. To argue with her now would only exacerbate his torture.

"How can you be so certain she's coming here?" he demanded.

Missus French grew quiet, needlessly pulling her gloves higher on her wrist, a nervous habit. She closed her eyes and audibly expelled her breath. Then she raised her eyes to her offspring, who was attempting to see through a squinty right eye, rubbing the eyebrow above the left which was closed tight, tears pouring from it.

"I know it," Missus French said in measured, low tones. "This is my punishment. Our punishment. Years ago, I made a…a bad decision."

She paused while that sunk in, then completed her revelation: "We'll never be free until we have her. Never."

"I thought you incapable of making a bad move," Devereau said. Defeated, he knocked the trunk off the stand, spilling its colorful contents onto the floor. Then, half blind from pain, he stormed out of the room, cursing and crying.

Missus French sat staring at the floor, contemplating their dire situation. She, who had taken everything she had coveted in life. Who had married the late Mister Clayton French, a plantation-owner from a wasteland called Turkle. Who had buried him and taken possession of his property, expelling a horde of defiant relatives. Who had subsequently acquired the best land in her corner of Lethe Creek County and had taken control of the local bank. Who now owned the mill and other local cornerstones. She had only one desperate, highly dubious gambit left to play. Otherwise, she and her son were trapped.

If only I could free Devereau. But that can never happen.

Chapter Five

The slicing, wind-blown downpour whipped through the night as the ungainly caravan of rider, men afoot and overloaded wagon bumped along the muddy road near town. For the fourth time in the last hour, one of the wheels became mired in the morass. Its drenched passengers reluctantly abandoned the tarps over their heads, so inadequate against the driven fury, and jumped onto the road, sinking to their ankles. Rivulets pouring off their faces, they put their shoulders to helping the mules pull the wagon free.

Riding at the head of the assembly, Hurst tensed, the urge to gallop away from his latest hare-brained scheme warring against the vision in his head. The rain was lucky for them; it would keep most people indoors. Hearing them, locals might stick their heads out to see who passed by, but a concerted confrontation in such conditions was out of the question. *Well,* he resolved, *Turkle had to see them some time.* "The town's coming up," he shouted through the sheets of rain.

Hurst was trembling, and not because of the cold. In despair, he wondered how he could have talked himself—and these men—into this. Now it was too late. If their scheme was exposed or the authorities took exception to them, his chance companions might have to pay dearly. And it would certainly be worse for him. He shut his eyes.

Hurst let visions of his plantation wash through his mind. He knew the next part would be the hard part, the deadly part. He'd have to get that killer Chickasaw to sign a paper for the land, then somehow have it validated by officialdom in Turkle. And that was before getting tools, seed and food to live on. He had no idea how he was going to do any of that.

He glanced back to reassure himself that his fevered imagination hadn't conjured his partners. But there they were, footsore, soaked, and disheveled. He tried to build his courage, picturing himself as the hero in books he'd read. Sitting bolt upright in the saddle, proudly erect, he became a storybook general riding in vanguard of his conquering army toward some rich citadel on the horizon.

They passed a pack of trash glaring threateningly at them from behind a shed. The men had slit, snake-like eyes. Clearly they were too closely related. These were the type of neighbors folks wished would go broke quickly and move on, only they were as slow at being self-destructive as they were at anything else. Hurst didn't want them sneaking around

DarkHorse.

Seeing Hurst and his minions, one of the trash picked up a musket, another a pitchfork.

"Don't worry, boys," Hurst shouted through the sheets of rain, "They're dangerous now, but I'm going to gentle them!" That would make the snake-eyes think twice before disturbing them.

Isaac, skinning the wagon, snapped the reins, *crack*. The mules started, then continued at their same fatalistic pace.

***

It had come to this, shivering under a leaking blanket with the nighttime storm blowing through it, groundwater rising to soak her. The fire she'd built had degenerated into a mass of drenched, blackened sticks in a muddy pit. A dry blanket in a warm cabin would be a relief, but she couldn't take that chance. Not here.

She had made it this far by avoiding people along the way, and using guarded words upon her rare encounters with strangers. But now that she was getting close, she had to be even more careful. New Orleans may have sent a rider ahead to warn that she might be headed to Turkle. Where else would she have gone?

She tried to think of what she might do next.

In the past, planning had been her forté. Planning had enabled her to run her husband's shipping concern, one of the largest in the Gulf of Mexico. Early in her life, planning had enabled her to escape who and where she had been, taking her to whom she had become. Unfortunately, she no longer knew who she was. And now that she was nearing her destination, she had no plan to rely on. The irony inherent in her predicament made her curse herself.

Who had she ever truly been? A poseur? A lower order of...of what? Since that day in New Orleans when she lost the life she believed would forever belong to her, she had lost all sense of herself and her belief in her power to persevere and adapt. What little strength she once had, that small piece of iron in her soul that she had gained through so much struggle and sorrow and hardship, was missing. She didn't know if she would ever recover it.

Since that day in his study, when she had acted irrevocably from the deepest anger a woman can know, leaden thoughts of escape into death kept invading her mind, becoming more persistent; waves of storms worse than the ones chilling her flesh. She was losing the will to keep those feelings at bay; there wasn't much left to hold them off.

39

***

"There it is!" A delirious Hurst stirred the roan into a gallop.

Behind Hurst, the rest of his weary, wet companions sighed, relieved to have arrived. As if to offer a ray of hope, the rain ceased its pounding.

Hurst turned off the road and crashed through the undergrowth, then drew rein. There it was, just as he remembered: a large, open plot surrounded by giant oaks. The two-hundred-yard clearing was cut by crystal steam. It was Chickasaw land, but adjacent to the old road to the county seat. Perfect.

After all these years of drifting, maybe he had found a home.

Chapter Six

The cloud-obscured moon doled out faint light, as if it was lying at the bottom of a muddy creek. Even so, Hurst could make out the land's gentle slope bedded within the encircling trees. On that rise they would build their mansion. Over there, the stables for horses and other domestic animals. And there, he'd lay out formal gardens.

"Hurst! Durk!" Big Josh shouted, running to his side. But Hurst could not tear his eyes from his vision.

Isaac pulled up the mules, wrapped the reins around the brake and climbed down. Everyone gathered by Hurst, sitting his horse, staring into what seemed empty space.

"So this is our plantation," Big Josh said, incredulous. He'd understood that the land was going to be raw, but he hadn't pictured this.

"Yes!" Hurst said, his excitement unchained. "We just have to fix it up. See, we'll build the mansion over there…"

"Ain't no house or field on the whole damn place?" Isaac said.

"It's a forest!" Hurst replied, spreading his arms to take in the whole miracle. "Look, there's good oak and cedar for lumber; that stand over there will just about do it for the house. And see, a clear, freshwater stream. Everything we need."

The old man in the house servant livery pointed at Big Josh. "Fine mansion, Mister B-Big B-Boss Man!" he mocked. Then he headed back to the wagon mumbling under his breath. "What can you es'pect from damn fool field hands?"

Bammer broke the silence. "We ain't got no food, rifles, seed, no *money*, nothing!"

"I tole' you, the man's out his head," Isaac sneered.

Angry and despairing, the men began to complain at the top of their voices.

"Quiet!" Big Josh ordered, silencing everyone. He lowered his voice: "We here, that's a f-fact. Now, we can do this or we got to turn ourself in. What you want to do?" He waited, frowning, looking from face to face until everyone nodded. "Now I wants me a fire." He turned a cold eye on Hurst. Like everyone else, Big Josh had been filled with doubts from the first. He knew Hurst was withholding something, and he was angry at himself for not asking the right questions. He doubted Hurst would have lied straight out if he'd been challenged. If it had been any other man, any other kind of evasion, if it had been different circumstances, Big Josh wouldn't have been quite so reluctant. Well, he was going to get to the truth before they took one step further.

"Why s-shouldn't we throw you in the s-swamp!" Big Josh growled between his teeth, bluffing.

Hurst tensed. "Cause I'm the best damn man in Miss'ippi for keeping up a fire," he laughed, putting on a brave face. "You said you wanted a fire, now didn't you?" Then he pushed between the men to the wagon and grabbed an ax from the wagon bed.

"There's good hardwood over there," he said, heading toward the west end of the clearing. "And don't take any rotted wood or someone will see our smoke from the road."

Big Josh put a hand on Hurst's shoulder, stopping him. "What else you the bes' man in Miss'ippi at?" he asked ominously.

Hurst thought a minute, but he couldn't come up with any other attributes that would sit well with his partners. Most of his best methodologies had to do with deception, and he figured he shouldn't reinforce their thinking of him in those terms just now.

"We're always gonna need someone knowing a good fire," Hurst said. "Hell, you can't have a kiln without a good fire, now you know that." Training his eye on Big Josh, he asked, "You been owning a better plantation than ours before, have you?" No one had an answer for that.

But Isaac hadn't finished. "Who going to be the boss?" he asked, his face hard.

Hurst saw every eye look toward Big Josh. The big man might emerge as the natural leader when they were farming and building the house, but Hurst might need room to maneuver and didn't want his hands tied. "Ain't you had enough masters and bosses?" he asked rhetorically. "We all got jobs to do."

"And your job is to be master?" Isaac snorted.

"To play master, Isaac," Hurst said, "but we'll agree on things." He paused, thinking, then added: "Anybody want to explain to the lawyers and sheriffs and such what we're gonna be doing out here, I'll call you 'master'." There were no takers.

Hurst felt euphoric. He would make it happen. He would at last fill the great void at the center of himself, where he dwelt in limbo, sheltered from both hurt and happiness. He would learn to actually live his life for his own purpose, not as a mere appendage to other people's whims and greed. Yes, one morning he was going to wake up and know exactly what he wanted that day. And he would act on that knowledge, regardless. He would, for the first time in his life, be a whole person, not a woodland squirrel grubbing for nuts and avoiding the foxes of the everyday world.

That had always been his Dream. A mansion and a plantation would make it possible. He had people with him now who might become his friends, maybe he'd even find a woman to love him. And if he believed in the Dream, even for a time, then lost the mansion and plantation and partners and the woman, perhaps he would not lose himself again.

"Does we own this piece of ground?" Big Josh asked in a voice that brooked no evasion. "Does we? Or is we s-squattin'?"

Paper! All this, and it hinged on a piece of paper that he didn't have. There was no other way.

"I'm gonna get the papers we'll need," he said, continuing on toward the stand of cedars. *No need to tell them how long the odds against him were. And what failure might mean to all of them.*

Big Josh gruffly stomped over to the wagon bed and grabbed what few tools they had, but seeing no one was following, turned back.

"Y'all c-come help us. We ain't your slaves, *partners.*" He gave a few sharp directions and everyone was instantly in motion. Big Josh handed out the tools, and each man went to work. Some grabbed tarp and rope to build temporary shelters, while others dug a pit in the damp, clay earth for the fire. Solid Bammer cut saplings, while Long Lou cleaned them for poles. Isaac took the last ax and followed Hurst. Nearby, Little Turby unhitched the mules and led them and the horse to the shelter of a large hanging willow.

Walking toward the wagon, Old Moses brushed against Big Josh's shoulder. "Set a tarp on the wagon so's I can keeps dry," the former houseman said.

Big Josh took Old Moses' shoulder and squared him around. "Ain't you gonna help?" Big Josh asked, glaring.

"I run the mansion, Big Boss," Old Moses said sarcastically. "Send me my two upstair maids, will you." Then he brushed Big Josh's hand away and climbed in the wagon to wait for the field hands to finish up.

Once settled under a blanket and tarp, Old Moses let his consternation get the better of him. What a fix old master and these field hands had gotten him into. He cast about for ideas on how to escape his predicament, but nothing came to mind. He soon tired of worrying and let his thoughts drift.

Old Moses remembered fondly his days as the General's man, the days of Jezzie in the kitchen, when he kept the key to the liquor cabinet. But those times weren't coming back.

Then a notion lit upon him, bringing an image of the only civilized, warm shelter in the whole county: the French mansion Isaac had been talking about. A peaceful smile came over his face as he dozed off into another world, a place where once again he was a respected man, a man needed by quality folks. Yes, sir, that French place, now that's how it oughts to be.

***

The morning sun glimpsed through the gently drifting clouds. The men worked the campsite lethargically, exhausted, like ghosts drifting through the rising mist of evaporating rain.

Hurst reached into his jacket pocket and removed his last gold coin; when it was gone, they were dead broke. He set his lucky piece on a stump and placed his pistol muzzle directly on it. Then, closing his eyes, he pulled the trigger, shooting the coin dead center. At the pistol's blast, every head turned toward him.

"To catch a fish, you've got to have bait," he explained. His partners shrugged and went about their business.

Satisfied with the dent he'd made, Hurst pocketed the gold piece. Little did his partners know, but this golden talisman would transubstantiate their rude camp into tilled bottomland and a gleaming mansion, and his partners from slaves into free men.

His plan stretched even his own credulity. There were two deadly swindles to pull, and either one would require more luck than he'd ever experienced. It was bad enough that he had to get Wounded Wolf to sign over the land. He also had to convince the government agent to transform the dubious document into a deed.

"I'm going to get a paper signed on the land from the Chickasaws," he announced. "And see about manumission papers for you'all, too." Then he mounted the roan.

Big Josh grabbed the reins. "If you thinking 'bout a reward, you better be thinking 'bout your neck broke. I get in reach of you, p-partner."

"Why would I trade a whole-herd-of-horses plantation for a horsefly reward, *partner?*" Hurst replied. "I won't argue I'm not strange, but I will claim I ain't stupid."

Big Josh released the rein, and Hurst turned the roan.

"What'll we' do for food?" the beanpole, Long Lou, asked.

"I done been corn-and-possum-ed out," Bammer said.

"You can kill a deer," Hurst said, anxious to be off.

"Kill a d-deer? How?" Big Josh asked. "We not a pack of dogs."

"No, partner, you're *men*." Hurst slapped the pistol into Big Josh's huge hand. At least the rusty firearm served some purpose.

The large man examined the gun, then handed it to Bammer. "This thing couldn't kill a c-coon. More likely gonna blow off your hand."

"Plenty of game out here," Hurst said distractedly, spurring the roan. He'd only ridden fifty feet when he reined in, turning back to gaze at the site of their future glory, perhaps for the last time.

Watching him go, Old Moses brushed the collar of his soiled black coat. "Wish we could catch the General's chef," he muttered in his superior manner.

***

Big Josh planned to stay. *Black men were simply property, like mules and axes,* he told himself. Whoever ended up owning this plantation would need Big Josh to finish it and run it right. That was safety of an order no paper could bestow.

He stepped through the underbrush until he reached a clearing beyond the reach of camp sounds. Alone with the birds and his thoughts, he settled himself upon a fallen cedar. He put the paper on his lap and dipped the quill to begin his lists: who fit what job, what supplies the plantation would need, in what order they should proceed—just like he did on General's place. He'd learned long ago that a day of planning saved weeks of stupid work that had to be undone and fixed over. It was exciting, albeit solitary work.

No, their white partner hadn't returned; that was concerning. The others were growing more worried by the hour, but he could quiet them. Hopefully, Durk wasn't killed already.

First he would teach Little Turby, with his quick, incisive mind, everything he could about running a plantation. That was the future. Next…

His concentration was broken by a crash of branches as Isaac tore through the brush. He grabbed the quill from Big Josh's hands. "Put this on your list," he growled, jabbing the quill down hard, breaking the point. "One white man to play master."

"Isaac," Big Josh said calmly, taking back the quill, "if you wants to g-go, *go*, my blessing. Run whiskey to the Chickasaws." Big Josh took his knife to whittling the quill point sharp. "Now, if you stays, you gone to be Durk's bes' friend." He pointed at his eye, instructions to watch the man. "Being the white man gonna be hard. Just keep him out trouble bes' you can. And member, when you round wh-whitefolks, you a slave."

Isaac absorbed those words. Then he wandered off, mulling out loud, "Why I gots to be the white man's friend? Cause nobody wants to be, is why."

When he was gone, Big Josh dipped the quill. "Neither of them gonna be much farming use nohow."

Big Josh chortled, surprising himself, which became a roaring belly laugh that echoed through the oak, cedar and pine around him. With great strokes, he began crude sketches of their future home, what Hurst called "the mansion", dipping and drawing, dipping and drawing. The simple farming plans could wait.

May as well enjoy imagining Big while he had the chance.

Chapter Seven

Death waited for him at every turn.

After an hour's ascent through heavy forest onto the ridge, Hurst reached The Great Tree, called the Place of Signs by the Chickasaws. The Signs foretold to a traveler what was in store for him spiritually, and in his degree of welcome by the inhabitants. A tribal elder had led him there as a boy and taught him what each possible Sign meant: the markings on The Great Tree, the arrangement of sticks and rocks, everything. He hadn't been told if spirits were supposed to have organized the Signs or if the tribe or its ancestors did it for them. He certainly hadn't been told of any signs for the Chief being a scar-faced murderer.

He drew rein, hoping for warning or guidance. He was shocked to find the Great Tree rotting where it had fallen. Uprooted, it had toppled and crashed through dense underbrush until its mighty top branches were sunk into wild scrub and pine.

Had it been torn out by a terrible storm or a vengeful haunt? He tried to read the ground, but the random stones and sticks littering the earth were in complete disarray. If a message at all, they spoke the language of a madman or of a violent, indifferent nature. This was a Sign that Hurst seemed to understand. He rode on, lost in memories of old heartbreaks. He didn't believe in magic or ancestors. Yet, it was as if the Great Tree had spoken directly to him.

Hurst would have to ride into the swamp and find the Chickasaws.

**

As the hours passed, advancing clouds smothered the moonlight, cloaking the twisted swamp in blackness. And still Hurst hadn't found the men of the village. He began to fear he would get lost in the vast tangle. He'd hunted this swamp and knew what terrors lurked there: panther, quicksand and cottonmouth. Even indigenous Chickasaws had disappeared in its expanses at night, never to be found.

After what seemed like hours, he was relieved to hear a steady pounding perhaps less than a mile away. He took a deep breath, then spurred the horse, leading it around bog and flooded backwash, toward the sound.

Then he was among them. The night drums cried to the forever skies, pounding in pride a declaration and a warning to the skies and to all biting, crawling, creeping, scratching creatures in the darkness. Beware: this territory is Man.

Hurst strolled among them, greeting old friends, learning the fate of those long gone. The Chickasaw story had become a sad one. The tribe was shrinking rapidly, as was the land they inhabited. They seemed to sense that the rising tide of white men had put them on a course to extinction. And that there was nothing they could do to reverse it.

***

In an instant, fast and rough, Wounded Wolf sprang from the shadows, knocking Hurst to the ground and landing on top of him. The Indian's knees trapped Hurst's arms, his weight pressed him down. Hurst felt the cold steel of a knife at his throat, smelled the heavy odor of drink on his assailant's breath. The drums stopped like the sudden silence at an execution.

Hurst fixed his eyes on the face above him and, seeing the scar on the cheek, believed with a rush of fear he was about to die. The two stared at each other in the moonlight.

"Dark Horse, my old enemy!" Wounded Wolf laughed heartily, rising awkwardly from drink while sheathing his knife. Hurst noted his bronze chest exposed beneath the open red velvet waistcoat.

Once released, Hurst rose and brushed himself off.

"You must be crazy to come near me!" the Chief said, his words slurred.

"Been a long time," said Hurst.

Wounded Wolf's eyes grew cold, like a hanging judge contemplating sentencing. "You steal my black white men," he pronounced.

"That's just what I wanted to discuss with you," Hurst replied tentatively.

"Come," Wounded Wolf said between clenched teeth.

They reached an isolated clearing a quarter mile away. Hurst tossed a log on the dying fire, while the hulking Chickasaw passed next to him, casting a flickering shadow on the leaves overhead. Then the Indian sank heavily into a great chair resting on the leaf and twig-strewn earth. With his chin held high, Wounded Wolf proudly settled his broad arms on the carved, velvet-tufted armrests. Hurst examined the fine chair, not knowing its origin, but certain of how it was acquired.

"So you're the Big Chief. How did you manage that?"

Wounded Wolf flashed his knife, then sheathed it.

"You've been around bad white men too much," Hurst said quietly.

"Learn much. No good for a boy," Wounded Wolf replied. Then his eyes narrowed. "My mother love you better than me."

"Do you have a woman?" Hurst asked, changing a sore subject.

Wounded Wolf examined scars on his forearm and elbow. "Cruel white woman, I run her off. She had many storms in her head; cut me."

The Indian's hand fumbled beside the chair until he located a jug. Lifting it high, he drank deeply, then offered it to Hurst. Hurst took a sip, feeling it burn down his throat, then passed it back.

Hurst reached in his pocket and pulled out the coin he had dented, absently playing with it to draw Wounded Wolf's attention.

"Why did you steal my black white men, Dark Horse? You had to know I would catch you."

"I have a plan."

"Plan! You mean you have one of your tricks. I know you."

"How did those men have the misfortune to wind up with you?"

"Cards, on a riverboat." Wounded Wolf whipped out his knife, demonstrating his speed. "The previous owner did not play his cards with a firm hand."

A natural killer, Hurst thought. *No wonder his own people are terrified of him.*

Hurst nonchalantly flipped the coin, letting Wounded Wolf watch it gleam in the firelight. Wounded Wolf liked shiny coins far better than paper. That preference made it difficult to deal with him at times, but it also led the Indian to bad swaps.

"You don't have any papers on them, I guess," Hurst said, his heart dropping.

Ignoring the question, the Chief rose and began pacing, making compulsive stabbing motions toward Hurst. "Ah, Dark Horse," he spat in frustration. "You saved me from that lynching near Memphis. But now I owe you a life and cannot harm you. And because I cannot kill you, I must kill you. It troubles me at night. You see?"

A quick move and Wounded Wolf caught the coin in midair, then examined it closely. "What is this?"

"My lucky piece."

"What is this dent?"

"Saved me from a bullet. Owe it…"

"Your life. I will trade for this coin, Dark Horse. A horse for it."

Hurst stretched, impatient. "I've already got a horse. I'll wager you for it."

"But you always cheat me."

Hurst stood as if prepared to leave. "Well, I don't care if you have nightmares about not killing me."

Wounded Wolf contemplated the situation, drinking thirstily. "How will we wager?"

"We could race horses," Hurst proposed.

Wounded Wolf took a great swallow, tilting his head back until he tumbled off the chair onto his back, splashing whiskey on his face. He coughed, laughing. "Not race horses, no."

The competition wound its way through the night. The moon emerged from behind the drifting clouds like a waking mistress, lighting the living night of pure forest fragrance. Wounded Wolf peeled off his waistcoat and breathed deeply to inflate his chest.

"I'll race you to that tree and back. I'll wager the coin against two of the men."

As the contest roared through the hours it was no longer a test of two men, but of two boys, a rivalry begun thirty years earlier; winding its way from clearing to clearing, the two combatants dwarf-like beneath the profound, brooding, solid walls of giant oak, cypress and gum, and the impenetrable cane breaks flanking the moccasin-infested bayous. As the night progressed, both men seemed to get drunker, but Hurst always let his opponent demand the jug—until Wounded Wolf no longer bothered to share.

The battles were heated, often just skirting the edge of violence, as Hurst won steadily, for larger and larger stakes.

Abruptly, Wounded Wolf had enough of losing. He became intimidating, pushing Hurst, his hand fingering his knife. The man's rage was coming.

Hurst lowered the bet considerably and allowed himself to go on a losing streak. During this turn of fortune, he complimented the prowess of his opponent and offered drinks to the man's string of victories. So the moment of the knife passed.

The competitions degenerated into the pursuits of idling boys: spitting for distance and accuracy, rock-throwing, stick fights, knife-tossing into targets, single fall wrestling matches, and bets on imprudent acts of bravery resulting from dares—all followed by Wounded Wolf drinking expansively to victory or bitterly in defeat.

Then Wounded Wolf found some reserve of clarity in his drunkenness, and Hurst began to lose contests he needed to win. He tried to summon his strength, but the day's riding and the drain on his will had weakened him.

The whole gamble would soon be over. The more he thought about losing, of having to start over, with nowhere to go and not even a dented coin to get there, the worse he felt. He might starve to death. He pictured himself an old man in ragged clothes in a cheap tavern in some strange, desolate place, bragging about how he once almost owned a plantation, and hearing other dusty old drifters laugh at his story and refuse him a drink. He was overcome by a sense of aloneness, as the awful vision engendered painful waves of despair.

A large mass of passing clouds caused the moonlight to desert the arena. The two returned to the fire, throwing on fresh logs and covering themselves in blankets.

Wounded Wolf reached into a deerskin sack and pulled out a carved box, its original paint worn away. His curiosity roused, Hurst leaned closer.

"You remember this; it kept us from killing each other during long rains?" Wounded Wolf asked, handing the box to Hurst.

"You don't mean…?" Hurst opened it. The very chess set he had exchanged squirrel meat and pelts for from a friendly white trader.

"I won it from you, Dark Horse. You remember?"

Hurst pulled a checkered board from the sack and laid it on the stump between them. Then he pulled out the rough chess pieces, each made from carved wood debris and shipboard materials.

"One game, for the life I owe you," Wounded Wolf said with deadly seriousness. In this game, they played even.

"All right, one game. I'll wager all I've won so far, the land and the coin, against the rest of the land across the northern branch." Hurst withheld mention of his new partners, knowing that Wounded Wolf no longer remembered or cared about them.

"It is too much," Wounded Wolf replied.

Hurst began setting the pieces on the board, the black-stained ones nearest himself.

"The People never cross the river anyway. The place is crawling with white men."

Across the river branch dwelt rough, hungry men who, through fear or sheer brutishness, sometimes shot Chickasaws they chanced upon. The Indians had long since moved south.

"Look," Hurst pointed out, "where will you go if the People get up the nerve to run you off? This way, you'll have a friend on the other side."

Wounded Wolf drank deeply, then dropped his chin onto his fist, thinking.

"White or black? Your choice," Hurst offered, watching Wounded Wolf's eyes. Choosing white—with first move—would give the Chief the advantage. Wounded Wolf grinned craftily. "You choose," he said.

"Okay, I'll take black magic; you go first," Hurst ventured.

Wounded Wolf slammed his fist down on the stump, knocking three pawns onto the ground. "No, I will take black!"

Reluctantly, Hurst turned the board so that the lighter, tan-stained pieces were on his side. "All right then, I guess I'll have to go first."

Hurst lifted his king's pawn and slammed it forward two squares, making a solid *thunk* on the wooden board. The battle was on.

Hurst played an unusually passive game, especially with first move, sacrificing a pawn here and a minor piece there to gain time. Instead of attacking, he patiently held back, subtly building up his power: piling paired rooks on an open file, quietly adding threat after threat, aiming one power piece after another at the very heart of Wounded Wolf's king-side stronghold. Hurst could feel his gathering power straining to be unleashed.

On the other side, as an effect of his drinking, the Chief played an impulsive game, tending toward random, intuitive incursions into Hurst's territory. Repeatedly grasping his wooden queen in his large hand, he charged around the board, slaughtering minor pieces indiscriminately like a mounted armored chieftain slashing through a wave of ragged villagers; leaving his own defending pieces without cohesion.

Then the match was over. With the confident abandon of irrepressible local superiority, Hurst hurled his long-restrained pieces at the black king. In lightning-like strikes, heedless of cost, he rapidly pulverized the black defenses, until finally he slid a rook to the eighth rank. The black king had no escape.

"Check and so forth, mate," Hurst announced.

Wounded Wolf scanned the lost position, growing furious, the victory he imagined stolen from him. In an instant, knife in hand, he leaped across the board, scattering the chess set. Landing with his full weight on Hurst, he wrestled him down, bringing the knife to his throat. Hurst fumbled for the coin and hurriedly displayed it.

"Wait! You win the knife fight! The life is yours!"

Wounded Wolf hesitated, then grabbed the coin and drunkenly rolled off Hurst. Working unsteadily to his knees, he held the gold piece aloft, issuing a bloodcurdling cry.

Hurst worked himself up, while the man who had nearly been his executioner drank to victory and collapsed into his chair.

Hurst pulled paper, ink and a writing quill from the bag on his saddle. Using the chessboard as a writing surface, he scribbled out an agreement, signed it, and offered the quill to Wounded Wolf. "Now you sign, and the land is mine, and the *life* is yours."

"I put the black white men on this paper, too. I'm gonna need them to grow corn and make squeezin's whiskey. Give you a cut."

"I can trade the black white men for gold," Wounded Wolf objected.

"And do what with the gold? Get so much you have to give it to the banker? The white man gives his gold to the banker, and soon the banker has the white man's land, too. You want to lose your land, Chief? Where will the tribe go when the banker has it?"

Wounded Wolf swayed unsteadily, stabbing his knife into the ground. "No, the banker will not get this land."

Wounded Wolf stared at the paper, his head reeling. He had learned from bitter experience that when the papers come out, he often got cheated. Wounded Wolf put the knife to Hurst's chest. "Why do you need this paper?"

"Gonna use it to keep white men off the land."

"Yes, a paper is the only way to make them listen."

After a long, silent pause, Wounded Wolf made his mark, and Hurst folded the paper, placing it in his pocket. Satisfied, Wounded Wolf started to fall over, but Hurst propped him up.

"Now you return the life to me and we are even."

Wounded Wolf slapped the coin into Hurst's hand, then slowly toppled over into the peace of a deep sleep. "Thank you, Dark Horse."

Hurst kissed his lucky piece, congratulating himself: *The perfect fleecing!—the skinned party thanks you for relieving him of his britches. He probably won't remember the details tomorrow anyway, if he remembers much at all.*

Then he felt a chill, wondering if he'd done something dishonorable by taking land from the people who had saved his life. But, he reasoned, the Chickasaws never venture that far north anymore. It was abandoned land, and this simply kept the rich plantation owners from getting it. Besides, now he could give his partners their freedom and a place to live. He shrugged off his misgivings, telling himself he'd done something commendable.

A thief's justification, he thought bitterly. *And this makes me the lowest kind of thief.*

*** *

As the sun rose toward mid-morning, Hurst drew rein behind a stand of sycamore and brush, holding his breath. He was played out, with barely the strength to sit upright in his saddle.

The air was thick with evaporation from the previous night's deluge. He could sense the world warming in anticipation of spring: soon the forest would explode into a panoply of green and wild color; Chickasaws, farmers, and slaves would sow fields; animals and insects would rut. The soil on *DarkHorse* would be broken.

From his concealed perch, he heard splashing in the stream ahead and, determining its direction, quietly flicked the horse along to get a better view, wondering: *Is it a robber? Killers?* Then a vision materialized.

The first thing Hurst saw was the horse lazily grazing on the wild grasses. A massive thoroughbred with slick black muscles, the magnificent beast was road dusty but looked to be worth its weight in gold. An expensive saddle of a quality he'd never seen, constructed with artistically carved, fine leather workmanship, rested on the bed of vines beside the horse. Next to both sat a monogrammed leather traveling bag, the rope used to tie it to the horse still knotted to its handle.

Then he saw *her*. Clearly, he must be losing his mind.

Chapter Eight

Framed in the bright sun shimmering on the water, he saw a woman kneeling on the bank washing her long dark hair. Unaware of the interloper, she stood, tossing her locks, a vision in bright halo and water-splashed sparkles. She turned to walk up the stick-strewn bank toward a dying fire, toweling her head, holding herself erect with elegant dignity, so graceful she seemed to float.

Hurst's eyes widened: rich, thick tresses, dark oval eyes, distinctly chiseled facial features. *Why here?* he wondered. Her presence on Chickasaw territory made no sense. He spurred the roan forward and crashed through the hedge to get a closer look, then drew rein.

She wore a plain, straight-legged riding outfit, and had just slipped on a matching jacket. The suit's borders were stitched with gold thread in classical Spanish patterns—material not made for hard travel. But these were clearly road-worn; her classic go-for-a-jaunt boots mud caked.

He'd seen women like her before; recalled leaning on his broom one night across the street from the New Orleans Opera House, watching the carriages of the gentry and wealthy merchants arrive, imagining…

He held her carriage door, a gentleman in every respect. From inside the carriage, she daintily offered her hand. He took it as she descended to the footstool, toes pointed like weightless porcelain, petticoat like sweeping wings.

When he reached her campsite, in a clearing beneath the sycamores, the woman turned sharply, aiming a pistol at his heart. "I warn you, I'm an expert marksman," she claimed with shaking voice.

His reverie shattered, Hurst calmly slid off the roan, then raised both hands, as if well-practiced in surrendering.

"Please don't be alarmed. I'm a gentleman, ma'am," he said, tipping his hat and brushing dust from his coat.

"A gentleman?" she replied with an amused smirk, noting his swamp-damaged suit. "Obviously of the finest breeding."

Hurst squatted by her moribund fire and began to poke and blow on its coals, adding wood. "You don't need a pistol to invite me for coffee," he said with a broad smile.

"Don't think I won't use this," she added, indicating the pistol; her brow creased.

"I don't believe you are the kind of person to mistreat a loyal servant—as I am yours." He bowed from the waist with an awkward flourish. *Expert markswoman, ha!* he thought, dismissing her claim.

The woman lowered her pistol and sat on a log.

Hurst looked closely into her frightened eyes; a known look. *This woman is running, in fear, has been for some time.* But there was something else, too, something that jolted him. He was overwhelmed by the urge to protect her. But from what?

Hurst examined her pistol, admiring its workmanship. Carvings of elk and deer were worked onto its barrel; its shaft was polished to a shine.

Somebody was awfully proud of that. Then understanding struck him. *This pistol is half of a matched dueling pair. Where is the other?*

"I do need a gentleman to aid me," she ventured.

"My name's Hurst," he said, forcing a smile. "Durksen Hurst. And yours?"

"I'm sorry, I can't tell you that, Mister Hurst." She smiled apologetically. "I hope you are not offended."

"I must call you something."

"All right. My name is Antoinette, though if anyone asks, you don't know me."

"Antoinette, then."

They both stared at the fire. Finally, he broke the silence. "You're a little far from home," he said, "on Chickasaw land." He noted her alarm. "Don't worry, Chickasaws wouldn't harm a woman."

The woman tried to sound casual, "Ah, what's the nearest town, Mister Hurst?"

"Durk, please, ma'am. A little place called Turkle. Turkle's the backwoods word for turtle. They are kind of hard-shelled," Hurst said laughingly, hoping she would smile. But instead she reacted with barely suppressed intensity to the information. "You're from New Orleans?" he asked.

The woman grew quiet, dropping her eyes. Her chin trembled, before she forced a smile. "From no place quite this rustic, that's for certain."

"These wilds are no carriage ride through the Quarter," Hurst said, probing further.

This woman seemed to be masking a profound sorrow that fit her better than her tailored riding outfit. He had detected it the moment he met her, and her weariness was at least as grave as that that he saw in his shaving mirror. He gave the ground between his boots a long, questioning look, but the Earth offered no clues to this mystery.

All he knew was, if she would stay with him, he would never let anything hurt her, if he could help it.

Not knowing what to say, he blurted, "I've got land for my plantation not far from here. You can hide out there as long as you need to."

Plantation! Why did I say that? He knew his boastful claim was nowhere near a certainty, but he had already convinced himself of his destiny. He'd always known his mother bore him to do something remarkable, something unique. And this *DarkHorse* plan felt like the surest thing he'd ever chanced—crazy or not. And wasn't meeting this woman proof? Certainly, his grand schemes had crashed and died before, usually because they were impossible, but not this scheme, not this time.

"Your plantation? Have a string of slaves on it, do you?" she asked sarcastically.

"Not slaves, no," he said, contemplating how much to admit. Then he figured, sometimes the greatest reward comes from the most perilous exposure. "Don't believe in it. Everybody's the same on my place, black and white."

Momentarily taken aback, her eyes softened and her face relaxed. "That is unusual," she said, setting the pistol aside.

They had something rare and substantial in common; he'd struck gold. "What brings you here?" he asked.

"I have compelling business."

"Legal or illegal?"

"No one can know I'm here," the woman cautioned. "Understand, Durksen? Not a word."

"My word of honor."

"Just so you're warned." She paused to let that sink in. "I need to see a family by the name of French. For a private discussion." She placed a hand on her pistol, a clear sign of bravado.

"French!"

"You know of them?"

"Antoinette, if that is your name, those Frenches are no people to cross."

"Would you at least guide me to their property?"

"The safest way I can." He tried to guess what could account for the determination in her voice and eyes. He was good at reading people's motives; he'd had to be to survive, but he couldn't figure this woman.

"I've got some business in town first," he added, "but you'll be safe with us in the meantime."

"Tell me about the Frenches," she said.

***

The sun felt good on Big Josh's muscles as he slammed the hoe down. Hard work passed the time—gainfully, he hoped. It also kept his worries from eating him up, and helped him ignore the hunger in his belly.

Big Josh paused to wipe his brow. Would the man return? What if they were caught, with no white man to claim them? And being caught, what if the townsfolk found out the General had been murdered? All frightening possibilities. If Durk Hurst showed, would he have the courage to vouch for their tale or would he disavow any knowledge of them?

Well, nothing to be done but to hope. Big Josh swung the hoe in a great arc and brought it down with all his power, driving a deep wedge in the damp earth. Then he yanked it up, leaving a broad depression.

Big Josh's mind drifted into memories of his own son, James, whose birth had taken his mother's life. The boy had shown signs of developing into everything a man should be: strong, clever, hard-working. But James simply could not stomach injustice on any level, could not bear to be still when he witnessed capricious woundings to any man, much less to a woman. And so his James was lost forever, like the boy's mother before him, leaving a hole in Josh's soul that would never heal. He had been too late to save him.

What we gonna do now? He sighed and again brought the hoe down, hard.

***

They sat in the shade while the horses watered, Hurst holding the slack reins of the grazing roan while she held her thoroughbred.

"You must have left in a hurry," he said. "Were you married back home? In New Orleans?"

"Well, yes, and no." She blushed, realizing he'd tied her to New Orleans!

"Yes and no?"

"I'm a widow, Mister Hurst," she replied in a tone that discouraged further inquiry.

Her face darkened. She had watched in horror as he died, the vision marked indelibly in her memory. His final suffering was almost never out of her mind. She had loved him, and yet she had stood there and watched the life seep out of him; watched him struggle vainly to resist death's tightening grip until he coughed and shuddered.

"You were saying, Mister Hurst, a plantation?" she asked, forcing the conversation back onto his dubious claim. Let this disingenuous man reveal his secrets first, if he dared. "Tell me about your business in town."

"Going into Turkle may be the foolhardiest thing I've ever attempted," he said with gravity. "More dangerous than I would ever choose to do. There's a killer in the heart of even ordinary folk, but I've got to get a proper deed on my property."

"You talk like you've been there before."

"Not for thirty years."

***

1829

It was a good house, an awful good house for a one-room cropper shack made of slapped-together, weathered old boards. The floor was dirt, like in all the other towns they'd lighted—the boy, led by his father. But the shack sat up on a rocky hill, so rainwater didn't swell up from the ground to chill the boy's bare feet quite so much. And the wind didn't blow through the gaps in its walls as hard as it had in some. A good house, but not a home. No, none of these drafty hovels had been home since he'd buried his mother four years back, when he was just six. He hadn't caught the name of the town she died in, nor even the state, and his father wouldn't remember, so there was no sense in getting beat for asking.

The boy had spent the day wrestling against the terror rising up the back of his neck, keeping busy in a vain effort to clear the threatening clouds from his mind.

In the afternoon he'd trapped and cleaned a squirrel in the woods out back, so meat was simmering in the pot in a residue of ground meal, the last scrapings from the sack. His stomach growled, but he held off so the two could eat together. It smelled good. He dipped a finger and tasted the juice-soaked meal. As the shadows lengthened, he pulled out his treasured book, with its missing cover and loose pages, and untied the rawhide strip holding what remained together, but the fear gripping him wouldn't let him puzzle out what the words on the pages meant.

That morning, his father had awakened with steely fire in his eyes, a look the boy had seen before many a catastrophe in their lives. Instead of the man reaching for his coveralls and heading to the fields, he propped the mirror shard on the kitchen table and meticulously trimmed his unkempt beard, gulping whiskey from his tin cup and cursing under his breath. Then, face glowing bright red, he pulled on his black going-to-church coat and preacher hat. The boy pleaded for him to stay home, but was slapped away.

There was no stopping him. When his father wore the black coat and hat in the morning, the boy knew he was going to town for the sole purpose of preaching against what he called "the abomination of slavery", and to warn of a coming apocalypse wherein fantastic sums of men would die in battle and bring utter devastation on the land.

It was after these missions to town that packs of men would sometimes come to finish the job at night, and the pair would have to flee.

Night fell and hours later the boy was still waiting. His stomach growled as his nerves felt the seconds, then the minutes, then the hours drain away. Growing heartsick, he let the fire below the pot die. Wrapping himself in his torn quilt, he took up the rusty musket as he had been taught to shoot and positioned himself at the window to watch the weed-grown clearing outside. He prayed his father had lost his passion on the ride to town and had instead taken up drink, as sometimes happened. Or perhaps the hard, wiry man, whose body had survived so much hardship and injury, was being treated peacefully for bruises and cuts on a doctor's cot, if they were lucky.

The boy was rail thin from his own inner energy and from lack of regular solid eating. Built for fast running, in the wilds he could cross ribbons of water by leaping barefoot from stone to stone upon surfaces too narrow for all but deer to traverse. He knew the woods intimately. They were a source of food and a fine place to explore when he wasn't working the field. And he was good at hiding out in them from groups of armed, angry men.

He fought to stay awake, but dozed sitting up. The musket fell, and the rattle jarred him into consciousness as he saw a rider galloping toward the shack, bareback on a bag-of-bones. He knew the man's bearing, the jacket flapping in the wind. His heart sank.

The rider neared the cabin and drew rein, stretching his neck to listen. With a cry of relief and grief, the boy ran from the shack to the man's side, his bare toes not feeling the nubs and stubble about the littered ground. "I ain't asleep, Pa!" the boy shouted, grabbing a rein.

His father dismounted. "I tole ya' to stay in there!" he said, striking the boy. Then yanking the horse with one hand and the boy's collar with the other, he pulled them toward the shack.

The man stopped again. The boy began to speak, but was silenced by his father's rank sweat and leather-smelling hand covering his mouth. Both listened. They could hear the rustling sounds of horses, mules and men approaching through the brush. A shot rang out and the two ducked.

"Why'd you have to do it, Pap?" the boy cried.

Ignoring the outburst, the flushed, rough-faced man ripped the musket from the boy's hands and whapped the horse's flank with the stock, causing the frightened beast to jolt away.

"Get to the Chickasaw village!"

"I want to stay with you!" the boy shouted, but his father's glare made its point, and he tore through the undergrowth.

At last the boy got to an outcrop where he felt safe enough to look back. Through his tears he saw the shack burning, its flames lighting up the sky. It struck him fleetingly that his prized book was in there, and that he should have eaten. Then the fire's true meaning struck him. He'd never see his father again. He was alone.

"Pap," he cried quietly. "Why'd you have to be so mean?"

Chapter Nine

The figure on the horse, bandana across his face against the night's raging storm, passed the darkened courthouse and continued across the square. Oblivious of the downpour, he sat erect, facing straight ahead, but watchful out of the corners of his eyes. Somehow, he had to turn the signed paper folded in his pocket into a deed.

The patchwork hamlet was typical of small Southern towns; begun with big intentions, but stunted over time due to the way its denizens conducted business. Turkle was founded almost fifty years before as a gaggle of nondescript, one-story buildings coalescing around the junction of two rutted roads. The primary road carried cotton-laden wagons from the county seat in the east to a makeshift landing on the Mississippi further west, then back again carrying goods from St. Louis and Vicksburg. The other road drifted in from the north to join the first.

Over the years, the town had grown by a kind of alluvial accretion from the central square along staked-out mud streets. Buildings appeared with designs determined solely by the whims and means of their owners, limited by available local materials and skills, resulting in a rough coherence of style. Now Turkle consisted primarily of cramped rows of small, wood-frame houses with peeling whitewashed shells. On its more prosperous boulevards, larger dwellings nestled on flower-cultivated lawns, with swings dangling from their covered front porches.

Outlying Turkle was once populated by a number of plantation mansions, but now only one remained intact: the French place. The others had long since been abandoned and scavenged until they were nothing but collapsed shells with orphan chimneys beseeching a deaf heaven to come take them.

Hurst was grateful for the rain, a fine excuse to cover his face. Although it had been thirty years since he'd escaped Turkle, he still feared someone might recognize him, which could lead to unknown consequences.

He tried to find a scintilla of courage among his chaotic, frightened ways of thinking. He had never been one to trust fate or believe in supernatural powers. If these existed, which he had good reason to doubt, they had proved unreliable. But with his recent run of good fortune, he began contemplating the idea of destiny itself, whether he was being guided by some sort of benevolent hidden forces. Dismissing these notions, he reminded himself not to become complacent—a shortcoming often characteristic of his past endeavors.

Maybe, he thought, the juncture at which he now found himself was due to something other than luck or fate. Maybe this strange predicament was merely an outgrowth of his aberrant nature. Certainly, his life had been a peculiar one. He was plagued by an unceasing sense of impending catastrophe stemming from a nomadic father who constantly railed against a nation damned to implosion. His gentle, but unfulfilling, folding into a raw Chickasaw tribe tormented by an encroaching white civilization merely exacerbated his feelings of estrangement from any human community. His self-learning had been idiosyncratic as well, a stew of randomly acquired books, from cheap adventure stories to ancient philosophy. Not to mention his hardscrabble life as, in effect, an itinerate pitchman.

His fearful mind became flooded by myriad potential exigencies, any one of which could cause his downfall. And there were certainly dozens of demons lurking unseen, waiting to crush him. One wrong move, and he might have to make another skin-of-his-neck escape; this time encumbered by a whole coterie of black-skinned soil busters on foot. Not a good prospect.

Yet standing against these terrors, there was Antoinette waiting for him back at the rough squatter camp that he already thought of as *DarkHorse*. Her presence overrode all trepidation, compelling him irrevocably forward.

But disappointment, his tireless familiar, never ceased stalking him. Truly, Antoinette was in all probability an apparition, a phantasm spawned from his own fathomless longings. And like his wishful plantation, she would soon vanish into the ether, just as she had appeared.

***

The drummers and drovers ambled onto the gallery of the boarding hotel like damaged ships listing in a gale, bellies overfull to the point of misery from Miss Olney's cooking. They stumbled onto the seats, benches, kegs and the washtub, groaning and holding their ample stomachs, belching and picking their teeth with satisfaction.

In a daze, the men sat watching the torrents of rain run off the overhang in miniature waterfalls. The periodic lightning flashes, followed by hollow thunder, lit the familiar ramshackle structures about the town square: the livery where they quartered the steeds of their trade, the matched mules and flea-bitten horses; the well-worn steps of the country store whose scrawled ledgers held debts accumulated a nickel and a dime at a time by the sharecroppers and forty-acre freeholds; the town hall; and the sheriff's office with its jail. From the decayed, tar-roofed shack of the blacksmith, furious clangs, mighty hammer-blows, and grunts emerged, a sound totally incongruous with what the town knew as suppertime. This day, the smithy had a special job to finish.

Devereau French emerged from the boarding hotel door, his feet light on the planks of the porch. When he traveled in rain he always left his favored white steed in the French stables and took the old phaeton with a mare to pull it. That day, one of the phaeton's wheels had broken down, and the severity of the downpour had trapped him at Miss Olney's until the blacksmith completed his repairs—at a special price, of course, considering the time of day, the urgency, and the resources of the customer.

Having nowhere better to go, French had consented to join Miss Olney's lodgers at dinner while he waited. Miss Olney fussed over her honored guest, yet she was still able to scrape together enough to feed French's servant and armed guards in the kitchen.

"Lovely repast, gentlemen, as I told Miss Olney," French remarked cheerfully, leaning against the wall because nobody offered to rise and give the honored dinner guest a seat. The men merely grumbled politely, considering the introspective time of day.

French sensed this was further evidence that he'd never acquired the common touch. "Sure raining a heap," he ventured, a pained expression evident on his face.

"Seems like," a man responded and hawk-spit over the rail.

French's face flushed. This interlude was becoming interminable. Well-educated as a child by tutors brought in from Memphis and New Orleans, he was eager to converse about art, music, philosophy, literature, but he had no counterpart in Turkle to share these. He may as well live among livestock. The discussions at Miss Olney's table were little more than grunts as her boarders stuffed their mouths, getting their dollar's worth on the price of the room. French had breached a number of enlightening subjects, but he may as well have been speaking Latin—of which he was capable—or living on a desert island. The weather, the price of hogs and corn, and ridiculous gossip were all that anyone at the table had any interest in. He was beyond his wit's end.

At once, the men at the boarding hotel roused themselves, sitting up and craning their necks. Lightning revealed a momentary glimpse of a stranger riding toward them.

"'Nother one of them river rats blowed to this a-way," one man concluded.

The stranger drew rein immediately in front of them and pulled down his bandana. "Where do I register a deed?"

One of the men resting in a heap belched directions to the Honor Store.

There was something about the stranger that intrigued him; a sensitivity in the rider's face; a tired wisdom in his eyes, as if the man had intelligence, knowledge; a strength to his jaw; the shape of his lips. The possibilities created by the fact that the rider was a pariah, an outlier like French himself, only whetted his fascination. And triggered the unbearable screams of fear screeching into his ears. *Please. All I want is what any of my slaves have! What any French slave already has! Yet, it's impossible.*

Overwhelmed by curiosity, French yelled into the boarding hotel, a high-pitched, frantic demand for his manservant to bring him his umbrella. In short order, French's pair of armed guards followed, wiping their mouths on their sleeves. Taking the umbrella, French sloshed onto the street, heedless of the thick mud on his boots, waving his guards to follow.

Seeing that something unusual may be about to transpire, Miss Olney's guests and their acquaintances followed, grinning and making faces behind French's back.

The rider didn't need to turn his head to know he was leading an unwanted parade down the street; a rowdy crowd, an aristocrat followed by armed men. This was the worst possible happenstance for what he planned to do. It felt like his luck was about to run out, but he knew if he turned back to the campsite, he would not have the element of surprise when he returned to get the deed. Turkle would be prepared for him.

He steadied himself, taking a deep breath. This was his only chance.

***

The Senior Deacon, a 72-year-old widower, slept the dreamless sleep of the self-righteous and unimaginative in the old wooden frame house where he lived in the back rooms with his granddaughter, Ellen. In a land where people struggled ceaselessly to get along or to build empires, the Senior Deacon had built his commercial establishment in defiance of all practicality, untroubled by his tenuous grasp on solvency.

Ellen was a mousy, quiet girl of indeterminate age (she was actually 17) who wore plain, shapeless clothes that had come to hand by luck, charity, and her own skill with a needle. Living almost entirely indoors, her skin was spectral white, with a smattering of light freckles. As if to accent this ghostly effect, her hair was wispy white-blond, with eyebrows and lashes so light she appeared to have almost none at all. No one ever spoke about Ellen's long-absent mother, nor the father who abandoned them when she was born.

The two of them, grandfather and young woman, comprised the sum total of Turkle's abolitionists. The pair generally kept this view to themselves, however, enabling their neighbors to tolerate their heresy as merely another eccentric notion of the hare-brained family.

The pair eked out a modest living in the house's converted former reception parlor. In this cramped space, they derived a stipend serving as the local government records office. The grandfather called the room's other enterprise "an honor store", a business patronized almost exclusively by members of his own church. The honor store consisted of shelves on three walls, which held a meager collection of cheap goods, tinned meats, and fabric, plus a chaotic assortment of handmade curio items and broken tools long abandoned there on consignment by the town's desperate, its widows and unlucky sharecroppers.

It was Ellen who determined the honor store's prices. She based these entirely on her mood, instinct, inspiration, or desperation, whichever was in ascendancy on the day she chose to mark the honor store's goods.

The store's other furnishings consisted of a table, upon which sat a cigar box for the money, a guest chair, and a rocking chair in which the Senior Deacon sat from daybreak to dusk reading his Bible—the old Bible with the vain, vengeful, violent God.

The prune-faced Senior Deacon called his establishment an honor store because customers were expected to take whatever they needed and place their payment in the box, on their honor, at the times when he and his granddaughter were in church, which was often. It also meant that members of his church with no money could take anything useful or edible without paying. The assumption was that the honor store would be repaid in better times, a good feeling both sides of the imaginary transaction chose to believe, but neither ever expected to be consummated. While the customers browsed, the Senior Deacon never looked up from the page, and the embarrassed customers would have to clear their throats to make him realize they'd made their choices. If they had no money to pay, he would write single-word descriptions of their selections on a scrap of paper and place it in the cigar box without ever mentioning a dollar figure.

At the end of each day, the Senior Deacon would rise from that day's reading, remove the handful of coins from the box, then take the hand-scribbled pieces of paper and toss them into the stove fire where Ellen was cooking their supper. In this way, he trusted in God to account for his customers' finances, sort of making Him the supreme bookkeeper for the store. The Senior Deacon's objective was a firm throne on the other side of the grave, where money had no meaning, and he believed his single-minded mercantile practice established a substantial credit balance there waiting for him.

Their survival was aided by the pittance received from the town for keeping its more obscure official records, the ones too insignificant to file at the county seat. This, too, was Ellen's sole providence, and she kept the almost worthless dusty papers in meticulous order to occupy her endlessly solitary days.

A loud pounding on the honor store's front door woke the deacon. He lit his bedside candle, put on his robe and passed through the living quarters, shooing the frightened but curious Ellen back to her room. When he reached the front window, he pulled its faded lace curtain aside and peeked out. Staring back at him from the other side of the glass was the face of a stranger.

"Got to register a deed," the man said.

"Come back Monday," he replied. The Senior Deacon shook his head in disgust. Then he noticed quite a gaggle of people standing on his porch behind the stranger. Straining his eyes to see into the darkness, the Senior Deacon made out Devereau French. This was a different matter.

"Let me get my pants on," he growled, and dropped the curtain.

Seeing it was official government business, Ellen threw on her robe, which she tied tightly and buttoned at the neck so she was covered modestly.

Hurst waited, trying to act calm, sneaking sly glances at his unwelcome entourage. Harmless, mostly, except for the single dandy, who was flanked by unwholesome-looking armed riffraff. *What kind of man dressed like that—and had armed escorts—in this part of town?* he wondered. This was a terrible omen.

The Senior Deacon shuffled in his slippers to the cramped office, followed by the granddaughter. Hurst followed along with his unwanted retinue. While the old man lit the rusty lantern, once rescued from the consignment pile, Ellen seated herself at the desk, blowing dust off the large books the town had entrusted to her.

"Now, let's see what's so important we miss sleep before Sunday Church," the deacon said.

Seating himself opposite Ellen, Hurst reached in his jacket and pulled out the paper. With a grand flourish, he flattened the agreement on the edge of the desk and laid it on the records book. Brushing Ellen's hand aside, the deacon picked up the wrinkled document and disdainfully studied it, then his eyes widened. Seeing his distress, three townsmen crowded behind him to read over his shoulder.

"The whole Chickasaw forest this side of the river!" one of the locals exclaimed. There were awed gasps, wild whispers and whooping it up among the startled gathering—all except the quiet, thoughtful Devereau French.

"Well, after all these years, Turkle now has two great landowners!" another townsman shouted, eliciting a laugh from the gathering.

"Looks like the man stole a bigger chunk from them Indians than your granddaddy did, Mister French!" the third man proclaimed.

Hearing the name, Hurst stared at the man they addressed. So he was the one who ran the town; the last of Turkle's once lusty, violent, seemingly monolithic French tribe. Small, smooth-faced, and immaculately dressed, he didn't look much like the Great Man of anything.

At Antoinette's urging the previous night, Isaac, the local partner, had regaled everyone around the campfire for hours with tales of the notorious French family; for decades an insatiably greedy, drunken stain upon the town's propriety. Apparently, years ago the current Missus French—a French by marriage only—through clever maneuver, routed the whole clan from Turkle, casting them piecemeal to the four winds until only she and her son remained. How much of Isaac's stories were exaggeration, sheer speculation, or the truth, Hurst couldn't tell, but he wondered what chance *DarkHorse* would have to survive against a woman of such cunning and foresight.

"What do you mean by that?" French asked, suspicious.

"Where'd you think all your *French Acres* come from?" a townsman replied. "Your great-grandpappy run a horse race with the Old Chief. Or didn't your momma tell you?" The group snickered, then grew quiet.

The Senior Deacon strained to read the crude contract in the dim light. "Hurst, eh?" intoned the Senior Deacon knowingly, his frown suggesting he might remember the infamy associated with the name.

Unaware that he was transacting business with the town abolitionist, the only townsperson once sympathetic to his father, Hurst shifted his feet. Searching the faces around him, his gaze fixed on the weapons held by the riffraff.

"But I guess that ain't nobody's business," the deacon said. Then he paused. "Slaves, too?" The deacon peered over his spectacles, inspecting Hurst from top to bottom.

Hurst saw the Senior Deacon's thoughts in his eyes and breathed a sigh of relief. "Well, I wouldn't…I wouldn't call them slaves," Hurst said.

"Then what does this paper mean?" the Senior Deacon demanded.

"Because…" Hurst paused to figure out what to say, but it was a tricky situation with so many people watching. "Because I'm going to sign a paper," Hurst ventured, raising his eyebrows toward the Senior Deacon. "I think you understand."

"You won't have to pay me a dollar for that," the Senior Deacon said, initialing the paper. "It's a service I give free of charge that none take advantage of—especially not our town pride here," and he nodded toward French, the biggest slave owner in the region. "Shall I fill out those papers now?"

"I'd rather they be given the quiet dignity they deserve, without so many gawkers around," Hurst said. "I'll be back for them."

The Senior Deacon gave him a baleful stare. "You know where to find us, Mister Hurst."

The Senior Deacon nodded to Ellen, who wrote some words in the book, then turned it around and slid it across the desk, offering the use of a pen. While she filled out the official deed, the stranger signed his name, struggling through it a few letters at a time. That done, he added the name of his plantation, writing it as one word with two capital letters, *DarkHorse*, which a bystander hanging over his shoulder noted aloud.

The stranger flipped a dented gold coin onto the desk, where it clattered to a stop. "For the deed," Hurst said, growing confident.

The Senior Deacon pushed the deformed coin back. "I offer this service on your *word of honor*, Mister Hurst," he said balefully. "Assuming a man like you has honor."

Hurst nodded thanks.

Ellen passed the deed to Hurst, and he folded and placed it in his jacket. Then he picked up his coin and, out of habit, bit it. He flipped and caught it, admiring it in display for everybody in the room. "Sorry to wake you, deacon." Hurst rose to leave.

French's armed riffraff anxiously brushed their pistols with their fingertips.

"Mister Hurst, wait," French said.

Chapter Ten

French fanned a large wad of high-denominated paper money near Hurst's face. "Your business in this town is not nearly done, sir. Since that land is legally yours, I can turn it into some real gold, real fast for you." French paused, his face showing extreme anguish over the offer he'd just made. *Do I want to enable him to just ride away, never to be seen again?* "I'll make you my livestock contractor," he added, a note of desperation in his voice. "You'd own your own, very profitable business."

Hurst didn't want to be French's, or anyone's, toady. But selling the land was his chance for a quick coup with a profitable getaway. He and Antoinette could begin a new life somewhere with a handsome stake. Knowing how tenuous life is, how hard it is to hang onto any enterprise, how extremely long the odds were against *DarkHorse*, he was severely tempted to take the man's gold. He might have, but something nagged at him, burning in his neck. He had promised his partners, and they had shown him good faith. As jaded as life had made him, he couldn't bring himself to abandon them.

But there was more to it than mere loyalty to men who had trusted him. He discovered he had been carrying an ancient longing to prove to Turkle he was a man to be respected, not a drifter destined for ignominy. And how better to gain respectability than to be thought of as a plantation owner, which is what Big Josh's scheme entailed. No, he had to gamble everything. Fool that he was.

"The bank will cash out your deal Monday morning, more gold than you ever imagined you'd see," French continued. "You could buy your first stock, trade horses, cattle, be an important man."

"Save it. That's gonna be the *DarkHorse* plantation."

"Oh, a plantation!" French laughed, taken aback. "Encumbered by all that tall, green cotton." The gathering chuckled nervously.

The belittling words burned Hurst. He knew he should keep quiet, be polite, but he couldn't control himself. "That's right, Mister French, and I'm going to build a mansion. Bigger than yours. Hell, bigger than the courthouse."

"More fabulous than Solomon's Temple," French retorted. The laughter behind French became more genuine.

"I'll have you out to tea," Hurst said angrily, "if you don't end up murdered like your daddy did." The late Mister French's death was the one story that Isaac swore was true and contained so many details that it sounded plausible to Hurst.

One of the town's hard taboos having been broken, the room instantly hushed. No need to get a French unsettled, which could make regular folks suffer. Two townsmen urgently pushed Hurst toward the door. "You get on out of here," one said, "if you know what's good for you. This town won't tolerate that kind of talk to Mister French."

"What did you mean 'my father murdered'?" French called out, his smooth, pale face reddening.

"He didn't mean nothing, Mister French," a townsman replied, trying to calm him.

"He said my father was murdered!"

"It was just white trash talking," another man said soothingly. "It ain't nothing."

French composed himself. "This is your only chance, Hurst. If you won't sell, I'll see that you never get a seed loan in this town. I'll starve you out."

Hurst tipped his hat while allowing himself to be edged out the door. He had done it and was making a clean escape. "Been a pleasure, Mister French," he said with a sneer, crossing the threshold.

An honor store benefactor through the church, French threw his stack of money down on the table and strode off, followed by his riffraff. "Arrogant fool!" he said between clenched teeth. Trailing after him, the townsmen mumbled apologies to the Senior Deacon, but the elder had already turned his back on the gathering and was headed back to bed, leaving the pile of paper dollars in the haphazard fashion they'd landed, spilled onto the table and fallen onto the floor.

"Get back to bed," the Senior Deacon growled.

"It's just what I'm doing, Grandpa," the diminutive Ellen replied, scurrying to her room in back, her bare feet feathery light. She closed her door behind her, then, climbing into bed, blew out her candle and pulled the covers up to her chin.

She closed her eyes, letting herself sink into the darkness, but she couldn't stop thinking about what she'd just witnessed. If what she understood was true, in the coming days she was going to sign manumission papers, actually freeing human slaves—something she'd never been asked to do. After 17 years of little more than the honor store and church, this late-night encounter was more exciting than a Chautauqua tent revival! She knew it had special meaning; it was a Sign of something extraordinary. Yes, somehow, in some way, her destiny was changed. God had certainly spoken to her through that Mister Hurst's voice, if only she could understand what He meant.

***

Outside in the moonless night, the heavy rain had passed, leaving a hardy drizzle in its wake.

"We need to talk business, Hurst," French commanded, as Hurst mounted the roan.

"I'm minding my own," Hurst replied, playing aggressively while on a roll.

French nodded to his riffraff, who pulled their pistols from their belts and boots, leveling them at Hurst.

"I built that road," French said, referring to the road that passed through what was now *DarkHorse*.

"Sure kept your hands clean doing it."

"It's my road," French insisted.

"You can take it off my land any time you want," Hurst replied. He had to risk an immediate exit; he closed his eyes and spurred the roan. If they shot him in the back, so be it.

"You'll do business with me or this town will expel you like swamp debris," French shouted after him. When the rider did not turn, French paused to consider the situation, then signaled for his men to replace their guns. Furious and frustrated, he stalked back to Miss Olney's. "Oh, but we will do business," he grumbled under his breath, "formal and informal. There will be no seed loan without me, and worse!"

Behind him, one local turned to his neighbor, nodding toward Hurst. "We best make sure he don't mind us on his land fore we go huntin' that a-way."

The townsmen hurried through the rain, returning to the comfort of Miss Olney's benches, kegs, and barrels. While they shook out their hats and dried themselves as best they could, French disappeared into Miss Olney's, followed by his attendants.

Indicating French, one man said, "I imagine that forest looks pretty good to a man who's got a sawmill lying idle."

"Right!" interjected another. "Didn't French ride off to get the lumber rights from them Chickasaws a few years back? Disappeared for a long time."

"Sent his riffraff back and stayed out there alone, is what I hear."

"That ain't like French. He's naked without them hired weasels."

The conversation paused while the men contemplated this startling new feast for a town ever starved for gossip. Throughout the countryside, in every hamlet and county seat where folks lit pursuing their business, there was going to be plenty of livened up speculation and envious chatter.

"Stranger's got the timber, and French has the mill," one man said somberly. "But I wouldn't count on good mill pay any time soon."

He spit his toothpick over the railing. Almost in unison, everyone spit to affirm that unfortunate, but logical, conclusion.

"Life ain't gonna be pleasant for one of them two."

"Or, more likely, it'll be bad weather for both."

***

On the road, Hurst felt the resurrected rain blow in his face, into his eyes, the cold soak into his bones. Yet something was warming him; he felt euphoric. He had met the first two tests, and now all they had to do was the impossible; against some fearsome headwinds.

Riding out into camp, he tied the roan and ducked into the waist-high shelter the men had built for Antoinette out of view from their camp; the large clearing he, and he alone, called the "mansion site". She could see the strain in his face, around his eyes, the exhaustion in his sore, deliberate movements.

"I have the deed in my pocket!" he exclaimed.

She was tolerant of his close presence, watching him stretch out within touching distance in the cramped space.

He rested only a moment, then opened his heart to her. Waving the deed around, he told her about his Dream—a secret he had never revealed to anyone. He began slowly, then the words began to tumble from his mouth of their own accord, as he released a stream of long-repressed ideas and images, alluding to a fantastical-sounding plantation. To her startled ear, his entire monologue was a wild hash of grandiose phrases and animated gestures, devoid of any logic or rational possibility, thrown together for the sole purpose of impressing her.

"You're a partner too," he said. "No obligation on your part."

So that's where his verbal pyrotechnics were leading; he meant for her to share in his swindle. "I decline, Mister Hurst," she said. "I sympathize with your aims, but my personal business will absorb my time." She let that sink in; it was imperative that he didn't misunderstand.

"All right," he said. "But you're still a partner."

"Are your partners free men now?" she asked.

"I have to go back for that. There were too many people around; Mister French was there."

***

She watched Hurst split a log with the ax and lay one of the resultant shards neatly on the pile, watched his partners work about the clearing, hewing saplings to buttress temporary shelters and doing a multitude of tasks to make their situation livable.

Yes, his "partners." When he first told her about his scheme, she thought he was crazy. But now that she was seeing it with her own eyes.

Of course, it was all a house of cards that would succumb to the slightest of breezes, much less to the force that society can bring to bear against an unnatural organism in its midst.

Regardless, she had decided, if they were to aid her in her plan—vague and rudimentary as it was—she would have to tell them everything, and soon.

If she could use these men without harming their interests, all the better. She would do what she could to keep them from falling into danger on her account, but she must go on.

She would have to wait until Hurst learned more about the Frenches, apparently only a mother and her son. But what did she have but time? Time, and the will to go on; to somehow get to them; to take them by stealth and surprise, pistol in hand. She had no idea of how to do that, but what other choice did she have?

She looked at the men around her, realizing she was starting to feel compassion for them, even empathy. She too had been treated shabbily by an aristocratic New Orleans society to which she was alien, even if she had deceived herself into believing she was not. These men were far more alien to society; had been treated more callously than she ever had, even at the tragic end.

And what about the stranger, Durksen Hurst? What were these odd feelings that had intruded into her thoughts about him? Back in New Orleans, if she'd passed him on the street, she would have brushed by him, an inconsequential encounter. But she realized she had begun to care what happened to him, to them all. She thought it amazing that the changed circumstances of a few months could wreak such an upheaval in her view of the world and the people in it. She would think about that…someday.

Chapter Eleven

The morning appeared brightly, a portent of an incipient spring. Devereau French hurried down the hallway to the mansion's main marbled entrance hall. What he saw there made him come to a halt. An elderly black butler was busy polishing a bust of French's father. The massive head sat on a centrally placed marble column in the otherwise empty room, like a talisman planted in the desert to ward off intruders.

Transfixed, French stood there for a long time, watching the dark hand emerging from the white cuff manipulate the rag, contemplating the face of the man he had never met. Was this a cruel face? A sensitive one? What had it been like for this man to go on a merry lark to New Orleans? And to end up marrying his mother? Why her? What had it been like for the two of them to lie together in the night, his sainted father and the reclusive woman with the great mind and lost soul?

More importantly to Devereau, was the man this bust replicated one who could have inhabited the father-dream he'd wrapped so much of his untapped love within all these years?

"Must have been a lot of excitement around here when my father was…was murdered," French commented casually.

The butler paused briefly, then continued polishing, his strokes now slow and deliberate. "Don't know nothing about that, Mister French," he said. "I weren't in the house that night."

"In the house! He was killed in the house? But Mother said…"

The man was in terror—and not of French. "Please, Mister French. I don't know nothing. Please, sir."

French stared at the bust a moment longer, then continued out the door. The foolish lawyer in town who gave him so much advice, much of it bad, once said, "Your enemies will sometimes tell you the truth that your friends won't." French decided to speak to that lawyer. But he already knew that the man would never violate a silence, however implicit, imposed by his mother.

He looked at the slip of notepaper he held. In his mother's shaky script, it read: "COME UP NOW."

He felt his stomach tighten, felt his chest clench. He began to grow dizzy, had to resist throwing up. Gritting his teeth, he crumbled the note and tossed it on the floor. He gave the bust one final, longing stare, then ran out the door into the sunlight.

His eyes, not having adjusted, were blinded by the flash of white light pouring from the sky, which caused French to trip on the verandah steps. He tumbled down all five, landing hard in the dirt, knocking the wind out himself and scraping both hands bloody. Catching his breath, he covered his face and began to softly sob.

I will not answer your summons, his mind screamed, *I will not answer your summons. I will not!*

***

For the third day in a row, grandfather was gone to church, there to spend the day fasting and praying. He had been troubled lately by thoughts of a sin he believed he had committed with a girl long ago in his youth. She had initiated it, but he had done it.

Ellen was alone and bored; even her favorite stories in her Bible couldn't rouse her. Nobody had come into the honor store that day, typical of the lightly patronized establishment, and she suspected nobody would. Even if anyone did chance upon the store, she reasoned, it was an honor store, wasn't it? Customers could take what they wanted without her help. Knowing her grandfather wouldn't return until supper, she put down her Bible and went to her room, leaving the store unattended.

She kept it hidden behind the back panel of her chifforobe. When she was little, she'd discovered that the inner panel of the ancient piece of furniture came loose, and since that day she'd hidden small treasures there. At first, as a small girl, she had hidden little trinkets of which not even her grandfather would have disapproved. She felt good and warm to know that she possessed things in a place only she knew of, away from his prying eyes.

But "Lilith's gown" had magic. She only wore it in secret, on the rare occasions when she had the house to herself. She had made it entirely from material she had acquired by stealth. She'd sewn it secretly, too, into the magical garment it was today, working her needle and thread during the interludes when her grandfather wasn't home and hiding it away before he was due back.

The skirt was cut from a full young girl's dress she found at the annual church bazaar. Made of a silky, shiny material so soft to the touch that it enchanted and fascinated her, the cloth was a stark change from the coarse clothing her grandfather's beliefs and their poverty forced her to wear. The dress it came from was too small for a young woman her age, but she knew her wizardry with a needle could make it into something wondrous and supernatural, clinging to her bony hips, revealing in the mirror what curves she had.

The blouse was made from gossamer lace curtains of a light, white cotton that once hung in the little storage closet off the kitchen. But that had been five years ago and she'd grown since then, not so much in volume compared to the other girls her age—the strapping farm daughters who cooked fatback and helped in the fields—but greatly in proportion for a girl who was slight enough to fit into the tiny, constricted world she inhabited with her grandfather.

Now that she had begun to fill out, the blouse was so tight across her chest it no longer reached to her belly button. Besides, she could see through the flimsy material, which presented no problem to her as a child, but now she could see the dark oval outline of the pair of them through the material, as if she was naked.

The first time she wore the skirt and blouse together she had stood before her mirror fascinated, watching herself turn and move for hours. She'd spent that day feeling free and wild, euphoric to be alone, admiring herself and brushing her hair, or lying on the bed and dreaming about stories in the Bible in which the kings of old were smitten with sultry queens and other such things, pretending she was one of them. She'd never before known this private excitement, but she had since repeated it every chance she got.

She heard the door to the honor store open and boots walk in. She froze, still as a post, holding her breath, hoping whoever it was would take what he wanted and leave. Then she heard a voice calling out for her grandfather: the stranger who had registered the deed late in the night before Sunday church.

She was in a panic. She wanted to hide Lilith's gown and replace it with her plain dress. But his second and third calls sounded so plaintive, yet so sweet, that a wild notion took hold of her, spinning her secret thoughts out of control.

**

Hurst thought he heard movement in the back room, as if a child was moving haltingly across the ancient floorboards on tiptoes. To pass time, he drifted around the room, studying various items that amused him, fingering them absently and placing them back on the shelves. Then she was there.

She was so light on her feet he hadn't heard her come in. One moment he was alone, another, the pale-skinned wisp of a girl was standing by the doorway to the living quarters. He made her out in the dim light, what looked to him like a small, colorless-white pubescent girl wearing a costume of sorts. The shape of her small, lithe hips were visible through the clinging material. The blouse was even more revealing.

"What do you want?" she whispered, the words struggling out of her constricted throat through the dusty, motionless air.

"The Senior Deacon said he'd give me some papers. To free…to free my…my slaves."

"You sit down." She pointed to the guest chair and scurried from the room. He sat as he'd been instructed.

Once she passed through the curtain to the living quarters, she pressed her back to the wall, trying to catch her breath, her mind racing. What was she doing? She'd let him see her wearing Lilith's gown! What if he told someone? What if someone came into the store while she was busy with him? She'd look foolish rushing from the room. But when the fear wore down, she controlled her inspired excitement. She had a charged feeling in her nerves that was far in excess of her nakedness within the gown.

Now for the first time in her life she was going to do some paperwork that was more than a mundane title to a scrub farm or the other formalities she made official for a quarter or a dollar. This time her own practiced handwriting was actually going to free some of God's children from bondage, just as Moses had freed his people in the Book. Now was the singular moment in her life, and she was thankful her grandfather wasn't there to spoil it. She gathered all the dusty, yellowed, cracking parchment certificates they had for this purpose, forms that had been lying unused for years. Taking a deep breath, she glanced down at herself, noting how her secret circles had begun to blossom. Then she re-entered the honor store.

He watched her glide in, papers in hand, still wearing the fabulous outfit.

She pushed the empty moneybox aside, laid the papers on the table, then sat across from him. Without a word, she inked the pen and started writing the date on each of the official-looking documents.

"How many people are you going to free?" she asked.

"Twelve," he said. He pulled out a piece of paper with a list of names scrawled down its length in his own hand, and counted them one at a time. "Yes, twelve is right."

"Twelve?" The young woman's brow creased with concern. She licked her finger and counted the pages, one by one. When she got to the last one she cried out gleefully, "Twelve!" And picked up the pen again. God would not leave her short of manumission forms.

"Name?"

"You mean, mine, or the—?"

"Not yours."

He handed her the list and watched her write out the first name in her neat, artistic hand. As she wrote, he became distracted, staring at her blouse. Thoughts bubbled in his head and his face grew flushed. She wasn't unattractive, not unattractive at all.

Before he knew what was happening, she turned the sheet around so he could read it. Then she rose and went behind him to stand over his shoulder. He tensed, holding his breath. In that close proximity, he could smell the fragrant lilac powder she wore interwoven with the dusky smell of the clothing that had lain hidden for so long in the cramped confines of her chifforobe. She leaned across him and pointed to a line on the bottom of the page, her body pressed against his.

He inclined toward her to make the contact more solid, feeling her rapid, sweet breath on his neck. They stayed this way for many long seconds, then her voice broke the stillness.

"That's where you sign," she said, pointing.

She dipped the pen and placed it lightly in his hand, leaving hers to linger on his. He felt her skin against his, her soft fingertips, her warm palm. Then she withdrew her hand. He signed his name and turned to look more closely at her, his mouth dry.

She returned to her chair, sat, and filled in the names and date on the other documents—as he looked her over, his breathing growing faster, shorter. He loved to watch her smooth fingers draw words like poetry on the page, loved to see the writing motion cause her right breast to jostle ever so slightly. When this ceremony was done, she turned the whole stack toward him and offered the pen.

"Sign them, just like the first."

He pulled the stack to his side of the table and began to affix his signature to them. She watched him, admiring his rough hand struggling on the page, his broad lips spelling out the letters. Heart fluttering, she drank deeply of his squinting dark eyes, the lines and sorrow around them like a handsome prophet in her Bible. When he was done, he set down the pen and they both rose. She was staring at him, her eyes alive, almost too much so.

"They's set free, just like white men is," she exclaimed, her exuberance unrestrained. In one motion she rushed up to him and threw her arms around his neck, then kissed him quick and hard on the lips (the first man, excepting her grandfather, that she had ever kissed). Then she nestled into his body and squeezed him with everything she had. For her, it was like the stars opened in glory and light, like the magic in the itinerant stump preacher's words in the Chautauqua tent as she prepared to sing her favorite hymn; like Sunday church social suppers with other people her age who weren't making rude remarks at her; like the smells and tastes of all the church social foods that she could not afford. It was sparkles and fireworks, like a dream she once had.

He felt her body against his, slight, but a woman's body nonetheless, and pressed his hand against her tender, skin-and-bone back. Then she backed away from him, crossing her arms across her chest, staring into his eyes. As if suddenly startled, she covered her mouth with the back of her hand, seemingly about to break into tears.

"Don't you never tell no one you been here today," she pleaded. "But you can come back."

Then just as suddenly as she'd rushed to kiss and hold him, she turned and fled from the room, her footsteps quiet as a ghost.

Hurst stood there, stunned, not knowing what to do. After a while, he took up the papers, left the house and mounted the roan for the ride back to *DarkHorse*.

On the road, he imagined his partners' gleeful celebration. They were free men, legally non-chattels, if no one examined the situation closely. But as Hurst thought about it, he realized it would be a quiet, bittersweet moment, a cold comfort for them. In their vulnerable situation and sitting on land coveted by everyone in Turkle, especially by the Frenches, Big Josh's admonition that they must keep their freedman status a secret made sense. *They'll be free men pretending to be slaves!* This realization deflated him.

The irony was, if someone like Mister French had signed the papers, Hurst's partners would be in the clear, able to do whatever they chose. Unfortunately, it was Hurst who had signed and, though his partners could now be considered free—through some leap of faith or twist of imagination—they couldn't reveal it to anyone. The charade would have to be maintained, and Hurst couldn't see the end of it.

Yet, he figured if he ended up hanged or imprisoned or run off, at least Big Josh, Isaac, Little Turby, and the rest could pull out these papers to complicate the situation; they would have some kind of a chance; they could say he had misled them.

Besides, the girl hadn't charged him the dollar.

***

In her room, the Senior Deacon's granddaughter lay face down on the bed, crying in fits. After almost half an hour she was able to rise weakly, utterly shaken, to remove and hide Lilith's gown. Then she put on her nightdress and took to her bed with feverish trembling.

After dark, her grandfather returned from church. When he smelled no supper cooking, he hurried into her room only to find her in bed, claiming she was sick. It seemed forever before he quit asking if he could help and departed, closing her door. His arrival had opened her nerves again.

On the one day she had been granted dispensation from her little life to actually *free* a dozen of God's creatures, she had despoiled the whole august event by wearing the harlot gown. And to top it off, she had dishonored the honor store! She knew she was bound for Hell. It was the most confusing thing that ever happened and, at the same time, the greatest tragedy of her life.

Then she received divine guidance. The idea came to her like Heaven's light and filled her every pore with soothing warmth, like a hot bath. Yes, there was one way to redeem herself; to do so in full! She was only grateful that at last she knew what that one desperate act would be, knew what ultimate sacrifice would be required of her. Her plan would take time and some degree of subterfuge and risk, but she steeled herself for all that. There were many women in the Bible who had done bad—even using their womanliness—to do good in the service of the Lord's purposes in eternity. For the first time in her constricted life she knew she was destined to be one of these women, to be His instrument. She only wondered why the idea had never occurred to her before. It was almost as if…almost as if her encounter with the stranger had been a Sign!

Of course, the question of Hell still stood between her and her objective. She was certainly going to have to endure much, much more than a single kiss. But if God meant her heroism to be rewarded with Hellfire, well, she was nonetheless determined to sacrifice her immortal soul to fulfill her quest. Besides, would God punish a girl for doing His will?

Yes, she would free all the slaves in Turkle. She didn't know how one converts seduction to manumission, but that clean-shaven Mister French was just the King she needed to be her instrument, and God's.

And Lilith's gown had been the inspiration and the catalyst.

Section II

Threadbare Illusions

Chapter Twelve

March, 1859

Devereau French wrote a formal invitation to supper on good watermarked paper in his elegant hand and handed it to Annie, who opened the bedroom door and called. A small barefoot boy ran up the dark hallway to answer her summons. Taking it, the boy picked up his candle and hurried away.

Up one shadowy, frightening hallway and down the other, he crossed the entire vast house until he reached the door to Missus French's room. There he was greeted with knowing nods by her two manservants. When the boy held up the invitation, the pair declined to touch it with a wave of their hands. The boy thrust it at them, but they again refused, shaking their heads and shying away.

"You the one done brung it," the oldest one said.

As the boy struggled with this terrifying impasse, the younger of the servants, tiptoeing, placed his ear against the door. At last, he signaled the boy forward. The boy gathered his nerve and tapped lightly on the door.

An angry growl came from within. Hearing this, the boy opened the creaking door and stepped gingerly into the room. After pausing to let his eyes adjust to the dark, he worked his way along the path that passed between the warehoused paintings, statues, strongboxes, silver sets, and jewel cases. When he reached her chair, he laid out the invitation on her chessboard. Missus French held her candle above it, then looked up.

"Is it day or night?" she asked.

"Supper gone be 'bout a hour."

Missus French nodded assent, then returned to her thoughts. The boy waited nervously and, seeing she would say nothing else, hurried quietly from the room to pass word along to the kitchen.

***

Mother, at the head, and offspring sat three chairs apart without speaking at the table designed to seat fourteen Frenches and related guests. The flames of candles positioned on the oak surface fluttered in the draft that seeped in through leaded glass windows encircling the large room; their faint luminescence utterly failing to break the gloom.

The tension between the two was almost palpable. Missus French knew she had not received the rare invitation because Devereau wanted company. Supper was not a social event; they both preferred eating alone (with only the servants at elbow to do their bidding). But Missus French hoped Devereau's purpose was to discuss business and that she could somehow turn the meeting into a chess match. It had been so long since they had played.

A cook held the platter as the servant forked two bloody slices of top round and placed them on Missus French's plate. The servant then picked up the gravy boat and delicately spooned the rich brown sauce thick with mushroom and sweet potato chunks onto the slices.

Satisfied, the cook carried the platter to where Devereau sat glowering at his mother, as though seeing her across a barren field in winter. He selected one slice of burnt meat and waved the meat platter away. The slightest sign of red always killed his appetite, and the cook had been careful to scorch his extra lean piece.

Devereau cleared his voice, but his mother, absorbed in supervising the cutting of her meat, did not notice. Gathering his courage, French called to her twice more before he got her attention.

"Mother, what haven't you told me about my father's death? You said he was killed in an accident."

As the word "killed" echoed and died in midair, Missus French's gloved hands fumbled her fork, dropping it into her plate. "In a hunting accident, that's right. What is this foolishness again? Is someone giving you wild notions?"

"I've asked others," Devereau replied defensively. "Even the town drunk is afraid to discuss it. What is it you—and everyone else—have been keeping from me? The lawyer tells me that word may get around in a small town, but secrets about a person can be kept from that person forever. Someone can live his whole life being the only person in town who doesn't know."

"The lawyer is a long-winded ass," Missus French replied. "And you, wasting time listening to him." Missus French fiercely eyed Devereau. "Oh, I see," she said, "it's that stranger, isn't it? Listen, you get rid of him and take that land. You hear me? I don't care how you do it. He is some kind of Indian, I hear, and a great danger to us, a *great* danger."

Devereau simply stared at her.

As Missus French feared, it was *that* problem again. She scowled and signaled for her man to wipe the gravy off her fork handle, to protect her white gloves.

While Devereau meticulously carved his piece of meat, carefully cutting away every speck of fat, his mother stared through the dim candlelight at his troubled face. Etched into his soft features were the years of desperate loneliness he couldn't escape—and from which she couldn't release him. Despairing, she felt the painful prick that stung her heart every time she contemplated her long-suffering child. Yes, it was all her fault, but what else could she have done? Nothing, under the circumstances; the alternatives would have been far worse, likely fatal. What could she do now to free the child? Almost nothing.

Almost. But she still had one possible counterattack that might turn the whole game their way, a brilliant gambit that she had been painstakingly ruminating on for *over thirty years*. A saving grace that, if she could effect it, might fulfill all their fondest desires, transforming the French mansion into the loving home it had never been. If only Devereau would be patient and trust her just a while longer.

No further words were spoken between the two diners that evening. They would not play a game of chess.

***

Big Josh rubbed his massive arms to get his circulation going. The mid-morning air was cold and damp, and the long idleness demanded by their discussion with the woman had given him a chill. He looked to the distant trees circling the campsite, barely hearing the words. The place was his, theirs. He was free—at least for now.

Big Josh had known it was coming. He could see it in the woman's eyes, in her mannerisms. Right after breakfast Hurst rode off to explore good hunting sites. She waited an hour, then told Big Josh to gather everyone around to hear the truth, her truth.

He knew what she was doing. She wanted to tell them first, without Hurst to interfere. If they didn't want her there, she would leave immediately, without Hurst to stop her.

Besides, everyone would be more forthcoming without Hurst. Slaves by necessity lived their lives hiding their true feelings from white folks. Even a strong man like Big Josh often found himself doing it out of habit. Certainly their circumstances had changed, and Hurst was far different from the General and his crowd, but their white partner surely couldn't change the color of his skin any more than they could.

He stared at the woman as she revealed her predicament, barely hearing her story. Her presence could constitute a fatal risk. She could stay, but only at a safe distance from the "mansion site". That way, she'd be able to flee if they were surrounded, but close enough to join them any time she felt compelled to.

For Big Josh, living on *DarkHorse* was so different, he felt a sort of vertigo. Added to that, the woman's horrific revelation had exacerbated his already terrifying sense of isolation. And if Big Josh was shaken, how much worse was her predicament affecting his partners? Two of the men seemed already near wit's end.

Big Josh climbed down from his seat, resolved not to think about the perilous quagmire they were in. They had a job to do, to build her a better shelter. Yes, his partners were in turmoil now. They had little to eat, but they would get more—or die of starvation. He would simply go on. What else was there to do?

As he headed for the woods, he tried to evaluate things, to establish a simpler reference for their lives. Certainly, clearing the land was like being back home. Yet they were far more than miles from civilization; it was as if they had arrived in some distant country or on a deserted island. And that was disturbing, more than anything else.

***

She had to tell him. Alone. As evening fell after the much-abbreviated supper, she agreed to go with him to see it.

They went on foot, with him leading her along pathways he'd discovered. After the first quarter-mile they began to talk fitfully, then more fluidly. At first, his remark on the beauty of the night and the living green Eden around them missed its mark. She agreed, but not wholeheartedly, believing he had an ulterior motive. But the further they walked, the more she was swept up in their surroundings, the full moon, the quiet words between them, his boyish laughter.

Another side of him showed through, and this touched her. Of all the men she had known, the elite of New Orleans, society gentlemen, rich merchants, political powers, carefully groomed and polished men vain about their actions and deeds, Durksen Hurst was one of the few who wasn't entirely self-righteous about his activities or his mission. He was completely obsessed with what he was attempting. But still, he was different.

He remarked again on the majesty of what they were seeing, of what surrounded, actually breathed about them, and she could sense his deeply felt reverence for it. She realized he was one of those rare, restless individuals who had spent all his hours—growing up in the Chickasaw village, in the white world, throughout his wanderings in the South's cities and hamlets—trying to piece together patterns, to contemplate meanings, rather than simply careening from one moment to the next, blindly chasing pleasures and enduring pains. He'd told her that's when his reading compulsion had captured him, and she could see the proof of it in his words and thoughts.

The sun went its way, and the darkness seemed to unite the vine and brier to the trunks of the ash and gum trees bordering their pathway. After struggling through the denseness, they emerged to the moon touching upon them through the trees' dappled shadows.

When they reached the place, the moon lit it like a gallery painting. The grotto was just as Hurst described it: a subterranean-fed waterfall tumbling over a steep outcropping of wet rock into a deep, clear pool. Surrounded by lush ferns and a smattering of wild flowering plants, the whole tableau was embraced by encircling great cypress and ash. She thought it breathtaking, a vast change from the dusty country roads and fetid swamps she had traversed over the past weeks.

"See, I told you," Hurst said, his eyes twinkling.

The woman from New Orleans took a few steps away and sat on a large, dry boulder to admire the scene.

"It is lovely here," she mused. "Lovely."

"People wouldn't believe the things of beauty that can be found on *DarkHorse*," Hurst uttered softly, hoping, but the woman was not going to accept such a tone.

"Mister Hurst," she said, growing serious, "I want to know if you plan to keep your word to your partners."

"Antoinette," Hurst said, "I've never cheated anyone. Kind of. What I mean is, I've been cheated—" He stopped, unable to explain the distinctions. He walked to the pool's edge and looked at the moon's reflection rippling in its dark waters. What could he say to make her trust him?

While he attempted to gather his thoughts, she extracted paper money from her jacket. She peeled off a number of bills and extended them toward him. He hesitated, unable to either move or take his eyes off the money. She urged it toward him.

"Here, don't be a fool."

He approached slowly, staring blankly at her. Why was she trusting him now? He had known in the back of his mind that a woman like her might have money, but he had ignored that thought because it placed such a distance between them. Still, he was shocked to see so much of it in her hands.

"Antoinette, you just bought yourself a full partnership in our plantation," he said, attempting a smile. This offer solved everything. He could accept her help and at the same time attach her to *DarkHorse*. He imagined her in his arms, but she didn't even return his smile.

"I do not accept, Mister Hurst. This is a purchase price for your aid and discretion. When I explain my circumstances—and what I'll need you to do for me—you might ask for more than I have to give you." Still he held back. "Never mind," she continued. "Here. This will get *DarkHorse* started. It's all I'm willing to part with."

He took it, thanking her in the name of the partnership. Then he looked at her again, his heart swelling at her closeness, which shone in stunning relief against the wasteland that had been his previous life. Money or no, she was now part of his great fantasy life.

"Listen, I meant that about you being a partner. I dreamed about this so long, about how this would be, but now that it's coming to pass… I mean, you could live like a lady again and—"

"No, stop." She couldn't let this go any further. "Durk, I haven't led the easy, innocent life you think I've led. I'm not what you imagine."

"Hell, I'm not what *anybody* imagines," he replied. He had to see how she felt about him. He leaned forward to kiss her, but she stopped him cold with her hand, pulling back.

"There's something dead in me," she said. "Maybe forever."

He stared into her eyes, half-elated, half-resigned to losing her. "That deep sadness in you," he said. "I wish—"

"Don't. Wishing only makes it worse."

"You're right," he admitted. "I wished for you long ago."

"Not for me, you didn't. Not me."

***

"His family was old money, the New Orleans DuValliers. Perhaps you've heard or read of them. He owned a whole fleet of trading ships."

"Your husband? And you shot him?" Hurst felt his heart lock up in mid-beat. He resented this man who had had her love.

"In stone cold blood."

"And?" he said.

"I didn't stick around to see if it was fatal, but I believe it was."

"But…but, why?"

She rose and walked to the pool, staring blindly into its waters, trying to decide how much to reveal and what to conceal.

"He was a good man, but he'd been sick, on death's doorstep at one point. I know that can change a man.

"I was unerringly faithful to him. I did love him." She knew she was obscuring the story in a flurry of words. She would simply have to buck up her courage and be out with it.

"Anyway, one of our young belles found herself with a loaf in the oven and no ring on her finger. I know his legacy had been on his mind." She paused, unable to speak.

"Don't tell me," Hurst said tenderly. "This young woman took a fancy to the DuVallier money. I guess many a man's been a fool for that."

"Her family—the *right kind* of family—spread stories that my great-grandmother was a slave. They had documents, from whatever source, if they were genuine, I couldn't know. Of course, being an orphan—"

"You had no way to dispute it," he said, furious at the injustice.

The telling of it was going to be more difficult than she thought. She cleared her throat, then continued:

"At first, I didn't care about the tales, one way or another, until I saw their effect on my husband. Then, I was repulsive to him, to all our friends and acquaintances. He refused to touch me. He ordered the servants to displace me from our bedroom, to keep me out of his sight. I went to his office, but he refused to receive me. And it wasn't something we could discuss, because there was nothing I could prove or disprove, even if I had wanted to."

She remembered the eyes upon her, his eyes, everyone's, as if some miniscule portion of her that wasn't human had gained ascendancy within her and transformed her into an ogre.

Hurst opened his mouth to speak, then hesitated. Whatever its source, her skin was the most desirable thing he'd ever beheld, but he couldn't say that.

"I take people as they are, good or bad," Antoinette continued, "but the law in Louisiana sees it differently. You know, the law states that, in marriages like he now believed ours to be, the husband can declare a divorce whenever it suits him." She snapped her fingers. "That quick. Just sign a paper. Forget the marriage ceremony in the Grand Cathedral, conjoined for eternity by a special dispensation of the Bishop himself and sanctified by all that is holy. Forget...everything." She paused, fighting to maintain control.

"No, mine was no side-door marriage, not that that would have been an impediment. There hadn't been any need for that as I was a well-known, relatively successful businesswoman when he met me."

Hurst knew of the New Orleans practice of side-door marriages. He'd had friends who'd resorted to that very institution to sanctify their love. New Orleans had a large free-black population, the largest in the country. Over the years, in fact, many free blacks had grown quite wealthy, owning great estates and successful businesses. Free blacks also dominated many highly skilled professions, including creating much of the decorative wrought iron throughout the city.

When couples of mixed background married, however, they were joined in ceremony at the side door of the church, held on the steps outside, an expedient the church took to protect their immortal souls while not disturbing society's racial notions. Other institutions, like the formal quadroon balls, supplied opportunities for the substantial classes of both races to meet, from which many unions were created that defied the years.

"Of course," Hurst added, venom in his voice, "it's men like Mister DuVallier and his friends who write the law. I've seen enough of that." He stopped, trying to see it through her eyes, to understand how much it must have hurt her. The silence became unbearable. After a long hesitation, he asked, "Did you have children?"

He had struck the heart of the matter. Her lower lip trembled, and she attempted a brave face. "Yes, my precious Louis Edward. He's three. Louis Edward is a little slow—a sweet, loving boy, but slow." She fell silent.

"When I lost my humanity, our son became simply one more of my husband's chattels and, at that, a visible reminder of me. And given Mister DuVallier's preoccupation with his own death, with his legacy, our rumor-tainted little boy wasn't a very prized possession.

"Then he received an offer from a place called Turkle and saw a future for his son, far away from society."

Overcome with grief, she covered her eyes.

"I'm sorry, Antoinette," he whispered.

He realized then she was doomed; there was no way to stop her. He'd seen it often. No man could replace a good woman's feelings for her child. Some women were willing to throw over their children for a man, but in his experience he knew that was often based on a vain woman's feelings for herself—and the man's money. Always on the hunt himself, he'd played the pretend-to-have-money game with this type of woman, but it seldom lasted for long, nor returned much satisfaction. You need proof with a woman like that, and the proof always ran too dear for the return.

On the other hand, he'd always found a good woman's faith to be very expensive in other, less material ways. The game of honesty had always been a tough one for him to play; he believed he just didn't have the instinct for it.

But this woman had exposed those honest instincts, raw, confused and deeply buried as they were. At once, he found himself in unexplored waters, with the stars overhead in unfamiliar patterns. He knew his need for her, when drawn to the surface, was going to be painful. But what could he do? Yes, he despaired, a hustler in love is doomed. Doomed, like every other fool. Doomed, like this woman's foolhardy quest.

He clenched his teeth, missing her already. He wondered what other surprises awaited him. A loss like this, a wound beyond any happiness he could hope to achieve, wasn't what he had planned. He knew a bad bet when he saw it, but couldn't stop himself.

***

The bright sun high in the sky was growing hot against their skin. Little Turby, afraid of being left behind, stumbled through the forest undergrowth, hurrying to keep up with Big Josh.

Ahead, Big Josh crossed the wide, shallow ford using broad strides, stepping from rock to solid ground to rock to keep his boots dry.

Unexpectedly, he heard a splash and a groan behind him and turned to see Little Turby struggling to raise himself from face down in the water.

"You needs to take off your clothes 'fore you takes a bath," Josh needled him. For being so dang smart, Little Turby sure been having troubles out in the wild.

Little Turby, already suffering cuts, scrapes, bruises, and strawberries all over his hands and arms and legs and knees, didn't show any appreciation for Josh's humor. He wiped his face and glasses with his shirttail, then brushed the mud and leaves off his clothes as best he could.

Big Josh chuckled watching him, thinking warm thoughts about the bright young man. Then, seeing Little Turby was fit to travel, he proceeded. The long hike back was giving him time to think about their life in the wilderness, with few tools, little food and no money. He was free, but free to do what? Starve to death? Get arrested? Get hung?

Breathing the free air, he wistfully imagined Ceeba at *French Acres*, working in the fields this time of day. To the Frenches, she was just livestock, like a plow horse. But to Big Josh, she was everything love had to offer, her great round eyes, her sweet lips, her soft skin. He had to see her soon or he'd go crazy.

His thoughts drifted to back home. He remembered his loving momma and his kinfolks, his friends and the people who lived in the quarters. He remembered Libbeth, the woman he once lived with. But with General's place sure to be broken up and auctioned off, all were surely gone now. Where? He'd never find out, never see them again. It was a place more lost in time than in distance.

The past.

His nature was to love life, even on General's plantation. Not that the circumstances couldn't have been better, but even back then, in spite of his enslavement, he couldn't stop himself from loving at least the active completeness of his days, the waking in the morning with jobs to do, with things to get done.

He'd been born on the plantation and as a little boy helped his momma and daddy at picking time. When he was still very young and shy, the older boys teased him because of his stutter and his size, calling him a fool—at least, until he grew too big to tease with impunity. Being young, he believed they were right. But he proved to be nobody's fool.

By the time his daddy died, Big Josh was already a hardworking, bright, practical sixteen-year-old, and the hurtful comments ceased. Later he'd been made field-boss, then at thirty-seven, the big boss of the whole plantation who ran everything, including the white hired hands.

He liked everything about getting work completed. That was his nature. He liked using his hands to tool a gin or drain a field. He took great pride in what his strong body could lift. *Need two men to get it loaded? Just watch everyone's face when I totes it by myself.* He also liked figuring out new and better ways to get the desired results from materials and instruments intended for other purposes. Nobody could figure out how to do things like Big Josh, no sir.

Most of all, he liked using his heart. He liked helping people in time of need. He loved and respected people and liked feeling that they loved and respected him back. All in all, Big Josh knew that, given the chance, there was nothing he couldn't do. Nothing, except stop the General's losing.

That had been the General's downfall, the losing. The General could afford to pay dearly for the chance to win, for the chance to feel good about himself, feel pride. But when the losing meant so little, it was hard for the General to concentrate his mind on the winning, not that the winning meant much to him. So the General drank, to enjoy the moment and not feel the pain of defeat. And then it just got to be the habit of drinking and bragging and hollow laughing and chancing—and losing. And now the General was submerged deep in the Chickasaw swamp, as if he meant to put himself there in the first place.

Big Josh neared the last trap, bone weary, his hungry stomach pinched. Empty, too, like the others. They'd set this trap right on a trail well-worn from paws and hooves and covered it with leaves, but nothing.

Little Turby examined the area. "We could dig a deep pit here," he said. "Cover it with branches. Catching a bear would feed us for days."

"A bear?" Big Josh said, frowning. "And who' going to jump down in there and kill it? You?"

Turby's face fell. "Maybe...maybe it'll starve to death 'fore we do."

***

Spring was in full gallop, making the hardship more easily borne. That night, most of the partners went directly to their lean-tos and wrapped up in blankets, tired and sore from a long, hard day, and still hungry.

Antoinette sat with the remnants—Hurst, Big Josh and Isaac—at the long common table they'd fashioned. Big Josh explained offhandedly what work he would expect from everyone when sunrise came, mentioned Hurst's coming trip to the county seat, but the talk was merely to pass the time.

They couldn't avoid forever what was on everyone's mind: *DarkHorse's* chances for survival.

"Durk," Antoinette suggested, "I think you have to make some kind of deal with the Frenches to have any chance."

"I'll never deal with those people," Hurst replied so vehemently that Big Josh and Antoinette were taken aback. Without realizing it, he had inherited his father's deep-seated disdain for aristocrats, and all of his experience had never disabused him of it. And the Frenches were the embodiment of his anger and frustration toward the whole class. He knew he wasn't playing this smartly, but he couldn't help himself.

"Mister Hurst," she reasoned, indicating the land around them, "the Frenches can end all this nearly any time they want. You're going to have to come to some accommodation with them. Think of your partners."

"It's going to take all we gots to beat the swamp and all," Big Josh said soothingly, "without rich folks throw'd at us, too. A d-deal with them peoples might even h-help Antoinette here."

"It was the damn *Frenches* killed my father," Hurst said, spitting their name. "If they didn't pull the trigger, they were behind it. I can't just smile and shake their hand.

"Look, Missus French has something in her past that's worse than a scandal. My father used to talk about it. When I've got proof of what she did, they won't be able to touch us."

He turned to Antoinette, to try to make her understand. He had it all planned out—well, not planned out, but he had a hope of how it would be when he beat them.

"And you'll get what you want, too," he told her. It was the only way he could see to do everything at once. This way, she'd be satisfied and stay.

"You s-scares me, Durk," Big Josh said. "I'd rather do it Antoinette's way, the careful way."

"Blackmail is a double-edged sword," Antoinette added.

Isaac had heard enough. He spit out the toothpick he'd fashioned and rose to his feet. "Yeah, you try to get in bed with Mister French," he said scornfully. "He be waiting for *you*." Then he stomped off to his blankets, lay down and turned his back on them.

Everyone watched him go, then trained their eyes on Hurst. But Hurst had figured out how to end the discussion. "Y'all are welcome to make any deal with the Frenches you want," he said. "I'll sign any paper you draw up."

"I see," Antoinette said. "Mister Hurst has had a plantation only a few days, and he's already got 'rich-man's folly'."

"What do you mean?" Hurst asked.

"Durk, I've done business with men of means and influence of every kind, and I've seldom known even the best of them to compromise when pride is at stake. They'd rather doom themselves and everyone around them than change their ways. The whole country will be soaked in blood soon enough to prove that."

"You mean all this war talk?" Hurst asked. This was another problem down the road that he was attempting to ignore.

"Talk?" Antoinette exclaimed. "The fools are hell-bent to ride on white horses under brave banners, sabers waving and plumes flying, and bring this land to waste and ruin. To drown their fortunes, families, and lives in rivers of blood—and nothing will stop them."

She stopped herself before she took this to what she saw as its inescapable conclusion. Yes, she knew these scions of the South. She'd seen how prone they were to zealously believe a host of mutually exclusive ideas and not be troubled by the inherent contradictions. She knew they'd justify their actions with good words, representing noble ideals, words like "God" and "honor" and "country", but for every man who used those words honestly, she'd heard five scoundrels use them falsely.

Yes, they will use the word "country" to render their country asunder, embrace the word "rights" to deny others the most basic rights, wave the word "God" like a banner to justify motives and actions that God would turn from in disgust and sorrow. They would rush ahead in complete blindness to recurrent fateful consequences, until their whole system of beliefs imploded…and never question their actions.

Finally Big Josh spoke up.

"So you think war c-coming?" Big Josh asked. It would be just like General's losing.

"Count on it, Josh," Antoinette replied.

"And I see it, them rivers of blood gonna wash away *DarkHorse* and *French Acres* both," Big Josh said. He stared at Antoinette, seeing that was what she thought as well.

"I could be wrong," Antoinette said, regretting her outburst. It was going to be hard enough for these men without the sense that they're doomed to failure hanging over their heads.

"You ain't wrong 'bout n-none of it," Big Josh said.

Sad that she'd been such a fool, Antoinette rose and walked off into the encircling oaks at the perimeter of the clearing, headed for her distant shelter. Why couldn't she keep her mouth shut!

***

Big Josh glared eye-to-eye at Hurst. Hearing this woman whose opinions he respected—and who gave them money!—say their *DarkHorse* enterprise was headed for disaster had chilled him to his soul. Antoinette had called it "rich-man's folly", but Big Josh had seen many a poor man and a slave, too, come to a sorrowful end because of it—revengers and revenged alike. "All-folks' folly" was more like it.

He watched Hurst lower his eyes, watched his mind working, this man who'd gotten them official-looking papers that said they were free men, a great boon whether the manumissions were of any practical use or not. More than that, the man had given them *DarkHorse* because he needed them and believed in them, as no white man had believed in them before. No, Big Josh would speak his mind, but he would never force Hurst to deal with his sworn enemies.

He watched Hurst rise and, crestfallen, saunter away slowly to his blankets—as if the world weighed on his shoulders, and he knew he wasn't strong enough to bear it. After Hurst was settled, Big Josh sighed wearily and did the same, Antoinette's words crashing in his ears. Tomorrow was going to be a long, difficult struggle for Big Josh's body and his brains, and he knew the "heart" part of his strength was going to be dragging a particularly heavy burden.

Chapter Thirteen

The breeze was light, and he felt an occasional spray of pin drops on his face; the residue of the previous night's storm blowing off the leaves of nearby oaks and cedar. He could breathe and feel the whole green morning. Soon the last traces of winter would pass and the world would abandon its sad narcosis.

He fixed his hat firmly atop his head, straightened his coat and strode purposefully—a bit magnificently—to his horse. Isaac and Big Josh were on the road to the county seat, riding the mule-driven wagon, but the roan would easily catch them. His heart swelled: seeing Antoinette, old feelings came back from his boyhood Chickasaw days, as though the world was painted new. He never felt so alive!

He climbed into the saddle, gazing at her one last time for courage. She was the grandest creature on earth, a gathering of starlight. She had confided in him.

"I'll find out what I can," he said.

"Remember," she cautioned, "you must be completely circumspect in your inquiries. Absolute discretion. You understand?"

"Don't worry, I've been sly before."

He gave her a gallant hat-tip and rode off. Nothing would stop him. He had money in his pocket and new friends. The most majestic woman in the world waited for him. Hell, in only a few days, he was already the wealthiest damn man in all of Miss'ippi!

***

Big Josh and Isaac arrived at the county seat seed and feed store in late-afternoon. They felt a bit of pride wearing the new clothes Hurst had acquired for them at a country store outside Turkle, though both pants and shirts were ill-fitting. At least these weren't frayed, with holes and tears.

Hurst had ridden ahead to do his slippery-like business, leaving Big Josh most of the money for their purchases. Big Josh knew it would be dusk before the wagons were loaded and the three of them were back on the road. But hope meant the hunger didn't hurt so much.

Isaac looked into the eyes of the white men hanging around the barn-like front of the store with its dry-grain smell, idling away the wait for their purchases to be brought up, squatting as country men do or sitting on the barrels and benches. As Big Josh drove the wagon closer, the white men, one by one, turned their heads, until everyone was staring at them. Isaac felt a chill. He knew they were measuring these two strange, raggedly dressed black men, trying to read their intentions. He tensed up, in spite of the fact that he knew the wagon and money would offer some measure of legitimacy to their presence.

Big Josh spoke to Isaac quietly, soothingly, as one would to a skittish mule, but Isaac still felt like leaping from his skin and running away into the woods. He saw a glimpse of a black face looking out from the barn loft near the hanging pulley that was used to lower the sacks. Then two other black men wearing aprons showed in the opening, and together the three watched expressionlessly as the new dark faces pulled up. Isaac fixed his eyes ahead on the mules, not looking to either side. Neither facial tick nor smile crossed his face, nor did he speak a word. For a slave, even a pretend one, fresh news had to await private times.

Big Josh turned the wagon, directing the mules to the hitching field where other wagons, horses and flea-bit mules waited. As their progress slowed, Isaac thought about their predicament, the illusion of fear and the reality of danger. He'd always been afraid, living out in the Chickasaw swamp, existing on hunting and the corn squeezings trade. He feared there might be a reward offered, that someone might turn him in. But he wasn't most afraid of punishment, he was terrified of being enslaved again, at the mercy of men who regarded him as nothing more than an ornery mule.

"I sholy wish we could do something," Isaac said, "to get folks to leave us alone."

"Do what?" Big Josh asked. "If white folks wants to come after us, they comin'."

"Hurst needs to figure some way to keep folks off'n us," Isaac grumbled, hanging his head.

Isaac had an idea! Hurst wanted to make himself into a tall story? Well, Isaac decided he was gonna help him—and help all of them stay alive at the same time. When Big Josh pulled up, Isaac hopped down, unhitched and tied up the mules.

"I'll be back," he whispered to Big Josh.

"Where you going?" Big Josh asked.

"It's for *DarkHorse*," Isaac said and hurried away.

Big Josh merely shrugged. He didn't need no scarecrow to load the wagon.

***

"Yes, sir, Master Dark Horse take care of that white man, that fast. It was like the man was hit by lightning. Yes, sir."

Isaac grinned and studied the faces of the three aproned men who had watched from the loft. His plan was working. When word got around the slave grapevine and out to white folks, why, wouldn't nobody take a chance on crossing Durksen Hurst. Either that, or...

"Why, 'nother time three robbers stop Master Dark Horse on the road, and he ain't even got his pistol with him. Yes, sir. They thought gettin' his gold was gonna be some easy pickin's—*but they was wrong.*

"Somewhere deep down South," he said to the yellow-eyed white men squatting back of the hitching yard, passing a taste of the squeezings, "they's the graves of four bad white mens—and here, my master still breathing God's good air."

The slave in the apron spoke with animated intensity, watched silently by two country farmers leaning against the building. Isaac enjoyed the dramatic tone and fierce arm-waving that accompanied the man's tale.

"Whens they peek up over the log, why he put one right in they eye. All six of them, one ball each. Bamm, he' gone. Bamm, bamm, bamm, bamm. Dead, dead, dead, dead. Bamm! And that man, Dark Horse, still laughing!"

***

Durk Hurst went looking for Big Josh and Isaac. They had what they needed and all they had to do was ride off. He'd been in such fine fiddle that day, playing the town while checking around for information, that he'd made a purchase beyond the plan. He'd happened upon a little house where two widows lived by selling knick-knacks. Widows were often a good source of information—true, false, or exaggerated—plus his few dollars were burning a hole in his pocket. So he'd bought all five of them for four bits. They were lying in a corner of the widow's house, probably untouched for months: a dusty pile of old books, some schoolbooks, some just for reading.

Their mansion was going to have books for anybody who wanted to read them. Including Hurst, of course, who was beginning to think about what landed gentlemen do.

Hurst also acquired what Antoinette wanted, the homespun secondhand dress and a worn bonnet. He thought the notion foolish. Might as well put a plow hitch on her thoroughbred and sell it for a mule.

But she wanted as much cover as possible, even from a distance. It was her money, after all. He guessed her size from the pile of discarded calico patterns by holding them against himself, drawing odd looks from the widows. He imagined they had never seen a man hold up dresses against his own body. They'd gotten a chuckle out of that, which turned his face red even as he laughed with them.

Hurst turned the corner, and the waiting men all jumped to their feet.

"Well," Isaac snickered, "there the legend now."

"Evening, boys," Hurst said cheerily.

"Yes, sir, Mister Dark Horse," one of the locals stammered. "Y-you wants to sit here?"

Hurst looked at Isaac, hoping to get some hint as to why people were acting so oddly in his presence. But Isaac only clicked his tongue and headed off to join Big Josh. He'd tell Hurst about this new trick later when they were away from town and could laugh all they wanted. It would be a "rolling on the ground" story, and he was half-ready to bust out laughing right now.

Then Isaac tried to predict what Big Josh's reaction would be. Maybe the big man wouldn't see the funny side of it. Maybe he'd be angry, angry enough to pummel Isaac.

On second thought, Isaac decided, *I don't think I'm gonna tell nobody. Let them find out for theyself.*

***

"They're back! They're back!" Little Turby shouted, running to gather everyone together. When Isaac pulled up the wagon, Big Josh climbed to the back.

"Help me unload," his big voice boomed, and everyone hurried toward him, smiling and chattering with euphoria and relief.

"County seat sure was friendly taking our money," Isaac said.

As everyone unloaded the firearms, tools, and supplies, Hurst rode up to Antoinette and dismounted.

"Well, you had the money and you came back," she said.

"Think I'd become a 'runaway master'?"

"Did you learn anything?"

Hurst picked up the tin cup, dipped it in the cedar bucket, drank and wiped his mouth with the back of his hand.

"I went to the courthouse, the post office—hell, I bought the law a slice of peach pie. Nothing about you. Nothing."

Antoinette turned away, her mind racing. Then she turned back. "Could it be possible the Frenches are suppressing it? Why would they do that?"

Chapter Fourteen

It was another unpleasant morning, like so many lately. Missus French sat at her desk examining her papers by candlelight. But she could not concentrate. She kept glancing at the door. Finally, Devereau French, dressed for riding, strutted into her suite, and made his way up the treasure alley to face her.

"What is it, Mother? I'm busy."

Missus French sighed and pushed the papers aside. "Your croppers and hands are leaving for their annual hunting trip. They're going out there to get that man's permission to hunt on his land. You go out there with them. She may be hiding out in that cesspool."

"I'll gather up some bodyguards," French said, his brow creasing.

"No, fool. Why don't you send a parade ahead of you? You'll go with Bake. Alone. I want her brought here. Unless you're afraid." She glared at him.

Devereau responded to the affront by shaking his head "no," holding in the desire to lash out.

Missus French opened her top drawer, pulled out a pistol, and slid it across the desk.

Devereau stared at the cold piece of worked metal. Pistols weren't allowed in the house for fear that one of his terrible headaches might drive him to shoot himself. Yet she was giving one to him.

"Here. Maybe this will make you feel more manly," Missus French said.

***

The steel gray cold returned in the night, and the following morning felt like spring had deserted Turkle.

Hurst carried a bucket with their midday meal out to what Antoinette called the bower, and they both ate it wearing their coats, blowing on their fingers to keep them warm. When they finished the cold vittles, they talked about the meaning of certain lines in her book, which she had lent him the day before. That night he had lain on the ground reading it, wrapped in a blanket near the fire, while the others slept, until he, too, fell asleep.

The book seemed filled with excitement and wisdom. He could feast on its pages for years and never fully suck all the sumption out of it. He also felt flattered that she was willing to share this part of herself with him. And sitting closely beside her, her ladylike fingers pointing to the pages, was like nothing he had experienced. He hoped these discussions would become a habit for as long as she remained.

A dull glow through a weak layer in the clouds indicated the sun might be directly above them, but it supplied little warmth. Their breaths hung in the air together as they talked, attempting to glimpse understanding between the lines of the printed page. When Hurst grew animated about a passage, Antoinette answered his gestures quietly, explaining the author's meaning.

Hurst sat erect and perked up his ears. Isaac was riding hard toward them on the roan, a rifle tied over his shoulder with plow line. Hurst rose, offered Antoinette his hand, and pulled her to her feet to await the fury of dust, hooves, and horseflesh roaring toward them. The roan skidded to a halt, and Isaac slid off.

"White folks coming!" he said, deeply agitated. "And they gots rifles."

Hurst looked wistfully at Antoinette. He hadn't had many moments like this with her and he didn't have much hope for many more. For the past two weeks Big Josh had been pushing everyone hard, day and night, to finish the outside shell of the mansion, until everyone was living in a foggy kind of continuous walking exhaustion. Spring was coming and planting time would overrule any work on the house.

Under Big Josh's steady guidance, they had cleared a number of acres of good bottomland not far off, where they would soon break ground. Hurst's chance to sit and peacefully discuss Antoinette's book with her was rapidly disappearing.

"Damn," he said, his brow darkening. With a sense of foreboding, he gazed at Antoinette one last time, to chisel her face into his memory, knowing that after she was gone time would erode her features until she became merely a feeling, like everyone else in his past. "I guess I got to go play Master. Take care of her, Isaac."

Isaac gave Hurst a contemptuous stare. He didn't like being told to do the obvious by anyone, much less by this poseur.

Hurst took the reins of the roan, mounted, and galloped off. Then Isaac turned to Antoinette. "That fancy one is with them," Isaac said. "French."

It was time. Antoinette handed Isaac the book. "Give this to Durk, will you, Isaac?"

"You can't leave him just like that, without saying nothing," Isaac said, but was ignored.

Once mounted, Antoinette reached in her bag and checked her pistol, making sure the alien instrument was loaded, then rode off.

Isaac watched her disappear, his mind racing. Early on, he had figured out where he was going to hide from any point in and around the "mansion site". Now he ran off to his predetermined refuge.

If there was trouble, Isaac was willing to go back to living as a fugitive around Ironhead and the surrounding swampland, hunting, trapping, and growing corn for squeezings…and being lonely. Just as he figured, loneliness would always be his lot in life. But he'd chosen being isolated over slavery, and he couldn't ever go back.

***

So's we was all packed up and ready to go—all the croppers and such, and the handymen and overseers and menfolks that works for the Frenches. That's a lot of folks. Jake Dill come with us this time and he brung his boy, Fordel. We always leave 'bout three weeks before planting, so's Martha filled me a lunch pail and I had my new smooth bore I got with the egg money last November.

Now we didn't know if he was still alive or not in the first place. Turkle ain't seen him since he done registered that deed at the honor store. Hell, he was dead or give up the ghost for all we knew. Oh, we heard stories he been up to the county seat for his needings; buying a new hame string and such, but you never know 'bout what you hear from folks. Story got back to me he didn't have nothing but a goldpiece when he first come to town, so's I ask you, where did he get his folding money? See? Maybe with his pistol, taking folks by the side of the road, or maybe on one of them riverboats with them drunk fools ready to toss away their gold and cotton and ever'thing else just to say they done it.

Well, we was on the road, the whole pack of us, on mules and horses and what-all, with all our gear piled in Hollib's wagon, but that weren't all this time. Mister French shows up to join us. That's right, Mister French.

He don't say how he know'd where we was going, 'cept his momma probably knows every sparrow that falls in the forest even if the Lord God Hisself don't. But there he was, on that fancy white horse, riding out to wild Chickasaw land that has that man living out there, nobody knows how or if.

Anyhow, guess what Mister French don't have with him on this hunting trip? Just guess…a rifle! So we said, come on along. How could we say no? We all work for him one way or t'other.

He's all jittery. And you know Mister French, when he's jittery, he talks. Here one minute nothing but mules and horses clopping along and a wagon creaking down this old run-down dirt road runs to the county seat, and then he starts filling the whole damn woods with words.

And then we done hear'd it. Coming from up ahead, jest south off 'n the road, past a stand of gum and maple. A-choppin' and a-hammerin' and a-sawin' and I don't know what all, like they was building a ship or something out in this empty part of the woods. We all just stopped and looked at each other.

So's Bake goes ahead. That's right, Bake! 'Cause Mister French was there, you see, and election time's coming up. Bake, a scout? We just hoped he wouldn't get lost 'cause he had one of the jugs. Then Bake comes back and says, "Fellas, you won't believe it if you don't see it yourself, and even then you might not."

So's there we was. Sitting around some big log table near some lean-tos he done set up for his slaves and such. And standing right behind us is the biggest darn—just a mountain of manflesh. His arms across't that barrel-chest of his, grinning and listening, like maybe he wanted us for supper.

There they all was, working like a anthill. Not saying no word, neither. Hauling bricks from a kiln and splitting logs and dragging them with the mules and cutting and sawing and I don't know what-all.

And there he was, sitting that roan, his back straight and his chin up like this, one hand on his hip and t'other holding the reins. Lord have mercy, if 'n that man can't strut sitting a horse.

Now one of his slaves has a rifle strapped to his back, tied up at barrel and stock with plow-line. So's Mister French give Bake this look. "Why, he's given them firearms, Bake!"

"Can't think of a law against it, Mister French," Bake says, shifting his guts and reluctantly handing the jug to Nordly.

"I made you the law!" French said.

Bake looked the operation over. "Seems to have them under control, Mister French."

And then Willie Earl pipes in, with his eyes popping out in his amazed way, "Never even says a word to them!"

"Sure got them trained," Stebbens adds.

And you wonders how the hell he done that, 'cause I think ara another man would take them mess of rascals into the woods and give them guns, there wouldn't be enough left to bury in a bread box, but he done somehow tamed them like that man trained that dog in that traveling tent show that come through two years ago, you'll remember.

"Look at it," Wilber Snood shouted. "That thing's gonna be bigger'n the French place. Hell, bigger'n the courthouse!"

And so it was. He'd got into the oak and maple 'round his clearing and had the struts and the roof already in place and was bricking and planking the sides. Say what you want about Mister Dark Horse, but there it was.

So's then he was sitting down at the table with us. And French narrows his litty-bitty eyes at Hurst, and says, "You ought to mix-breed your wild stock with my tame, Mister Hurst. I'll sell you some heifers for your studs."

"I'll consider it, French," Hurst replied. "After all, what good's a man's work without a woman to share it?"

So's French's face boils a bright red, and he touched his hankie to the corner of his mouth. Then he turns to Bake, who's working his heaping plate of vittles and the jug, and brushes his ear with a finger, like some kind of signal. See?

Then Bake kind of shifts his weight to see if he could still move his body in the direction he wanted it to go, looking kind of hurt 'cause he was supposed to actually do something besides eat, drink, and try to stay on a horse while it did all the walking. So's Bake smiles at him—Mister Dark Horse—and says, "Sorry to bother you, Mister Hurst, but I wonder if you'd mind me having a look around. I'm just trying to keep it friendly."

Well, Hurst glances out the corner of his eye at one of his whatevers hauling kindling, and the man smiles back, so's Hurst says, "Well, friendly is my way toward these good folks. Sure. Make yourselves at home."

So's Bake searches these lean-tos and the house, and comes back. "She ain't here, Mister French. Least, if she was, she's gone now."

"He's hidden her somewhere," French replied. "I want you to arrest him!"

"But we don't have no proof, don't you see," Bake said. "Now, if you wants me to get a warrant from the judge—" But French don't say nothing back, so it all passes.

***

It weren't long 'fore we was back on the road heading toward some-a the best hunting we done in years.

So's we stopped to blow the horses and mules. And out of nowhere French says, looking right at Dark Horse, "Awful strange things going on out here, Hurst."

"Sure glad you're here to notice, Mister French," Hurst answered, taking two nervous swallers from the jug. "By the way, gentlemen," Hurst added, making his pitch, "I have a surprise for you—and all the men of Turkle."

"Not another surprise!" Walter shouted, and everyone but French laughed.

"I'm going to dedicate a place way back, about three miles south of town, as a hunting lodge for all Turkle," Hurst said. *"There's a deserted road right to it. You can hunt, fish, stay overnight. You never know what you might find to amuse yourselves,"* he added, raising the jug. *"No women, though, you understand."*

"That'll sure save us this long ride out here," French said, then spit in an effort to fit right in.

"We can race each other in to church Sunday mornings!" Nordly shouted to laughs and hoots.

"Just so the womenfolk don't find out what goes on!" Scugg said.

"Only men hunt, right, boys?" French added, but no one even chuckled. Instead, everybody just quieted down. But Hurst wasn't through.

He give French a angry glare, like *'Frenches be damned,'* and says, *"And I'm gonna give big share lots. Big ones. Good bottomland near town, and supply cotton seed. You clear the land, you get two-thirds of your crop!"*

Well, ever'body starts talking all at once't, all riled up. Stillins says, *"What? What did he say?"* But he missed the whole damn thing 'cause he was staring into space like he do, not one earthly thing in his head.

"Sure beats the forty points French is paying his croppers," Scugg says. *"But sounds pretty risky to me."* Of course, living out there and clearing wild land and all, jest for a dicker more bushels.

But Hurst weren't close-dealing on this offer, no sir. He may be a fox, but he ain't no hog. So's he says, *"After five years, you own the land! I'll sign a paper. Heck, I got plenty of land."*

Free land! It was like we all done been struck by the Word! Well, ever'body starts a-whooping and a-yelling to beat the band.

"Well, that'll attract some attention," Strophe said.

"Ah, attention," French says. *"Just what you wanted, Mister Hurst. If you can get by on a third, I'll let you run French Acres for me."* But French can't touch that offer.

That Dark Horse, he is sho'ly one shrewd customer, he is. Gots him more land than a man could ride across't in two days, considering it's woods and swamp and what have you, and he's gonna be making money by giving away no more than if a French give a hundred dollars to the honor store.

Yes, sir, he sho'ly is one slick character, he is.

***

Well, it ain't more than a half hour and a doe must have wandered within shooting distance of the Dill boy's stand. Wouldn't you know it, he brings it down on his first shot. Right through the heart; it never know'd what hit it.

Well, the boy starts a-whooping and a-hollering 'cause he's got first honors, and on his first shot on his first hunting trip. So's we all come a-running and ol' Jake Dill is beside hisself, like it's some kind of sign or something.

So's Jake's gonna show the boy what to do. He puts his fingers in the doe's nostrils to brace the head and slits its throat with his knife, all proper and such. And naturally, the blood come a-pouring out. So's Jake Dill says, "Your first kill, boy! Now here's what the Chickasaws do when a squirt becomes a brave." Like we do with youngsters, you know? So's Dill dips his hands in the doe blood and smears it all over the boy's face.

"Now, you're a real hunter," Strophe said, then turns to Nordly. "Won't be long, he'll be huntin' them two-legged does wearing skirts."

Well, I turn my head and there's ol' French turning five different colors. He goes over to where Bake's a-snoring all peaceful-like and shakes him. "Bake. Bake, damn you," French says.

But Bake ain't gonna be woke up now, so's French heads off back to the wagon to get his horse. "Sorry, folks, but I...I've got business—" French said, and without another word, rides off.

"That French," Nordly joked, watching him go. "Wonder why he come' a-hunting, but don't fire no shot."

"Guess he don't need the meat," Strophe said.

***

Dusk rapidly closed in, the sun's retracting tendrils leaving bloody claw-marks upon the clouded sky. The final residue of daylight drained quickly behind the western hills, drawing with it what little warmth remained of the day.

On the abandoned, overgrown road to practically nowhere, the pair of rheumy-eyed, sallow-skinned swamp rats in the ragged-legged britches held out their hands. Repeating his earlier words of caution, the well-dressed man in the bowler hat counted bills into their waiting paws. As soon as they had the money, the two recipients snarked and chortled, but didn't shout, as the man had instructed them not to do.

Moving with bodies in full ambling celebration, they mounted the saddleless mule, one behind the other. Glancing back with disdain at the fool who had handed over such a rip-roaring sum for such a simple tracking job, the pair dug the mule's ribs with their bare heels and rode off to drink and gamble away every last penny.

Ignoring them, the well-dressed man placed his wallet into his jacket and mounted the healthy steed. All in all, it was shaping up to be a highly profitable day's work.

***

The sun went into hiding, taking the day's tolerable warmth, and her courage, with it.

Hidden in the foliage on the hill, Antoinette sat watching the road stretching to the west through a break in the trees. Hurst had chosen the spot well.

She placed her husband's elaborately carved dueling pistol in her lap and shoved her icy fingers in her jacket pockets for warmth. But the cold damp earth only laughed at such attempts and simply found other unguarded parts of her body to attack. She adjusted the blanket on which she was sitting, silently cursing the wetness rising through it.

It was a long, brutal vigil. She began to worry that perhaps French had already returned home, that perhaps she was waiting in vain for a rider that had long since passed. She tried to figure out what she would do if French was surrounded by guards. Would they be armed, for hunting if for nothing else?

Then she saw a lone, small figure on a white stallion approaching from the east. Rising quietly, she untied the thoroughbred and led it slowly down the hill. She paused momentarily to gauge the rider's progress, then continued, trying to time her approach to coincide with his passing, so that she could take him from behind.

She reached the last stand of trees faster than she expected and halted to check her pistol. Without her own clamor to drown out the sounds about her, she thought she heard a rustle of what could have been horses directly behind her. Her heart sank.

"I'll ask you to drop that, please, madam," a deep voice said in a New Orleans accent.

She dropped her pistol and raised her hands. Behind her, two men wearing suits and bowler hats sat on well-fed horses, aiming pistols directly at her. So this is what it had all come to, a foolish, wasted effort! Why did she ever think she could overcome such odds?

The largest of the two rode past her down the hill, while the second signaled for her to follow the first. She obeyed, leading her horse on foot.

The large man cleared the trees below and galloped to the road, where he drew rein.

"Mister French! Mister French!" he shouted, firing his pistol into the air. When Antoinette and her second captor reached the road, French rode up and drew rein.

"What is this? Who are you?" a startled French asked.

"They're obviously from New Orleans, Mister French," Antoinette said, choked and furious. "Come to take me back."

"Not exactly," the large one said. "We represent a private firm, hired by Missus Marie Brussard French. You're to be taken to *French Acres*."

"A private firm?" French said, bewildered. Then a realization worked its way across his face, rapidly becoming fury. "Oh, I see. We'll put an end to this."

***

French drew the pistol his mother had foisted upon him, rode up to the captive woman and, sitting the white, pressed its barrel directly to her forehead.

If she is counting on my being reluctant to use this pistol, French thought, *she is underestimating my determination to be free of this cursed town. Everyone thinks I'm a coward. But I'll close my eyes and pull this trigger, and then I'll be free! Mother won't have any more excuses to keep me here.*

Antoinette watched French's face, but seeing no mercy there, closed her eyes, resigned. *Perhaps it is better this way,* she thought, *quick and over.*

Then she was filled with remorse. She wouldn't be alive to protect Louis Edward; there would never be anyone to protect him. She thought longingly of the helpless little boy.

French looked down at the woman and saw the waves of sorrow cross her face. *Shoot this lovely creature? Wouldn't it be easier just to defy Mother and go? No, it would not.*

French studied Antoinette trembling before him. This woman was flawlessly attractive. French began to grow jealous and resentful, asking why all the happiness on this Earth, all the warmth in the world, is the private possession of people like her, whose flesh covered their bones in just such a manner? Why can't a plain person have just a moment of that warmth, of that happiness?

In his frustration and confusion, without thinking French closed his eyes and unconsciously clenched his fist, accidentally squeezing the trigger.

Chapter Fifteen

Hurst returned to *DarkHorse* after dark. Flushed from conquest, he quickly launched into his tale, but wasn't permitted to finish.

"You offered them w-what!" Big Josh roared. "We told you not to attract attention, and now you go and upset F-french and the whole d-damn town."

"But Josh," Hurst argued. "Every one of those folks that comes over here is one more on our side. 'Cause if *DarkHorse* ain't legal, French will take away their land, too. See?

"Not only that, but we've got more land than we could ever work. Why shouldn't we share it, give other people a chance like we have? And make some money at the same time?"

Big Josh looked around the table. "All right," he sighed, too tired and heartsick to argue any more that night. "I'm willin' to wait on this. But if Turkle turn on us, you g-gonna see we get North—and I don't care how you d-does it!"

"I already done promised that," Hurst said.

Big Josh scowled, and everyone returned to tending the fire, skinning the kill, carving the flesh, chopping wood, cooking. Big Josh gave Hurst a doleful stare before stomping off to be alone in the woods, to think…and to decide.

Hurst spotted Isaac. "Where's Antoinette?" he asked.

Isaac slid the book across the table. "Here, she give you this."

Hurst's face whitened, as if he'd been slit open at the stomach and all his blood had drained. His heart stopped beating as he picked up the book and stared at it, then he tossed it on the ground.

What did he think he was doing? A great plantation owner with a lady to call wife! That was the dream of an ignorant boy who didn't know the difference, not a grown man.

Without a word, he stumbled away and sat propped against a tree, watching the fire's cinders and sparks fly up toward the dark leaves, glowing against the encompassing night.

All the blackest days Hurst had ever known—and there had been many—came rushing upon him. Those first days without his mother, the night Turkle killed his father. And now this.

He pushed himself blindly to his feet and staggered off toward the woods, stumbling on roots and gullies. Behind him, his partners watched until he plunged between distant maples and disappeared.

Shaken, one by one the partners caught their breath. First Big Josh had stormed off, angry and distressed, then this display of utter hopelessness from Hurst.

Bammer drifted over to whisper to Isaac, but Isaac pointedly ignored him. Instead, he picked up the book and stomped off to see if their sick mule had died yet.

***

She shut her eyes, squeezing her hands tightly into fists. But all she heard was a loud *click*. Shocked that she had felt no searing pain, nothing beyond the cold barrel pressed against her forehead, Antoinette slowly opened her eyes to see a confused and frustrated French looking back at her.

Then French's face changed before her eyes. "Bait!" he screamed. "Like a lamb tied to a stake to attract a she-wolf. Mother, goddamn you! You gave me an unloaded pistol. I could have been killed."

French turned to the detectives. "You tell my mother I'll have nothing further to do with this," he said. Enraged, he threw the pistol into a ditch and mounted the white stallion. Gritting his teeth, he whipped the horse's flank and raced off.

Antoinette caught her breath. She was still alive. Headed to the Frenches, a prisoner, but alive. She could not, however, conceive of a plausible hypothesis to explain what she'd just witnessed.

***

Clutching her jacket about her, she held her hands to the candle sitting on the frail, marble-topped table. She blew on her fingers, momentarily moderating the cold sting, then tucked her hands into her pockets.

A candleless chandelier hung over the table, obviously not used in some time. The room's fireplace, too, was smooth and clean in spite of its blackened brick surface. The bed was old, but the spread and pillows appeared fresh. The room had been cleaned recently. Had someone prepared it for her capture? Not French, she deduced, given his reaction on the road. Perhaps the mysterious Missus French?

She went to the window and pulled back the curtain. The window was barred and the grouting that held the bars in place was fresh. She peered to the ground below. There, two riffraff talked together, one squatting on his heels, leaning on a rifle, while the other sat with his back against a fence, rifle across his lap. She had heard from Hurst that the French place was crawling with armed guards, and everything she had seen so far confirmed that rumor. She let the curtain drop.

Except for the table and chair, the bed and a night stand, the room was bare. She contemplated breaking the table somehow and burning it in the fireplace for warmth, but thought better of it. Then she crossed the room to the door and tried the knob. It was locked, as she assumed it would be. She knocked and waited, then repeated it more loudly. Finally, she heard heavy boots outside the door.

"When will Mister French see me?" she asked.

"I give him your messages, girl. He come when he's a mind."

She struck the door with her fist, then buried her forehead in her arms. What did the Frenches plan to do with her?

***

They sat with two candles burning, one on either side of the chessboard. The game progressed for an hour until it became clear to Missus French that Devereau had blundered and couldn't hold out much longer. Still she patiently played on, waiting for him to broach the subject. This would give her the advantage because he had spoken first, but she waited in vain.

Time passed. Her pieces progressively tightened the noose, constricting his space and mobility. At last, she began to fear he would simply turn his king on its side and rush from the room, with nothing decided. So she mentioned Antoinette first.

French looked away from the board, his face red with hurt, vengeful, hateful. Then he replied: "We'll see how proud she is when she's headed back to New Orleans in chains."

"That would free up Mister DarkHorse for you, wouldn't it?" Missus French parried, then thrust again. "Perhaps you want to go out there and be his plain-faced squaw. Listen, I know what you're thinking. He'll make a bigger fool out of you than the other one did."

"Mother! I...I—" But French could not continue.

Missus French laughed, then spoke directly, pointedly: "Send her to the hangman! You'll keep her right here. She can run *French Acres* for us."

"Her?" French sputtered, aghast. "Run? This proves you've gone insane."

But Missus French's forces were too well-positioned for such amateur flailing to have any impact on the game. She drove the point home: "She ran DuVallier's shipping empire for more than two years while the old goat convalesced. Hell, she's a better businessman than he was, better than you are."

"How...how do you know that?"

"I know. You do what I say—if you ever want to see New Orleans."

The indisputable argument. Defeated, French sunk back into the chair as they both mentally turned his king on its side. Triumphantly, Missus French mused, "Yes. She could be quite useful. If a hint of scandal develops, it might even supplant the old rumors."

"All right, make her your offer," Devereau snarled.

"No, you will come to agreement with her. She is your charge. I want nothing to do with her. Make it clear: I don't even want to see her. You understand?

"You always wanted a friend," Missus French continued. "How well, and how soon, she runs *French Acres* will determine when you can be spared to go your merry way. You have to figure out how to build a friendship, a sort of partnership based on trust, with her."

"A friendship? With a murderess?" Devereau exclaimed, mortified.

"It will be a good lesson for you," Missus French replied. She watched Devereau's face twist in confused thought, turning the multifaceted conundrum over in his mind.

The matriarch then returned her attention to the chessboard, calculating a swift, clean conclusion to the messy conflict. It was time to impart some wisdom to this dull, confused, hopelessly dreamy offspring of hers.

"Beware of traps, Devereau, and don't expose your queen."

***

Anyways, so's I was loading up bricks from the kiln onto the wagon, leading them lazy critters by the halter, smacking them on the snout to get them to tote it up to where ever 'body was laying 'em on the walls of what Hurst calls the mansion and we all call the house. Long Lou kind of got into his rhythm, you know, and Big Josh, well, he doing more than ever 'body else. And Isaac, well, Isaac is Isaac. One minute he laying on bricks like he crazy with it, fast and hard, the next he don't want to do no more; even Hurst getting more laid on than him. And Hurst is like he been lately, you know, all in a sulk since that woman done gone. But he a partner, too, as Josh always say.

Anyways, so's all of a sudden up here rides Little Turby on the roan a-shouting and a-hollering and waving his arms around and laying his heels into the poor thing.

"Josh! Durk! They comin'! From even outside the whole county! They like locusts!"

Well, we's all ready to 'scape off 'n into the swamp. So's Big Josh grab the reins. "Settle down, Turby," he say. "Who coming?"

But Turby is so shook up he fall out on the ground and cain't catch his breath. Finally, he able to spit out. "White folks! Moving in! The whole west wood is full of 'em! And more coming all the time!"

Well, when we hear'd that, we was all looking to run, I mean a passel of white folks coming! Must have been happening for days. We was all shouting at once't, 'Where we gonna go' and all such. I start thinking 'bout that rope ever'body been talking 'bout waiting for us somewheres. I weren't even gonna take no mule to slow me down, no, sir.

And Isaac gives Hurst that Look, you know. "They coming on your land deal, Hurst. We was hiding out. Now he gots the whole damn place crawling with white folks."

And sure enough if it ain't that crazy offer he done made to those folks who come hunting, and if we ain't in it now. I mean, I was scared like a pit full of snakes, see?

So's Big Josh frowns and says, "Well, we gonna have white folks growin' cotton for us. Guess the Great White Master gots to get more papers signed." And he don't look happy about it.

***

"I'm Durk Hurst, the owner of this plantation. You're gonna have to sign a paper to stay here." He grinned apologetically, extending his hand.

The man looked Hurst over, from hat to boots, then spit. "You tellin' me you the boss-man! Ha! I only do business with Mister Dark Horse hisself, not no riffraff." The man shook the ax, "Now you git off'n my land."

"But I'm Mister Dark Horse, I mean—"

"Mister, if you thinks I is stupid enough to believe that trash like you is some kind of plantation owner, my boy here got a musket ball—"

Being called *trash* made Hurst's ears burn; it was the one insult he couldn't bear. His instinct was to unleash his tongue to cut the man to pieces, to show how much smarter he was than his detractor, but he was going to need peace with this man, with all these men to make his plan work. Besides, the man's ax helped dissuade him.

Hard as it was, he had to swallow the curse and dream up a backup gambit.

***

Big Josh noted that the family had already fashioned a makeshift house with a stovepipe protruding from its tarp roof and judged the work a good start. He dismounted, walked up to the man and extended a contract paper toward him. The man made no move to take the paper. Instead, he spit tobacco juice and said: "You Mister Dark Horse's boy?"

113

"Yes, sir. I w-works for D-dark Horse," Big Josh replied.

"Well, I'll sign that there paper, then."

Big Josh put the paper on the stump they'd been working with their mule and handed the man the writing instrument. "Right there."

The 'cropper took the writing tool, made his *X* and handed both back to Big Josh, who placed them in his sack. Then Big Josh examined the area, appraising its potential for good farmland, seeing what it had and what it needed. He looked the family over, estimating the amount of work that could be gotten out of them.

"You got plenty of hands here," Big Josh said with businesslike gravity. "*Master* say you got all the way up to that river bend; wants you to build a dam over there; dig ditches over 'cross there to drain that area. When you done, you' have you some rich bottomland. Yes, sir, rich bottomland."

"Mister Dark Horse is a good man," the 'cropper exclaimed, "a good man! You tells him, Bobby Jim Martin says there's a drifter coming 'round with a paper, claims *he's* Mister Dark Horse. Looks like trash to me. You tell'em for me. Name's Martin."

Big Josh merely smiled and nodded. *Yes, sir,* he tickled himself thinking, *it's a damn good thing we gots the real Master Dark Horse and not no trash pretending to be what he is.*

The legitimate representative of the true Great White Master mounted the mule and headed off to meet the next family gonna be cropping on their property, and someday, in five years, owning their own piece, too.

***

Missus French sat motionless in the phaeton, wrapped heavily in blankets against the chill. From her vantage point, she examined the fallow French fields that stretched to the horizon, inwardly fuming, calculating her lost income. Her liveried driver squatted beside the phaeton, heating bricks in the open fire he'd built. Even under the thick blankets Missus French's knees hurt with the cold, and her fingers inside their mail-order fur gloves still felt the chill. Her driver picked one of the hot bricks out of the fire with the tongs, carried it to the phaeton, and placed it with care under the blankets by her frozen feet, then returned to wait for the others to heat.

As he came over the ridge, Devereau French spotted the phaeton and rode up at a leisurely pace, attempting to appear nonchalant. Once he reached his mother, he drew rein directly in her line of sight, so that his horse completely blocked her view. He waited for her to say something, anything, to acknowledge that he was there; that he had acquiesced to her summons after receiving the good watermarked notepaper, written without salutation and signed with her standard single-stoke *F*. But Missus French's eyes never moved, as though she was able to stare directly through the horse's powerful, sweating body. Her facial expression didn't change, but remained hard, implacable.

"What are you doing out here, Mother?" French asked.

Missus French's thoughts continued to dwell upon her impotent rage, as her calculations raced through various dead ends and failed scenarios. She knew what Devereau was thinking. Buy more slaves to farm this land. But even he was bright enough to realize that was a foolish proposition. Pay full price now? When slaves would certainly be a buyer's market when the war started?

War? Yes, she thought, *they've been preparing for this for decades; they won't be turned back now. Otherwise, what was the point of all the hunting and riding and shooting? War is the embodiment of all the Southern ruling class's best attributes. Just look at the lavish considerations paid to state politicians so that cotton growers could entitle themselves with military rank: colonel, major, even general. To bet against war would be foolhardy.*

And if the North won, which, however unlikely, was always possible? Then all the slaves would be emancipated, which would result in their total loss with no compensation. No, *French Acres'* policy had been to sell slaves when a good price was to be had and to replace that labor with white sharecroppers. They would do the opposite when the slave market dropped. That was only good business, and there had been no reason to consider changing it—until last week when most of their white hands ran off seeking free *DarkHorse* land. Besides, unlike the other planters, she felt a nagging aversion to slavery, as did Devereau. But she told herself she owned a business, not a charity.

"That man has stolen all our sharecroppers," she complained. "Hundreds of our acres will have to be abandoned, to lie fallow! What are you going to do about him?"

"I've sent him messages that I'm willing to negotiate, but he ignores me," French replied.

Just what she had feared! The child didn't know enough to protect himself, didn't have the heart to persevere. And she hadn't been able to force those characteristics into him.

"Negotiate!" Missus French exclaimed. "Don't you see that only one of us can survive? Every day he grows stronger, and *French Acres* slips further into oblivion."

Missus French gave Devereau a piercing look, then attempted to conclude the futile conversation. "You see to lancing that boil. I don't care if you have to lynch him, shoot him, burn him, and throw his ashes in the river. Your father would have put a bullet through his eye."

French swallowed hard. "But I'm not my father's son, am I, Mother?" He turned the white horse and galloped away.

The driver snapped the whip and the phaeton's motion forced Missus French back into the seat. She was mortified. The child would never understand, even if he knew the truth.

Chapter Sixteen

The plates were heaped with fresh venison. Meat was cut and hungry bites were downed, but Hurst noted the mood about the long table was cooler than the evening chill. Finally, Big Josh asked what the problem was. Eyes searched eyes, until Little Turby spoke, as though from the mouth of babes.

"The white folks been asking about the seed Hurst promised them, which we ain't got no money for."

"Those folks clear that land and we ain't got no seed, we be lucky if they just stretch our necks," said Isaac, slamming his palms on the table.

The sound of metal against tin ceased, except from white-haired Old Moses, who never stopped his constant and considerable volume of chewing and swallowing. Partners stared at the table, at each other, at the darkening sky.

Hurst lowered his head, cupping his brow with his hand so no one could see his panic and embarrassment. He felt like he'd been stabbed in the heart. As he'd done before when he was on a winning streak, he had gone one step too far and run their chance of gaining something solid into the ground. He'd gambled away *DarkHorse*.

Finally, all eyes rested on Big Josh, sitting at the table's head. Big Josh searched all their faces for one idea. But every face he saw was a blank. "W-what' we g-gonna do?" Big Josh asked.

Old Moses forced one more bite into his mouth, overstuffing it so that his cheeks popped out, and fought to force the under-chewed chunks down his throat. Finally, he pontificated, as if to a group of ignorant children. "We needs us a bunion."

"A bunion?" Isaac exclaimed, flabbergasted. "What you talking about, Moses?"

With every eye on him, Old Moses majestically laid his fork and knife neatly beside his plate, pulled out his handkerchief, and delicately patted his lips.

"Sees, back home, that how the General lose the plantation. Old Titus what work in the kitchen had a bunion, but Titus get a chilling and die. Then Master start drinking and Missus start crying and ole' General ain't got no more plantation lef'. See? No more bunion."

"What you sayin'?" Isaac asked.

"I d-don't understand," Big Josh told Old Moses.

Old Moses merely sneered to himself and replaced his handkerchief in his pocket. Then he turned to Big Josh: "Try to explain things to field hands! See, you gots to trade you the cotton contracts before you seed the fields, like the quality folks does. That's how General get his money." Old Moses had accompanied the General to the cotton broker's office every spring to carry his bottle and to watch him forward-sell or -buy huge cotton contracts, which would be consummated after harvest.

Listening in fascination, Little Turby realized the partnership had a resource to help Hurst improve his shabby display of playing Master.

"See, Durk," Little Turby blurted out, "Old Moses live up to the big house, so he can teach you 'bout being a gentleman."

Hurst grimaced. If these men could see through him that easily, so could everyone else.

"Great!" Isaac said. "We gots the fool leading the madman!"

"Hush, now, Isaac," Big Josh ordered. "All right, M-moses, tells us 'bout it."

Old Moses lifted his nose at Isaac, then proceeded. "See, that cotton trading is kind of like gambling on the come. Big money, too. No trifling in that game. Old Master like it better than cards."

Hurst jerked his head up, his face instantly animated. "I heard of this cotton trading." If outsmarting plantation owners at their own game might save them, well that's one thing he was willing to try. Perhaps he could raise the stakes and win it all back for them. Now he just had to figure out how to get a seat at the table.

Everyone started talking at once, but Big Josh shut everyone up. "But what does a b-bunion have to do with it?"

"See, if it going to rain," Old Moses continued, "Titus' bunion hurt. The more rain coming, the worse it pain him. So he say, 'I cain't walk upstair today, General.' So's then General know'd it was going to rain and he buy cotton or sell it, one or t'other, I can't remember which. Yes, sir, Titus' bunion make the General the talk of the cotton brokers. But then Ole' Titus die, and here we is living in a swamp. No more bunion."

"Boy," Little Turby mused, "if we had one of them bunions."

Right then the normally placid Bammer shouted, "I does! I gots a bunion! Hurts me terrible-bad sometimes."

"Let's see it, Bammer," Long Lou exclaimed.

As Bammer worked to pull off his right boot, everyone sprung up from the table and hurried to surround him. Bammer took his boot off and placed his foot on the bench so everyone could squeeze close for a look. Wiggling his toes to display a thick knob on the big toe, Bammer said, "There it is, the meanest ole' bunion this side of Jordan."

Big Josh rolled his eyes, his mind drifting to the old days back home, remembering with sorrow and terror the General and his losing. "Oh, Lord, a bunion! We' gonna lose this plantation faster than the General lose his."

But no one was listening as Bammer merely wiggled his toes.

***

Rain drizzled intermittently on Hurst and Big Josh all morning as they rode along the overgrown, deserted road to the county seat, but a half hour out of town the rain stopped and the sun cleared the clouds. This suited Hurst's mood. He was going to push the clouds of Antoinette's loss out of his mind and attempt to make the day a memorable one.

The clever county seat cotton broker ruined everything. As Hurst and Big Josh entered his office, the man didn't even attempt to rise from his plush leather chair to offer his hand. Uncertain of what to do, Hurst sat tentatively in the opposite chair and made his pitch, leaving Big Josh within a foot of the door and a quick escape. But the broker simply looked down his nose at Hurst.

"Surely, sir," the broker said, "you don't think you can come in here and expect me to pay you large advances on some imaginary cotton crop on your word alone."

Hurst was taken aback, but desperately pressed on. "Everybody in the county knows about *DarkHorse!* Over in Turkle. I'm the owner, Durksen Hurst."

But the broker's face didn't change. Instead, he placed his fingertips together under his chin, displaying his manicured nails and diamond rings, considering. "I've heard rumors and tales around the courthouse. But the man I've heard about would be much, well, taller than you... and considerably larger. Now if you had documentation such as letters of credit from the bank or simply a note from Mister French would do."

A note from Mister French! Now that cut it. Hurst rose, fuming, his heart plunging into the pit of his stomach. Jamming his hat down on his head, he said, "Let's go, Josh." But Big Josh was already out the door.

Joining him outside, Hurst asked, "What're we gonna do?"

Big Josh thought about it, then came to a decision: "I must be crazy as you is, but I thinks we gonna have to chance Turkle."

Hurst shuddered. But it was that or give up, and it was too late for that. He walked to where they'd tied the horse and the mule. "Back into the fire," he said.

Big Josh only spat.

***

The local cotton broker's office was much different than the one at the county seat. Smaller, constricted, with fewer windows to let in the bright afternoon sunlight, here the balding local broker, wearing rolled-up shirtsleeves, sat behind a paper-piled desk in a simple storefront office.

"If you default," the broker said, "I take *DarkHorse*. You understand?"

Hurst stretched his back, compensating for the hard guest chair and the long day's riding they'd done to get there. He glanced at Big Josh, whose stoic face remained frozen, unmoving. Hurst nodded reluctantly and signed the paper.

Across the desk, the local broker lifted the nearest stack of papers and, placing them precariously crossways on top of another pile, cleared a spot to write. Then he reached in his top drawer and, after shoving papers about, pulled out a small rectangular piece of paper with an official seal at its head. He set the official-looking slip of paper on the cleared spot, wrote a few brief words and numbers on it, signed it, and handed it across the desk.

Hurst accepted the slip with shaking hand and looked it over. He saw written on it the number representing the dollars they had agreed upon.

Amazed, Big Josh studied the paper over Hurst's shoulder. Hurst glanced his way, but Big Josh merely shrugged. They both studied Turkle's broker, but he simply replaced the original stack of papers in their vacant spot, as if the matter was already concluded. Finally, Hurst cleared his throat. "What is this? I want cash money."

The broker grinned smugly, replying with subtle sarcasm: "If you take that over to the bank, they'll give you your 'cash money,' Mister Hurst. The bank's been doing that for folks, oh, must be for two or three weeks now."

"I know, but I heard Missus French owns the bank," Hurst responded.

"That is written on my account," the man replied. "They'll honor it."

"Le's visit the bank," Big Josh said.

***

Outside the broker's office in the bright sunshine, they felt it was safe to talk.

"I'm going to deposit most of the money in the county seat bank. The bank will give me a paper, which I'll show to that Lethe Creek cotton broker. Hell, that paper will be almost as good as a note from French."

Big Josh was ahead of him on this trick. "I see," he said. "You going to sell more cotton contracts through the county seat broker and get us more money, double or triple up. I just ain't so sure—"

"We'd better keep some goldpieces hidden around *DarkHorse*, too," Hurst said, attempting to circumvent the big man's doubts. "No sense in going broke simply because you put too much faith in a bunion, no matter how well-proven that investment technique."

They reached the mansion site bone weary. They'd ridden extensively the last two days, to the county seat and back yesterday, then to Turkle, returning today. Tomorrow they had to ride to the county seat and back one more time. This being a rich cotton trader required an awful lot of hard riding.

Supper was just finishing when they rode up in the darkness. Everyone sat at the long table in weary repose, unable to move or speak. Bammer who, without Big Josh, had done most of the heavy lifting that day, laid on the ground beside the bench, his eyes closed.

Isaac watched the pair dismount. "There our prodigal wheeler dealers! Did you get it?"

Hurst grabbed the bills and gold coin from his pockets and dumped them onto the log table. "There it is, gentlemen!" he said. "Cash money on the barrelhead!"

Like lightning, all was pandemonium as everyone began talking at once. The pile of money seemed to materialize from a dream none of them had dared. They could barely believe it. Hearing this, Bammer opened his eyes and saw the pile of gold and paper. He rose as fast as his sore body would allow and hung on the edge of the circle of wide-eyed plantation owners, pushing his way closer for a touch.

Big Josh sat, leaning back, feeling like he was floating lightly in the air, as if for the first time he was truly free. He stared at Hurst in amazement. Why, the crazy white man had gotten them to a place where everything seemed possible. From the beginning, he'd known Durk was rare for a white man, but now he was seeing how singular the man truly was.

Crazy? No, Durk was far beyond crazy. He was, in fact, building his own world, with rules that seemed to defy nature, and he had taken them with him. This was something! *Someday,* he determined, *Ceeba gonna be with me, even if I have to buy her from French.*

"We can really buy the seed!" Little Turby exclaimed. "*And* finish the mansion!"

The excitement infected Hurst, too. He realized the money spoke better for him than any of his fanciful words or speeches. "See, I thought we could put the gardens around the stream," he said, demonstrating. "Over there. We could build little bridges over it. We could hold big parties!"

But nobody heard. Everyone was drifting off to gaze at the land upon which they'd worked so hard, seeing it through the new eyes of inspired imagination.

Little Turby rushed to Big Josh's side, his swift young mind working: "We could have a big circle drive up from the road."

Big Josh swept his finger along the line of the mansion. "And p-put wide balconies looking over the g-gardens."

Everyone wandered off in bands of twos and threes, talking excitedly. Meanwhile, Isaac made certain every note and coin was placed securely in a saddle bag, while his mind cast about the periphery of the site for the best place to stash it. When he had the table clean of any possible medium of exchange, he threw the sack over his shoulder and headed off.

***

Finding himself alone, fatigue, fear, and a sense of loss overtook Hurst. He flopped down on the bench, elbows on the table, and rested his head in his hands, covering his eyes. "We're only missing one thing." Need of Antoinette was almost beyond his ability to bear it.

He wished he could give every cent to save her from the Frenches, to have her by his side. But he knew money couldn't do that. His only chance was a risky plan he'd devised, and that would require confrontation with Turkle's supreme family—a final wager that he promised himself would be his last, if he survived it. It was a long shot, but it was the only ball in his pistol.

He had never felt so sorrowful and afraid.

***

As the afternoon sun poured through the window, Devereau French watched Turkle's balding cotton broker. The even-spoken man's livelihood was primarily dependent on the Frenches' confidence in his ability to sense the general direction that cotton prices would tend. This meant calculating and balancing how bounteous the degenerating soil would prove against the many pitfalls that might bedevil anyone who owned land and cotton.

Over the years, the man had established his worth in this task to the ever-demanding Missus French, as he steadily increased her margins on the finite resources she encompassed, enabling her to become an apotheosis of business acumen for all Southern landed aristocracy. Indeed, the pair, Missus French and the now middle-aged, pear-shaped man, constantly had to conspire with a network of ever-changing intermediaries and dupes to conceal their strategy, lest a secretive string of purchases become a general buying fever or a subtle sale become a frenzied selling panic, leaving them owning a declining asset. And now, at her behest, he dealt with her son, still representing *French Acres*.

"All he wants to do is forward-sell on his next crop to buy seed, like everybody else," the broker said in his flat monotone.

"Simply refuse him," Devereau suggested. "I'll back you up."

But the man remained calm. "I can't, Mister French. Practically everybody in town has some family on his land. I'd be run out of Turkle. Besides, I've got his plantation on the note."

So the man would not take sides. Too many local people had taken up Hurst's offer, and being a churchgoer, the broker would not go against his principles to cause them harm. French considered all the angles.

"So he's speculating on the cotton market. How much has he lost?"

The man inked his pen point. "I wouldn't say he lost, Mister French."

Winning, that was the Frenches' province! French figured that the broker had probably advised Hurst and was even now advising him, probably correctly. But what could French do? The broker was too valuable to the French interests to be cast off. They would be cutting their own throats by disassociating themselves from him. And that would only hand Hurst an advantage.

French was struck with an inspired strategy based on a hunch that, this year, the broker, who believed the price of cotton would go down, was wrong.

The world price of cotton had been rising steadily the last couple of years, a trend that the broker said was probably caused by the European mills laying in an extra supply—in case war broke out in the United States and shipments were interrupted. During this period, the Frenches had cashed in substantially on this rising trend by buying in the open market, a gamble jokingly referred to as a "farmer's hedge"—both owning the crop and having bought the forward-selling contracts, too. Yes, it had been a prosperous time, with the French family doubled up in the market.

But the broker was afraid of the risks this year. War-talk and the general excitability of the populace made him nervous. Plus, another consecutive year of rapidly rising prices seemed unlikely.

French understood the man's reluctance to recommend the double purchase again. But he wasn't troubled in the least by heated talk among the lower classes of people. As for war starting? Didn't war always drive up the price of goods, sometimes to astronomical heights?

For once, French would prove them all wrong—and with his own money. Mother could not stop him from doing it, and it would win him enough to be free of her completely. And Hurst, the seller, would be the big loser; he'd be at French's mercy.

French pulled out a check from his inside breast pocket. Seeing this, the broker quietly handed French a pen, knowing it was good business to shut his mouth when French was laying out money.

French wrote out a check and signed it. "All right, buy all he wants to sell. But he can't find out it's me on the other end of his trades."

"So it's you against him," the broker mused. "And if he can't deliver?"

"I'm sure he has some land hereabouts to cover his dealings—this check ought to cover the note you hold on *DarkHorse*. You see, my friend, the deep pile of gold always wins."

The broker nodded knowingly, then signed over to French the note Hurst had signed for *DarkHorse*. "Indeed," he said, "the cream does settle to the top."

***

French stepped out of the broker's door and took a deep breath, relieved to walk away from that paper-crowded little hole of an office. The spring day was almost perfect, warming after a night of light rain. The main street's wooden sidewalks bustled with life. Women in their homespun and store-bought dresses and colorful spring hats shopped the General Store and small storefronts in clumps of three and four, talking and laughing. Nearby, men in their broadcloth suits, farm wear and shirtsleeves gathered at the courthouse steps trading mules, swapping stories, discussing planting, cotton prices, politics and the possibilities of war. French shrugged off the scene and continued on his way to the bank.

There, he learned that Hurst had left only a small deposit to establish an account, withdrawing the rest in cash. He did the necessary calculation and concluded that he was going to have to ride to Lethe Creek to duplicate the secret arrangement with the county seat cotton broker that he'd established with the local broker; he would play against Hurst from both points. He asked the bank president a few other questions and, satisfied, headed straight to his white stallion.

"I've got you hooked: French take all."

Yes, it was *French Acres* against *DarkHorse*, indirectly, underhandedly … just the way Devereau liked it.

Chapter Seventeen

She saved twelve sheets of salvaged notepaper from the aging, discolored stack which the honor store sold at twenty a penny: twelve, one for each apostle in the Bible. Paper was one of their slowest moving items and, in fact, were it not for its scatological uses, would barely have sold at all. She would hide the sheets in the chifforobe before her grandfather returned and he would never miss them.

She knew her chance would come, and it did. That morning the Senior Deacon went to church without breakfast for one of his day-long fasting and prayer sessions. She heard him from her bed, but when he looked in on her she pretended to be asleep. Then, hearing the front door shut, she scurried to the town records in her nightclothes. She was going to work on it all day, not taking time to even eat. She was moved by God and would not feel hunger. Time was crucial. She had so much to do, and this was only the first step in her plan! She only hoped no customers would chance into the store that day.

She opened the bottom drawer and drew out a pile of yellowed, musty records that had accumulated over the years to gather dust in the honor store, then inked her pen. They were the bills of sale and registrations for all the French slaves going back three generations. First, she must take an inventory of which living slaves the Frenches actually owned. The task would be highly detailed and tedious, but she had always been extremely meticulous with all the town records, especially these.

Then would come the tricky part.

***

The loneliness took him that day, took him hard, harder than it had ever hit him before. Loneliness had gathered like a thundercloud in the back of his mind during all the long days of hard labor, swelling in his heart over the endless, solitary nights. He'd fought the fearsome beast, struggling with all his might to keep it at bay. But now he kept hearing a voice, his voice, saying repeatedly in his head, *She's gone, and she's never coming back.*

Sweat pouring off his back and arms in the afternoon glare, he placed the wedge of wood on the stump and whacked it with the ax, splitting it into kindling. One after another, whack, raise, whack, clatter, pile it, pick up a new one. Place it on the stump, whack. He did not see or feel what he was doing; no longer paused even to drink from the quarter-full jug of squeezings sitting beside him.

He was six-years-old. He entered the dirt-floor cabin and stood awkwardly just inside, afraid to go further. From the doorway, he saw his little mother with her high, angular cheekbones, lying on the cob mattress, eyes not quite alive, as if they were clouded over. Each night, he had so loved to watch her brush her long black hair, sitting before her small mirror set on the kitchen table. Now her bangs were pasted with sweat against her forehead, her tresses a tangle on the bed. She sensed him there and attempted to smile, sweetly calling him "my baby boy." But he could see she was in terrible pain—and soon she was gone.

The next day was the gloomiest, overcast day he could remember. He was out back of the one-room 'cropper cabin digging the hole, using the shovel with the loose handle. Every so many scoops, the blade would come off and he'd have to jam the handle back on. As he dug, he remembered playing tag-touch-tree with her and not letting her take a shortcut. Waves of sadness came over him as he remembered her laughing appeal to let her skirt the rules this one time, but he refused to allow it. As if winning mattered!

As he dug, memories of her came fast and furious. He couldn't shake the sight of her emaciated body lying on the bed, her flesh barely causing a ripple in the quilt. Finally, he collapsed on the dirt pile and broke into tears, the second to last he ever shed, as either a man or a boy.

His father came out to check on the grave work before setting off. He didn't yell or hit the boy that day. Instead, he gave a quiet, stern order to get the hole done, and then he was gone, taking the last of their edible meal from the bottom of the bucket to trade for a badly needed jug. Crying blindly, young Durk rose and continued to dig, drowning in a sorrowful, bottomless sea.

And now Antoinette was gone too; that's how it always ended. Always. Hurst threw the ax aside and picked up a piece of kindling from the pile. In his rage and drunkenness, he flung the kindling strip into the kiln fire. Then he took another, and another, and another, and threw them all savagely into the fire until the heat drove him back. But that wasn't going to stop him. He grabbed another piece and threw it, then picked up another and…

Big Josh grabbed his hand. "Hey, Durk! We'c-cutting off. Ain't no b-bricks in there no-how."

Big Josh placed his massive arm around Hurst's shoulders and, half-supporting him, led him to the supper table. There he plopped him down and sat beside him.

"He' been like this for days," Isaac said, joining them.

"You c-can't do nothing 'bout her," Big Josh said.

Isaac brought up an idea he'd been working in his head. "We can probably get word to her through the grapevine out at French's."

Hurst turned to Isaac: "You aren't afraid to go out there?"

"Listen, we all g-gots womens out there," Big Josh said. "Where you think we' disappear to those Sat-day night and come back late Sunday?"

"But—?" Hurst began. Then he began to understand why some of his partners looked so exhausted Monday mornings—and always on the exact same days when the mules wouldn't work. They'd been riding out the whole way, socializing with French slaves.

"Don't worry," Isaac sneered. "White folks don't see us no how. That's how the grapevine know everything."

"Let's do it," Hurst said, a determined look in his eye. "Besides, I figured out what I'm gonna do on my Missus French Plan."

His Missus French Plan! Hurst had been mumbling about this secret "Plan" frequently in recent days, but no one had had time to listen to his ramblings. Now he seemed serious about pursuing his scheme to confront the Frenches. Whatever that plan was.

Big Josh and Isaac eyed each other, wary. Having access to money had made their partner reckless. They'd often joked that this crazy white man was going to get them all hung. Unfortunately, the jest was beginning to look prophetic.

***

She poked the fire, its flames reflecting on the window against the black night backdrop, waiting for dinner to be brought. Bored and anxious, she picked up one of the books they'd left for her. She'd been reading only a few minutes when she heard the key at the door.

They wouldn't tell her where they were taking her, which frightened her. Carrying a lantern against the gloom, she was led by three armed men down the hallway to a circular staircase. This she descended, and continued down a first-floor hallway, until they entered a large dining room.

The room was dimly lit by two candles stuck in a large silver candelabra. It took a moment for her eyes to adjust, until she made out French at the head of a long table. Two places were set in fine China. French waved the three guards away and signaled for her to sit.

Holding her still-trembling hands in her lap, she examined the man who had aimed a pistol at her head and pulled the trigger the first time he'd seen her. His features were indistinct through the shadows, but she drew upon her memory to fill them in. Neither of them said a word.

The soup was brought into the dining room by a black woman servant. This was repeated for six courses, with servants silently carrying in newly-cooked dishes and carrying out empty plates. To match the servant's muteness, neither diner spoke throughout the meal.

After the two finished eating, a liveried black manservant refilled their wine glasses from the decanter, first hers, then French's. The servant then lit a cigar for French and left, closing the door to the kitchen behind him.

Antoinette broke the silence by protesting her captivity, trembling with rage and frustration, but she didn't get far.

"My hospitality is certainly more gracious than you'd find in New Orleans," French broke in sharply. Then he softened. "I…I'm simply trying to be your friend."

"You certainly have an endearing manner of showing it," Antoinette replied with venom. The room fell silent.

"Never mind. I want to make you an offer, Missus DuVallier, a very generous one," French said with hesitation. "My mother—and I—are aware of your shrewd business acumen. We…we want you to stay here and run *French Acres*, all our properties. You'll be quite safe. But there's one condition."

"And that is?" Antoinette asked, her eyes narrowing.

"You may not leave the grounds without my permission…and you must definitely never have any contact or correspondence with Mister Hurst. Never. If you do, I'll have you on a steamboat to New Orleans—and it won't be for the social season."

Antoinette sunk back in her chair and took a sip of wine. She had learned to expect anything from these people, yet this extraordinary offer took her aback. What did they really want?

Had she misunderstood their motives? Were the tales and rumors about the Frenches simply so many apocryphal stories, devoid of any truth? Was this person actually, at his core, benevolent? If this offer was legitimate, what could be behind it? She concluded the offer had to have been the mother's decision. And if French's mother had a hand in this wholly unexpected proposal, why hadn't the woman spoken for herself? Then she remembered the stories labeling the mother a recluse.

"Why would you want me to run your plantation?" she ventured. "What about you?"

French laughed, puffing on his cigar to display his calm confidence. "Do you think a little backwater town like Turkle can satisfy a person like me? Don't you think I want to see New Orleans and other civilized points, just as you have?"

So there it was; he needed her in order to pursue his own interests. The rural plantation was his prison, too. She realized this offer put her in a position of strength, and summoned her courage to press on.

"First tell me, where is my son, Mister French?" she asked.

"Louis Edward is well and happy," French said, forcing a smile, his voice shaky. "Look, I can understand your desperation—"

"You couldn't. Ever."

But French was prepared. He reached inside his pocket and displayed a parchment document. Then, rising from his chair, he walked to where she sat and with shaking hand laid the paper beside her, before returning to his chair.

"Ah, but I do understand," he said with a catch in his throat. "You see, Antoinette, Mother *acquired* Louis Edward for me, yes…and I adopted him."

Antoinette studied the document. The adoption paper listed Louis Edward DuVallier as the child, Devereau Brussard French as the legal guardian, with French's signature on the bottom.

"Those papers are in good order," French continued. "In fact, it's amusing. Here we've only recently met, and legally you and I are Louis Edward's mother and father."

"Just met, and you would have murdered me," Antoinette countered. She paused to clear her thoughts. The person across the table was trying to make some sympathetic connection to her, but was his awkwardness merely social clumsiness, as it appeared, or was he hiding some devious motive?

"Please, Mister French, let me see my boy," she asked, her voice softening.

French took a long draw of the cigar, contemplating his reply. He knocked off the ash with his little finger and drank deeply from his goblet. "Of course you can see him…as soon as he returns."

"Returns?" Antoinette said, her voice rising. "He's not here?"

"Well, it's Mother, you know," French said, stumbling through his answer. "She's not…not very partial to children."

"Where is he?"

"H-he's in school," French stuttered. "A g-good school—in New Orleans."

"In New Orleans, the one place I can't go? School? He's three years old!" Antoinette said, cornering him.

French spiked his cigar into his wine glass and snapped to his feet. "You will see him when I do," he shouted, voice breaking. "And that's all I'm going to say. Make up your mind. One of us is going to New Orleans. It's either going to be you, in chains, or it's going to be me. Is that clear?"

French stormed across the room and picked up the adoption papers. Then he circled to the kitchen door and threw it open, freezing the manservant and two cooks with their ears pressed to the door.

"You can sneak up the south steps and tell Mother that I've made her the offer," French told the startled servants. Then he strode to the room's main doors and threw them wide open. In the hallway, the three waiting riffraff scrambled to their feet and, receiving their orders, entered the dining room to escort Antoinette back to her room. But Antoinette wasn't paying any attention to them. Instead, she watched French's almost disjointed, unnatural gait as he walked away into the black emptiness of the French mansion.

***

Early as it was before breakfast, Hurst saw motion in the storefront office that belonged to Bake, the sheriff. Seeing Bake was there, Hurst sucked up his courage and entered. He uncovered a quart jug, plopped it on the desk and slid it across. Then he pulled up the secondhand kitchen chair Bake kept for guests, spun it around backwards and sat straddled across it, his arms resting on its back.

Bake lifted the jug and sniffed it, then took a swig. "Hmmm. That's that good copper kettle going 'round," he said, his visage brightening. Affecting a stern pose, he added, "You done right to turn it into the law."

Bake pulled two mismatched glasses from his side drawer and planted them on the desktop's worn, stained surface. Then he filled them, sliding one across to Hurst. Both raised their glasses before draining them. *It's a start,* Hurst calculated.

Hurst eased into the conversation by making small talk, and soon they were passing hunting stories back and forth. Some of Hurst's were toppers, and many were actually stretched versions of tales he'd heard other people tell. Still, true or not, with the haze of good squeezings settling over the proceedings, the sheriff was mightily amused.

"Listen, Bake," Hurst said, gathering his courage, "I know all about Missus French and her late husband."

Stunned by the statement, Bake swiped his mouth with his sleeve, then set the glass down, friendly no longer. "Well, if you know everything, that certainly overtops the nothing I know," he said.

"That's not all you know," Hurst replied, digging in.

"Listen, I like living in Turkle, and I ain't gonna cross no Frenches—like you shouldn't neither."

But Hurst had anticipated the sheriff's reluctance. "I understand that. Then could I just kind of poke through the jail's old records, sort of quiet-like?"

"I'm warning you," Bake said, his eyes narrowing. "When I smell smoke, I keep a' eye out for burning *trash*."

"Then just tell me one thing," Hurst ventured.

"Nope," Bake replied, rising. "I don't know nothing about no Frenches."

Informing Hurst that he was late for breakfast, Bake shooed his guest out the door and headed directly to his boarding house table. As Hurst headed the opposite way, he silently cursed his own impatience. How could he be so stupid? By coming when the sheriff was hungry, Hurst had turned the odds against himself. Plus, he'd shown his hand prematurely. Well, he told himself to keep up his courage, this was only the opening move of a very long game.

***

French's sporadic attempts to learn something definitive about his father's death were bearing no fruit. He went to the lawyer, but as talkative as the lawyer was, French couldn't get anything useful out of him. Rather, the man's continuous stream of prattle proved even more vacuous than usual. Further inflaming his curiosity, lately French had begun to pick up word that the stranger was inquiring about the same subject. Thoughts of his father's death began to trouble French's dreams, leading to bloody nightmares.

The newspaperman set the lantern on the desk to light the otherwise deserted office. It was late, and he wanted to get to bed, but he couldn't refuse this guest. He explained how the yellowed old editions were ordered, then backed off to allow French to take a chair.

French licked his fingers and went through the entire stack, not finding what he was searching for. Frustrated, he started at the beginning and went through the stack again, taking more care, with no more luck than before. Frantic, his fingers ran back and forth through the pile.

"Wait a minute," French said, "the whole year's missing! My father's death, my birth announcement, everything."

The young editor merely shrugged. "I haven't touched these since I

131

bought the paper, Mister French. Maybe the *County Seat Courier—*"

French stood up, kicking back the chair. "I doubt if Mother overlooked that, but there are plenty of mute birds that money can make sing."

***

The basement of the county seat courthouse was dank and chilly. The night law clerk worked the rusted key into the locked trunk and labored to turn it. Nothing. Growing impatient, Isaac took over and struggled mightily with it, making so much noise that the other two feared someone might hear. Finally, the lock made a *click* and Isaac threw open the lid. Relieved, the clerk set his lantern beside him to search through the sealed, yellow envelopes. This was it! He held it close to the light.

"You guessed right!" he exclaimed. "State of Mississippi versus Marie Brussard French. That's your Missus French's legal name, all right. The judge must have ordered it sealed."

Isaac deftly lifted the envelope from the clerk's grasp and handed it to Hurst. Then he handed the clerk the money.

Hurst stared at what he believed was the end to the Frenches' dominance over Turkle. His hands trembled as he broke the seal and pulled out the ancient watermarked papers. Then, straining his eyes to make out the words, he saw that this was indeed the document. He scanned through the decree, his eyes feasting on one luscious revelation after another. The more he read, the faster his heart beat.

At long last, he thought euphorically, remembering his own father's ignominious killing. *This will prove to everyone that the Frenches are no better than anyone else.*

Impatient to be away, Isaac yanked the papers out of Hurst's hands. Startled by the sudden motion, Hurst seemed to comprehend what had happened, but his eyes were far off.

Hurst knew from chess that a threat is often more powerful than a threat actually exercised. That is because a threat always limits your opponent's options, forcing him to focus his attention on what damage you *might* do to him. Whereas, once you execute your gambit and do your damage, your opponent is then free to resume contemplating his own attack against you. Often, in fact, his counterattack catches you temporarily exposed. But that was pure theory, and what was real now was what Hurst felt in his heart. A lifetime of hurt was at stake, and his heart said to bludgeon the Frenches bloody with these papers.

***

Easter, 1859

"I don't see why I have to go to church simply because *That Man* rose from the dead."

Missus French always resented this annual ritual. But Devereau persisted, cajoling her to dress and get to the carriage waiting out front. They couldn't be late to church.

"The town's got to see you at least once a year, Mother, and Easter is the only day they are willing to tolerate you." French looked sourly at his own black suit, which he wore only for this occasion each year so that his mother's black wouldn't stand out quite so prominently.

Heading to the church, the pair rode in silence inside the ornate carriage, a remnant of the old days, brought out specially for this purpose. Each stared moodily out of opposite windows, lost in thought. The heavy traffic of slave-driven cotton wagons had etched deep gullies in the road, causing the carriage to lurch back and forth.

"Your fine stewardship of the roads is noteworthy," Missus French said sarcastically, irritated at being jostled about.

She turned to watch her child staring dreamily out the window. *Why was this one foisted on me?* she asked herself. *Why one so weak? So cowardly? So totally unable to grasp the simple nuances of life? Oh, the child had assets. Intelligent, well-read, even clever at times. Good with numbers and a nose for the cotton market. But one so unsuited to be my offspring!*

"I know about your dealings," Missus French blurted. "That devil out there has a stake pointed at our heart, and you put enough money in his pocket for him to survive."

"I made a brilliant deal," French said, slapped from his reverie.

"Brilliant, ha!" Missus French retorted. "If he smiles at you, you'll give him the deed to *French Acres*. Hell, you won't own a pasture to bury me in. A true French would simply eliminate him with one swift act. Oh, but I've spoiled you too much for that."

French scowled and turned away toward the window. To oppose a man who had accomplished such extraordinary feats using methods so foreign to French would be foolhardy. But he couldn't believe his mother was that shortsighted; she was up to something.

They rode the rest of the way without a glance or a word between them. Easter was always such a heartsick day for poor Devereau. Their black clothing was so absolutely appropriate.

***

The liquid, clear sunlight suffused the green lawns and the wooden church, promising the resurrection of life after the dreary, deprived winter. The women in their finest Easter bonnets and the men in their best Sunday black coats greeted each other pleasantly, drinking in the warmth and the neighborly congeniality, as if a magic euphoria, a readiness to grant life a new chance, had taken control of the air itself. But their pleasant bubble was soon to burst when the stranger intruded, bringing in his wake an angry disturbance.

The townsfolk gathered around Durksen Hurst to watch him hammer the faded, yellow-brown legal documents to the church doors. He pounded each nail like a man possessed, his eyes aflame, as if expiating all the considerable pain in his life in one mad rush. When he finished putting up the last one, he turned and, in a brief, impassioned speech, told the churchgoers what the documents said and what they meant.

He had expected that, after seeing the proof embodied in these papers, the citizenry would rise as one, demanding that justice be brought against the Frenches. But to his utter frustration, their voices grew hushed. Could he have miscalculated? His heart pounding, he thought about gathering the papers and disappearing back to *DarkHorse*, hoping word of what he'd done wouldn't get to the Frenches. But maybe the people were merely shocked. Maybe they would catch onto their role in what he needed done. Maybe they would have to see the whole drama, his confrontation with Missus French played out before they rose against her. He had to see it through; there was no other choice.

Just then the French carriage pulled up, and the crowd fell silent, like the moment before an execution. The French servant on the top seat climbed down and set up the steps at the carriage door, while the crowd separated to let Hurst pass through to face his nemesis.

Missus French's head poked out through the carriage door.

"There she is," Hurst shouted, his voice hard and angry, "the woman who killed her husband and took all his land, like it says on these legal papers! She cut him over fifty times before they could stop her."

"Well, you certainly practice what you preach, don't you, Mother?" French growled angrily.

"It's time to debunk your fairy tale, child," Missus French said coldly. "Well, you're man enough to take it—I hope Hurst doesn't find out, or there'll be a scandal to beat all scandals!" Having said this, Missus French broke into loud, throaty laughter.

Hearing her wild derision, the crowd—few of whom had ever heard her voice—began to speculate in excited whispers, which created a rising buzz like a violated beehive. This Easter would be one to remember, the antithesis of Easter.

"Stop that laughing," French demanded. "It's a monstrosity when you do it. Stop it!"

Stepping grandly from the carriage onto the top of her portable stairs, Missus French blinked at the sudden exposure to the morning's full light. But her eyes soon adjusted, enabling her to see the colorful Easter crowd at her feet. An amused smirk crossed her lips.

"Yes," she announced, "I killed the late, sainted Mister Clayton French. I slashed his throat with a piece of broken mirror, then cut him over and over and over. When the staff ran in, my hands were in shreds."

She dug her left thumb under the wrist of her right glove and with difficulty wrested it off. Then she held up her hand for all to see. The scars in her gnarled palms and fingers ran so deep they deformed her entire hand.

The crowd surged forward to get a better view of the deformed fingers. So that explained her perpetual gloves.

***

He burst into her room, reeking of alcohol and countless other unsubtle odors. She lay on her bed where the three French relatives had left her—not crying, never crying. Her eye and arm were bruised, her nightgown torn and bloody, her advanced pregnancy apparently intact. He stopped, focusing his eyes on her, swaying on his feet, his stomach rumbling. Then he saw the state she was in and knew what had happened. And the rage hit him, a rage beyond morality, beyond conscience, the rage of a wild stallion protecting the viability and survival of his seed against wandering stallions. In blind fury, he went after her.

She tried to run, but he was big, with long arms and strong hands. He caught her by the shoulder and hit her on the face with his fist. She tumbled onto her dressing table, causing her tiny bottles full of gentle scents to crash about her.

He came again. She tried to rise, but too late, he was upon her. In her desperation, she reached for the nearest object and hit him a glancing blow with her hand mirror. Further enraged by the sudden pain, he ripped the mirror from her hand and brought it down upon her head, breaking out of its center a large, triangular-shaped, jagged shard. Throwing the mirror aside, he came again.

Only later did she remember what followed. Somehow, after he had beaten her into unconsciousness, she woke on the floor to discover him asleep on the bed. Then she was upon him. She only knew she had the shard of glass firmly in both hands and that she was using it to repeatedly slash his throat as he fumbled at her through his drunken slumber.

There was a lot of blood, more than she believed two people could hold. At some point she must have struck his jugular, causing his blood to gush forth. She didn't stop even when he ceased to struggle, even though her hands were cut to ribbons.

In the hallway, a 'cropper wearing a black coat and preacher hat had taken advantage of the big party at the house to sneak a drink for himself. Hired to do odd jobs around the mansion, mend furniture and paint walls, he was slinking around, looking for an opportunity to steal. Hearing noise from the master bedroom, he crept up to peer through the crack in the door. He discovered her partially undressed lying on the bed. Instinctively, he opened the door wider for a fuller view before he realized what was taking place inside the room. Being drunk and seeing blood everywhere, he made a startled cry, which caused the woman to turn and see him.

The man mumbled an apology and backed away.

***

"Drunkenness? Sudden madness?" a bewildered French managed weakly from his seat in the carriage.

"Sobriety, sanity," Missus French responded, raising her voice so that the whole crowd could hear. "The entire episode was nearly premeditated murder. I thought of little else for the two years we lived together—and you were conceived. You complain about missing your youth. I was only nineteen when I killed that beast."

"See, she admits it!" Hurst shouted, trying to recover the initiative.

"Admit it?" Missus French replied. "I boast of it! Do you think he kept his cruel depravity in my bedroom? Turkle had endured him for years. Do you think there was one soul to avenge him—even one human being who wasn't celebrating that monster's death? Why, Turkle practically gave me a medal."

The crowd knew many versions of the story through gossip and tales. Indeed, the murder, once almost legendary, was now so much a part of the town's general lore and historical fabric that it was rarely mentioned. But now the crowd perked up its ears to hear the tale directly from the woman herself.

"Listen," Missus French continued, "if you good people want me to let his family come back to Turkle, if you want Frenches slithering about everywhere like snakes in a swamp, you tell me. If you want your daughters raped, your sons beaten and shot, your farms burned, you tell me. I'll put them up.

"Now I think you've seen enough of me."

Shouting orders to be taken home, Missus French climbed back into the carriage. Hands trembling, she pulled the curtain before covering her eyes with her handkerchief.

On the lawn, an utterly mystified Durk Hurst couldn't let his lifelong dream of victory slip away that easily. Seeing the driver mounting to the seat, and desperate that the confrontation not end so indecisively, he ran forward and yanked open the carriage door.

"I want to see her," he demanded, clenching his fist.

Inside, Missus French wiped her eyes, then retrieved the pistol she kept secreted under her seat. "Here is your chance!" she urged, shoving it into Devereau's hands. "Self-defense, damn it! Self-defense!"

But French pushed the pistol away. Instead, with shaking hand he reached inside his coat pocket and pulled out a letter written on fine linen stationary, a letter he carried with him every time he left the house. He handed it to Hurst.

"The widow DuVallier's given us instructions that she does not wish to be bothered by you," French said, now fully composed. "There, in her own hand." French gave his mother a sly grin. "Women have such lovely script, don't you think, Mother?"

In spite of her distress, Missus French smirked at the remark—and at her child's quick recovery.

"I've written friends in New Orleans to check up on you," Hurst shouted to Missus French.

Grabbing the letter from Devereau French, Hurst gave him a look strong enough to pierce him through his back. Then he read the note and realized what he was holding. His heart stopped beating, his eyes watered; he had to fight back the urge to scream and curse.

His head pounding, unable to think about anything but the fact he'd lost Antoinette, he slammed the carriage door shut.

He'd needed a clear win—fully expected a complete victory. Instead, he had discharged his lone shot and wounded only himself, perhaps fatally. The two sides were bitterly trapped in a mutual death grip. And the French family held all the weapons. He only had to wait for the consequences to crash down upon their heads.

What was he going to say to his partners?

Chapter Eighteen

On the long ride back to *French Acres*, Devereau French sat sullenly in the carriage, his chin on his fist. "How did you…? Why didn't they…?" he blurted, breaking the silence.

But Missus French was tired from all the excitement and dismayed by her son's innocence. Keeping the truth from him had oppressed her since the beginning, but now she was relieved it was out; she wished she'd shattered his illusions long ago. Perhaps this shock would jolt him out of his timidity, would make him into the kind of man she wanted.

"The law can't hang a pregnant woman. Even lynchers won't do it. His *male* heir was in my belly. You! Understand? Now, is everything clear? Do you want to know more? There's still one small detail."

French turned away, submerging himself into one of his infamous sulks. This explained many things, but not everything, not at all.

The "small detail" troubled him and, as his imagination took free rein, he considered all the ramifications. He looked at his mother, but her glazed-over eyes told French she was in another time and place. He could not speak to her when she was like this.

French's thoughts turned toward breaking free from his trap, from his mother, everything. He glanced once at the pillow that now concealed his mother's pistol, feeling its closeness, coldness, its finality. He would think of that pistol often in the days to come.

***

Durksen Hurst rode the long, foliage-lined road home as the sun sank lower in the sky behind him, his hopes for a quick and decisive resolution to *DarkHorse's* uneasy existence dashed. Dashed, too, were his hopes of seeing Antoinette, at the very least to say goodbye. He felt she was trapped now because he hadn't been strong or smart enough.

He remembered how his father had told him the apocryphal story of the murder that had taken place thirty-odd years before. He wondered whether the part his father claimed in the town legend was true or, like many of his father's tales, contrived just to make himself important in a world that hadn't much use for him. The stealing part of the tale had a ring of truth, but now he realized the rest was probably extrapolated from common stories around Turkle. The man had been adept at stealing, but never at telling the truth.

Yes, stealing had been his father's one consistent enterprise. But Hurst found he never could steal, and this backwardness led to beatings when his father perceived he had missed opportunities to acquire other people's property, as was often the case.

Now Hurst felt his life had come full circle, befitting his father's intended legacy. Hurst had indeed stolen, stolen more than his father could have ever dreamed of stealing. He had appropriated land from the very people who had given him shelter during his darkest desperation, who had raised and nurtured him—they were people he loved. Hurst wondered what hardships the Chickasaws were doomed to suffer because of his acquisition of their land. Hell, he'd stolen more from them than any of the planters who, as a boy, Hurst had learned to hate. He despaired that he wasn't a better man than his father, merely a better thief.

He hung his head as he rode, watching the streaking pattern of leaves and stones on the ground as they disappeared behind him. He simply couldn't raise his eyes to see the trees, sky, birds or wild animals. He wasn't worthy even of their company. His trip home was slow and agonizing.

***

Devereau French threw the jacket on a chair, then crossed the lush bedroom suite to the full-length mirror. Night would soon be here and with it the melancholy that never departed.

Home, my prison cell. All the pain I've borne within these walls, all the solitary years forced to masquerade as her son, and years ahead with no relief.

Drying her eyes, Devereau unbuttoned her frilly white shirt with the lacy cuffs and took it off. Then she unpinned the thick, strong band constricting her breasts and began to unwrap it. The band was long, and unwinding it took time, but she was in no hurry. Like every other night, she had nothing to look forward to but more solitude. Finally exposed, she stared hard at her breasts, wrinkled and distorted from their tight wrapping.

I've spent my adult life obscuring these! They're not much to hide. I hate them.

Look at that miserable creature staring back at me— gaunt, pale face, an unlovable face—nothing like a man's and a colorless imitation of a woman's. Hair like straw. Body that could only be described as nondescript, undesirable by any standards.

Even my mirror is a bad liar, just like my mother, and no one has been fooled but me. And for going along with Mother's lie, I have lost my chance for a real life, to be a wife, to be a loving mother to my own child, to not be alone!

With a gentle tap on the door, old Annie quietly entered, closing the door behind her. Draped over her arm, Annie carried a frilly ball gown that smelled of cedar. She tiptoed across the Persian carpet to deposit the dress onto the bed.

"You lied to me! About my father's murder!" French lashed out, slapping Annie's cheek hard, driving her crying into an armchair.

"Your mamma tell us!" Annie pleaded. "And you was a child. Honey, she was just trying to protect you." Tears rolled down Annie's face.

French softened and handed Annie a clean handkerchief, then returned to her reflection in the mirror. Her eyes welled up until her own image was blurred beyond recognition.

"Lately, Annie, I just don't know."

Annie wiped her eyes and blew her nose. "It's that new man out there, ain't it? Lawd, if this one ain't as bad as the last. Baby, why don't you tell your mamma you wants to be what you is? All men ain't like your daddy— or that devil you run off with that time."

"And be a laughingstock?"

Devereau snapped out of her stupor, horrified at her outburst at Annie, despondent over exposing her hidden reserve of cruelty. She'd never spoken a cross word to this woman who had raised her from infancy and was her only confidant.

Devereau had only seen Annie cry once before, on the day she had returned from what she thought of as her "exile". Tears had fallen down Annie's cheeks as French came riding toward her, the prodigal child reappearing. Back then, she'd disappeared for four months, and no one at *French Acres* was sure she was still alive.

The horse she rode bareback had picked up a stone, but she urged it limping on. French Acres *couldn't be far now; she vaguely recognized the fields she had passed the last two miserable hours of riding. Her cheekbone was swollen the size of an apple and throbbed with every jolt and bounce, burning like fire. Her lip had stopped bleeding, but was also swelling. Her arm, having taken her weight when she had been thrown to the ground, could barely move.*

Then she saw the old mansion ahead. She turned her horse off the road to approach the house from the rear. The horse resisted, limping and stumbling, but French was a horseman—or rather a horsewoman. She forced it onward. Slaves working around the house stopped what they were doing to stare silently as she rode by, dressed in a stolen, oversized

Chickasaw man's clothing. When she reached the kitchen, she slid off the horse and cried out.

Then, her shoulders shaking with sobs, she stood safe in Annie's soft embrace. Annie led her upstairs and drew a warm bath. She brought food. Devereau cradled her head against Annie's large bosom, and Annie listened as she told her everything—where she'd been, what had happened.

But that had been then. Now her feelings were hurting just as badly.

"Honey," Annie said soothingly, "they's a lot worse things to be than a rich, pretty, young white woman. Your mamma made you a boy to fool all them folks. All that French land and money sittin' here," Annie said sadly. "Why, you knows them folks would just have brushed off a stranger-woman and a girl-baby and took it. But having old Mister French's boy-child needing a mamma to carry on, now that was how folks say it oughts to be.

"I knows it's hard, but, baby, if you was a girl, with the way things is, them folks would have hung your momma. Well, maybe she' be better off, way she lives. But where you be then? It ain't so easy being a chile with nobody in this world."

***

The careworn country doctor finished wrapping the baby girl in a dirty jail-house towel. He clicked his tongue, then carried her to where the mother lay drenched in sweat, her long, jet-black hair plastered to her forehead. Even with the shadows of jail bars across her, wrapped in dirty sheets, her unpainted face lined in pain, she was still the most breathtaking woman he'd ever seen. He tapped her shoulder and she opened her large, oval, dark eyes.

"A healthy baby girl," he said. "Too bad you landed here for the delivery."

He attempted to lay the bundle at her side, but she pushed it away with her thickly wrapped, damaged hands.

"A…what? Oh, no, absolutely not," she said, as if rejecting an opening offer to a dubious deal. "Doctor, I'm told you love to fish. I'm going to see you get to fish as much as you like for the rest of your natural life. And you won't have to worry when you're away because I'm going to personally see that the cause of most of Turkle's violent injuries are eliminated."

Then she reached up and took the baby into her bandaged mitts.

***

She stood before them in the judge's chambers wearing a change of clothes, a beatific, gentle smile on her face, the child in her arms. The baby suckled on her naked breast, leaving the judge and town dignitaries on the panel speechless, swallowing hard. Above the infant's head they could see the dark of her broad nipple. Though decorum had been broken in a wholly unanticipated way, neither the judge nor any of the others called her attention to that fact. Without blinking or looking aside, the dignitaries merely whispered to one another to pass the pitcher of water, which they consumed prodigiously.

Her disheveled hair had been brushed, but not washed. Her face was without makeup or powder, but her beauty remained. Finally, when the babe was done feeding, her breast was fully revealed, and then disappeared as she refastened her buttons. The judge cleared his throat.

"For the record, my dear, what is the child's name?" the judge asked.

"Devereau Brussard French," she replied.

"Devereau," the judge repeated, beginning to write, "isn't that Miss Faragut's name? Well, it could be either, I guess. If that's what she wants to call the boy."

"There's only one French worthy of running French Acres, *" the young woman told them, as if lecturing a group of schoolboys, "and that is my son, Devereau French. I'm going to kick the rest of these flat-headed French fools off his property and out of this town for good.*

"Think about it, gentlemen. Your families will be able to walk the streets at night."

"That's an awful lot of wildcats for just one housecat to scare off," the judge said, sarcasm in his voice thick as molasses.

"If the court gives little Devereau documented legitimacy, I'll outsmart them."

"Outsmarting them won't be a stretch, but that will be the least of your problems."

The judge and the panel eyed the doctor, seeking his thoughts. The doctor nodded. "I believe the child doesn't carry the French madness."

The judge hurrumphed, looking the woman over carefully. "If the boy is indeed the son of a French—but that is not for our determination. If we questioned the paternity of every boy who wasn't as crazy as his father, we'd have a town full of bastards. That argument ain't neither practical nor desirable, as it would turn our wives into women of debatable morals, and they wouldn't stand for it."

The room filled with laughter until the gavel sounded. The judge and the noteworthies looked from the doctor to one another, the same conclusion in every mind. This was obviously a case of self-defense, but the stranger-woman from New Orleans couldn't herself profit from killing one of their own, a white man of substance. That would set a dangerous precedent. However, the innocent boy harmed no one. He should inherit his father's legacy. The woman could serve as the caretaker of the child's estate until he reached his majority. After all, doesn't a boy need a mother?

Every man on the bench was thinking about how he might aid this poor, defenseless woman, and how he might benefit from such service to the French Acres *estate. Further, they hoped such a woman might find good male friends amongst their gathering, or at least one good male friend. At least before she squandered or was swindled out of the boy's legacy by some slick stranger from out of town.*

Plus, she'd promised to rid the town of those quarrelsome, degenerate Frenches. Not that she had much chance of succeeding, but it was certainly worth letting her make her pitiful attempt. The judge brought his gavel down hard a final time.

"To protect the innocent child, this case shall be sealed and remain so in perpetuity. Case dismissed! Boys, bring out the jug. I ain't been this thirsty for a long stretch."

***

"But look at me, Annie," French pleaded, crossing her arms to cover her naked breasts.

"Baby," Annie said gently, "you let your pretty hair grow out and put you on a fine dress, you'll have every nice man in the state after you. Trust old Annie." She straightened the dress and left the room.

Alone, French removed her trousers. Then she removed her codpiece and buried it in a drawer. Wiping her eyes clear, she picked up the dress and held it to herself, searching the mirror for any kind of femininity, any glimmer of attractiveness.

Her face hardened. "I'll investigate you, Mother. I've been your slave too damn long."

Chapter Nineteen

Sitting behind her desk, Devereau French adjusted her smoking jacket before sealing the letter. It was past midnight, but she couldn't wait another minute to enact her plan. Once the letter was sealed, she handed it to the sleepy messenger.

"You tell that lawyer I want to know every detail of Mother's former life, and I want to know it yesterday. You hear me. Then you ride back here as fast as you can."

"Yes, sir, Mister French," the man replied, yawning and scratching. He placed the envelope in his leather pouch and, yawning more broadly now, shuffled from the room.

When he was gone, Devereau sat back in her chair with a deep sigh. She reached across the desk to lift the lid of her humidor and pulled out one of her favorite cigars. She started to reach for her butt-clip, but thought better of it. Instead, she bit off the end of the cigar and spit the acrid, foul-tasting tobacco onto the carpet. After sniffing the cigar, she lit and puffed it into burning, coughing harshly before her throat adjusted to the scorching bitter smoke. It felt good between her lips.

She sat puffing, her brow creased, another irony to her situation not escaping her. "Here I'm stuck in purgatory—while my hands get to visit New Orleans."

***

It was already past midday, and they had far to travel. Big Josh sat the roan and Little Turby the mule, wearing their best suits. They wouldn't reach the French slave quarters until past sundown.

They hadn't gone visiting their women friends there for three weeks. Work was harder with spring seeding, so this night was special. Tied to the saddle were buckets containing their best foodstuffs, along with a jug and knickknack gifts from the county seat.

Hurst held the animal's rein, nervous as a rabbit at a wolf-dance. He handed Big Josh the note that contained all his hopes and dreams, before Big Josh offered Hurst some reassuring words and rode off.

Hurst returned to the table, sitting with his chin on his fists, alone. The fire was dying and the air was growing cool, but he didn't have the energy to get up and put on another log. He wondered, even if the note did get to her, even if she saw his message favorably, how long would he wait for a reply? Would he ever receive one?

***

Big Josh was peaceful and full, and a bit loose from the spirits, feeling safe in the night. He leaned back, picking his teeth with the gold toothpick Hurst had bought for him at the county seat general store. At the time, Big Josh said the gift was unnecessary, but he didn't refuse it.

He gazed across the one-room cabin at Little Turby and Turby's young woman, who both stared shyly at the ground. The skinny girl's hair was tied into two knotted pigtails. Big Josh caught Little Turby's eye, and nodded to the boy that it was probably safe to take his girl out into the night air. Little Turby spoke softly and she nodded in response. Hand-in-hand, the two young people went out the door.

Big Josh reached into his jacket pocket and set Hurst's note on the table. Then he placed his toothpick in his otherwise empty watch pocket and examined the confined space around him.

I came from a place just like this, he thought. *Same small improvised fire, same pallet on the floor, same broken-and-repaired table once discarded by whites. Same third-hand clothes everyone in the quarters wore.*

Ceeba came through the door carrying stove wood in her arms, the kettle full of fetched water in her large hand. While she got the fire going, Big Josh untied the paper package he'd brought and opened it up to reveal the coffee. Real coffee, a handful! Ceeba made a pleased exclamation and went to stand beside Big Josh, laying her arm on his shoulder as he embraced her waist. Then he handed her the note.

She picked it up and slid it into her bosom. Following her hand with his eyes, Big Josh kissed the note. "I g-gots another message on my lips to put with that one."

"Get on away from me, fool," Ceeba laughed, playfully fending him off.

"How you g-gonna get word to her?" Big Josh asked.

"See," Ceeba explained, "Eulunda's sister is with Oral in the stables, whose Aunt Sissy works in the kitchen. Well, Sissy's man, Dooley, is a upstair man, and he can get word through Annie, who takes her meals."

"I could just kiss you," Big Josh said, smooth as honey. He tried gently to pull her toward him, but she resisted, in no gentle way, breaking away to check the kettle.

"Aw, Ceeba. Someday, honey, you' gonna live in the *DarkHorse* mansion w-with me. We' have a f-fireplace by our bed and—"

"Yeah, you get me off this French place, Mister Big Talk. Y'all come 'round here wearing them fine clothes, with all them wild stories 'bout things that can't never be. Live in the mansion! You think I'm a fool? Josh, I don't care 'bout no mansion or no shack neither, if we could be together some way. But you' there and I'm here."

"But, Ceeba, we can't— Can't you just wait for me?"

"On your promises? Here? Why, a woman like me don't know what might happen to her. Don't you see, Josh, there can't be no mansion for us dark folks. I'm sorry, but that's just the way things is."

Big Josh sunk down in his chair. Being here with Ceeba was good, but it wasn't near as good as being with her at *DarkHorse* would be. He could make good bottom land out of a swamp; could practically lift a mule; could do almost anything a man can do. But he couldn't arrange to have the woman he loved—the woman who loved him, who would willingly go with him—ride with him the few miles back to *DarkHorse*. And that was a damn shame. Big Josh looked deeply, almost imploringly into Ceeba's eyes, but all he saw was a misty reflection of his own sorrow. And that was a crying damn shame.

***

That night Devereau French—wearing her finest man's suit—arranged a solitary dinner with Antoinette. At French's instruction, the servants had the fireplace roaring, the dining room filled with candles and the curtains thrown open to allow the moonlight inside. But the quarter moon in a cloudy sky did more to accentuate the gloom outside than to brighten the interior. The world never let her capture the mood she wanted. She could almost hear her mother laughing from the far end of the house.

Down the long table, Antoinette picked at all seven courses of her dinner in virtual silence, with only nods and whispered thanks to the servers. She didn't know why she had been brought here. No word passed between them until the plates were taken away, the port poured, and her host's cigar lit.

"You knew the odds against you," French said, blowing a smoke ring and watching it dissipate. "Why did you take such a chance coming here?"

"Because I swore Louis Edward would never have to endure what I have," Antoinette replied sharply, without hesitation. "Just so you're warned, I mean that, Mister French."

French was taken aback by the sudden vehemence of her response. She absently fingered her knife, then set it down, her curiosity aroused.

"What do you mean? Tell me. Please," French asked softly.

Antoinette examined French's face, then spoke haltingly, her throat constricted. "My mother abandoned me when I was a child. Really, she gave me over to a—a horror!"

"What do you mean, a horror?" French asked.

"I can't talk about it. Ever. Some may criticize me for marrying Mister DuVallier, but he was really very kind before he got sick." She paused to collect herself.

"Do you remember her? Your mother?" French followed.

"Yes. I see her like a picture in my mind, but it's probably more imagination than her," Antoinette said. "I often wonder how the world would look to me if I'd had my mother. What I'd be."

"Believe me, a mother is not necessarily a blessing," French said sarcastically. "'The sins of the mother,' you know."

Silence. Then Antoinette turned her dark brown eyes on French. "Speaking of mothers… Strange, I haven't met yours."

"Let's not speak of her!" French shouted as if stung. Then, regaining her composure, she forced a smile. "But we're talking," she said in a condescending attempt at friendliness. "Now, what do friends talk about?"

"Why, whatever's in their heart, Mister French."

French instructed the armed riffraff to remain by the dining room doors and, holding a lantern, led Antoinette into the long-abandoned garden that lay beneath her bedroom window. Almost thirty years had passed since anyone had crossed that threshold and the space had become an overgrown mélange of thorny briars, weeds, vines, and twisted trees with no discernible pathway. Enough bare spots allowed them to work their way within ten feet of the brick wall. There, French stopped, searching the barrier for the boarded up archway she once had passed through, but the night was too black to make it out.

"So, tell me about Mister Hurst," French blurted clumsily. "Is he as remarkable as they say he is?"

"Who?" Antoinette responded.

"Don't be coy," French said with a manufactured, trilling laugh. "He's survived this long on my sufferance. Tell me."

Antoinette searched French's face—cheekbones, lips, eyes, skin—then a smirk lighted on her lips.

"Oh, you know the type, I'm sure," Antoinette said in a voice that suggested a confidence between old companions. "Rough on the edges, but underneath, sweet and soft as a virgin's dream. And, you know that white stallion you ride?"

"Yes, Insatiable," French stuttered, trying to follow the sudden conversational tangent. "Insatiable is the finest stud in Mississippi."

"Your one true love, and I know you must love to watch that horse put to the test," Antoinette said, barely containing her laughter. "Well, Hurst's not unlike Insatiable."

"You're making fun of me!" French shouted, red-faced. "Here I've tried to befriend a low-class—Take her away! Get over here!" French called to the waiting riffraff.

Two men hustled through the garden, cursing the thorns and sticking undergrowth until they reached the pair. They led Antoinette away, re-entering the house through the open doors, and passed Annie, who stood watching.

"Don't pay no mind, honey," Annie said to Antoinette. "That child jes' been 'lone too long."

* * *

Finished brushing her hair, Antoinette lit the bedside candle and climbed into the fresh white sheets. She stacked her pillows and settled back, pulling up the covers. Comfortable, she reached over to her nightstand and picked the top book off the stack.

Her youth had been lived entirely from one book to the next. Residing in hotels and pensions across Europe, she was usually actively reading three or four at once. She purchased them at local book shops in whatever city or village she found herself. Most were in the language of the country of the moment, but she sometimes managed to acquire English editions, especially of the better-known works.

The elderly man she was forced to call "Father" always hired a private tutor for her from among the local student population, so she became fluent in new languages more easily. Yet she and the man never stayed in one place for long. No matter how placid the setting, he would eventually worry that the locals were becoming suspicious. Fearful, he would pack and the two of them would flee. Even today, when she recalled this constant running and hiding, she still trembled. But what could she have done? She was a child, and he was all she had in the world.

She laid the book face-down on her lap, the words on the page not strong enough to keep her from being drawn back.

She was four. Early that morning, her mother bathed her for something she promised would be very special. She remembered how much she loved the way her mother meticulously combed her long black hair, which reached far down her back. Then she was dressed in her prettiest red dress, white pinafore, and shoes. She knew something exciting was waiting for her.

Finished primping and fussing over Antoinette, her mother took her small hand and led her to the French Quarter. He lived on a quiet, well-kept street, with his house, ominously, the sole long-neglected on the street. The interior of the house reflected the outside. Heavy shades darkened the rooms, and colorful vases full of flowers from the back garden specially cut for the occasion failed to bring cheer. The furniture and paintings on the wall were exquisite, but old and dusty. The man, too, reflected his surroundings. He was immaculately groomed and dressed, but his well-tailored clothes were from a bygone age, matching in some sense his wispy mustache and gray-white hair.

The man handed her mother a check, which she tucked into her purse. Then, with a quick hug and good-bye, her mother placed her little hand in the man's dry, furrowed palm, and left.

After a time, the man became frightened by the neighbors' questions. Soon they were on a ship to Europe, by way of Cuba. Her heart broke beyond pain or hope. Once aboard, she knew she would never see her mother again.

Years later, as an adult, she spent a year searching for her mother, not even knowing the woman's name, but her mother had vanished.

Yes, she knew, the lonely little girl had taken refuge in her books. Books had certainly saved her life, her sanity. If, indeed, she was sane.

***

She was awakened from a troubled sleep by a groggy armed guard who smelled of rum. Over the man's shoulder Antoinette made out a black house servant in nightclothes, holding a candle, and a second armed guard carrying a lantern.

"Y'all come on with us'n," the guard said.

"Where are you taking me?" she asked, terror in her eyes.

"Why, to see the Queen of Hellfire."

"You the first outsider been in her room anybody can remember, least since I been working the house," the second guard said.

"Put on your wrap, ma'am. We be waitin' rat outside in the hall."

***

The house servant bearing his candle led Antoinette into the gloom. The vast suite seemed more warehouse than habitation, smelling of dust and dampness. Antoinette tugged the man's sleeve to stop him in his tracks; then, guiding his arm, directed his candle above a number of paintings leaning against the nearby pillar. One by one, she examined the few within reach.

The beauty of what was in her hand took her breath away. A possible Honoré Daumier, perhaps an early El Greco! And what appeared to be a sketch for a greater work by Michelangelo! And the sculptors represented…a possible Donatello? The person who bought these did so by extensive travel or through a series of well-connected surrogates. The suite was too dark to identify the other paintings and statuary farther off. Clearly, though, the artwork was priceless. More importantly to Antoinette, the objects displayed a knowledge and sensibility far beyond this isolated hamlet, or that merely revealed someone's prescient investment acumen.

"Quit gawking and get over here," Missus French called.

Antoinette released the servant's sleeve and followed him to where Missus French sat positioned at her chessboard, clad in black. *Could Louis Edward have visited this dark, dusty space?*

"Sit down, Missus DuVallier," Missus French said, indicating the chair on the opposite side of her board. Antoinette sat behind the black pieces as requested, while the servant left the room, closing the door behind him. Only one candle remained, contorting their faces like some monstrous gargoyles in the flickering shadows.

"My son's offer to you includes one of those paintings. A fine gift for a trustworthy hired hand, wouldn't you say?" Missus French said smugly.

"Where is my son, Missus French? I must know." Antoinette insisted.

"Where did Devereau tell you he is?" Missus French replied, as if answering an inquisitive child.

"I want to hear it from you."

"He is quite safe, I've seen to that. Now, next subject: Devereau made you an offer."

So this woman, sitting in the stygian dimness, surrounded by a museum's worth of beauty and riches, is going to be as devious and obstructionist as her son. Antoinette tried another approach.

"Why did you take my Louis Edward?"

"Why?" Missus French chortled. "That boy has your husband's blood in his veins! DuVallier blood of the deepest blue."

"Yes, and my blood, too. You seem to know so much about what transpired in New Orleans, down to my son's status. You do know why my husband was divorcing me, don't you?"

"Nonsense, I don't believe a word of it," Missus French said dismissively. "You're as pure as I am. The family of that debutante he impregnated spread those rumors."

"How do you know about that? Answer my question."

"I was born and reared in the French Quarter and have many correspondents there still. When you and Louis Edward lost your husband's favor, I merely took advantage of the situation to acquire a child for my son. You have noted how isolated poor Devereau is."

"The tragedy is, Missus French, that you are just as alone as Devereau, yet neither of you can stand to be with the other." Antoinette saw this truth stung Missus French deeply.

"You suspect my motives," Missus French said, sounding hurt.

"I suspect your veracity," Antoinette replied.

"One day you will learn, my dove, that your suspicions are so far afield as to be irrelevant."

"I am sure your altruism is the talk of the county," Antoinette said sarcastically. Still tired, afraid, and confused, her mind raced. *What could the Frenches' motivation be? Perhaps Louis Edward was still Mister DuVallier's legal heir!* With Devereau now the boy's legal guardian, Louis Edward was the ideal pawn for the Frenches to acquire the DuVallier Empire. *Had this predatory woman pounced on the DuVallier fortune?*

"Now that Louis Edward belongs to Devereau, Missus French, I assume your attorneys in New Orleans are in court attempting to retrieve my son's legacy: my late-husband's shipping empire, his estates. You are seeking these things, are you not?"

"*Preparing* to seek, my dear. You mean, are my attorneys *preparing* to seek his patrimony in the courts."

"Preparing? I'd think you'd have filed the papers some time ago. Why haven't you?"

"Why? Because, my flower, your husband isn't 'late'? He is still in grave danger, he is bedridden, but you are not a murderess yet, only an assailant."

Antoinette was bewildered and dizzy. After all this time believing she had killed her husband, hearing he was still alive disarmed and disoriented her. *Not a murderess? Can I believe this revelation?*

Missus French grew wistful, almost tragic. "Of course, I don't need to accept additional risks by going after your husband's assets. You see the proof yourself. Nevertheless, even if your suspicions are true, you must accept that my best interests lie with the boy's well-being." The older woman's voice caught, and she lowered her head, her eyes downcast.

Is this acting? Antoinette wondered. *Or does Missus French really care for the boy? But it almost sounds like she has already lost—or given up—*

Louis Edward.

Antoinette studied Missus French through the confusion and flickering darkness, focusing on her face. Her face was strong, perfectly formed, appearing lined more with will than with age. Likewise, her eyes were vortexes of despair, desperation, and volition.

This woman seems oddly familiar. Yet I have never met her. But she knew memory, faded over time to shadows, can become more iconography than real.

"Look," Missus French continued, squirming from Antoinette's attention, "you are a stranger to me, yet I am being extremely benevolent on your behalf. At great risk to myself, I am giving you a place to hide from the consequences of your actions and a chance to perform honest work; for good pay, considering the demand for your services at the moment. You could still be a fugitive, you know."

"That is true," Antoinette replied, growing contrite, "and I am grateful for that."

"I can understand your chagrin, my sweet," Missus French said sympathetically. "We held you like a prisoner, but we had to make certain you were tame before we gave you the run of the place. After all, you shot your husband, and you were lying in wait to kill my son when you were captured."

"I wasn't going to kill your son," Antoinette said, but then conceded. "However, I can see why you may believe that."

"There is more, Missus DuVallier," Missus French said, seeming to search for the right words, or to introduce a new gambit.

"Yes?" Antoinette said.

"You must understand, I am concerned about an heir to *French Acres* to follow my son. Being no toady, you probably understand why." Missus French studied Antoinette's face for her reaction, but the guest was playing her cards with a straight face.

"Louis Edward could inherit everything you see in this suite…and a majority share of the Turkle Bank…and the mill. It goes on and on.

"Besides, you may grow to like Devereau."

"He and I will never be friends," Antoinette asserted. "However, if I do accept Devereau's offer, this will be purely a business arrangement. I want nothing else to do with this sordid madhouse."

"I never expected that," Missus French said. "But Louis Edward, with his DuVallier blood, might do quite nicely as a future French heir. That has always been my intent."

"So back to my original question: Where is my son?"

"You know the DuValliers first-hand, Antoinette. While your husband believes in fair dealing—much of the time, anyway—many of his kin would slit a priest's throat for a sip of Holy Water if their meat was served too salty."

"And more," Antoinette acknowledged. "They were a selfish tribe, like any family connected to wealth."

"So what reward have the DuValliers placed on your son's head? Do you think they'll wait for your husband to shudder and expire before taking precipitous actions? The adoption documents we signed lead directly to Devereau and me, and now you've drawn further attention, which could bring the authorities into our lives here. You did notice all the men I've hired to protect us."

So why wasn't Louis Edward here? Was Louis Edward alive and safe somewhere, hidden from the powerful DuVallier clan? Was he already dead—perhaps his murder arranged by the DuValliers? Had he been sold by Missus French to an acquisitive family with its sights aimed at the DuVallier fortune? Or had she sold Louis Edward to the DuValliers to ensure their interests?

"Where is he, Missus French?" Antoinette pleaded. "I have to see him."

"I can't tell you that. Look, my love, the minute they get their hands on you, you are quite doomed."

"Yes, I'd certainly never see light again. A life in prison is the best I can expect; a hanging the likeliest outcome."

"I can't take the chance that, to save your life, you might reveal Louis Edward's location." Missus French's voice grew tender. "I'm sorry. I know how that feels."

"You can't know."

"Ah, but I do." Missus French's eyes were on fire.

"I still can't understand why my husband turned our son over to you, Missus French," Antoinette said.

"Mister DuVallier does love the boy, but he knew he would have to give him up for his new wife. With us, the child has a new life in a Godforsaken country so far from the Garden District that his mother's taint is washed clean, lily white. I paid a dollar to make it legal for the privilege of having us raise Louis Edward."

For the first time, Antoinette studied the ornate chessboard between them. The position favored Missus French's white pieces so strongly, it was doubtful, sans some catastrophic blunder, that the black pieces—whomever

Missus French's imaginary opponent was, whether devil or God—would have the slightest chance. Then Antoinette's eyes fixed on the two gold-leafed, porcelain female figurines, the set's "kings." Missus French's white monarch, safely behind his/her fianchettoed bishop, looked invulnerable.

"So why save *me* from my fate?" Antoinette asked.

"You are an intelligent woman, you'll understand. You overcame much in your life, just as I had to do."

"So?"

"So, Devereau is not a good businessman," Missus French said matter-of-factly. "The whole plantation barely drags along on its last dollar. He is as cruel to the slaves as he is capable; he orders them beaten on rare occasion, but no profits. Cruelty just doesn't come naturally to Devereau, and he just can't fake it. So I guess, perhaps the plantation needs an iron hand, perhaps yours. You see, our motives for our offer to you are not completely benign."

"I wouldn't imagine they would be," Antoinette said.

"I see you studying the board, dear," Missus French said, her voice lightening. "Are you a strong player?"

"I have played, but I will never play against you. I don't need my spirits crushed for your pleasure—any more than you already have crushed them."

Hearing this, Missus French's face hardened to steel. Her voice grew cold, inflectionless. "All right, make your decision. But understand these two inviolable rules: I don't ever want to see you again, but it is possible I may call for you some day; then you will come. But if you get the notion to try to see me, you'll be sent back to New Orleans. I'll throw you to the DuVallier wolf pack."

"I understand."

"Second," Missus French added, "If I ever find out you've met or corresponded with Mister Dark Horse, you are on your way to New Orleans as well.

"I'm sure you don't need these stipulations in writing." She pulled the cord to her bell in the hall. "Get her out of here!" she shouted.

***

She would do it; in the morning she would accept their offer, and tomorrow she would run the French empire. Missus French's description of how Devereau French allows his slaves to be treated made up her mind—and she knew the woman told her that to influence her. Regardless, if the Frenches didn't like her methods, then she would tell them to find someone else.

Tomorrow she would ride out to the fields to link up with the main French overseer. If the Frenches believed—hoped?—she'd run everything from her room like some poor crippled creature, they had a lesson coming. To ride in the fresh air would be wonderful after her confinement. Once out on the plantation, she would gather everyone together, black and white, to issue her first directive: No longer would there be any abuse, beatings or intimidation of anyone on French Acres, slaves or hired hands. Anyone who violated this order would be gone. Period.

She placed the candle on her night table and climbed into bed. Satisfied that she had a plan based on principle for her first day, she prepared to read until she grew sleepy. If the anticipation she felt would let her read, if it would let her sleep.

***

"Since I am now the top overseer," Antoinette announced to the crowd, black and white, standing around her near the stables, "things are going to be different around here."

***

Devereau French, wearing one of her regular riding suits, lay on her stomach beneath the forest's covering foliage, a catalogue-bought brass spyglass to her eye. She changed its angle to reduce the glare from the sun, until through its eyepiece she could see a shirtless Mister Dark Horse off in the distance, chopping a downed tree with irregular, barely effective strokes.

She adjusted the lens to get a better view. After fiddling with the lens for some time, she finally brought him into focus, but even such a fine spyglass as this had its limitations. She concentrated on watching him, savoring the bittersweet moment, her heart pounding inside her breast.

She thought she heard a sound. Rising stealthily to one knee, she listened intensely, fearful, but the birds were making too much racket to ascertain if she was alone.

Reluctantly, she rose and walked back to her stallion and slid the eyeglass into the saddle pouch. She mounted and rode off with deep sighs, wondering, plotting her next move.

Tonight would be another of those melancholy nights she so dreaded; standing at her bedroom window, staring into the shadows of the overgrown former garden below. *Thirty years of disuse*, she thought bitterly. *Just like me.*

***

Deep in thought, Hurst walked away from the house onto what he called "the drive"; still nothing more than a rutted path from the dirt road.

Waiting for the French/Turkle ax to fall had made sleep difficult, had worn him down. He'd grown fatalistic merely to continue on.

Distant enough for a full view, he turned to gaze at his magnificent mansion, *their* mansion, in the morning light, to savor the sight. It was still mostly a rough-hewn shell, unpainted, cut from ancient trees that had stood within shouting distance of that very spot.

He thought about the joyful day they'd first moved into the structure. It had had a roof, but was largely unfinished. That was when his partners began sarcastically calling it "the plantation-owner quarters" to distinguish it from the "slave quarters" they'd come from back so many miles, so many months. He studied the big house critically. *My monument.* He laughed scornfully.

Actually, the building had its merits. It was imposing for a house built by field hands and a no-talent drifter, considering it was based on plans partially scratched in the dirt with sticks and measured out in boot lengths. An irregular, sloping brick chimney, drawn from a kiln they'd fashioned themselves, warmed a second-story "study" with crude floor-to-ceiling bookshelves, but few books…yet.

He turned away to the *DarkHorse* gardens. His eyes wandered over the precise patterns cut in the earth for flowers, shrubs, and saplings they'd staked out and hoed with icy fingers, shivering in their thin, frayed clothes through that first winter. When he first went out in the cold to work on it, his partners thought he was crazy. They'd argued that this potentially fecund patch could endow them with corn, beans, and vegetables to supplement the game that their guns supplied the table. But seeing he wouldn't be convinced, they came out, away from the fire, to work beside him, to see that it was done right, to take pride in it, too.

He sighed. *If only we had time…*

But Durksen Hurst knew time would inevitably ride down every man, no matter how swift, and there were no more swamps or plantations in which to hide.

Section III

The Shuttered County Cotton Exchange

Chapter Twenty

November, 1860

Hurst woke in a hazy, warm fog and wanted to linger in bed. Her cabin was cold, but her covers were cozy and restful. Only when he was done again, and she had risen to prepare breakfast—with her kids running everywhere about—was he motivated to get up and dress. A widow, she was at least five years older than he, but she had a lot of spirit. More than enough spirit for him. She seemed so happy with everything he did and wanted, even just his naked, needing presence to break her loneliness and boredom. He didn't care that he was merely one of a series of her fleeting encounters, wedged between his most recent predecessor and some forthcoming youngster fresh from behind a plow. She didn't seem to care that he seldom thought of her; she only wished he wanted her more often.

He just couldn't seem to make himself hurry out to *DarkHorse* this morning. The French ax hadn't fallen yet. Over so many months, the *DarkHorse* partners had begun to believe they might safely escape conflict.

He tarried at a little store on the purlieus of Turkle. There, he noticed the old owner and the two customers talking at once with excited animation, half angrily, half enthusiastically. He didn't like the looks of it.

He laid the two dollars on the counter for his purchases. As the storeowner counted out change, Hurst noticed a special edition of the *Turkle Tower*, with a large banner headline framed in special artwork. This edition was obviously meant to be a keepsake, a family heirloom. Hurst shoved the coins back to the storeowner and picked off the top sheet.

"That damn fellow won't leave our rights alone. Folks is mad as hell," the man said.

So that's why everyone was so upset, Hurst thought. He'd been afraid it had something to do with him, that he was in for some kind of trouble, afraid the sheriff and some of French's riffraff were waiting in ambush for him, rifles at the ready. Fortunately, it was nothing more than some political shenanigans.

He tapped his index finger to his hat brim in salute and strode out the door. Pausing, he leaned against the post and studied the bold headlines:

LINCOLN ELECTED
—States Threaten Secession—

Black Republican Befouls White House

So that's what the fuss was about. That fellow Lincoln got himself elected president way up in Washington. If what Hurst saw was any indication, the poor devil stepped into a hornets' nest. These Mississippians can be real trouble once they work up a sweat. Well, Hurst would read all about it when he got back home. Relieved that Turkle had something to distract them from plotting against *DarkHorse*, he folded the flimsy sheet and stuck it in his coat, then mounted the roan.

Luckily, it had nothing to do with him.

***

Big Josh and Isaac felt it. Folks at the county seat seed and feed store were riled up enough to spit. Anger was thick as sausage gravy. Nobody, neither the clerks nor the customers, could talk about anything but that Lincoln fellow.

A slave was sent to load for Hurst, but the man froze in his tracks, astonished, as the three *DarkHorse* inhabitants, white and black, took hold of the sacks and implements they'd acquired and began filling the wagon themselves. They moved quickly, speaking quietly among themselves, Big Josh and Hurst carrying from the barn to the wagon, and Isaac hauling up on the bed. When the slave understood what they were doing, he joined right in, moving hurriedly. In ten minutes, the work was done, and Hurst was pulling on his good going-to-the-county-seat, master-type coat.

A town boy approached and stood anxiously by, trying unsuccessfully to get Hurst's attention. When at last the men stopped to confer, the boy tugged on Hurst's sleeve and handed him a pink envelope.

Hurst looked the envelope over, then, detecting a strange odor, sniffed it. An odd grin crossed his face. He tore the envelope open, pulled out a matching pink sheet of paper, and read it. Isaac and Big Josh watched, eyeing each other.

"Who gave you this, boy?" Hurst asked.

The boy pointed to a spot where the road disappeared into the trees, but no one was there.

"Y'all go on back without me," Hurst said. "I got a little business in town tonight."

"W-watch out for that c-county seat town business," Big Josh kidded. "You liable to lose you britches."

***

Backlit by a host of candles, Devereau French stared into the hotel suite's mirror, critical of her appearance, yet feeling slightly euphoric. She checked the pins holding her piled and clipped wig in place one last time. The hotel was the oldest still standing in the county. Though it smelled a touch damp, it was well-appointed with ornate carved wood molding and bright wallpaper of intricate patterns. The satin pillow-covered lounge in the main room, added during the hotel's latest renovation, was comfortable. Beside it sat a champagne bottle in a silver bucket.

She glanced at the bed beside her dressing table, a high, large four-poster, with curtains of velvet overlaying a gauzelike cotton drapery. She turned back to examine her dress's low bust line, her stomach tightening. *If only*, she thought.

***

She sat on the lounge, nervously smoothing and spreading her dress. A knock at the door caused her heart to flutter. French hid the pistol under the pile of pillows, glad she had brought it, and leaned back, neatly folding her hands in her lap.

"Please, come in," she said sweetly.

Hurst entered the room, clean-shaven and powdered fresh from the barber. Locking the door behind him, he turned and saw her. The woman was exquisite. She wore a sweeping purple velvet gown. The sparkling jewels on her slender neck descended into the smooth cleavage of her half-exposed bosom. Her young, fresh face boasted tender red lips, deep green eyes and auburn hair piled high. A rich ruby dangled from her forehead. He was shocked that the invitation represented so fine a lady.

"Excuse me, Miss. I'm Durksen Hurst," he said hat in hand, eyeing her anxiously. "The owner of the *DarkHorse* plantation? You sent me a note?"

"I'd know you from reputation alone, Mister Hurst. Please, join me."

She rose grandly and offered her hand. Hurst crossed the room, eyes fixed on hers. His face was not all that was flushed.

"My name is Charlotte, Charlotte Brussard."

Hurst raised her petite, ivory hand to his lips, but felt riding calluses on her fingers and palm. Choosing to ignore this, he tenderly kissed her knuckles, as he'd read about in books with knights. He hoped she wouldn't object.

"Please call me Durk, ma'am."

"And you call me Charlotte. Let's have some champagne. Please, sit here beside me."

She sat back, her body covering the pistol. When he joined her, she pulled the champagne from the ice. Working and twisting expertly, she popped the cork, causing bubbling liquid to explode from the bottle's mouth. Laughing, she covered the spray with her lips, gagging as it spewed down her throat. When it slowed to a trickle, she wiped her wet chin and breast with her fingertips. Then, with a luring smile, she offered her delicate fingers, which he drew to his lips.

"My favorite part!" she said, inching closer to him. He took the pair of flutes from the table and held them for her as she poured. Then they clinked glasses and raised them. He waited until she sipped, then threw back his head and drained his. Seeing this, she laughed melodically and followed suit, downing her own flute to the bottom. The swift drink made her dizzy, but exhilarated.

Hurst looked her over suspiciously, his brow knitting.

"You'll excuse me, Charlotte, but you surely resemble a gentleman who resides in these parts."

Her face flushed, and she cleared her throat. "Mister Devereau French, that scoundrel," she said teasingly, forcing a smile. "I ought to. We're first cousins. I'm stopping to visit him on my way home from Europe."

"French's cousin!" Hurst said, a sly grin spreading across his lips. "Maybe I'm gonna enjoy this. Are you close to them? French and his mother?"

"That gruesome pair!" she replied, her laughter trilling. "They both ought to be locked up in a madhouse. This visit is merely a family obligation."

"So, you said you know my reputation. What have you heard about me?" Hurst asked, returning the conversation to his favorite topic.

"I've only recently landed from the continent, but I have heard tales of your prowess with the ladies; although it's not always rose petals and silk sheets, I understand."

He didn't know who'd spread such ridiculous stories, but he saw no reason to disabuse her of the notions.

She sidled up to him, and he put his arm around her, resting his hand upon her soft, bare shoulder, stroking it gently, admiring its velvety feel. He began to look her over, his eyes wandering to her low-cut dress, noting that she had a small birthmark on her breast that stood in display against her white flesh. He reached toward her, inserting his finger just below the bustline's hem, and tenderly touched the birthmark with his finger.

"My, that's a pretty little thing," he said.

Without a word, she melted into him, trapping his hand against her breast. She looked tenderly into his eyes, and he looked deeply into hers. Then she kissed him—but he drew away, uncomfortable.

"Why, you're shy," she teased. "And here I've heard you're such a dangerous man."

"I'm not shy," he replied, flushing. He'd show this French cousin!

"Good. Because I know some things they do in Europe that you country boys never dreamed of."

She turned her mouth up to him and closed her eyes. Their lips met, lingered together, and he pressed forward, squeezing her tightly. They parted briefly, examining each other head to foot, then their lips were together again as though drawn by magnets.

Madness followed, fast, hungry, and hard.

He was upon her, and hands, mouths and bodies touched, grasping, moving, urgent. She was small and maneuverable, and he ceased exploring only when she pushed him back. He opened his half-shut eyes to see why, but, too late, she was already upon him, in control, tearing at his clothes and her own, never stopping, all hands and mouth and soft flesh. The flutes fell and broke, but neither of them slowed as the two submerged themselves into the vice-like grip of passion, their hunger for touch and taste soaring, insatiable, blind and furious. The lounge became too constrained to hold them.

Without a word, they stumbled together toward the bedroom as a tangled, clutching mass, lips locked, lust-blinded, hands groping, clothes flying. When they bumped the bed, he lifted her and they fell onto it in a heap. Then he was headfirst into her body, beyond hunger, beyond avarice for the wealth of her soft skin. It seemed as if his feast would never end, that his desire would never die.

He paused to catch his breath, gripping the nape of her neck, and then she was at him, strong and unrestrained, on top of him, beside him, below him, everywhere, rubbing and touching and tasting him. He fell upon his back, letting her come at him again, letting her begin her entire journey top to bottom. Then she rose upright from her knees, lingering above him for a moment, looking down at his face, his body, before blowing out the candle on the nightstand. As she was twisting away from him, he admired her sleek, slight body, its curves and hollows and delicate signatures. He put both his hands upon her, drawing her to himself. Then the second candle was extinguished and there was darkness, violent, piercing, clinging darkness.

A mutual conquest, each seemed eager to destroy the other.

***

The dawn crept in through the narrow gap in the curtains. French woke and rolled onto her side, to the middle of the bed. Hurst was asleep. She raised herself onto her elbow, to admire his face. His beard had grown bristly, but it was not an unhandsome face. She lightly kissed his forehead, waking him gently from his dream world. He gradually focused his eyes on her and smiled. They kissed. Parted.

"You see," he said, "What is a delicacy in Europe is merely a staple where I come from."

Then she fell hard at him, again fulfilling her craving and her desire.

Later, he rose from the bed to dress as she lay watching.

"Durk, tell me," she ventured, "merely in the interests of any progeny that may result from one of our liaisons, you don't have any 'surprises' in your past?"

"Progeny!" Hurst exclaimed, taken aback. "Now wait a minute. You're getting far ahead of me."

"Just answer the question, please."

"Well," he said, confused. Did she mean his father? His checkered past? His plebian nature? Or did she mean...?

She felt her face flush, as her heart stopped beating. "I mean, any surprises in your blood."

"My mother was mostly Indian, I think," he said.

She let her breath out, feeling her pulse return. "Oh, that doesn't matter. Indian children are so, so loving," she said wistfully.

He studied her fair-skinned face, with its thin lips and nose turned up, all aspects in accord with some ideal created by society and implanted in his and, he believed, in everyone's mind. *Here's how people with money are supposed to look*, he thought bitterly. Lily white. Such appearances, the shape of flesh stretched over bone, made you a welcome guest at sumptuous parties in great houses, allowed you to dance with women like this who wore jewels and dresses worth more than his horse. This appearance made people ignore your flaws, trust your motives, and believe your lies. Farm wives offered you dinner with the family when you hadn't eaten for days, while men offered you work. Young women wanted to bear your children. Hurst was forever excluded from that identity because of his Indian face; his rough, fast way of moving; his nervous manner and speech.

He turned to study himself in the mirror. High cheekbones, flat nose, thick lips, skin tinted bronze from the sunlight, dark eyes, too, somehow not right. His stranger's face might steal your chickens, damage your house, rape your wife, or injure your children. This face belonged to a lower creature, to a servant, never to a master.

She rose and went to him, naked and barefoot upon the cold carpet, and wrapped her arms about him. She tried to turn him, to pull him toward her, to kiss him, but he turned his back to her and continued dressing. She'd cut him at his tender spot, and the sunshine had disappeared behind the clouds.

"Every child is loving," he snarled, "if you give'em a chance. Been around a lot of Indian children, have you?"

"What's the matter with you now? You weren't so distant a few minutes ago."

He handed her a robe, which she slipped into and returned to bed.

"Charlotte," he ventured, wistfully thinking of Antoinette, "You're a fine-looking lady. Very fine. And this was a fine time we had, but, see, there's this woman. I mean, with the Frenches owing you money, I wondered, maybe you can help her."

That touched it off. French threw the empty champagne bottle they'd shared the night before, hitting him on the calf hard enough to sting.

"Why you!" she screamed. "You've got your nerve. Here, you're in my room, drinking my champagne—"

"Look, you invited me," he answered heatedly.

"What did I expect!" she said, furious. "You're nothing but trash. Ignorant trash."

Trash! That ended it. "Ignorant! You're lucky you're a woman. At least I'm not—what you are."

"You could never be what I am," she said. "You'd better find yourself a stupid farm girl or town hussy. Get out! Get out of my room before I cry out!" She threw a pillow at him, then picked up the other.

"You Frenches are all alike," he said, as he yanked on his boots. He pointedly did not look up to see her glaring at him, red-eyed and hateful. Shod, he stomped for the door.

"I'll show her who's trash," he muttered under his breath. He knew what he had to do!

***

Staring at herself in the mirror, French removed the pins and then the wig ever so slowly. Tears forming, she removed the eye makeup that she believed gave her an air of depth, of mystery. The lip color that broadened her lips, making them more sensual. The red on her cheeks that gave her color and vitality. The face powder that gave smoothness to the raw, sun-freckled flesh of her face. She washed away the perfume, her hint of provocative femininity, and removed the robe, which laid bare her white shoulders, her long neck, the roundness of her bosom.

She had almost looked like a woman. Almost. This person in the mirror had been her, but posing.

Suddenly, she was gripped by fear. What if he had seen through her disguise? He had relished exposing her mother for an act most of the town had known about for decades. How much more might he revel in belittling her for her demented, lifelong masquerade?

The risk she took had been insane! Was she doomed to exposure, to unbearable humiliation before all of Turkle, the whole county? She'd never be able to look anyone in the eye again, not even white trash, not even her own slaves.

And then there were the legal aspects! Her mother's ascendancy as the matriarch of the family was based upon a fabrication, a false primogenitor assumption from the day of her birth. If she were exposed, would she lose the plantation, everything?

She unlocked the chifforobe. Blinded by crying, she took out by feel her riding suit, stained and sweat-smelling from her ride from *French Acres*. The shirt, jacket, pants, boots. The long band to wrap around her breasts. And the codpiece.

She had never felt so humiliated, so lost. Getting what she desired so desperately, needed with all her being, was proving to be a myriad-headed hydra with razor-sharp fangs.

Chapter Twenty-one

Hurst studied the manicured fingernails of the county seat cotton broker as the man filled out the check. Hurst was fascinated that the man, by merely adding a few zeroes, could make the number they'd agreed upon into a real piece of cash. The cotton broker signed his name with sweeping, stylish strokes ending in a swirling flourish. Then he slid the negotiable paper across the desk. Hurst looked it over and nodded. This kind of money would show the Frenches and everyone else.

The two rose and shook hands, and Hurst left, strutting. Pleased with himself, the cotton broker wrote out a note, placed it in an envelope, and sealed it. He then waited to give Hurst time to complete his transactions at the bank. A short while later, after checking to see that the man's roan was gone, he summoned his fastest-riding messenger. He was willing to pay the boy five whole dollars to ride all the way across the county to *French Acres*, on the far side of remote little Turkle—with a dollar extra to ensure his silence.

***

On the road, Hurst's anger cooled, and he began to worry that perhaps he'd done a foolhardy thing. What would his partners think? What would Big Josh say? Had he jeopardized their plan out of pride and bullheadedness? He'd have to consider the possible consequences of his rash act before he reached *DarkHorse*.

Maybe if he came up with a new scheme, a bigger plan to obscure his rash act…

Riding hard, Hurst made the mansion site just as the evening meal was about to begin. As he tied up his horse in back of the kitchen, he noted the leavings from a fresh-cut deer carcass. Long Lou must have gotten lucky on the hunting stand that morning. The timing of his arrival seemed fortuitous because Hurst knew fresh venison would put everyone in a good mood, which would consequently make it easier to reveal what he'd done. He pulled the saddle bag from the roan's haunches and went inside, tense as a tugged wire.

When he entered the kitchen, his partners were sitting at the big round table, dishing out the cooked venison, gravy-soaked meal and collard greens. Hurst was long past hungry and the strong odor of pan-fried meat and the rest made his mouth water.

"Well, here our b-boy now," Big Josh joked through a mouthful. "Them t-town ladies make him miss work."

"I'll work Sunday," Hurst said, knowing full well they had already been working Sundays and would continue to work them for some time to come.

Hurst hung his hat on the back of the remaining chair. Then with a great flourish, he slung the saddle bag from his shoulder and poured the paper money and gold coins onto the table, letting the sight speak for him. But no exclamations of joy erupted this time; instead, the room grew quiet, as everyone looked fearfully at Big Josh to see his reaction.

"Where this from?" Isaac asked accusingly.

"County seat broker," Hurst replied. "I'm tired of trifling with these small time locals."

Big Josh swallowed his bite and reluctantly laid down his fork. "You m-mean we owe more c-cotton, Durk! What if the crop ain't good?"

"We leave him alone for one night!" Isaac added, then turned to Hurst. "What do we need all that for?"

"'Cause. 'cause we do," Hurst said, going over in his mind the way he planned to relate his newest Big Idea. If he could get them to buy it, he'd be home free and able to simply let the ridiculous new scheme die out through neglect. "Maybe I'll run for gov'nor or something."

"Gov'nor!" Isaac shouted, his voice halfway between laughter and tears. "Boy, you sure know how to keep out of sight."

The room grew restive. Hurst plopped down into the remaining empty chair. Long Lou, sitting beside him, dipped the scoop into the pot to fill Hurst's plate, but Big Josh caught Lou's wrist. Startled, Hurst looked up to see Big Josh's frown. The big man would have his word before Hurst took a single bite. This was not what Hurst had hoped.

"What you gonna do, g-gov'nor?" Big Josh asked sarcastically. "Free my people? Stop this war c-comin'?"

The questions took Hurst by surprise. He had planned to slowly work up to those potential benefits himself, to save them for last to nail down his argument. But Big Josh, anticipating Hurst's strategy, had gotten him off track, and Hurst wasn't sure how to work his way back. Besides, it was obvious that none of Hurst's partners would believe such nonsense anyway. Free Miss'ippi's slaves! Stop the war! Him, Durksen Hurst?

"Hell, somebody's got to do it," Hurst replied. "You know what Antoinette said."

"He stop the war, ha!" Isaac jeered. "He want to give big parties in the gov'nor's mansion for all the fine white ladies while the country burn down, is what he want to do."

"You got to stop gambling with our crop, Durk," Big Josh almost pleaded. "P-please."

Hurst was rocked to his core. Why did he always ruin everything? No angle was going to get him out of this predicament. He should have tried the truth first. He rose to his feet, grabbing his hat. He wasn't going to eat any venison that night.

"Fact is," Hurst said, "the price of cotton's gone sky-high 'cause of all this war-talk, and I'm just cashing in for us." Then he turned and stomped out of the room, concealing the despair on his face.

Why do I try to prove my wealth in other people's coin? he wondered. *I don't care about the money; that's French's counting. Except for Antoinette, I've got what I need already: friends, food on the table, and honorable work. And I've probably thrown it away to impress the Frenches, who I hold in the filthiest regard. I'm the biggest fool in Miss'ippi!*

"Damn!" Big Josh said, slamming his fist on the kitchen table so hard everyone jumped. "Just like General. Whitefolks just g-gots to grab and takes alls they can, till they ain't got nothing left."

If Hurst didn't come through, if *DarkHorse* didn't make it, they'd likely be sold off, manumission papers or no. They'd be slaves again.

Isaac stared glumly at the money. "Wish we could use this gold to buy us a new master," he snarled.

***

Devereau French signed the check and slid it across the desk to the county seat cotton broker, thus replenishing the once-substantial, but now overdrawn account French had set up for this purpose.

"You sure you want to continue with this?" the broker asked. He'd never seen a French, son or mother, so hooked by a risky ruse.

French gave an enigmatic, malevolent smile. "You have to break a wild horse before he gentles."

***

When Big Josh rose from bed it was still the cold pitch before sunrise. Carrying his boots to keep quiet, he left the mansion shell by the back porch before stopping to pull them on. Then he wandered off, through the cedars, past the laid fields, and into the wilderness, where he spent the day intermittently wandering or sitting as the mood took him, half thinking, half not.

Here they were, fixing up the mansion facade, while hanging over their collective heads was a stone bigger than a mountain, powerful enough to crush them at any moment. And nobody had enough strength, shrewdness, or foresight to forestall disaster when it came calling.

Nothing had changed. Ceeba was still those miles away. He still had to sneak past French overseers and riffraff to see her.

Later, Big Josh returned to the house feeling worn out and heartsick. Scraping the mud from his boots on the step, he entered the back door, heading toward his room. As he passed through the kitchen and its cooking smells, he absently nodded to Little Turby and Bammer, barely noticing that they'd stopped to stare at him.

"What is it?"

Little Turby held a new special edition of the *Turkle Tower* to his face. This meant, he noted, that Hurst had been to town for supplies.

He stopped in his tracks. Directly below the newspaper's elaborately decorated border, its banner headline read:

MISSISSIPPI SECEDES FROM UNION
Is War Coming?

"We done quit from the Union," Little Turby said. "It's right here."

Big Josh took the newspaper, wadded it up and, swinging open the rusty stove plate, threw it into the fire. Then he left the room, not glancing back.

As he climbed the stairs to his bedroom, the realization of what was about to happen crashed down on him, stunning him like a sixteen-pound maul blow to the head. Nothing would ever be the same again. They lived in a land that, because of its declared intent, was broken off and isolated from the world, floating loose in a sea of slavery—beyond redemption or salvation. They'd never be free, and he'd never be with Ceeba. He felt like burning the mansion and drowning himself in the river. This was sho'ly the death of hope.

***

Isaac smashed the last nail with all his might, giving vent to the deep-rooted terror, rage, and sorrow threatening to boil over in his head. That killed his last plank, and the roof was patched, as far as he was concerned. Now all he had to do was wait for slow Hurst to finish his part, and they'd climb down together. He turned around deliberately and settled himself on the second-story roof of the mansion, wrapping his arms around his legs and resting his chin on his knees.

He watched Hurst attempting to patch in his nervous, careful way, thinking they could certainly get by without him.

Isaac was ready to shuck all this and go back to living in the swamp, if that would tone down the fear so it didn't hurt so much. He could live by himself with the anger and the sadness; he'd always lived with them two pains. But this terror was another matter. He didn't know if he could live for long with it smashing against him.

He could sense it everywhere. Even Big Josh had been acting strangely, skittish. He sensed it in town, too. The white men couldn't talk about nothing else except guns and fighting. He could plainly see they was getting worked up to do something extreme and glorious.

Hurst hadn't brought this war turmoil on them, but he'd made their vulnerability worse. He'd done taken crazy chances without talking it over with his partners, and now they were in grave danger.

It was getting to be almost impossible for Isaac to control his rage. He was sorely tempted to crash Hurst in the back of the head with his hammer and throw him off the roof. Hell, couldn't they simply conceal Hurst's absence, pretend they had a master? But part of him knew that wouldn't solve anything. Besides, Hurst was the best friend he ever had. He was the first person Isaac could talk to, who listened to him, who took seriously what he said. And he never thought he'd feel that way about any white man, even Turkey John, who mostly liked to talk and rarely listened. Yes, they'd pulled off many tricks together, including *DarkHorse*—the biggest trick of all. But still the urge to crush his friend's skull burned in him so badly.

When Hurst finished, he sat down next to Isaac, still breathing hard. Isaac attempted a smile, but Hurst could sense the anger and fear troubling his friend. Hurst looked away, off into the distance, drinking in this dominant view of the mansion site. Then he pointed out vistas that, if captured on canvas and constrained by a painter's frame, could adorn the wall of any palace: the place across the dirt road where the woods began, the foot trail disappearing into the distant cedars, the *DarkHorse* sign hanging from the arch—all of it exquisite beyond language. It was as if Hurst was saying to Isaac that they were able to drink in this breathtaking panorama because they were sitting atop a creation they had built with their own hands, a monument to themselves, and so they were somehow entitled to do so.

It was this humble gesture by Hurst that enabled Isaac to restrain himself and not kill his friend. It wasn't much, but the way things were going, it was a great relief.

***

At noon the next day Hurst stood in front of the Lethe Creek County Courthouse, his mind working. The planters, traders, and farmers surrounding him were absorbed in their own ends, so the communication between him and the cotton broker was not seen. The broker, wearing his finest broadcloth coat, glanced at Hurst. Hurst's eyes scanned the crowd rapidly. Then, without making eye contact, Hurst brushed his ear with a finger. The broker immediately pointed to the trader standing on the steps.

Hurst nodded to the broker and turned away, pushing through the crowd to his mount, consumed by his darkest fatalism. If he was going to lose everything, he decided, he may as well increase the stakes, even if failure meant an end to all his dreams. He'd always known it couldn't last.

Now he was done for the day. He'd have to wait and see.

***

April, 1861

Big Josh set the lantern on the verandah railing, pulled the folded up sheet of paper from his back pocket and sat back in the rocker. He'd tried not to think about what Little Turby said at the supper table about the word going around the slave grapevine, but these rumors filled his mind, filled everyone's mind.

The *Tower's* headlines read:

FORT SUMTER SURRENDERS
Union Fort Falls.
Yankees Defeated!!!

So they was going down that road, was they? And them rivers of blood Antoinette was talking about gonna start flooding the land.

***

Celebration! The town square was lit up brighter than the Fourth of July. Men carried flaming torches, fired rifles into the air and waved newly-sewn Confederate flags.

The young cocksure who had been voted to lead the Turkle contingent, climbed the courthouse steps to the message board. Men shouted and women waved handkerchiefs as he held up the *Turkle Tower*—its first two-pager ever. He ripped down every piece of paper on the message board and, when the surface was clear, nailed dead center with the butt of his pistol that day's special edition. The board displayed the largest banner headline the paper had ever produced, with letters so large they could be read (by those who could read) twenty feet away:

WAR DECLARED!!!

A great cheer arose, as rifles and pistols fired into nothingness. The local band (of three musicians) struck up *Dixie;* people sang and waved flags in time to the tune. During the firing, one young man discovered his pistol was so rusted that, when he pulled the trigger, the powder merely flashed, and the barrel fell off. Fortunately, his hand was not burned badly enough to miss the following day of work in the field with his pap and mule.

***

LINCOLN ORDERS BLOCKADE!!!

***

She lay awake in bed. It was as she predicted, divine intervention: the South was about to plunge into the cataclysm. She was ready for the next step.

Lilith's gown was packed. All she needed to do was catch a ride out to the French mansion with the first wagon. She'd have the driver leave her off about a mile away so she could prepare. Then she'd walk the rest of the dusty road by herself.

There, she would enact her plan to free all the French slaves.

Yes, she would make this town a better place, holier and true. A lump rose in her throat.

Chapter Twenty-two

The day broke sunny, clear and mild, a vast deception by the free-flowing blue sky upon those minuscule figures struggling in the ruts and ridges of the brown earth below. Sundays can fool you like that.

Big Josh was relieved to find Hurst and Little Turby reading together in the garden gazebo they'd erected. He called to Isaac, and they walked that way together.

"He driving me crazy with all his gold-piece-size words," Isaac said.

"He trying to make hisself believe his own legend—which we d-done made up," Big Josh said. But he knew it was more than that. Hurst was trying to make himself believe *DarkHorse* would survive.

The pair confronted the two figures reading in the gazebo, their grim expressions making it perfectly clear they were deeply troubled.

"We got important news," Big Josh said.

Hurst and Little Turby set their books in their laps.

"Ah, gentlemen, you're looking prosperous this magnificent morning," Hurst announced. Seeing their demeanor, he knew he would have to display strength.

"Will you quit talking like that!" Isaac said with a threatening glare.

"D-durk," Big Josh said, "the white folks have d-done declared war."

After a pregnant, stunned pause, Little Turby caught his breath. "My God. What 'bout us?"

Hurst laid his book aside. "Slaves will build mansions for other slaves to burn," he said, rising, gesturing as if to a large gathering. "Nevertheless, *DarkHorse* shall ignore this conflagration."

"Oh, yeah, *gov'nor?*" Isaac shouted. "Our whitefolks running off to join."

"Our folks?" Hurst said, flabbergasted.

"Who you th-think's gonna fight? French?" Big Josh said.

"But who'll feed their families?" Hurst asked, his voice high-pitched, breaking. "Who'll tend their cotton?"

"That's what I mean!" Isaac shouted. "They all be off playing soldier."

"Speaking of c-cotton, Durk," Big Josh said in even tones, trying to calm the growing hysteria. "You been hanging 'round the county seat cotton exchange a awful lot lately and bringin' money home. What we doin' in them markets?"

"Sale, good sir," Hurst pontificated, trying to regain control of the conversation, "and none too cheaply! Secret transactions through fiduciaries with powers of attorney. Fancy rich folk dealing; y'all wouldn't understand."

"You b-been sellin'? M-more?" Big Josh asked, incredulous. Now the reason for Durk's activity at the county seat was clear. The three partners stared at Hurst.

"The price has been going up, sky high. I've been getting more and more advance for each sale."

"D-durk," Big Josh said, "the grapevine says French has been buying. He buying."

"What, French?" Hurst asked, his face turning red. "Buying?"

"Every b-bale you sold, he bought it," Josh answered. "He planning to clean us out. W-what if we can't deliver all the cotton you done promised?"

"Then they'll—" Unable to speak, Hurst stared at his boots.

"Will they take *DarkHorse*?" Isaac asked. Hurst didn't reply.

Big Josh and Isaac groaned loudly. The four looked at each other. Then Little Turby had an idea. "Can we buy it all back?"

Hell, they'd contracted to deliver more cotton than they could ever grow. Perhaps they could buy contracts to cover their obligations and go back to even.

Hurst took a deep breath, calculating rapidly, then exhaled for long seconds, completely deflating himself. "The price is too high," he said. "The cotton market would have to go down for us to cover."

"Why, you!" Isaac shouted, unable to contain his fury. "Here we had our own place! Trash! Trash!" He grabbed hold of Hurst's collar, but Big Josh restrained him.

Stung by the insult, an enraged Hurst tried to get at Isaac, but Big Josh stopped him with his free hand, interposing his large body between the pair.

"Swamp rat! Swamp rat!" Hurst shot over Big Josh's shoulder.

Big Josh pushed the two apart, and gave them both his infamous 'dark look'. "Now, listen, you two. This is not the way *DarkHorse* do things. Stop!" He squeezed them so hard it hurt.

"Should I change my methods now?" Hurst shouted. "I won us this place, didn't I?"

"And about to lose it," Isaac answered vehemently.

"Now, th-that's enough," Big Josh said, giving both a final severe squeeze.

Isaac stared balefully at Hurst, but then a sly smile spread across his face. "Why, you right," Isaac said. "We ain't give golden tongue a chance yet. Sure, Great White Master here gonna talk Turkle out of going to war."

"Isaac," Big Josh said, his eyes narrowing, "ain't nobody can talk folks out of getting themselves killed when rich folks tells them they ought to."

But Isaac ignored the caution. Shaking himself free, he circled Big Josh and placed his arm around Hurst's shoulders. "Yes, sir," Isaac said, smooth as honey. "Ain't nobody can outtalk our boy. He gonna make a speech, turn fire into ice. Yes, sir, fire into ice."

Big Josh watched Hurst's face sorting through doubts, then lighting up. The man was swallowing the flattery, his oratorical proficiency confirmed by his harshest critic.

"Durk, you stay away from them soldiers," said Big Josh. Then, seeing his words had no effect, Big Josh stormed off to the mansion.

Little Turby swallowed hard as he watched Big Josh disappear into the house. He could feel the end of *DarkHorse* rapidly approaching, and nobody had any idea how to stop it.

"I got to save us," Hurst said.

***

Hurst gestured passionately, trying to block the road to Turkle. Shuffling toward him, *en masse*, through the dust of the half-formed dirt road were the men who only days before had lived on and worked the widespread *DarkHorse* lands. The men had a determined, jaunty swing to their gait. A home-sewn flag flew above their heads, and though they'd all had their wives and mothers dye their work clothes butternut, each wore his own hat, adding to the impression of a bedraggled, raw mob. They carried their various makes of vintage rifles and muskets awkwardly, in no discernible pattern, either slung upon a shoulder right side up or cradled in the arms like a hunting rifle.

"Just hear me out! Please!" Hurst pleaded.

"Let's hear him," someone said. The band shuffled to a halt, while with shaking hands the legendary Dark Horse removed a sheet of paper from his pocket. He had practiced all through the previous night in the woods so as not to disturb his partners. Determined to roll the dice, he plunged into his speech.

"Friends, neighbors, future *DarkHorse* land owners, please hear my pleas," Hurst began in his best stentorian voice. "You are now faced with the most momentous choice a man can face: between war and peace. Sirs! There is a time for fighting—"

Hearing the word *fighting*, the men broke into wild cheers and shouting.

Fighting is what they wanted and were ready for. Life had been hard for these men, from the hurtful pinch of childhood hunger in dirt-floor shacks, to the never ending struggles against poor soil to feed their families. Paying work, the kind that put actual folding money in their pockets, had always been hard to get, in good years and in lean, a condition only exacerbated by the uneven competition of plentiful slave labor. Yet they'd never understood the connection, or felt any empathy with the slaves' suffering. Rather, in their deepest hearts, they felt an affinity with the master, whose position and wealth they dreamed of emulating, and whose skin was, after all, of their own hue.

Hurst waited until they quieted down, cleared his throat to cover his fear, and continued. "A time for fighting, as I said, and a time for reason. A time to plow, and a time to plant—"

"What in hell are you talkin' about?" a man shouted, his query followed by the crowd's grumbling assent.

This wasn't going well, even though he'd stolen parts of his speech from books, he felt the full weight of consequences if he failed. *It's the damn speech,* he decided. *It's too starched collar. I've got to speak from my heart, use that old Durk Hurst magic.* Regaining his composure, Hurst wadded up the sheet of paper and threw it aside.

"Aw, hell. Folks," he said. "This is crazy! Y'all moved onto *DarkHorse* and turned a swamp into good bottomland, into fine farms and homes. Now I know you're brave and all, nobody in the world braver—"

That touched off the celebration again, as the men fired rifles and muskets into the air, and shouted from the sheer joy of knowing their chance to become heroes had come at last.

"But why do you want to run off and get yourselves killed? So French and me can own slaves? What about your families? Damn it, if it'll save one of your lives, I'd free all my slaves. They're free! I beg you, boys, return to your homes and fields."

Without warning, the company became an angry mob, shouting at Hurst, cursing and calling him names. Men in the front of the group pushed Hurst roughly aside, knocking him sprawling into the roadside ditch.

"But, boys," Hurst pleaded, desperate, "who's going to plow your furrows!"

"A man's gotta fight, Hurst! Coward."

"Dark Horse, you traitor!"

"Abolitionist! He a dirty abolitionist!"

Hurst rose from the ditch and, dusting himself off, shouted after the men who had become, in effect, his white *DarkHorse* partners, partners who were now deserting him and his cause for another.

"But your families!" he shouted after them. "The lawyer and the banker gonna steal all our land for the Frenches."

Behind Hurst, one last man ran up the road to catch up, one of the Stillinses that had begun to infest the southern edge of *DarkHorse*. Hurst climbed back on the road and blocked his progress.

"Judd, you got six little children. Hell, you can't even hitch your mule without breaking a leg."

"Outta my way, you pus'ule-gut pig-eye," Judd said, swinging his musket butt at Hurst's head, only to miss and fall face first into the dirt. Frustrated, the man rose and hurried to catch up with the others, tripping and falling again, his musket clattering on the ground. Hearing him fall, two men at the rear of the unit came back to help him.

Near the front of the pack, a young tough wearing a pistol in his belt, carrying the flag, turned to the man next to him. "We'll settle up with this Yankee-lover later. Like they did those two over in Benlow Bend." It wouldn't be long before word of Hurst's traitorous words got around.

Durksen Hurst fell silent, his throat tight, resigned to his failure as an orator. As Turkle's bravest disappeared down the road, he knew he was watching the last of his Dream march away to an ephemeral notion of glory.

***

They straggled in a mass down the road, sweating profusely in the heat, exultant to participate in the great enterprise. No more grubbing in the soil from before sunrise until past sundown simply to fall deeper into debt in the ledgers of the general store. No more staying up all night to nurse the sick cow. No more wrenching your back digging up a stump or plowing the fields, all the while overwhelmed by fits of desperation, of impending poverty or starvation, at least for the few weeks it would take Yankee courage to collapse; until they could return home to martial music and the banner-flying welcome of real heroes.

Yes, this would be like battles and wars in the big history books dating all the way back to the Old Testament. This would be glory and courage and will. They were defending the homeland, their helpless wives and children, protecting freedom and a bunch of other transcendent notions. Trumpets will blow, cannons, horses, and wagons move out, ships sail; wind-blown flags and generals with swords will lead straight lines of uniforms marching in cadence, their strength arrayed against firearms, men, and the same sundry, uniformed spectacle on the other side. This would test their hunting skills, their aim and stealth, against, not merely animal craft and sinew, but against the greatest, most deadly prey the earth can produce, a trained army of men; the most wily, courageous, lethal and destructive beast of all God's creatures. This was war, boys! And this war would be grand, the grandest of them all.

They were off to become as brave and durable an army as any civilized country ever deployed on a battlefield, an army matched in bravery only by their noble and worthy opponents who spoke their same language and prayed to their same God, in this contest for the ages that would alter for all future generations the destiny of the greatest country ever created beneath Heaven. Off to become foot cavalry, able to march with bloody bare feet twenty miles a day. Off to become sturdy, reliable infantry, willing to charge across open fields directly into walls of fatal fire, beneath the devastating, roaring explosions of steel-laden shells from massed artillery, while simultaneously keeping the line straight, heedless of almost certain loss of life or limb.

All this valiant willingness in spite of foreknowledge that the officer drinking in his tent the previous night had made a disastrous miscalculation and that the stated objective was impossible for mortal man to conquer. Off to huddle in dampness and bone-chill through the seemingly endless winter nights, without food or shelter or blanket for warmth, resigned to defy the certainty of final defeat rather than face the ignominy of surrender.

To suffer all this far from home and hearth, with nothing to drive them forward into those walls of lethal lead projectiles or to restrain them from running away from the advancing massed steel bayonets and balls, but manlike faith in the Great Men of Legend who rode tall on mighty steeds ahead of them. With nothing to compensate for the willingness to be torn and die bleeding or to forever struggle alone as an amputee or sightless beggar but an unquestioning belief in one's own untrained officers recklessly waving swords, calling for everyone to follow. With nothing to repel the black, implacable, relentless despair but the kinship of blood to the comrade beside you. All because these men with you, around you, every one, from the man sitting the glorious thoroughbred horse on down to the clumsy foot soldier, are heroes you love and trust and respect beyond question, because all your companions, of every rank, were certain to return to you that unqualified love and trust and respect, with merely one's life a small enough price to pay for such a dear, mutual conviviality.

To those that survived the war, regardless of the scars, destruction and waste, the preordained poverty, the loss of family and friends, of missing limbs, the cold sharp stone of bitterness and hurt, this war would be the singular, iridescent epoch that each would always remember silently, gratefully, and with a fond and proud swelling in his breast. This would be the time worth remembering, the wood smoke of the early morning campfires and the rush of excitement when it came time to defy death.

And to those who never returned—fully half of these would die from disease—they would rest peacefully a hero, too, their souls aware that their bravery and sacrifice would be immortalized forever in monument and artifact.

The Man in Washington knew this, knew the rivers of blood would soon begin flowing. That young boys would never know a woman's love, would never exult in the harvest wrung from the good earth by their own hands, would never feel their child's gentle touch, would never know a man's paycheck or a great book mastered; knew mothers and widows would nearly drown the world in tears.

He knew the Cause for which these men of Turkle would fight to be among the least worthy for which any people ever fought.

But what could he do to stop it? Like these heroes of Turkle, he could only endure. Endure, and supply the spirit and justification for enduring to the young men who must die in opposing that Cause. Endure, and embrace in his own heart the whole nation's hurt and pity and loss, lest the sorrow and despair drown the will and courage of the whole populace to resist that Cause. Endure, and bear on his mortal shoulders the sure knowledge that his failure, whether through some flaw in his wisdom or will, or through some fateful factor beyond any man's control, would forever bring down upon him all the derision and scorn of a bereaved and bereft humanity deprived of its last great hope.

And he knew that all the nation's men on both sides, from President to General to bugler boy to barefoot soldier from Turkle, Mississippi, saw his own place in the struggle in those very same terms, as if each man believed he and he alone was the bulwark responsible for all of the people's tomorrows. And, like every other man on either side in this bloody enterprise, only death was going to stop him from enduring.

Chapter Twenty-three

Dusk fell. Hurst had looked everywhere about *DarkHorse*, and he was growing desperate. Because Turby had taken the roan to town, Durk had hiked out to the fields and to the widely scattered hunting blinds, but no Big Josh. Then he remembered that sometimes the partnership's *de facto* leader went to the fern grotto waterfall seeking a place to contemplate their destiny, as had all the partners at one time or another.

Approaching the site, he heard stones being tossed into the pool below the fall and felt relieved. Pushing through the hedgerow, he saw Big Josh sitting on a rock, sulking, his chin resting on his fist. Hurst walked up behind him.

"Hey, Josh," he said.

Josh didn't answer. Instead, he angrily skipped a flat stone across the pool and watched it careen to the far side and out onto the rocks.

Hurst picked up stones and, seating himself beside the big man, began absently plunking them into the water. "I know I should have listened to everybody," Hurst ventured. "It's just, I get these ideas."

"It ain't that. Durk. You ain't the only one w-wants your woman with you. Here I'm doing everything a m-man can do…"

"Everything two men could do!"

"…and it don't matter. I can't even marry the woman I loves."

"I know it doesn't make sense," Hurst said, attempting to comfort him, afraid of where the conversation was headed.

"N-nothing makes sense no more. Nothing. I tells you, Durk, I feels like we just playing at a plantation—and I don't even like the thought of no p-plantation no more. You done your best, but we dark folks can't never be free with things like they is. Look, I been thinking about it. I got to get N-north somehow, to get in this war. I just want to end all this slavery—or die."

Hurst momentarily lost his breath. "But who'd run *DarkHorse*?"

"Them white folks got to run off and fight for they side, didn't they? Look, we all been talking. Li'l Turby, Long Lou, Bammer and the rest all thinking about coming with me. Everybody but Isaac, who don't believe the war will clear nothing up."

"Isaac and me by ourselves! Oh, we'll survive for sure," he said sarcastically.

The loss of Big Josh alone, not to mention the rest of his partners, would be the certain end of the Dream. Hurst's mind reeled, his suspicion and anger rising to fever pitch. His heart was flooded again with the familiar sense of hurt and betrayal, the sense that the whole world conspired against him. But he fought it this time.

Hurst finally collected himself enough to speak. "Hell, it's you who've been our strength and our brains both, Josh. I wouldn't last a month here without you. You don't want French to beat us, do you?"

Hurst looked imploringly at his friend, but he could see the big man wasn't moved by his appeal. Big Josh turned to look him in the eye. "I'm sorry, Durk. Look," he said, trying to offer him honey to down the bitter truth, "we love you for the chance you give us here. You a man belongs probably somewhere a hundred years from now, maybe more. But you see how it is. We's free, but can't be free here in our own home." He couldn't speak any more.

Hurst knew he couldn't dissuade him. Events beyond his control had determined that his partners and sharecroppers would desert him. He would be a landless, friendless stranger again, adrift in a world now consumed by the stark terrors and mindless destruction of war. He may as well go get himself shot with the rest of them. He hadn't cried since the day his mother died, and he struggled not to embarrass himself in front of Big Josh.

The two sat silently together, both staring into the ever-blackening waters as the sun sank below the horizon, drawing the night rapidly upon them. They both knew it was over.

Durk's thoughts turned to memories of his first days on *DarkHorse*. He remembered the night of their arrival in the pouring rain, seeing them as they had been, a wet, ragged group of scared men. He thought of moments good and bad, when he'd been working together with these men, the truest friends he'd ever had. He'd help them get what they wanted, and he would move on.

"It's all right, partner," Hurst said. "I'll get y'all North. But we've got to do one thing first."

He thought of their other partner, the woman, and her note that French had given him at the church. Since then, he'd heard the tales, gathered from tradesmen who'd ridden out to *French Acres*, that a dark-haired city woman was running the place, performing all the transactions and dickering, as if she was safe and happy—as if she was Devereau French's wife. He couldn't go out there to see her. But before *DarkHorse* came to dust, he wanted to make sure her life and circumstances were of her own choosing.

With determined fury, he told himself he could arrange at least that.

"Don't worry 'bout the m-money, Durk. You get us North, you can have it."

"Never mind. I'll use it to buy your women over from French."

Big Josh skipped the last of the flat stones he'd been holding and settled back. It took a helluva lot to be a man, and he didn't know if he counted as one yet, as judged by other people. Or even as judged by himself.

At eight-years-old, he was big for his age. He hadn't outgrown his baby fat yet. Big, and a stutterer. For that reason, he was reluctant to speak; people might think he was simple. Maybe he was simple. Whenever he tried to prove he wasn't a fool, he got nervous and stuttered so badly people's misperception was reinforced. Everybody teased him—the older boys, the white men who oversaw the pickers, and other children, mocking the way he spoke.

It was picking time. He was walking out to the fields one morning when he came upon a group of six older white boys waving sticks like they were swords, playing at war. All of them were taller than he was. One of them mocked him, and the others joined in, shouting in derision and calling him names. He could feel the heat of anger flood his face, but he cast his eyes on the ground ahead and kept walking. Mamma had told him not to mess with no white boys. But he could tell these weren't gonna let him live in peace.

He was surrounded before he knew it. When he looked up, one of the boys kicked him in the pants from behind and skipped away laughing. Another jounced forward and whacked him on the arm with his sword-stick hard enough to break it. The laughter and catcalls rang so loudly in Josh's ears that he was afraid he would have to scream to quiet them down.

And then, like a wild animal cornered, he butted them with his head, threw wild punches, kicked, and bit. In return, the boys broke sticks across his head and shoulders, punched and kicked and tripped and bit him. His blood and their blood was everywhere.

Then, they were laughing and he was laughing with them, as best he could through his painful ribs. They all tended their wounds. He had some bad hurts. He was bleeding and holding his side, where they'd kicked him when he'd first fallen down. He struggled home and wouldn't make it out to the fields for two days. But at least those boys didn't want to fight him ever again.

This encounter led to the hunts. The next time the six white boys went hunting in the woods, they invited him along. He stayed with them that first time for two days, until he had to get back to work.

Oh, he had to do the fire building, the cooking, and much of the carrying, but when they left the campsite to hunt, he went with them. When they settled, the leader of the boys even taught him to shoot using the boy's own musket. Certainly, they'd occasionally jest about his size and his stutter, but it was always friendly, no more cutting or vehement than how they kidded each other. All because he'd fought for himself. It was a sort of heaven in those woods, being one of the boys. Almost.

Hunting with those boys had made him feel like a man. But now he wasn't so sure.

Big Josh looked over at the man beside him. Durk Hurst was his friend, a white man who respected him as a man. And he was planning to abandon him to go North. But, goddamn, he was prepared to die to be called a man. He deserved *that* much.

Maybe such a decision made this war good in some twisted way. He didn't take back everything he'd thought about the war, but if war was what it took to wipe away the shame and the fear and the sorrow, so be it. If it took killing and dying so that no man would have to endure this helplessness again, so be it. But they surely, surely lived in some mixed-up kind of world.

* * *

When Hurst was discovered missing the next morning, a great fear arose. He wasn't at breakfast, even though he had work to do. Was he in jail? Or lying dead on the side of some road? Word from town that his efforts to stop the white croppers from running off to war, and that he was going to free his 'slaves', had spread, branding him a traitor to their whole civilization. Frighteningly, rumors were filtering in from throughout the region telling of dire consequences awaiting men who'd opposed secession or who'd hinted, however innocently, at the overthrow of the South's traditional system of labor. In these times, anything was possible. Wasn't that the way Durk Hurst's father had died?

Soon afterward, it was discovered that most of *DarkHorse's* money was missing from its hiding place. A deep gloom settled over the partners. The questions on everyone's lips, in everyone's minds: If Hurst was indeed a "runaway master", what would happen to them now? How would they get North?

The coolness eased in the afternoon, offering a hint of spring, a promise that winter wasn't eternal. It seemed time to take the fixin's to the far end of the garden, to cook supper down there in the old rock pit and eat at the old, weathered tables, like in the days when *DarkHorse* was new. Besides, if any malevolent white men came calling, it wouldn't do to be found living in the Big House with the white man gone missing. Everyone packed everything they would need if they were transplanted, and hauled their belongings to the old site. Then Long Lou and Bammer built the fire, and the rest went to work preparing.

The sunset and the evening warmth settled in, along with a sense of quiet. The partners lingered around the fire, talking. The stars appeared in the clear night, so rain wasn't expected to spoil the eatings. And Hurst still hadn't shown himself.

Long Lou gave a sudden "Hush," stopping everyone dead still. They heard a rider approaching, and the horse wasn't the roan. Everyone listened intently.

Then they heard more, the sounds of *many*. A heavily laden wagon pulled off the road, and feet shuffled beside it. "Shoes," Bammer whispered. The feet weren't bare!

"Run," Big Josh ordered with a whisper.

The partners scrambled into thick foliage that encircled the mansion site, hiding as best they could. Then they waited.

They saw the silhouette of the rider coming toward them, surrounded by a mass of dark shapes on foot. Even through the darkness, however, what they could distinguish made them feel oddly reassured.

"Why, it's Antoinette," Bammer shouted, recognizing the rider.

"And look at who she got with her!" Long Lou added.

Having seen the fire, Antoinette rode up on a French mare. Behind her hurried Ceeba and all the partners' women friends from *French Acres*. Each woman wore a store-bought homespun dress, matching bonnet, and new shoes.

Celebration! The partners rushed out of the woods, blind with happiness, like a sudden sea storm washing to shore. The women hurried to meet the men. When the two forces clashed together, there was tearful hugging and kissing, as the men held on for dear life to the women they never thought they'd see again, much less on *DarkHorse* ground.

"Ceeba! Now what you say?" Big Josh said, throwing his arms around her and lifting her substantial body into the air, light as a feather.

"I say, 'Here I am, baby boy.'"

Old Moses came last, stumbling through the undergrowth and cursing at the vines and briars grasping his dirt-stained, once white cuffs. Finally reaching the clearing, he stopped, fearful, before turning to sneak back into the woods. But too late. An old woman who seemed little more than twigs joined together at the joints, covered by wrinkled flesh, completed her painstaking climb down from the wagon and spotted him. "There that weasel!" she cried out.

Old Moses took off fast as his limp could take him, chased by the elderly woman. The group broke into relieved laughter, and the celebration continued.

"Antoinette!" Little Turby exclaimed. "You did it! You're back!"

"I'm not free to stay," she said. "Now, where is The Great Legend?"

"We ain't seen him all day," Big Josh said.

"And most of our runnin' money gone," Isaac added.

Big Josh raised a hand. "If he gone, even with all the money, he gone with my blessing. I don't hold nothing 'gainst him."

"I know about the money," Antoinette said. She smiled and handed a sack of gold coins to Big Josh. "He forwarded this to me through the slave overseer, to buy your women, which I have the discretion to sell. But he vastly overpaid."

The happy night was a time for music and dancing, to talk quietly and to look deeply into dark eyes long burned into the memory. Unattended, the fire burned low. With many more mouths to feed, they came to believe they were eating in just the right place, on the old log tables near the abandoned lean-tos in what they had once called the 'master quarters'. The mansion was far away, so far away it didn't even cross anyone's mind.

* * *

By the time the sun slipped behind the distant hill, Hurst's brain was played out. After his ride to *French Acres*, he'd spent the entire day at the fern grotto ruminating about everything: what he'd gained and how he was losing it, trying to figure out a way around the trap fate had set for him, trying to locate enough strength to go on living.

Now his mind was sidetracked again. As he steadily grew more maudlin, his thoughts reverted to that day on the road with the flags and rifles, and the rejection of his arguments.

He began to wonder about truth itself, its elusiveness, and the manner in which he usually approached it. He rarely succeeded in looking directly at the truth because it was like looking directly at the sun, blinding. Instead, he always looked away and caught it out of the corner of his eye.

If he misplaced an object, he always searched and eliminated every unlikely spot before he discovered it in the most likely place. He wondered if he acted in this circumspect manner because he couldn't bear the disappointment if the most likely place proved wanting.

The straight way got you there faster, but it often got you to the wrong place. Look at where Turkle's folks were headed. His way of doing things took longer, but it often got him to new places and, right or wrong, it was interesting to go to a place where most folks never went.

Hell, he thought, most people live their lives following the first glimpse of light they see, even long after the illumination had faded and disappeared—even after they discovered the shimmering glow was a phantasm leading to their demise.

Then he looked up and saw his truth, shining brilliantly through the twilight, seated on a chestnut mare with French markings branded on its hindquarter.

With a broad smile, he approached the chestnut. Then he reached into the leather bag slung over his shoulder and pulled out his pistol.

"What does this mean, Durk?" she asked, startled.

He slipped the pistol into the bag on her saddle. "I want you to make your own choice over there at French's."

***

He stared morosely into the grotto pool, beneath the black sky, the glittering stars. They spoke quietly, saying far less than they felt. After Antoinette explained why she must return to the Frenches, the words came more slowly, from deeper, inexpressible longings.

"Durk, I'm not ashamed of that blot on my pedigree. My *acceptable* ancestors were very unremarkable."

"Unlike you. At least you're not trash, like I am. That's what I come from, and I haven't broken it."

"Durk, trash could not have created *DarkHorse*. *DarkHorse* is a masterpiece. It's your masterpiece."

Hurst shrugged and turned away.

"It was you who had the leap of imagination," she continued. "Is there anyone else who could have done this?"

She saw in his face the excitement her validation engendered. Then his whole demeanor dropped; he hung his head. "We may not have *DarkHorse* much longer," he said. "You were right. War overtops everything—even Bammer's bunion."

He looked into her eyes, eyes he was afraid he would never see again. She looked back, her knowing sorrow etched in her face.

"I've got something hard to tell you," he said. "The men have been asking around the French slave quarters."

"What? What is it?"

"We hear French buried a child about the time we showed up. There'd been a sickness in Turkle; a lot of people died. I'm sorry."

She'd known all along. She had forced herself to deny it, but hearing it cross Durk's lips somehow eluded her defenses. She had tried to learn Louis Edward's fate, using the trust she built running *French Acres*, but she'd invariably find herself stonewalled by silence. The French slaves, like the townspeople and plantation laborers, could not be persuaded to discuss certain subjects in any depth.

Durk offered her his handkerchief, which she refused. Instead she faded into his arms. Finally, she regained her composure. Her arms dropped from around his shoulders and she drifted away, beyond the pool, to where it emptied down the hill and became a gentle stream.

He waited, not knowing what to do, then tentatively followed her.

"I heard that, too," she said haltingly. "But the burial could be one of Missus French's subterfuges. A slew of children died at the time. I wouldn't put a switch past her.

"But I didn't come all this way to be deterred by a rumor, Durk. I've still got to know. One way or... I'm sorry I've been so cold toward you, but this unresolved...I get overwhelmed with the blackest memories, from when I was little."

Hurst knelt beside the water. He absently picked up a seed and dropped it into the quick current, then watched it rush away. What could he say? He knew she was damaged, badly, and nearing the end of whatever held her together. He might lose her soon, as he might lose himself.

"Sometimes you've just got to decide to go on living," he said, realizing that truth was what he'd been searching for all day.

She sat beside him and stared into his eyes, stroking his cheek. No words could transverse the distance between their pasts and that instant. At last, she kissed him deeply. Separating, he looked quizzically at her, as if asking: What did this kiss mean? Good-bye? Condescension? A recognition that at least one of them would never break free from their hopeless fate?

She found the strength to answer. A simple answer, limited to the tiny speck of time they controlled, ignoring the vast hours and days ahead that they already believed to be lost.

"The answer is 'yes,'" she said. "Tonight. Whether I live or die tomorrow."

She kissed him again. If they had only this moment, then let it be free and carefree, unobstructed by thoughts of thwarted dreams. If they were only human, let them glory in their humanity. If they were only mortal, then let them revel in their mortality.

She dipped her hand into the pool, absently gazing at the distorted, turbulent image of the moon in its churning waters.

He watched the waves of sorrow and joy play across her face, her head bent slightly, seemingly peering through the shallows and rocks below into the land itself. He splashed her lightly to draw her attention. Startled, she raised her eyes, searching his face. He smiled gently, and she returned a smile, unable to mask her emotions.

He reached in his pocket and drew out a tangled mass of rawhide stripping he'd cut from deer hide, not gold or silver. When he unraveled it, she saw the famous dented coin he'd often bragged about, the precursor to his gathering legend.

He displayed it between them, a crude necklace, the quasi-legendary gold piece hanging from the rawhide strip, the roughest adornment ever offered to any woman who wasn't a Chickasaw, 'cropper, or slave.

"What's this, Durk?"

"My lucky piece."

"You mean your bragging piece," she said, smiling, turning to allow him to tie it on her from behind, feeling his warm breath on the nape of her neck.

"Thank you, Durk. I sometimes forget that all people…"

She straightened it so that he could admire it against her breast. Her face glowed faintly; she felt her decision to be there with him confirmed, knowing he was offering his only talisman to evidence the highly dramatized and apocryphal tale of his conquest of *DarkHorse*. He was giving it to her in the unreasoned hope that she would remember him if, by some improbable happenstance, she would become free one day.

She smiled and placed her arms around his neck, tenderly kissing his cheek, then held him with all her might. She whispered into his ear: "I've never been so proud."

She closed her eyes, pressing herself to him, engulfed in emotions, eyes moist. She tried to clear her mind and heart of the underpinning despair brought about by the tortured memories of the desperate acts of those last days in New Orleans. Surrendering to that moment, she willed herself to forget all the memories of the men of the great city left behind, banishing her bitter knowledge of subservience and betrayal.

Hadn't forgetfulness and pretending always been her redeeming grace? The young girl's escape when the men of means put the lie to anything resembling gentlemanly, courtly love?

Indeed, had not that self-deceiving quality brought her just to the edge of—what? Some sense of freedom? True autonomy in a world of demeaning visions of submission and pleasure? A chance to believe for perhaps one moment that she had never heard of compromise and sublimation; that she had never been initiated into their capricious abuse of intimacy; that she had never learned that a single rose and a delicately kissed hand entailed compulsion or surrender? Indeed, those very gifts— forgetfulness and pretending—forged and refined in sorrow and triumph, had nearly elevated her, returned her, to that young girl's belief that when you were swept away by your knight in his steed-drawn carriage, you were being whisked away to a castle on an impregnable cloud, pristine and unassailable.

She had almost been there, in control of her own destiny, perhaps within months of reaching that young girl's belief. Perhaps it was not in that castle on a cloud, neither pristine nor pure, but at least unassailable with her child, her glory and vision, in her arms. Then her world had collapsed, and she'd located his dueling pistol.

But tonight she would forget all that; she'd use her gifts with joy, rather than furious, secret necessity. Tonight she would clear her mind of her past as completely as if she'd just been brought naked into a world without caste or class, brought innocent and unstained without cynicism or bitterness into a world encompassed by this leafy grotto. Tonight she would give openheartedly and unselfishly, without remorse, as he was prepared to give to her.

Using the leverage of her grip upon him, she playfully flung him into the water, making a great splash. When his head cleared the surface, gasping, he looked up to see what he'd done wrong. But she was there on the bank, removing her riding garments in shadowy view for his pleasure and his approval. He watched in silence, awestruck. Just tonight would be enough, he thought, he'd have that. He began to unbutton his soaked shirt.

At last together in the pool, they pressed their warm skins together against the relentlessly rushing coolness, clinging to each other for stability against the flow. Their shared, rhymed breathing seemed to exhale the overarching stars into the profound blackness above, hurling the numberless, wildly-wheeling glistening sparks into the pitch night in symphonically spinning spirals, each distant glimmer matched, reflected below in the distorted swirling, cascading chaotic cold stream—the final residue of their mutually spent sigh.

So they became a magnificent, single being, soaring above broken destiny, transcending like a paired, Janus-like deity all the cheated mortal games, ascending in unison above the betrayal of their stolen fates. He died in her arms, and she in his. It took a long time to die, but it was restful and peaceful when the mutual passing was complete.

Tomorrow would wait for tomorrow; as One, they were dissolving in rippling waves, were blindly adrift on tremulous breezes.

***

Seldom was such a bright, shining morning suffused with the weighty clouds of so much loss. Antoinette sat the French mare. Hurst took her hand and tenderly kissed it, then pressed its softness to his cheek before reluctantly releasing it to an empty tomorrow.

"Will you come back? Can you?"

"I don't know."

She turned the mare quickly and was gone. He watched the clearing until he could see her no more and then listened until the sound of the mare's hooves no longer reached him. Still, he stood staring at the place he had last seen her. Then the view became too cloudy to see anymore, so he shuffled back to the pool to wash his eyes, truly alone.

***

This seemed like a good place with a woods to conceal herself. She made him stop the wagon about two miles short. "Stop! This here's it."

He offered to wait so she wouldn't have to walk by herself the rest of the way to the French mansion. But she ignored him, taking her bag from under her seat and sending him on his way.

Once the wagon was out of sight, she carried her bag into the bushes. There, she changed into Lilith's gown. Then she wrapped the long cape she'd fashioned from a thin, threadbare old quilt bedspread around herself and pinned it tightly together at four places. Sure that no one could make out what she was wearing beneath the cape, she climbed back through the bushes. Her skirt caught. She pulled herself free, tearing her hem. But she knew she was simply being tested. Once on the road, she headed directly for the French house.

It was warm going. She couldn't loosen her cape lest someone passing see her wearing the revealing garment. So she walked on, getting hotter and dustier. Nothing would stop her.

After a mile, her legs grew weary and she was burning from exertion. She laid her bag beside the road, brushed herself off, and sat down on a log to rest. She looked both ways, up and down the road, and, seeing she was alone, unpinned her cape at the neck to cool off. She wiped her sweaty face

190

with the bottom of the cape, dusty as it was.

She caught her breath and studied the fields stretching far off to the horizon, their furrows covering the gently undulating land. She shifted around to study the scattered woods behind her. She'd never seen wild land before and thought it a marvel. Already she had come so far from town. She'd never before been farther than the manicured grove where the church held its annual picnic. Now she had gone many times that distance and still had a goodly piece to go. She had always known the world was a big place, but experiencing it first hand was giving her a better appreciation of its vastness.

She spotted someone coming from town. The good Lord really meant her to free all the slaves in Turkle! She refastened her cape and watched the glacial progress of a tiny dust cloud in the distance slowly forming into a wagon with a single rider. Then she was able to make out the man sitting in the seat. Hiram Sparks! Of all people! She wasn't going to ride with Hiram Sparks. The man never stopped talking. She had thinking to do and didn't need his tinny voice echoing in her head all the way to the French place.

Hiram pulled up on the reins, looking her over. She was the first person he'd ever seen wearing a cape, much less one made from a bedspread; but though he spoke for many long minutes, he was careful not to ask her about that, and she didn't trouble herself to get in a word edgewise to explain it. Finally, after an extended, tiresome introduction, he got around to asking her what she was doing there.

"I'm just walking," she replied. And that was all.

In so many, many words, he asked her if she wanted a ride.

"No. You go on," she said.

He tried a number of clever approaches to change her mind—he'd sure like to have someone to talk to on the ride out to the French place. But she managed, when he ceased talking long enough to catch his breath, to repeat her instructions to go on. At long last, Hiram got her hint. She thought he'd never get done blowing through his teeth!

When Hiram's wagon was out of sight, she trudged on. She thought hard about why the Lord would send Hiram Sparks to her on this most auspicious day. Finally, she decided the Lord sent Hiram as a trial for her, to test her courage and judgment. But she was prepared to suffer the walk to remain clear of mind. From this trial, she now realized, she had been found pure in motive, true and trustworthy.

She also saw clearly that Hiram's appearance was a kind of Sign from above, an assurance that if she grew weary or lame, or encountered anything seemingly beyond her modest personal powers, the good Lord would supply anything she needed to get her through.

Yes, the Lord knew what He was doing. And He sho'ly picked the right person and the right way to free up all of Turkle's slaves. How He would free the rest of the people who lived in bondage throughout the South was His business. But He had proved to her, once again, that He had the foresight and the means to get it done. And it wasn't going to take no war and destruction to do it, neither.

***

She reached the French mansion at late dusk. It was the largest building she'd ever seen, after the Turkle courthouse, of course, but she was not awestruck. A pair of armed riffraff stopped her at the gate. Nonplused, she looked them squarely in the eye and told them in no uncertain terms she was there to see Mister French in private and wasn't leaving until she did, and that was that. Then she added, with all the fierceness the hot day and the long, dusty hike engendered in her soul, "When the Lord turned again the Captivity of Zion, we were like them that dream."

The riffraff looked quizzically at her, unsure of what to do next.

"Psalms," she said, identifying the quotation. "Now I got the Lord's work yet to do." She went on.

When she reached the front door, a liveried black house servant tried to block her way, telling her that neither of the Frenches was available to see anyone else that day. But she merely replied, "The Lord turned again the Captivity of Zion…" and continued past him without exegesis or explanation.

In the house, she found a chair and sat down. She told the servant to tell Mister French she was there to see him in private and would be waiting in that exact spot until she did. The servant tried to dissuade her, but she refused to reply. When the servant's face showed his utter frustration, she recited, "Turned again the Captivity of Zion…" and sat board upright, staring straight ahead, still as a statue. Seeing he could not convince her, the servant left.

In the next hour, night fell rapidly upon her, leaving her sitting alone in almost pitch blackness. But that meant nothing to her. She could outwait any French ever born and, besides, she had God on her side. These people may not know that now, but they would learn it soon enough.

She'd get in to see Mister French as soon as his resistance broke down. Then she would seduce him, marry him, and free all his slaves, and that would be that. It might as well be written down in the Good Book.

***

French saw the last tradesmen out and went directly to her bedroom. On the way up the stairs, she issued instructions that the honor store girl waiting downstairs be given a hundred dollars and the phaeton brought up from the stables to convey her home. Mister French could see no one else today and, if the girl still needed to see him, she should return tomorrow.

For two hours, French had made the messenger from New Orleans wait out of sight, in effect teasing herself, while she dickered with the craftsmen and suppliers over minor purchases of furniture and draperies for the house, pretending to hold on for the extra dollar just to delay completion of the deal. This teasing swelled her anticipation from mere titillation into an almost unbearable desire, like holding out a special bite she craved most to end the meal.

Reaching her room, she sat behind her desk, the prosperous businessman at his place of contemplation and paperwork. Straightening her suit, she rang the bell. Now it was time for her tingling bite.

The messenger was shown in, obviously agitated at the long wait. French signaled him over to give her the letter sealed by the hand of the New Orleans attorney who performed the investigation.

"What was New Orleans like?" French asked.

"It ain't Turkle," the man replied.

French waved the man away. Alone with her prize, French carefully knifed away the seal and slowly opened the letter, making certain she didn't tear it. Here was the truth she had been yearning for all these years, but was too cowardly to seek. She was so excited she had to read the first sentence three times before she made any sense out of it. Before continuing, she set the letter face down and took deep breaths, trying to settle her rattling brain.

She rose and went to her cabinet to pour herself a brandy, trying to control her anticipation, waiting only to reach a peak of pure ecstasy. She opened her humidor and selected one of her favorite Cuban cigars. Taking her time, she wet the rounded end exceedingly well, then played the match from a distance to make its flat end burn evenly.

Smoking, she took the brandy to her desk and took one sip, followed by a deep inhale on her cigar. Then she set the brandy down and lifted the letter. She could read it now. And she did read it, growing progressively more shocked and outraged as the pages turned.

The letter changed everything she had ever known and believed about herself. Everything.

Chapter Twenty-four

Devereau French brushed aside the servant's objection and entered her mother's room, slamming the door behind her. If Mother was asleep before, she wasn't now.

Missus French was sitting at the chess table, wide awake, when Devereau reached her. *Good!* Devereau threw the letter on the board, but her mother ignored the sheets of paper. Instead, she looked up from the game in progress, a vindictive grin on her lips.

"So, you're getting to the bowels of it, are you? And the prey's scent is making you *testy*. Man back from New Orleans, is he?"

Would the poisonous sarcasm never cease! "Mother, you are not a cousin to the Louisiana Fairchilds, nor to anyone else of note. Not only that, but, according to my attorney, you had an illegitimate child before you met my father."

Missus French pierced her with her stare. "That's right," she said, "a girl child: Antoinette. Anything else you want me to confirm?"

Devereau felt as if she'd been punched in the stomach. Unable to catch her breath, she managed to utter, "Antoinette is your daughter?"

"Yes, my daughter."

"Then it's true. But who was her father?"

***

They smelled of drink and tobacco—and money.

The four young men, for the evening free of family but intimately conscious of family fortunes, swaggered into the lushly appointed room, a room lit but dimly by strategically placed burning candles. Voluble and excited, they cast approving glances at the high-vaulted, finely patterned ceiling and its intricately carved cove, the gilded scarlet wallpaper, the myriad erotic curiosa, the paintings and statuettes of carnal women in exotic states of undress and repose. They joined in a banal toast and set down their glasses. Then, their courage reinforced, they glanced at the subject of the many rumors and stories they'd heard from friends and acquaintances. The sight froze them in mid-sentence, their words and laughter dying in the air.

There she sat, enthroned on a vast spread of rose-colored silk, piled red pillows supporting her back and naked arms, scanty sheer fabric enhancing bodily treasures beyond their imaginations. Her face was smooth and clean

194

of line, her eyes dark and deep, her lips rich and broad. If there was a goddess of beauty somewhere in the heavens, she had descended from her bacchanal empire in a cloud of moonburst and lighted like a feather upon this luxurious mattress. Not one of the four could utter a word.

With a gay laugh, she cleverly challenged their manhood and their courage. They looked from one to another, quizzical, uncertain. Then their hesitation was over.

They were upon her, roughly, all four, laughing and calling out, making wild animal and country noises, joining in her laughter. Their hands and mouths were everywhere upon her, as she aided them in recklessly tearing off their clothes.

It would be a night the four would remember fondly, evidenced only by a smile their wives would recognize, but never interpret. They would even make sarcastic remarks alluding to the sums two of them lost at chess against the hireling. For the woman, it was merely another substantial addition to her bank account. She was rising in the world, and rising fast.

***

"Her father?" Missus French sneered. "Antoinette was the daughter-in-common of an exclusive gentlemen's club I served in New Orleans—not that its *members* treated me like a lady. Until your bumpkin father carried me—his less than innocent pleasure—home to marry him. Ha! The fool thought he'd caught himself a gentlewoman. The late Mister French would never have approved of my past, of which your sister was unmistakable evidence."

"Does she know this?"

"No, of course not. Only you know."

Devereau's head was spinning. She sought for words vainly, until a few managed to stumble from her mouth of their own accord. "W-what happened to her?"

"I sold her," said Missus French, nonplused, "to a wealthy old reprobate whose tastes ran to pretty little girls. 'I ruined your life.' Ha!"

"You sold her, but how?"

"Because the law said I could, that's how. She was mine, wasn't she? Your report does note that I was the most notorious quadroon in the quarter, doesn't it?" With a quivering sigh, in deep agony, Missus French closed her eyes and, supporting her arm on the chess table, rested her forehead against her fist. Then she was still.

Quadroon? The word rang in Devereau French's ears. All her breath and strength fled. So that's what the letter's parenthetically enclosed paragraph, written in ambiguous, legal-sounding verbiage, meant! When French first read them, those few rambling sentences seemed somehow dark, threatening, but she pushed them away from her mind, partly in fear of what they were *not* saying. Now she understood the sheathed phrases and Latin terms only too well! Quadroon? She wasn't the person she always believed herself to be. Everything about her place in the world was gone in an instant.

No, it couldn't be true! She had a light complexion (but with underlying shades of darkness!), even freckles (not all red, some dark brown!), even a reddish tint to her hair—like her *father*. But what did she have of her mother's? She held her hand near a candle, squinting and cursing the darkness her mother lived within. Desperately trying to gauge her skin's color through the gloom, she rubbed the hand hard, as if lighter skin might flake off to reveal darker flesh as proof of the lawyer's cryptic claim.

Alternately, she saw lily white, then her flesh's dark shadows, back and forth, as the tiny candle flame flickered against Missus French's eternal night. If only Devereau could bring some light into this tomb! She wanted to rip down the curtains, but realized this would do no good. The room had no mirror, another of its inhabitant's oddities, as if Missus French might be repelled by her reflection or afraid she would make no reflection. Frustrated at her lack of proof, Devereau French collapsed into the adjoining chair.

Missus French lifted her head, a living creature once again. She reached into the chess table drawer and extracted a pistol, then slid it across to Devereau.

"Learn it well, child: The title to *French Acres* does not make us invulnerable. It's time for you to shoot Mister Hurst in the face. Or through the back of his head if you must, I don't care."

Devereau felt the blow land. She gathered her will, pointedly refusing to touch the firearm lying between them. Slowly recovering, she caught a glimpse of the strategy her mother had so carefully woven. With a searing anger, she retorted, "That would eliminate the embarrassing poseur for you, wouldn't it, Mother? Yes, I hang for shooting Hurst—or more likely, they shoot me 'attempting to escape.' Regardless, you bury my woman's body six feet down, and you've still got Antoinette to take my place."

She could picture Antoinette watching her coffin descend into the gaping grave; her mother wouldn't attend. And then Antoinette, her mother's daughter for certain—a mixed-blood, husband-murdering witch already running most of the French empire, could run the rest.

"What are you saying?" Missus French responded, shocked.

"Yes, I take your sins down with me, and your blood still prevails. Very clever. Except I won't sacrifice the crumb of life you've so graciously granted me to save your skin—whatever its tint!"

Yes, Devereau French saw her mother's scheme now in its entirety. The madwoman was bound to have a phony marriage certificate hidden somewhere, waiting, some elaborate, highly decorated piece of legal paper. Written upon it, in flowing, official-looking calligraphy would be two names: the now-late Mister Devereau French and, just below it, a fictitious name Mother invented to give Antoinette a new identity.

Mother would claim there'd been a secret wedding between Devereau and Antoinette. Who would dispute it? Who could believe that a lonely man like Devereau French would ever refuse the love of such a ravishing, sophisticated woman?

By revealing this fraudulent marriage document to the world, her mother would legally transform Devereau's half-sister, Antoinette, into her *widow*—the inheritor of her estate. Realization of the depth of her mother's cold-blooded plot against *her*, against her own daughter, made her nearly faint.

She now understood. The French empire, which had been registered in Devereau's own name since her majority, would now simply pass to Antoinette, French's presumptive widow. This would eliminate French's troublesome and highly risky masquerade from the mix, and pass the rights cleanly to the new *female* owner. Missus French would never again be threatened by her youngest child's tortured unpredictability, her unbearable discomfort at being trapped in her forced male role.

And to top it off, her mother could begin afresh with a new Queen of the Chessboard, one more compliant and grateful. This older, mature daughter, who had succeeded on her own without her mother's help, would be free to marry and to have as many children as she wished—and this freedom to have children, which had been denied Devereau so many years, infuriated Devereau far beyond jealousy and hatred, even beyond *murder*. Antoinette would continue her mother's bloodline, a bloodline further insulated from grief and discovery by the progressive legitimacy of future generations, and by the simple passing of time upon time. Her mother would be moored in safe harbor at last.

Yes, people would remember poor Mister Devereau French, strange man, tragically married to a courtly and brilliant woman, only to be hung—or shot—before he could conceive a son of his own with her. Hung or shot, only to have his awe-inspiring wife produce children for some Gloriously

Blessed Man who would marry the widow and, thus, gain with her love his stake in *French Acres*. And the man would probably gain *DarkHorse*, too, lands which poor Mister French would achieve for his mother by killing that Hurst fellow!

How ironic. I find myself hatefully jealous of the future husband of the widow I never had.

Across from Devereau, Missus French's gloved hands fumbled at the pistol. Then, taking hold of it, she slapped it into her daughter's hand. The sudden weight of the cold steel in her palm made Devereau instinctively cover it with her free hand.

"Use it, coward," Missus French barked.

"Never," Devereau replied, summoning her resistance.

"I'll see nothing happens to you," Missus French said reassuringly. "You're my own flesh and blood. Any jeopardy you might face would jeopardize all of us: me, you, Antoinette."

"Shoot Hurst!" Devereau forced a derisive laugh. Then she began to laugh richly, wildly, so hard she had to calm down before she could speak. "I've already slept with him, Mother. We spent the night at the stuffy old Grand Hotel at the county seat."

"Fool," Missus French said weakly, mortified. Her voice became shaky. "You can't do that. I'm sorry, but you can't."

"Why? Why can't I have him? That would solve everything: Antoinette can run *French Acres*; Hurst and I could have as many babies as I want, hide out somewhere comfortable, plush, when I'm swollen. Mother, I could have children of my own. My own children!"

Missus French paused, thinking deeply, her eyes cast down, refusing to meet Devereau's. "Certainly, you must see the manner in which Hurst is inordinately, unnaturally, fond of his slaves. Why do you guess his father preached so vehemently against slavery? Devereau, dearest, your combination with Hurst would doom us. People wouldn't stand for it."

"Wouldn't stand for it!" Devereau exclaimed. "This is one of your devious inferences, Mother. He's part Indian, so what. Tell me the truth, or we are done here." Devereau made as if to rise.

While Devereau watched her, Missus French twisted in her chair, her brow creased, and covered her eyes with her gloved hand. After a long silence in the darkness between the two, Missus French fixed her gaze on Devereau, as if to say, *You demanded this, be prepared:*

"People are attracted to qualities in another person which they see in themselves. Isn't that true?"

"Yes, I suppose so. Go on."

"The truth is, I kept Hurst's 'cropper father around the place to do odd jobs. Very odd jobs; it cost me a jug and a modest stipend, pocket money. He'd wear his stupid preacher outfit out to *French Acres* sometimes. Why I can't imagine. Devereau, it's possible, it's *highly likely*... The odds are *almost certain*: Hurst's father is *your* father. Any other prospect is so spurious, so ridiculous—"

"Now I know you're lying," Devereau said, her voice catching.

"You know it's true. Don't you see yourself in Hurst? I don't apologize. I needed what I needed in those days." Missus French settled back into her plush chair.

"Hurst's father was a hard drunk, mean; the kind of man you'd want on your side in a riverfront brawl. But he was amenable to my pleasure, like most men wished to be, with ruthless grasping hands like a man: in a closet, up the barn loft, hidden in the brush, even on a bed. Most importantly, he kept his mouth shut; that was all I cared about. I've had far worse. His field dirt and calloused hands meant nothing to me."

"L-lies, lies!" Devereau stammered.

"Lies? You look nothing like my late-husband. Go study his bust in the hallway; bring your precious mirror with you. Mister French was a fool. All he ever did was drink, hunt, and whore. Were it not for his family crawling everywhere about like lice and maggots on a ripped rat's carcass, I could have easily controlled the situation."

"Why didn't everyone see that I looked nothing like my... my...?"

"People only saw that I was ridding the town of Frenches. That's all Turkle cared about. Look, Devereau, grant that I know more about these matters than you."

"Yes, I am certain you do. Undoubtedly."

"Then believe me, when brother mates with sister, the offspring is born with pig or possum tails, or two heads, cow horns, or who knows what manner of monstrosities? Do you see yourself cuddling such a creature? How will Hurst feel about you then?"

"Is this true, about the children?" Devereau asked, shocked.

"I'm sorry, it is. Why do you think such carnal relations are taboo, forbidden? The very thought of it terrifies even the basest trash, who, as you know, aren't terribly selective during mating season. Name me one brother-sister marriage you've ever seen or heard of: trash, slave, riffraff, anybody."

Devereau was cornered. If she attempted to verify her mother's horrifying claim, they'd want to know why she was asking. Cornered, but not close to surrender.

"So is it the miscegenation or the incest you can't bear?" Devereau jeered, sneering at her mother. Grasping desperately for disbelief, she gathered her strength, preparing for war.

She would now play the one deadly power piece against her mother that she's held in reserve for these many months.

***

The girl had been told again and again to go home. Told she would be driven home in a French phaeton with a man to wait all night to bring her back in the morning if need be. And given money, too. Yet she continued to sit in the dark. That child was going nowhere.

The kindly, salt-and-pepper-haired servant lit the candles on the end tables flanking her chair. The flames cast shadows that distorted their faces into horrors, but at least now she'd be able to see.

Content that he'd done the right thing, the servant left the room, returning minutes later with a plate of warm food and a glass of milk. The milk was a rich beverage so beyond the girl's means that she only tasted it when it was a gift from a caring neighbor or plentiful at a church picnic in a good year on the land. The man set the plate and glass by her, then withdrew from his pocket good silver wrapped in a dense cloth napkin. Satisfied that all was well, he sat down in a nearby chair to watch her eat.

She ate delicately, picking at the slab of meat that was much too large and red for her, but relishing the vegetables and the milk. While she ate, she asked about her chances of seeing Mister French, but the man's reply was not promising. The servant explained that Mister French had gone into his mamma's room that night, and the girl sho'ly didn't want to see neither one of them Frenches after the two of them done been together. Especially the way young master could be heard shouting through the door of his mother's quarters. Folks that worked in the French mansion, even Annie, knew to stay away from the master then. But would a young woman wrapped in some crazy cape of old quilt, spouting the Bible, have enough manners and sense to stay away?

The young woman finished eating, deep in thought. She placed the silver on the plate, then drained the milk. With a faraway gleam in her eye, she stood, straightening the quilt bedspread cape covering the revealing Lilith's gown.

Before the servant could say a word, Ellen took a candle and was gone up the stairs, quilt cape swirling, and no panicked calling-after could stop her. The servant ran into the kitchen to warn the cooks.

***

"Our heart drives our lives, Mother," Devereau continued, "and mine needs Hurst. Your flimsy fabrications won't alter my course. You're lying for your own purposes. And I know why."

"Why would I lie?"

"Why," Devereau said smugly, sitting upright, straightening her back. "I know what you're concealing. I've known almost from the beginning; I uncovered it on my own."

"Go on," Missus French said. "Let's hear it."

"Hurst, along with everyone else, knows it was a French behind his father's gruesome murder. He even says so. That's why he's so set against us."

"The crazy drunk was talking too much, saying things he shouldn't."

Devereau leaned forward, fire in her eyes. "It was you behind that night they went out to his shack, you behind that night they burned him alive. Burned alive, my God, a man with whom you were intimate, or so you claim!"

"And you believe this, because…?"

"Not *believe* it—*know* it. Because the late-Mister French was already gone and buried—the date on his tombstone out in the family graveyard proves that. Your own hands saw to that. And you'd already dispatched his ignorant clan to the four winds; your prestidigitation in that triumph is legendary. What other French was left? It was you. He spoke against slavery, and in your devious way, you used it to manipulate the town to have him murdered."

"Slavery wasn't all he was raving about," Missus French said grimly, determinedly. "Those diatribes didn't matter to me. It was his sodden braggadocio about things between the two of us, me and him. He was casting light on the dark corner where my child hid. He said things that could have raised questions about your paternity, perhaps even led to exposure of your gender. Turkle's resentment against us has always been palpable, you know that. If such revelations, even such suspicions, became commonplace, it would have been open season on us, you and me: penniless ostracism at best, conceivably fatal. Above all, I had to protect you, my fair child. Above everything else, I must always protect you.

"You must extinguish Dark Horse, you must." Missus French stared at Devereau, but her daughter was unable to speak.

"Listen," Missus French said, "While Mister Dark Horse lives, his very existence will haunt you night and day. One bullet between his eyes, and you are free. Free of him."

"Never!" Devereau shouted tearfully. "I can't, Mother. I'm not cold-blooded like you."

"Quiet down, darling girl," Missus French said softly. "I only want peace in our family, between the three of us. Consider this: unlike you, Antoinette can have all the children with Mister Hurst that she wants. Her father, a nobody in New Orleans, and I are not related to Hurst. Isn't that true? Isn't she free to bear his children without fear of some Caliban being born?"

Furious, Devereau's face flushed bright red, and she covered her eyes. "Yes, she can," she mumbled.

"Devereau, dear, I warned her: if she has contact with Hurst, the sheriff will ship her to New Orleans. I did it for your sake, to keep them apart, isn't that true?" Devereau nodded wearily. "Where was she hiding when we captured her? Out at *DarkHorse*, that's where."

"Probably."

"He longs to be with *her*, not with you. Do you believe that?" Missus French paused, but Devereau remained silent, unable to deny it. "Perhaps you have reason to know that is true." A suppressed sob escaped Devereau's throat.

"Child, Antoinette recently sold *DarkHorse* some of our slaves. Fine, that is part of her duties. But she delivered them to him personally, and didn't return until the next afternoon. What do you suppose transpired out there at *DarkHorse*, given all the time they spent together? What do you suppose the two of them are plotting against us, against *you*?"

"Stop, please. No more."

Devereau rose shakily from her chair, the weapon cradled in her hands like a child. She felt her mother's glove pat the bundle. "It's loaded this time. Bring us peace."

Gasping for breath, Devereau stumbled from the room, blind in one eye from a scorching headache, her heart twisted by an iron vice.

***

Hearing the door close, Missus French returned her attention to the chess pieces. When she was young, in that house in New Orleans, while her whiskey-soaked clients dressed, she would always challenge them to a game for whatever stakes they felt brave enough to wager, cajoling them mercilessly until she'd cleaned their fat wallets. This gambit often proved more lucrative than her primary profession. Hard men, soft men, perfumed men, sweat-soaked men, tobacco-reeking men, everything she did was for her own pleasure, not for theirs—especially the chess.

She held Devereau's letter from the New Orleans attorney to the candle flame. When the parchment caught, she dropped it into a silver basin she kept by her side and watched as it was consumed. From beside the curling black ashes, she withdrew her elongated, tar-stained pipe with its diminutive burnt bowl.

No longer feeling like chess, or reading, she held the pipe to the candle until its contents glowed and smoked. Then she placed the stem to her lips and drew deeply.

"Devereau," she mumbled sadly. She paused, reflecting, as a troubled fog descended upon her. A single tear rolled down her cheek; she wiped it away with her white glove.

Now things were getting down to the endgame. She was attacking at just the right moment, exerting the power of the queen she'd held in reserve. She examined her daughter's position, but could find no flaw in her trap.

"You have no choice but to sacrifice your knight. But even that won't save you."

***

When Ellen reached the top of the landing, she saw many dark hallways and closed doors from which to choose. This place was larger inside than it looked from the road. She picked a direction at random and started forward, her thoughts racing to the task ahead of her. In respect of, and to mirror the silence of, the majestic mansion, she walked on her tiptoes, tensing with every step, as if she'd found herself in an empty church.

She'd never kissed any man other than that Mister Dark Horse stranger. Mister French, on the other hand, if what people said was true, had never kissed even one woman, and had blatantly refused every opportunity that had crossed his path. So seeing they had only one kiss between them, how was a just-grown, unworldly woman and a man like that supposed to find wedded bliss? Was that the way it happened to the women in the Bible? She'd never been told, and the Book didn't explain. Did God move both parties' hearts in an instant, and His will was done? Well, she decided, best leave the carnal part of it to the Lord.

She became lost in the labyrinthine mansion until, after creeping aimlessly up and down lightless hallways, she found herself back at the landing. She'd gone in a complete circle.

She paused, wondering if her plan was a mistake. But somehow she found the courage to continue, to trust in God's ways. And, as if to prove that point, after a short, uncertain venture down a different hallway, the next corner she turned produced a small black boy sitting half asleep by a door, waiting for any call from within.

She asked if the room belonged to Mister French, and the boy answered in the affirmative, warning that no one was permitted to cross its threshold that night. But the boy's words didn't faze her, nor could he lay a hand on a woman of her age and complexion. She continued on, heedless of his pleas.

She burst into the unlocked room, closing the door behind her. Then with a flourish she ripped off the cape, exposing Lilith's gown, all her physical treasures beneath it distinctly visible.

When her eyes adjusted to the light, she realized the room didn't match her imagination. True, it was enormous with plush furniture and a chandelier, but instead of being spotless, the floor was littered haphazardly with one of French's suits and undergarments, including some snake-like kind of wrapping bandage, all scattered as if removed and discarded while crossing the room. Well, maybe that would make her work easier, she thought to herself. She thanked the Lord for His foresight in the matter of Mister French's undressing.

Her eyes followed the rumpled clothing until they fixed upon the destination of this disorder, Devereau French lying naked on the bed, sobbing. But here, something was wrong, terribly wrong.

Hearing the door, Devereau turned toward her, shocked at being disturbed. The first thing the young woman noticed was French's eyes, which were full of heartbreak. Then she saw his body before he could cover himself. The body was like her own and shouldn't be. Mister French had breasts larger, with nipples more red and full, and hips more curved than hers. She thought fast, reaching deeply into everything she knew about men, marriage, and great women in the Bible who had seduced to the Lord's glory, but she couldn't remember any reference to such a thing in either the Good Book or in the Sunday school stories she'd been told as a child—nor in things shouted by her grandfather, who could never be held back on the subject of sin.

For what seemed an hour, the two stared eye-to-eye, hers determined, angry, and slightly confused; his looking back, filled with terror and tears, pulling a blanket to his throat to cover his nakedness.

Then she decided this plan wouldn't work. She had a better plan, a more direct plan, and she should have done it in the first place. She had chosen marriage because it didn't require her to break the law. But now that she thought of it, God had provided this war for a reason. Yes, sir, this war was going to fall right into her hands.

"You ain't gonna tell nobody you saw me wearing this," she decreed, giving the terrified Mister French a fierce look.

French merely nodded assent, clutching with trembling hands the blanket.

"Good," the young woman said, thinking she never should have taken Lilith's gown from the chifforobe. Well, too late now. She'd change back before the ride home in the French phaeton. At least she wouldn't have to wear that stifling cape any more.

She left the room. There was no future in this romance, no chance of love-struck persuasion to be worked upon this French, so she had other work to do if she was going to free the French slaves. God had certainly given her gifts beyond her sexual attractiveness. And another of those gifts was just what she needed to free up them Children of God.

When she was gone, French burst into tears again, tears so violent she thought she would break. Now somebody from town had seen her naked. Would this nightmare never end!

***

It was worse than being a child tied to a bed all night, a horrific night, with her few saving beliefs about herself vanished. Beloved father, who she had dreamed of for years, really a cruel predator; mother, a murderous wanton out to effect the death of her own daughter. She herself, likely descended from trash and who knows what. Hurst probably a half-brother, and untouchable for more reasons than that. The only thing that kept her from shooting herself was that her mother wanted her to do just that.

She was groggy from the long, exhausting headache but, though she hadn't eaten in many hours, she found she was able to rise from her bed without fainting.

She would endure, she decided; she must. She would endure despite the trap and find her own life somewhere, somehow. True, she could no longer resist her mother's monomania on the subject of Hurst. But perhaps she could eliminate him in a way that didn't doom her to join him in the cold ground. That way, she would simply dispose of the interloper and restore balance to Turkle. It was either that or end herself by her own hand, and she was not ready to die for her mother's pleasure. Not yet.

She wobbled over toward her chifforobe, catching herself from falling along the way by taking hold of her dresser and her desk. There, she withdrew her best suit. Though shaky, she was able to work her way back to her bed and, by taking frequent breaks to lie down, to dress. Finally clad, she crossed the room and leaned against her dressing table to admire herself in the mirror. As much pride as she'd had in this fine cloth, it merely kept hidden what she liked best (and least) about herself. Her woman's body. And now she knew it hid a truth even more damning to her than the shape of the flesh that hung on her bones.

Pushing the scattered clothes under the bed, she stumbled to the wall and rang for a servant before collapsing into an armchair. After an interminable interlude, the servant entered warily, eyes wide, trembling. The boy had been warned of French's mood by the other servants.

"Y-You rang for me, Mister French," the boy said.

French looked up, a fierce glow in her eyes. "Get me my messengers! Hurry!"

***

The tribe's hunt had been good that day; it was a night for feasting and drinking. In his lodge, Wounded Wolf sat on the blanket, old Chickasaw wisemen on either side of him, others around them, enveloped in a plentiful world. They heartily ate the cooked game and tasted of the jug. Then a surprise visitor from the outside world was announced.

A young brave led the terrified, bound black messenger into the hut. Wounded Wolf laid the haunch he was chewing back in the bowl and wiped his mouth with his sleeve.

The old Chickasaw turned to Wounded Wolf, narrowing his eyes. "You promised, *no more slaves*," the old one cautioned.

Wounded Wolf looked the trembling man over. Not much there. Knowing white people, he figured this man was probably sent because he was considered expendable. Whoever sent him wouldn't have to feed the poor devil any more if he failed to return.

"Why are you here?" Wounded Wolf asked.

"M-Mister F-French offer you a deal," he stuttered, "'bout your X on that Mister H-Hurst deed paper."

The man watched Wounded Wolf pull his knife from its sheath, rise, and approach. Shaking uncontrollably, the messenger closed his eyes and bit his lip. But to his relief, he felt the knife cut the rawhide binding his hands. When he opened his eyes, the Chief had returned to his seat and was taking a swig from the jug.

"Tell that cruel white-woman that the Chief of the Chickasaws says, 'Dark Horse is my friend. I am no longer bound *not* to kill him, so I have no desire to kill him.' Understand?"

"Yes, suh!" the man replied, wondering if he'd misunderstood the reference.

"Good," Wounded Wolf said, stabbing his knife into the venison. "There's the jug, there's the meat. Want to be my hostage?"

"Yes, suh," the man replied. "I kin sho'ly use the rest."

***

Bake hurriedly wolfed down the rest of his breakfast, stuffing into his mouth a whole gravy-soaked biscuit and two slices of bacon. Once he got that forced down his throat, he drained his coffee and, with thanks, headed out the door.

Mister French can't just ride in to the jail like folks would. No, I got to meet the damn dandy on a deserted road six miles outside town.

He arrived at the appointed place with a bad case of indigestion, to wait in the hot sun a half hour until French showed. This he endured by sitting on the stump he used to climb down from his horse. Then, without a hello or thank you, it was strictly business.

"I want you to arrest him," French ordered without identifying anyone. But Bake knew who he meant.

"But what has he done, Mister French? Don't you see—?"

"I don't care what he's done."

"But the law—"

"I made you the law."

Holding the reins, Bake climbed shakily up on the stump and worked himself from that height back into his saddle.

"I would like to remind you, Sheriff," French continued, "there's an election coming up."

Bake shrugged and turned his horse away, and said over his shoulder: "It's a free country, ain't it?"

***

French was undeterred. She still had a power piece on the board to break this game wide open. These early forays had merely been minor feints, simple attempts to pin Hurst's flank. Now would come the real battle for the center of the board, the time to crush him.

As she mounted, she considered every angle. She would play this better, more subtly, more sure than her mother ever had. She couldn't wait to see her mother's face when she told her. It would be her first major victory, a grand complete one. She hadn't made a single miscalculation.

Chapter Twenty-five

If the local cotton broker had come all the way out to *French Acres* on a Friday evening, it must be bad news. The man liked to spend his weekends this time of year at the house he'd built in the country. He should already be in the buggy with his wife and children, not sitting across the desk from Devereau French.

"There's a war on, Mister French. I warned you about buying too heavy in cotton this year. The price is dropping like a rock."

"But how can that be?" French asked, incredulous. *Didn't prices always go up during a war? The price of everything else, from seed to feed, had been rising at a breakneck pace since war was declared, so why not cotton?*

"But," French said, "the last two years…the price kept going up."

"My guess, them mills in Europe was laying up a big supply, figuring that war here was a shoo-in. That's what made that cotton price go up. Them English and Dutch probably got enough cotton stashed away to keep running for a year or two."

French's head spun. Her attack on Dark Horse had seemed so certain; Hurst had fallen right into her trap. With Hurst's speculative sales, he unwittingly owed to Devereau French more cotton than his land could ever grow, putting him at French's mercy.

But something was terribly wrong. If cotton prices continued to fall, Hurst would be able to buy dirt cheap the cotton he was obligated to deliver to *French Acres*, fulfilling his contracts. And Devereau would have to pay Hurst a huge premium for the now-worthless commodity. What could she have overlooked?

"It's the war, Mister French. See, the Yankee blockade done closed the ports. Cotton ain't worth nothing if you can't ship it to the mills in Europe or up North. It don't pay to ship it to the docks, just to pay more money to warehouse it.

"Face it, Mister French. There's no way to ship your cotton nowhere. You're stuck with it."

"But won't the government do something? Cotton is the South's life blood."

"I'm not sure the government wants to. I guess they figure when those English mills get hungry enough, England, maybe France too, will come in the war on our side. The Confederacy gonna need some outside help from those folks to win this war. It's diplomacy, you see?

"'Sides, if we ain't shipping cotton, we starve out those East Coast mills whose owners are all big Union politicians, governors, congressmen, and such. Let's see them Big Dollar Yankees back a war against us if their mills get closed down."

French's throat constricted so badly that she feared she would choke. When she lifted the water pitcher, her hand shook violently, spilling almost as much as she poured.

"So in effect, all the cotton I own—all that I've committed to buy from Hurst!—is worthless."

"You're obligated to pay him top dollar, too. Damn, if he didn't get lucky."

French's eyes darted about the desk as if searching for a chess piece mighty enough to turn the game all by itself. But there was no answer, no chess piece. She looked up at the broker.

"Then I'm ruined. Hurst has ruined me! Does he know?"

"Not yet. He comes into town on Mondays sometimes to check the market, but ain't seen him much lately."

French's guts burned like a red-hot boulder. She performed some rapid calculations, her mind traveling in whirling circles.

She was trapped: by her mother, by Hurst. She might indeed have to gun down Hurst—thus clearing the field for Antoinette.

From nowhere, she heard her mother's throaty laughter inside her head. Horrified, she clapped her hands over her ears. The broker politely lowered his eyes, and, seeing that, Devereau composed herself as best she could. All the while, her mind struggled within the wild din of echoing fear and hatred.

Eternity's staring us both in the face, Hurst. Better you than me.

***

Somewhere it was going to be a lovely night. Somewhere young men would stroll beneath the dappled new leaves in the moonlight, their arms around the waists of their tender young loves. Somewhere young men with blankets under their arms would stop in a field to kiss their soft-faced heartthrobs, their breath hot and sweet, their lips hungry, unable to wait for the seclusion of a stand of great oak to spread the blanket. Somewhere middle-aged farm wives would dry their hands after finishing the evening dishes and cast aside their aprons, to stand beside their husbands on the porch, watching the last glow of the daylight reflect pink on the clouds. Somewhere…

French straightened her suit, then checked the loaded pistol one last time. A tear welled in her eye and dribbled down her cheek. She wiped it aside.

"Well, Durksen Hurst, I will truly miss you. But if this pawn falls, she won't fall alone."

What if I shoot him and the woman, too? What then? Mother will be trapped, forced to save me or be cast adrift herself, old and alone, with no plantation to store her treasures. Perhaps they'll confiscate all her other assets, too. All confiscated from her and the murderer (me!), by our good friend the judge (ha!), by our loyal compatriots the banker and the lawyer (ha!), by the plethora of grateful tradesmen and suppliers whom both of us treat condescendingly like slaves (ha!), by the whole mass of little people in their little lives who undoubtedly respect the great Frenches and wish us well (ha!).

Then Mother, to save herself, will be forced to turn over her own king in defeat; to admit I have won, outmaneuvered, outsmarted, and outplayed the great master herself. Then Mother will have to admit I am the most courageous, the most ruthless, the most hard-hearted. Her only chance at survival will depend on keeping me—her only surviving heir—from the hangman. Then she will have no choice but to love me, only me.

She pictured her mother desperate to save her, savoring the fantasy. The endgame on the board would be clear of all complications. Cleared of Hurst and Dark Horse, of Antoinette, with only the two of them left to play the game.

And if her mother failed to save her? Then the old woman would get what she deserved. Perhaps the townspeople would discover the masquerade by which the Frenches had deceived them all these years. Her mother would be dragged into the sunlight.

She imagined her mother getting on a train to nowhere, forced blinking into the glaring sunlight, with nothing to her name but her black dress and eternal gloves. French almost laughed out loud. And then she thought of the rope waiting for her and of the gentle peace it would bring.

Someone tapped on the door three times: the messenger. She hid the pistol and shouted for him to enter.

She handed him the sealed envelope.

"Take this out to *DarkHorse*. Tell Mister Hurst I'll be unarmed, and I expect him to be the same."

***

He waited in the shadows of the town commons, leaning on the rough picnic table. An unopened jug sat on the table, unnoticed. His partners surrounding him barely spoke, and then only in short cryptic phrases. A perfect night to admit defeat and escape, if only they could.

He tried to focus on which tactic he would use. He must try to act warm and welcoming, but not humble or contrite. That would be taken by French as surrendering, and all would be lost. He must act strong and confident, but not arrogant or hostile. A man sure of himself, his position. And friendly; friendly above all—with a French!

He heard riders, then made out the white stallion leading a host of mounted men through the trees, emerging from the blackness of night. It was French, leading a group of riffraff. When they got closer he could see the group had rifles. French might be unarmed, as the note promised, but his *de facto* bodyguards had firearms aplenty. And Hurst and his partners had none. Hurst resolved not to be intimidated.

He nodded to his partners and they scrambled silently off to huddle together at a distance, near the woods. Then he picked up the jug and stepped into a clear patch of moonlight where French could see him. He whistled.

The aristocrat signaled for her escorts to dismount and wait, then rode on the white toward Hurst.

Reaching the table, French dismounted to face her host. Without a word, French reached into her jacket pocket and pulled out two Cuban cigars. She handed one cigar across, then tore out with her teeth the tip of her own, before reaching into her inside pocket for a match.

To stop her, Hurst pressed his hand against French's, flattening it against French's breast pocket. *Soft, an almost unmanly chest,* he noted. French yanked Hurst's hand away and backed off. Ignoring this, Hurst lit a match and held it to French's cigar, watching the peach-face puff and blow smoke, before lighting his own. Taking a deep puff, Hurst realized immediately the Cuban was too strong. He coughed and choked and was forced to spit. Bad start. Embarrassed, he saw French coolly blow a smoke ring.

Not to be outdone, Hurst popped the jug's cork and took a swig, then, wiping his mouth, handed it to French. French took a swig and coughed, then took another, before slamming the jug down.

"I'm certain we'll come to some mutually satisfying arrangement, Mister Hurst," French said.

"If that is possible," Hurst growled.

They sat on the benches, across the table from each other. French puffed thoughtfully on her cigar, then said playfully, "My cousin Charlotte tells me you have a way with women—although you're unsophisticated, like your kind."

Stung, Hurst answered, "Perhaps I just have better taste than homely French cousins."

Furious, French retorted, "I imagine a woman of her station can intimidate a man of your background."

"Her station ought to be in a back alley off Bourbon Street," Hurst snarled back.

"Let's get down to business," French declared harshly. "Do you ever wager, Mister Hurst?"

"When I wager, it's not a gentleman's bet. But, yes, I've been known to relish a risk."

"Here's the bet," French stated. "*Dark Horse* against *French Acres*. Winner takes all: our property, our forward-sold cotton contracts, everything."

"Everything?" Hurst sputtered. "All right, everything. Except the slaves. Took me too long to train mine."

"Fine. You can even keep the fillies Antoinette sold you for your studs. They're worth something; at least you won't be entirely broke. Agreed?" French spit in her hand and offered it to seal the deal.

So French knew Antoinette had been out to *DarkHorse*. Did that endanger her?

"Done!" Hurst answered. He spit into his hand and gripped French's, squeezing as hard as he could. The aristocrat struggled not to wince, fighting gamely to fix her poker face. After French managed to extricate her hand, she slipped it under the table to massage.

"Now, that's a man's bet," French said in her deepest voice.

Hurst slapped French on the shoulder, jolting her. "You're okay, French. One of us won't sleep too well one of these nights!"

"Or both of us won't," French replied, almost wistfully. Then French's face hardened. "You've won every battle, Hurst. But now I'm ending this war! Here's the contest…"

"One game of chess, winner take all," French said. "Turkle courthouse, witnesses and papers present; as soon as I arrange it, I'll send word." French flipped a coin and let it rattle to a stop on the table.

"Tails, I win!" Hurst exclaimed. "Looks like I got the whites on my side. That'll be a switch."

"You'll need any advantage you can get," French replied.

Hurst smirked and took a swig. He had French beat!

"What's so funny?" French asked, suspicious.

"When I was younger, I passed the time aboard ships playing chess. Hell, by the time we docked in New Orleans I'd won enough English gold to buy a horse!"

"Shipboard games mean nothing. I've learned from the best."

Antoinette had told Hurst about the Frenches' chess games. "You have a habit of winning, do you?" he asked slyly. "I hear through the grapevine that you've never beaten your mother, not once."

When he saw French's reaction to this remark, Hurst broke into conceited laughter. He'd done everything wrong, gotten himself overstretched in the cotton market, signed papers and made promises he'd never be able to keep. But if he won this one game he'd own so much property he'd be able to recoup everything, pay everyone off, and be scot-free.

If his partners still wanted to go North, he'd give them their share of whatever money he could dig up and buy them tickets on a riverboat. If they needed it, he might even hire a white man to play master to complete the charade.

If they returned after the war, they'd still be his partners, whether the South won or lost. He'd have his cake and eat it, too. And so would they. A dream finish to all their troubles.

His swagger was a mistake. French pulled a pistol from her pocket and placed the barrel between Hurst's eyebrows. He could feel its cold muzzle. "You've played your last trick on me," French said roughly. "Down on your knees, dog."

Seeing Hurst's predicament, his partners hesitated, then approached haltingly, knowing they were powerless, but not entirely unwilling to protect him. A line of riffraff muskets aimed at their hearts stopped them in their tracks. Their faces questioned each other, but none of them was willing to be shot dead to no purpose.

"On your knees, dog," French repeated.

Hurst refused to move, calling what he could only hope was a bluff. "French," he said, "everyone in Turkle knows you've never killed a living thing—and you ain't gonna start with me."

French cocked the hammer, her face tight, grim. Hurst stared at her defiantly. He couldn't show the slightest fear or that would encourage French to fire. And he didn't want French to have the satisfaction of seeing him afraid in his last moment.

They looked directly into each other's eyes, like children in a no-blinking contest. French's eyes reflected a mind going through somersaults so wild and uncontrolled that his hand began to shake. As clumsy-fingered as was French, a coward who had never manipulated anything but a pen, Hurst feared the slightest tremor might cause French to unintentionally blow out his brains.

But French's face changed. Laughing, French lowered the pistol, clicking the hammer down. Without a word, she jammed the pistol into her pocket and mounted the white.

"I don't have to shoot you."

Hurst was furious at himself. He'd bragged at the wrong time, a misstep he'd made before. Now he didn't know if French would be a man of his word, which would give Hurst his only chance, or if the aristocrat would play foul. He'd seen that "condemned loser" look in men's eyes before. No telling what a man will do to avoid certain defeat, especially with everything at stake. He'd scared the bird into flight right before he was about to spring the trap. Damn, would he ever learn to keep his mouth shut!

***

From atop the white, French saw, through her haze of envy and fear, Hurst's slaves walking toward him, sympathetic, apparently congratulating or consoling him in a way that none of French's business acquaintances or chattels ever had. French didn't like the friendly look of it.

Anxious to take the warmth out of what she was seeing, if only momentarily, she decided to play a trick on him. "Hurst," French shouted, "I'll send some men in the morning to haul your slaves out to my place. You sure drove a hard bargain for these worthless creatures."

Violently, a body slammed into Hurst's back, crashing him to the ground face first, making him eat dirt. Before he could recover his breath, he felt steel fingers on his throat, cutting off his windpipe. He gasped, but couldn't gain air.

"Trash!" he heard Isaac shout, his hands squeezing Hurst's throat. Hurst sensed running and shouts from all directions. He closed his eyes, gasping and choking, pulling vainly on the fingers gripping his neck. He felt he was going to pass out. Then he felt others tugging and grasping at Isaac, which only increased the pain. At last, Isaac's fingers were gone, and Hurst was gulping air and spitting out soil. Four hands pulled him to his feet. When at last he was able to straighten up, the sight greeting him was jarring.

Writhing in the arms of Big Josh and Bammer, Isaac was vainly attempting to escape, his eyes wild with fear. Surrounding Isaac, jabbing rifles into his body and face, were French's riffraff. Hurst tried to shove their rifles away from Isaac, but to no effect. These men, terrified and angered,

THE LIES THAT BIND

were going to keep Isaac in line. Would Hurst revenge himself upon his potential killer, as he should?

Isaac looked imploringly toward Hurst, while struggling in vain to break the hands holding him in place.

"My fault, gentlemen," Hurst said smoothly, feigning a casual laugh. "I done hit poor crazy Isaac on the head way too hard, way too many times."

But French's riffraff were having none of it. "He tried to kill a white man," one said. "We got to hang him or won't nobody be safe."

"Hang him or shoot him down, rat now."

"You're right, gentlemen," Durk replied, strutting around like a carnival showman, drawing their attention away from Isaac. He turned to Big Josh and Bammer, meeting their eyes. "All right," Durk ordered, "y'all take this mad dog home. I ain't gonna show him no white man's Christian mercy neither. He'll learn his lesson right."

Durk turned to the riffraff. "You boys don't want to see this," he warned them. "It's gonna be something terrible shouldn't no white man ever have to witness."

Durk's partners mumbled assent and dragged Isaac away, their hands clamped onto him like vices.

"Y'all ain't never gonna be lucky enough to get sold away from my wrath," Durk shouted after them. "French was just pulling your leg, making you think you're finally safe from me. But you ain't never gonna be safe from me."

***

French sat the horse, amused at what she had just seen, feeling better about her decision not to kill Hurst and Antoinette, at least not yet. *Why,* she thought, *he's just a man, vulnerable and weak, and I'm about to beat him.* She watched her group mount their horses.

"Good-bye, Mister Dark Horse," she said, slapping the stallion's flank. She and her entourage rode away.

***

Looking after French, Durk's heart sank as he realized he had over-talked away his last chance, that he'd condemned himself to his greatest fears. He only wondered what French's self-assured remark about not having to shoot him meant.

***

French reached the three-pronged fork in the road and drew rein. Deep in thought, she ordered her riffraff to return to *French Acres* without her. As she watched them go, the questions arose. Should she play the chess game she'd contracted with Hurst? She felt she could win, but victory wasn't certain. All the years of consecutive losses to her mother began to sting her nerves like poison. She was afraid to go through with it.

Her new plan seemed promising, almost a certainty. She didn't know why she hadn't thought of it before. Perhaps the war had made it possible now, or perhaps she'd never been trapped against the wall before. Or, more likely, she didn't realize until now how much she really wanted to eliminate Hurst.

Mister Dark Horse, Antoinette, she didn't care if the pair of them died together.

Chapter Twenty-six

The paunchy, slope-shouldered reverend set down his pen with a weary sigh and drooped back in his chair. In the hours he had worked, the lantern had burned low and needed refilling, which would further break his concentration.

For the tenth time that night he picked up the envelope and pulled out the money to reassure himself it was still there, to bolster his courage for the task ahead. He turned the envelope over and absently examined the French family crest emblazoned upon it. He hadn't realized that Mister French thought so well of him!

All this desperately needed money merely to preach one sermon. He had preached so many over his adulthood, fifty-two a year, and finally— finally!—enough recompense for a brief respite from his poverty. He replaced the cash, and felt the envelope's heft, balancing it in his hand as if on a scale. He told himself, not quite convincingly, that he would be speaking only what the town had long suspected about the stranger.

He looked about the dark, almost closet-sized, windowless room where he and his wife had moved his desk—his sanctum, she called it—and despaired. He felt a worthy clergyman should work in a bright, airy, light-filled room laden with bookcases full of leather-bound volumes. *He*, on the other hand, had a tiny second bedroom designed for the child he and his wife never had, in the little house behind the church built by its parishioners. Rather than elaborate bookcases, *he* had a worn trunk full of yellowed, meaningless papers: a lifetime of garbled platitudes. End of his life. End of his line. End of his ancestors' obscure and unremarkable name. He didn't even blame God anymore.

Yes, but this sermon would be the Great Mover of men and events for which he would be remembered. He would stir the hearts of his placid, weary congregation as never before. His voice would be a prophet-like force that would inspire a never-to-be-forgotten upheaval, a turning point in the town's saga, yea, and make him a legend all the way to the county seat!

He stopped scribbling. It was wrong, what he was being paid to preach tomorrow (even if the money did come from Mister French). Or was it? He never could decide. That was a problem he'd always had with moral things and with the taking of actions. He could never figure out the right thing to think, the right thing to do or to advise others to do.

He was troubled by the certain knowledge that his words would divide the community. Lives might be destroyed, men and women might meet their Maker, Turkle might be changed forever. But now was his time, his one chance to do something that had some effect. For tomorrow's sermon would, indeed, embrace a subject of consequence. He'd waited his whole life for this opportunity.

***

It was a fresh Sunday morning. The sun rose through the towering white oak and cedar encircling the mansion. The whippoorwills were active and vociferous, and the squirrels and rabbits of the bordering woodlands were nosing about the gardens, a premium source of tasty tender roots and shoots.

The rumor through the local slave grapevine was that the town was coming after them, to bring down the edifice of *DarkHorse*. The whispers had become deafening.

Durksen Hurst stood in the mansion door, the only man to sleep in the house through the night. His partners had thought it wise to take their belongings to the old lean-tos on the west side of the site and stay there with their women—just in case. They didn't want to get caught in the house.

Their frantic preparations to escape, and their growing sense of terror, stirred Hurst's drifter instincts to run. He tried to force himself to silence the ringing cacophony of fear in his head that had so often warned him, so often saved him.

Is this where it ends? They're terrified of being made slaves again if we're captured. They're afraid I won't be able to get them safely North; afraid, too, deep down, that I might panic and abandon them in the middle of nowhere without a white man to front for them, leaving them to their fate with manumission papers, the manumit, that might not be honored without a white man to back them.

He stretched his sore body, deeply breathing in the crisp air, feeling the sun's presence lift the night's chill. "Here he is, The Legend, stepping onto his broad verandah," he mused with melodramatic irony.

He slapped his hand against the unplanned door support. *Solid,* he noted, bitterly amused. He reached into the hallway and pulled his waistcoat off the wooden stake one of his partners had driven into the mud chinking to serve as a coat rack.

Yes, it was a good, two-story home. And having to leave it would hurt.

He forced his mind to consider what had to be done in the coming days, feeling a catch in his throat. Ride tomorrow to the river landing to buy steamboat tickets—how far North could they get on the money they had?

Did they have any chance? The whole world was on fire now, with war beginning to churn up the green land like some gigantic wheel of death and destruction. And they were trapped in that world of lost mercy, a world being consumed by the lust for killing. Win or lose, in his heart he knew this would probably be the last morning he awoke in his—*their*—mansion. In fact, it might be the last morning he awoke, period.

He cast about for an escape plan. His gut told him to simply disappear, alone, unencumbered by a large group of black folks. His was the only life endangered. But he'd promised to get his partners—his *friends*—to safety, and he owed them that.

He tried to dream up some ruse to change the odds, but he couldn't concentrate. Another thought overpowered everything: Antoinette.

He remembered with tenderness and a bursting heart the first time he'd seen her, a woman with such terrible secrets. Frightened and out of her element, hiding near a backwater town, like a trembling doe pursued by wolves. He remembered her dark eyes, her face lovely as if made of stars.

Now, French's riffraff stood between them. "Maybe I'll just ride over there, unarmed. If they shoot me down, at least she'll know I came for her."

He pictured himself curled up on the ground beside his horse, gut-shot, unconscious, peacefully bleeding to death. *At least I won't die a broke drifter.* The prospect seemed soothing after so many sleepless nights.

But the others depended on him. *Stand and save the plantation...lead his friends to safety...rescue the woman...save himself, his only chance.* An impossible conundrum.

He glanced absently over his shoulder, reassuring himself that the surrounding woods hadn't slithered away in the night. *To escape into them from a mansion seems a contravention of nature*, he mused. *Unlike an escape from a dirt-floor cabin...*

***

Hurst turned toward the entrance to the mansion grounds, a huge stone arch that fronted the dirt road from town. He had built the oversized gateway to match his dreams, to make any visitor, welcome or not, immediately aware that, upon entering *DarkHorse*, one was approaching the largest edifice anyone in these parts had ever seen or heard tell of.

He contemplated the rudely carved, black horse gently swaying in the morning breeze below its apex: the symbol of his—*their*—*DarkHorse*. Long Lou, who had a way with wood, had carved it.

Yes, the plantation belonged to all of them equally. And the sign was everyone's, too. But he always thought of that one possession as particularly his own, since his partners had given it to him as a gift.

They can despoil my corpse if they catch me—I'll have no say in that. But I'll be damned if some loudmouth braggart is going to hang my sign on his wall as an artifact of DarkHorse's downfall. I'll burn it myself first. He grimaced, clenching his jaw, then forced his thoughts away from the awful possibilities.

With fondness, he remembered the overcast day they'd all gathered to hang it. Isaac had pointed out the two hooks fastened from the arch, and then produced the wooden black horse, a surprise that touched him every time it came to mind. But no one had remembered the ladder and they'd all had a big laugh about that.

When that oversight was resolved, the whole group had given him the honor of climbing up and hanging it. He argued that Big Josh should have the honor—*Big Josh, who, though he is my own age, though his skin is dark, is the father I wish I could have had.* But Durk's partners wouldn't be talked out of letting him do it. It was the first honor he'd ever been given, the first time he'd meant something to someone.

He'd climbed the ladder, awkwardly, unsteadily in his boots. Meanwhile, below, everyone shouted jests at his lack of dexterity.

"You better steady that ladder, or you'll have to get you another crazy white man to play-act master," he'd shouted playfully down at them.

Looking back, he wondered if that was when he began to see his dark-skinned fellow conspirators as fully human beings? Was that when he realized these men had become his family, rather than merely his latest string of accomplices? When he'd felt for the first time he wasn't completely alone? From a lifetime of suspicion, he knew the honor was artificial, merely a ceremony. But that day he found he didn't want to stay apart anymore. With heart bursting, he found himself wanting to fall into the arms of their constancy. Then the skies had opened up, drenching them all.

How to get it down? With no ladder, he took hold of a protruding brick overhead and tried to climb up, but his foot slipped and he came crashing down, landing on his ribs. He fought to catch his breath.

He heard a laugh. A few feet away, Isaac leaned against a giant oak, arms crossed, wearing his Sunday suit, his broad teeth showing bright in his shining black face.

"I'm pleased you think it's funny," Hurst said. "You could'a helped me 'stead of standing there laughing like a jackass."

Isaac pushed off the tree and approached leisurely. "Can't do nothing without dark folks, can you?"

Hurst sat up, ministering to his scraped palms. "Just help me up, dammit."

"We all gonna need that, Durk," Isaac said, no longer smiling. Isaac extended a hand and pulled Durk to his feet. Their hands remained clasped as they stood looking into each other's eyes, memories and understandings passing silently between them. Then he dropped Hurst's hand. "Give me a hand up."

Hurst bent over, cupping his fingers for Isaac's foot. Isaac placed a hand on Hurst's shoulder to steady himself, then allowed Hurst to boost him until he reached a break in the chinking and worked himself up, climbing toward the black sign.

Hurst watched him, his heart heavy with seeing Isaac wearing his suit so close to escape day. Suit or no suit, Isaac still looked like the same frighten-eyed man he'd seen in the swamp when they'd all first met. Their partners were leaving their suits behind on the chance that, if they were captured, they might evade the noose because they could be sold as slaves. Fieldwork, something they knew, was certainly better than death. But Isaac choosing to leave behind his work clothes meant he did not plan to be taken alive. Isaac had decided he would not, could not, ever be a slave again.

Isaac stabilized himself near the top of the arch, then worked the wooden horse loose from its hooks and let it drop, before climbing down.

They walked down to the lean-tos, where breakfast was cooking over open fires. "What you gonna do with the sign?" Isaac asked.

"Firewood," Hurst muttered, his throat tight.

"Firewood," Isaac said sarcastically, unable to hide his sadness. "Only thing you was ever good for."

* * *

She stepped onto the verandah and steadied herself, failing to rein in her fury. Like a criminal, she had loaded her weapon late in the night. And in town, the preacher, having accepted the money, was preparing to pull the trigger from the pulpit.

As French crossed the threshold, the bright sunshine blinded her. She stopped to breathe deeply, and noted the same surge of euphoria she felt each time she stepped outside, regardless of the season or time of day, on winter nights or in rain. She often wondered why she was so reluctant to leave the house. Yet, except for unavoidable excursions on business and her regular Sunday churchgoing, she seldom left the mansion. And she invariably returned as quickly as possible, hurrying through her external duties like a person possessed. A thought struck: *Am I becoming a recluse like Mother?* Then, a more terrible thought weakened her knees: *Am I becoming Mother!*

Tears caught in her throat, and she covered her mouth. *Never to see Hurst again? Never to…*

***

She sent for her driver, who brought up the phaeton alongside four guards who would ride beside her. She would not, could not, ride the white stallion today.

On the road, she closed her eyes against the glare. The pain was flaring up, beginning in her eye and already spreading to her temple and forehead. French slumped back into her seat, holding a handkerchief to her throbbing eye, from which salty water was pouring down one cheek. She struggled against throwing up. A headache was coming on, but she couldn't give in to it today. Headache or no, she had to make it to church.

In town, the thick sun embraced the wood-frame church, revealing all too clearly the winter-neglected whitewash peeling from its walls. The young men who maintained it in spring were busy at war, and nobody knew when they would return bearing laurels and honors; only that it would be by Christmas, hopefully sooner.

The phaeton worked its way through the tied rigs to the church door, which was thrown open to let in the air. From her seat, French could see the mass of heads inside. She had expected a crowd, but not like this. She was especially pleased to see that her invitation to the army training camp had been honored. Hell, they might be soldiers, but it was Sunday, too, wasn't it? They certainly may be useful…

***

Pausing a moment to admire the crowd, the rotund Reverend Cain subtly squeezed his jacket pocket to reassure himself that the bank envelope containing all that balm in Gilead, that long-prayed-for recompense, was indeed his. Gaining confidence from the money's heft, a half-smile raised one corner of his lip. He licked his stubby fingers and opened the large, leather-bound Bible before him. Then with decorous gravity, he lowered his massive head toward its pages, a signal for the churchgoers to be still.

Finally sensing they were ready, Cain lifted his head and proceeded, his booming voice resonant, urgent.

"I must apologize to the womenfolk in the congregation for the nature of today's sermon. I shall be as discreet as possible. But there are those who think that the devil has deceived this town, and the time for reckoning is long past."

An excited murmur spread through the packed pews in anticipation. The church's time-worn clapboard walls seemed to vibrate like a violated beehive. Rumors were the rural hamlet's lifeblood, and lately they were thick and hot as the sweltering air.

Eyes were everywhere—suspicious, vengeful, frightened. Brows were raised, heads nodded knowingly. Furtive glances ventured forth, then hid beneath bright bonnets. It was like First Mortals summoned to Olympus for a contest fatal and foreordained, and nobody wanted to miss it.

"My friends, my flock, perhaps the men of Turkle have kept Durk Hurst's depredations too well from our gentlewomen. But today, as a community, we must prick the postulant abomination of that man called "Dark Horse". We must expiate that demon and his cursed dark minions from our town to save Turkle from degeneration and damnation.

"Dark Horse," the preacher continued, "the sound rumbles from deep in the stomach and spits from the mouth like a curse! The very name speaks of a man unregenerate and irredeemable.

"Who is this Durksen Hurst, I ask you? Who or what was he running from that drove him to this peaceful country?

"He just appeared one night in Turkle, riding into the town square, a fugitive down to the last gold piece he kept pinned to his pocket. And next thing we knew, he owned the largest plantation in Miss'ippi, with a mansion bigger than the great French place—hell, bigger than the county seat courthouse!

"My friends, my flock, there's something strange going on out there between Hurst and his…those strange…whatever you might call them."

***

Her driver placed the stool on the ground, and she climbed down onto the solid earth, making her way to the church. Each step jostled her head, radiating pain from her temples to her eye and forehead. When she reached the church threshold, French threw her voice over her shoulder to the armed riffraff who'd accompanied her. "Cover all the doors!"

She disappeared into the church, and one of her riffraff turned knowingly to his companion. "The Devil owns the preacher in Turkle."

Eyes wide, the companion gestured as if shooting a pistol. "I hope Dark Horse don't pick today to start attendin' church."

"I don't need this job that bad," the first added. "Ain't no Dark Horse pistol-shootin' none of my business."

Overhearing, the third member of the band pulled his horse away from the pair. "I ain't staying here by myself. Y'all better let me know'd if'n you see'd him."

"Pistol-shootin' don't mean nothing now," said an old grouch, sitting nearby. "The preacher gone get the womenfolk stirred up against him."

Inside, the preacher paused as every head turned to the commotion at the door. Devereau French, every eye on her, walked up the crowded aisle, handkerchief to her forehead. She reached the empty French pew dead front center in the packed house and sat.

The preacher recovered his bearing, preparing for the grand finale of his sermon. He had the congregation worked up good, and he was poised to strike them in the heart.

"Now, with our young men willing to risk shot and shell, sleet and snow, to save our institutions and our land from those Eastern abolitionists; with our brave boys leaving their wives and sweethearts behind, that Unnatural Fiend, that Dark Horse, is left behind to prey on the innocent, the unwary…"

The people recognized his tone, anticipating the exciting conclusion to his furious exhortations.

"We know he's a traitor. He tried to get our brave soldiers, out marching on that road, not to fight. And that isn't the only time he's talked against this war. I don't need to tell you what they do with traitors.

"We know he's an abolitionist who wants to turn our way of life topsy-turvy. His every action tells you that. The way he talks to those devils, and the way they talk back at him. There's just something unnatural about it.

"That Lucifer, lurking in that Satan's palace he and his demons tore violently from that captive virgin bottomland and thrust down on the gentle earth, has seen his chance.

"He has repeatedly violated our sweet womenfolk with fornication and other depraved acts too gruesome to mention!"

Angry shouts echoed from the congregation. A young farm girl burst into tears. Her mother placed an arm around her shoulders, handing her a handkerchief. Women covered their mouths in a highly agitated state. Others took note of who seemed to be most affected by this issue for later analysis and extrapolation.

"He a sinner!" a man shouted.

"He the Devil!" a woman warned.

Satisfied the plan was going well, her head in agony, French rose and, nodding toward the preacher, tiptoed through the people sitting on the floor beneath the pulpit and out the side vestibule. Once outside, she circled the church and made her way back to the phaeton, to begin the long, jarring ride home.

By the time French's carriage was well on the road, the preacher was concluding the most successful sermon of his life. He'd done it. He'd actually moved his congregation. He signaled the matron at the organ to begin playing, and a solemn hymn began ringing throughout the church. To its heavenly tones, townsmen and an unusually preponderant proportion of townswomen and farm girls were leaving their pews, heading to the altar for their Sunday blessing. Many of these women were in tears, whether tears of sorrow, sympathy, or merely emotional release only they knew. Yes, today he had delivered a real church sermon. His place in town history was assured.

"Come, wash your sins in the tears of this pulpit! We're all guilty before the eyes of the Lord. That's right, ladies. The Lord, in his infinite mercy, will forgive our transgressions, great and small."

In the back, a freckled, rawboned farm girl of fourteen in pigtails and ribbons slipped from her pew and strutted toward the pulpit. All awkward elbows and knees, even her exaggerated hip-swinging came across as merely a herky-jerky disability, not an alluring prance.

"Now, don't act so proud, Lulabelle," the preacher said. "Folks know you just bragging."

But she was not to be denied, regardless of the facts. "Who says I ain't sinned more than Sarah Thompkins? You ask that Mister Dark Horse. He'll tell you 'bout Lulabelle Tarbid."

"A child!" a woman yelled from her seat.

"He's defiled a child!" another shouted, and the church burst into an uproar.

Lulabelle glanced out of the corner of her eye as she passed the pew occupied by Sarah Thompkins' family. As in a tableaux, she could see Sarah was trying to climb over her brother's legs, while the ornery boy was lifting his feet to raise her skirt. Sarah was intending to march to the pulpit, too.

"You liar, Lulabelle!" Sarah shouted, defending a dream she'd cherished for over three months. "He loves me, not you."

Why, Lulabelle Tarbid thought, pushing her way forward, *I was a-sinning before Sarah Thompkins even know'd what sinning was. Or at least I knowed what a-sinning was before Sarah Thompkins done knowed hit. And while Sarah Thompkins may have kissed a boy first, it was that scrawny boy with the crooked teeth from up yonder over to the mill. Whereas I done kissed a older boy first, and that's what counts in the world.*

'Sides, nobody could prove I didn't kiss that Mister Dark Horse right on his lips, especially that Sarah Thompkins can't prove it! And that's really all that matters.

"And who, dear friends, will protect the children?" the preacher bellowed.

"I ain't no liar," Lulabelle Tarbid yelled. "Me and that Mister Dark Horse done sinned more than once't!"

Chapter Twenty-seven

The slave grapevine was not often wrong about these matters. And it wasn't wrong now.

The chilly night was falling fast, and they could smell a hard rain waiting to burst. A violent nighttime storm would make their flight treacherous, cold and muddy. But maybe it would supply cover, even discourage halfhearted pursuers. And that might make the difference between capture and escape.

Big Josh sat back, his large fingers toying with a gold coin from his share of *DarkHorse*. His dark eyes roamed about the cavernous, unfinished study. The huge stone fireplace dwarfed the flames; clearly a typically modest Durk Hurst fire. There was enough wood stacked to last for days—and they planned to leave within hours—plus the man owned a forest, but Hurst had built the same fire he'd built on the first day they'd met. He surmised the humble flames were a runaway's concealment from discovery, or a poor man's adaptation to scarcity.

The partners sat around the large table, going over possible escape plans point by point, considering every contingency, but Hurst was preoccupied, only half-listening.

He would soon mount the roan and head for the courthouse in hopes of playing his chess game against French. He would go alone. What other choice did he have?

After hearing the reports coming through the grapevine, none of Hurst's partners believed this contest would even occur, much less save *DarkHorse*. They believed instead it was some kind of French treachery. Hurst knew in his heart that the game was rigged, but with everything he owned on the table, he had to play his hand to the last card. At best, the sheriff would be there to jail him and, so, save him from assassination. At worst?

They only had a thread of an escape plan. The journey would be long and hazardous, a large group of black men and women with one white man—if he was still alive and free—passing through the countryside, towns, and the Confederate army lines to the free states. Their unknowns far outweighed their hope. Nevertheless, to delay the inevitable despair, they continued the charade that they could control their fate, that they could make it North.

Everyone froze. They heard someone run up the steps. Big Josh turned toward the door. "Th-there Long Lou."

Long Lou rushed in, then stopped and bent over to catch his breath.

"The women hid s-safe up in the hollow with B-bammer?" Big Josh asked.

"Yes, sir, but the whole town and the army, too, coming up the road! I had to come the back way."

"The whole t-town?" Big Josh exclaimed. Everyone rushed to the window.

"I see torches—a whole mess of them," Isaac shouted. "And they got guns."

"Let's get to the holler," Long Lou shouted.

Everyone panicked, talking at once, and headed for the door, but Hurst blocked it. "Wait!" he shouted over the din of excited voices. "Y'all promised to help me."

"It's too late, Durk," Big Josh said, easing him aside.

"I'll explain to them," Hurst objected, frantic.

"He gonna try to outsmart them," Isaac snorted downheartedly.

"Durk," Little Turby pleaded, "those folks coming to kill you."

"They don't mean it," Hurst said, denying the obvious.

"Forget him! He done lost his mind. He can't let go," Isaac said.

"Get to the h-holler," Big Josh ordered, and everyone poured through the door. Before following them, Big Josh paused. "If you ain't up th-there, what can we do?" Then he, too, was gone.

Durksen Hurst prepared himself to face his sternest test.

***

A mob in the night is an ugly thing.

Hands shaking, watching from his study balcony, Durksen Hurst felt it coming—violent death. Livid, vicious, lit eerily by shadows and torches, it swept up the road in an undulating mass, like a flame-flecked, wan-speckled sea serpent emerging from dark waters. The snake slithered from the road onto the drive, rippling, transforming itself from flowing body into distinct, hatred-contorted faces. Its low, indistinct rumble became angry shouts and random shots. Soon they were close enough for him to make out individual faces, many of which he recognized from his forays into town, from his landowner contacts with them, or from negotiations with them on their developing plots of *DarkHorse* land. These last, the white *DarkHorse* 'croppers, would lose everything when he was gone.

He wanted to run; a rational choice. But he couldn't make himself do it, couldn't even look away. Fighting terror and reason simultaneously, he steeled himself to overcome by will what he told himself was merely temporary madness, preparing himself like a man confronting a child's tantrum. The angry voices crashed into the thick, humid air, shattering the lazy night into frantic, jagged pieces.

Still Durk stood his ground, now focusing on the rifles and stars-and-bars flags waving threateningly aloft. No matter what anyone thought, if he could make them understand and win them over, he believed his empire would be preserved for his return from the North. He hoped his plea would work better than the time he tried to stop the troops from marching off.

Someone in the crowd shouted, and the tide's vanguard came to a stop. Like a flood crest clashing upon a dam, a trailing wave splashed and spread throughout the front yard, trampling down the garden. Another man pointed at Hurst in the window. Others followed suit, until Hurst saw every face uplifted toward him. He held up his hand to silence them.

"Listen, men," he shouted, using his best voice, "just let me explain."

"He's a coward! Traitor! Fornicator!" the virulent mob shouted. "Why ain't you off fighting, Dark Horse? Dark Horse, you traitor!"

"But folks, listen!" Durk said. "If you do this, French is going to take all your parcels of *DarkHorse*! You'll be landless again!"

A rock flew past his ear, shattering the window behind. Other projectiles came at him; one hit his forehead. He reached up to touch the stinging pain, and his hand came away with blood. The mob howled.

"Hang him! Burn it down! Burn in hell, Dark Horse," they shouted.

They weren't going to listen to reason. Ducking from flying rocks and bullets, Hurst ran frantically into his study. Casting about, he picked up his leather sack, which held his favorite books and clothes. Then he turned, his mind spinning.

He was a boy, hanging onto the horse's mane for dear life as it spooked away. A shot whizzed near his head.

Sitting on the ledge he saw his father run from their shack, his body in flames.

He smelled burning and threw down the bag, already running. Into the hall. The smoke seemed to follow him.

He saw the townsmen surround his father's burning body, poking it with their muskets. Was his death to be so ignominious? He saw his own body dragged out on display, kicked and spit on by every hothead in the mob—an unbearable vision. He must survive!

He ran toward the back steps that led to the kitchen. His only advantage: they wouldn't know if he was armed, and that would make them hesitate.

He took the steps four at a time, as a thick cloud of smoke emanated from his study. Reaching the landing, he dashed into the kitchen. Smoke was pouring in from the dining room. He covered his mouth and nose with his sleeve and ran toward the kitchen window, ducking to not be seen. He could hear voices and shouts coming from outside the dining room, but none yet from the back. He hesitated, then raced toward the window and leapt through it, falling to earth as glass crashed around him. His arm hurt, and, trying to scramble to his feet, he grew momentarily dizzy, discovering his injured wrist couldn't support him. It gave out, and he fell forward. Using his other hand, he worked his way to his feet. He could hear the mob coming around the house, surrounding it like rising flood waters.

He tried to run, limping, hindered by a shooting pain in his ankle. He cut through the back patch, taking the shortest route to the woods. Stumbling over a bush and falling, hitting the ground hard, he tore his pants at the knee. Catching his breath, he sensed the leading figures in the noisy mob had reached the kitchen. He rose, pushing himself forward with his good hand, dragging his leg, running as best he could. Almost to the safety of the woods, he glanced back and saw someone standing on top of the kitchen stairs pointing after him. Afraid he would be shot, he plunged though a clump of bushes and rolled to his feet, bumping his injured ankle painfully against a boulder.

He turned back, squeezing between two oaks to see how close his pursuers were. No one was chasing him, at least not yet, but they had already torched the back of the mansion, needlessly pouring more vindictiveness onto the doomed home. Smoke and flames engulfed the house, pouring from its windows and raging on its roof. Durk took one last look.

Inside the mansion, the books on the study floor caught fire, their pages crinkling black as flames overwhelmed them. The great *DarkHorse* edifice was consumed by a wholly immodest fire, very unlike those Durksen Hurst had so often built on that very same land.

He crashed through the woods, struggling, until he reached the river crossing. He plunged in, wading through waist-deep water, fighting against the river's current. His foot slipped and he nearly fell face first into its rushing waters, but he caught himself, soaking his coat sleeves. He was tired and the river wanted to drag him down, to carry him away, but he fought on. Once across, he threw himself down on the bank and rolled onto his back, gasping for air.

Isaac watched from the shadows, holding the reins of the pair of horses. When he was sure no one was in pursuit, he broke clear of the concealing bushes.

The sound attracted Hurst. He rolled over painfully, cringing at the figure, until he recognized Isaac. Relieved, he exhaled, sighing.

Isaac pulled Hurst to his feet. Hurst smiled, realizing that Isaac had figured out the only escape route Hurst could use—if he did indeed escape—and had ridden there to wait. By the time Hurst reached this conclusion, he also knew the route by which Isaac planned to reach the hollow. But he wasn't going there, not yet. And there was little certainty he would ever make it there.

Hurst bent at the waist, hands on his knees, catching his breath. "It's gone, Isaac. They burned it down," he sputtered in a tortured voice. Isaac already had seen the sky alight.

Hurst straightened up and looked Isaac in the eye, heartsick. Memories of all the words of caution and doubt that Isaac had expressed since *DarkHorse* was created came hard upon him. Yes, Hurst had lost everything, had squandered their chance—if they ever truly had one. *DarkHorse* was gone, and they were flung into a world of chaos and strife. He wanted to apologize, to give some hope to Isaac. But what to say?

"I guess I better change my methods," Hurst said.

"You can change your methods, Durk, but don't never change your madness."

"*DarkHorse* still lives," Durk said, gripping Isaac's hand, thinking, *Now comes the deadly part.*

***

The black skies burst. The wind howled, blowing sheets of rain into their faces, as if they were riding into a solid sea. They reached the turnoff trail leading to the hollow. *If only the downpour would slow enough to let me breathe.* It felt thick enough to drown them. He slanted his hat to ward off the downpour, but nothing helped. Lightning exploded across the sky, illuminating the tangle of trees, vines, and creepers around them, as though they were lost in a nightmare world without end.

Durk turned the roan onto the road that led west. He knew he was making a foolhardy choice, maybe even a suicidal one. *Let death come now, the death of a hero. No man on earth can outwit his final fall. It'd be better than living with this hole in my heart.*

Seeing the direction Hurst was headed, Isaac hesitated, not willing to follow. "Where you going?" Isaac shouted through the maelstrom. "The holler's up that a-way."

"French's. To get her."

"Are you crazy! French's riffraff got orders to shoot you on sight." Isaac looked across at Hurst and saw something in Hurst's eyes he'd never seen before. He dug his heels into the horse's side to catch Durk.

"There are things worth dying for, Isaac," Hurst said, speeding up.

"Now I know you lost your mind."

Isaac drew rein. What should he do? Follow this madman to certain death? Or make it to temporary shelter at the hollow? Even if he made the hollow, could the rest of them make their trip North without a white man? Not likely.

"Durk! Durk!" Isaac shouted after him, trying to catch up. *Damn him. Why do he pick now to get brave!*

Section IV

The Padlocked Honor Store

Chapter Twenty-eight

The devil coming for his 'n, tha's for sho'. Storm and lightning and who don't know what all.

The other servants huddled around the kitchen stove, shivering with fear. They made so much racket that she sent them to their cabins to have some quiet. It was finished now. She could keep the pots hot, and dish up soup and coffee to Missus French's riffraff more easily without them underfoot. They didn't have to be told twice. They covered their heads against the elements and cleared out through the back door. She shouted a warning after them, then returned to her chair. Nobody with any sense, di'nt have to, was going to be hanging 'round no French mansion that night.

Finally alone in the near darkness, she threw a stick into the main stove and pulled her chair closer to warm herself, waiting on old reliable Fredric to come downstairs. She covered her aching knees with her blanket and rocked, humming to herself, waiting.

Riffraff everywhere! They be doing that old plan of Missus French's they sometimes play-act at, standing around idle all day with they muskets, while she keep up hot soup and coffee, every stove covered with steaming pots. Now she got to keep the hot liquids going all night.

It was terrible. Right now, Mister French is up in his bedroom screaming and crying like a wolf with its foot caught in a trap. And breaking things! That poor man done lost his mind over this DarkHorse business, that is for sure. Lord, what next?

Wait! Is that Fredric on the stairs? She listened intently, attempting to hear footsteps through the random sudden lightning cracks and the wild crescendo of thunder.

The bone-thin, white-haired old man entered. He had news. "Them up in the tower seen two riders coming up the road through that glass they puts to they eye. Can't be far off. One run down into the rain to tell the gate. Didn't want no French to hear."

"Now them riffraff all about the place know."

"And they scared, terrible scared."

"Um-hm," she said. This confirmed what she'd been saying all day. "He comin' for that woman." She filled a cup with soup and handed it to Fredric.

"You go watch upstair. Now go on."

She stirred the pots nearest her and sat down again to her vigil.

***

That morning Missus French had sent orders for every riffraff on the place to be dragged from his bed and rushed out to stand guard like chess pieces at their assigned places around *French Acres*. Missus French had designed this well-planned and -rehearsed scheme years before, calling it "contingencies and exigencies."

After she woke, Devereau French separately sent orders to do the same, only to find her mother had beaten her to it. When the rest of the plantation walked out to see the day, they found groups of grumbling riffraff, muskets in hand, strategically placed at the gates, key road junctions, barns, mansion doors, and even on a hill back of the house with a panoramic view. The least distrusted riffraff manned posts inside the big house, at critical points in the hallways upstairs and down.

The weakness in this perfect plan was the human element. The rain poured down on the ragged hirelings, lashing them with its fierce, bone-chilling wetness. The men huddled under tarps with their muskets, pistols, and knives, soaked and shivering, cursing their employer as swollen streams poured off their hats and ran down their necks. Their morale was low, but Missus French gave no consideration to the sensitivities of her chess pieces.

***

The interloper was vanquished, but in forging his demise her daughter had gone mad. Would Devereau run away again like she once had? Perhaps disappear forever this time? Would she expose her male charade? In this state, she was capable of any desperate act.

Would the other daughter desert her as well? The sole grandchild, Missus French's fondest hope, the little male blueblood, was buried. With *DarkHorse* annihilated, there was nothing left to bind Antoinette to *French Acres*. Truly nothing.

And *French Acres* itself? Her empire? A will-o'-the-wisp, dissipating like smoke. Its vast wealth sunk into slave flesh bound by the thinnest of threads, invested heedlessly over decades in unwilling bondsmen who were silently watching the horizon for a glimpse of invading blue hordes, ears alert for an inexorable, crescendoing cacophony of bugles, boots, hooves, caissons, and cannon. Waiting, eager to rejoice and, like her family, to forsake her.

Missus French slid the rook to the seventh rank and sat wearily back in her chair, closing her eyes. When she opened them again the chessboard was still there, its pieces still in the same position as before. She didn't know if she'd slept or not, but if she had, it didn't appear there'd been any chicanery against her. *So this is where the game led,* she thought. She had advantages—after all, a rook on the seventh rank can exercise untold power—but the endgame remained uncertain, problematic.

Was there any unforeseen, random move that would destroy the pattern she'd so carefully structured onto the resistant cauldron of conflict, a surprise blow that would wipe away everything she'd built? She studied the position.

It was hard for her to reflect on a chess game in a critically detached manner for any length of time. The game's beauty was far too distracting, too overwhelming, for her to remain focused on the simple act of winning. In the near-darkness, broken only by her single candle, the power vectors which surrounded each piece materialized before her eyes, becoming brilliant liquid light-streams. This is the way it came to her: as illuminated, ever-changing, ever-electric patterns that were beyond any other earthly beauty. Once she was able to fully concentrate on her game, undisturbed by sound or external light, she always began to see them forming, a metaphysical, almost blinding, pyrotechnical eruption.

In truth, she admitted, this is what she lived for, watching this celestial display. Yes, when she was young she believed her communion with men's bodies lit up the night as no other sensation could. In those days, there were men she desired, and she invariably captured their bodies as she wanted. So many men. She knew how to handle them, how to put them at ease, how to bring them under her control. And she had thrilled to the sparkles in her head created by the feel of their bodies beside hers. But as she grew older, playing chess proved far superior to all of that.

She discovered long ago that when she made love to a man, those bright sparks behind her closed eyelids were akin to twinkling points in the black firmament. Whereas the lights caused by the games of chess she played— after making love in the night, or waiting for her prey to arrive—were so much more luminous that they obscured entirely her physical passions. Yes, physical union could not compare to the thrill of playing this wondrous game.

In Turkle, for a few years after her husband was buried, she maintained her physical hobby with men. They would come secretly to her house, or under cover of darkness she went to theirs. She always preferred a clandestine liaison to any sort of open union, which enabled her to have a variety of discreet experiences. But there came a time when she realized these interludes merely interfered with her chess, and she decided to never again entertain a relationship of that sort. In keeping with her vow, she gave orders to her servants that she was no longer to be disturbed by her former lovers and went about setting up impregnable defenses against their entreaties. For a time, her former men friends continued to send urgent notes, often accompanied by lavish gifts, but she refused to acknowledge them—or to return their gifts. After a while, they learned not to bother and, reluctantly, turned their attention elsewhere. Then she noted with amusement that none were so pure of heart as to continue to romantically send flowers, much less gifts, until the day they died—as they'd so arduously promised. A false god, love, she deduced, laughing to herself.

The world? The world was nothing compared to these magnificent fountains of force shooting off inside her skull. All the money she had made? With men in that house in New Orleans? Here, in Turkle? All the land she'd acquired? All the opponents she'd defeated in business? All the power she'd acquired? The training of her daughter to run her empire? All enacted so she simply could sit here, undistracted; so that she could become immersed in, could become one with this ecstasy that was beyond any mortal ecstasy.

People? She knew she was the only one with the inner vision to see it, the only one sensitive enough to feel it, the only one intelligent enough to understand it. All the people she encountered—except the occasional chess opponent—were simply an irritant, a deafening noise in the universe that interfered with the quietude of her pleasure.

People, bah! She needed to play a flesh-and-blood human periodically to refresh her mind. It cost her fair sums to bring worthy opponents from far away to play, but that was her one vice, wasn't it? And wouldn't she recover her expense when she defeated them? In fact, her one great disappointment was that she hadn't attracted enough good players who could give her a challenging game. Still, the ultimate pleasure for her was to sit alone in this room, undisturbed by any human presence or sound, to witness the brilliant chess lights in their wild, dynamic action, to see them flying through the heavens, rising almost to infinity, streaking to the breathtaking height inches above the black and tan squares, day after day, night after night.

She sat admiring the electric red and white and gold and so-many-colored patterns shoot off, crisscrossing the eternity of her mind's eye into ever more fantastic ephemeral structures. She was able to see clearly all the possibilities. At first, the power vortex each piece exuded swayed this way and that from a windy draft of reality, altering imperceptibly the board's overall pattern. Then, as each piece exploded into its own lightning-like projection, she began almost mechanically to reshape the conflict. Using her brute will, she twisted, distorted, bent, molded, and, finally, like a great metalworker in the medium of red hot molten steel, fashioned all the power to her own ends. She was satisfied. None of the potential changes looked to be fatal to her.

No, no move appeared to be fatal. However, she could feel with her deepest inner sense that, unseen, under the totality of all this beauty, lurked a doom she'd prepared for herself from the beginning, a doom she'd been drawn toward like a moth to flame. She knew now she'd sought that doom that night when, as a thirteen-year-old girl with a full woman's body and a woman's eye, she'd left her mother's door for those big men with the callused hands and strong smells and tastes, never to return. She hungered after that doom in that house in the Quarter, seeking unnatural union with the lusting, sweating bodies of those drunken aristocrats. She'd grasped that doom when she married a French and moved to Turkle. She'd wrapped that doom ever so tightly in her fists when she murdered him. Then, with a steel-like embrace, she'd wrapped her arms around and pulled that doom down upon her body with all her might when she transformed her daughter into a defective son. And, finally, she'd sucked within her and merged completely with that doom when she opposed the stranger.

A final question arose, the thought of which made the lights flicker momentarily, letting the darkness creep in. Frantically, she willed the lights to reappear, and after what seemed hours of concentrated will, an eternity of single-minded desire, they did, flaring up brighter than the sun, as blinding as she'd ever seen them.

Yes, there was a question; there had always been a question. Had all the winning merely enabled her to doom herself? Or was the winning a trap—His trap—to keep her from that self-destruction she so passionately and hungrily hunted? Then she realized that, even if these questions were valid, no conceivable answer mattered.

All she could do was wait for His next move. Wait and fully experience with each desperate second left the Grand Show on the checkered board before her.

***

Antoinette approached from the shadows. Seeing her, the pair of guards standing outside Missus French's bedroom set down their coffee cups and held their muskets across their chests, blocking her.

"You don't want to go in there," the one with the pox-ravaged face stated.

"We got orders, Missy," the dumpy one said, grinning to reveal his missing tooth.

Reaching into her purse, she retrieved her pistol and stuck it in the first one's face, taking him by surprise.

"I have a personal invitation."

"Well, a-a personal invite," the man said, stepping aside.

She entered, pistol drawn. She located the figure silhouetted by the single candle and strode purposefully along the pathway between the piled objects.

The aging woman raised her head from the chessboard, as if awakened from a dream. Her eyes narrowed at Antoinette. "I told you never to come here. What do you want?" Missus French asked.

"Where's my boy, Louis Edward? He's dead, isn't he? Your servants say you buried a child."

So it was out of the bag. Missus French knew this accusation was merely a ploy; Antoinette couldn't know for certain. She'd assumed Antoinette would make inquiries. The servants would be afraid to talk, but Antoinette would deduce the truth from the way they avoided her questions.

"Where is he? And don't lie."

It must end here, Missus French concluded, *one way or another.* Antoinette's pistol would be the easy way out, a relief. "He's in the family plot," she blurted. "Under that large black headstone which attracts so much of your attention."

Antoinette had tried to deny this nagging likelihood for all these months, until she had absolute proof. She had believed Devereau French's lies because people believe what they need to believe. Now the awful realization that Louis Edward was indeed gone struck her a full blow. She gasped for air, her insides quaking. The room swirled, everything went blank, and she collapsed onto the floor, striking her head. The pistol clattered to the floor.

When she awoke on the dusty floor, her head was throbbing. She pressed her hand to the bruised spot, and pain shot through her. Coming slowly into consciousness, she remembered what Missus French had confirmed, and it all swept down upon her again.

For many moments she lay there, memories of her son running through her mind. Of holding him as an infant to her breast, of his first steps, his first words, of dressing him, of his tears and especially his laughter. She pictured his little dimpled smile, his smooth plump cheeks and satin skin, his lovingness. She felt her absolute need to hold him close, and felt the heartsick finality of knowing she never would again.

She wiped her face on her skirt and sat shakily against an iron-girded wooden chest. Why hadn't the woman called her guards into the room? The pistol lay where it had fallen.

Antoinette took up the pistol. She pushed off the floorboards and struggled to her feet, attracting Missus French's attention.

"How? What happened to him?" Antoinette asked.

"There was an epidemic. Children were falling like flies. Over twenty died in Turkle alone."

"There's talk among the servants that you gave Louis Edward your own medicine, and it killed him."

"Nonsense, slave talk. The child was dying. I made his passing easier."

"I don't understand why you made such an effort to purchase my son; it was a risk for you. That, and keeping me here."

"Because the boy was my grandson, that's why. My only grandchild."

Antoinette stared at the face in the candlelight as if looking into a mirror years into the future. But the woman she saw wasn't herself, didn't resemble the image she'd often dreamed of. Since the day she met Missus French she'd felt an occasional suspicion, but these she easily dismissed. Now the words precluded denial.

"You! My mother?"

"Don't act so surprised."

"How? Why?" Antoinette said, her voice cracking. "Why did you leave me with him?"

She was three years old, her long black hair cleaned and brushed, dressed in starched white for this journey, not knowing it was a one-way trek. After her mother gave her hand to the man, she knelt down and hugged her, straightened her bangs a final time, then rose and left. Antoinette had a new home, but it was an austere, lonely place. Gone were her companions, the children of the pretty women in silk robes and of the kitchen servants that ran with her through the house.

By her fourteenth year, the old man's grasping schemes had caught up with him. His stake was gone. His heavy drinking had become continuous inebriation. His weak constitution was breaking down. Irascible to the last, his words to her, always malicious, became more stinging, vile. Now he was always sick, always afraid of men he had reason to believe were chasing him.

Finally, returning to New Orleans aboard the ship from Havana, she leaned over the rail to watch him struggle briefly and then go down into the vast blue sea. For many long minutes she tried to fix the spot where he was swallowed under until the point receded and disappeared. Only then did she cry for help.

For the rest of her life, when she thought about that euphoric moment of knowing she was at last free of him, she believed he had jumped over the railing to end his suffering, but she could never fully dismiss the idea that perhaps she had pushed him.

"Oh, Mister Dupré," Missus French snorted. "I did it for your own good! It made you strong."

"You did it because he offered you a price," Antoinette said, gripping the pistol tightly. "You were getting married to move here, and I was an embarrassment. You probably squeezed him for every dollar."

Missus French settled back in her chair with a sigh, the consequences of her past standing angrily before her. She felt her heart tearing. How could she tell this child of her own sorrow and regrets?

"I've thought about you every day," Missus French lied, barely audible. Yes, she had Antoinette tracked in New Orleans some time after the young girl returned on the Cuban ship alone; had paid a lawyer to know where Antoinette was and what she was doing; had even supplied her with a modest annual stipend. But this enabled her to put the child out of her mind for long stretches of time, sometimes for years. When she did think of Antoinette, it rent her insides.

"A lot of good that did me. Why didn't you come back for me? Mother, why?"

She could not explain the practicalities to this child. This daughter had been so consumed with her hurt, she would never see Missus French's side. She grasped onto a random stratagem to touch the truth tangentially and hope that would suffice. "He wouldn't sell; then he took you off to Europe," Missus French ventured. "He'd grown fond of you."

"Fond of me!" Antoinette exclaimed. "From what I know of your methods, you could have found some way."

Ah, the child was going to question everything she said. If only she could find a truce that would allow her to retreat, not without loss, but at least with a chance to regroup.

"Too much risk—my connection there. And you were a girl-child."

So there it was. Her mother had been so preoccupied with her own survival, with her greed and her lusts, she had foregone any chance of rescuing her own daughter from her nightmare. She could have established Antoinette somewhere, anywhere! Living with a 'cropper family in the next county; even living in the slave quarters would have been better than her existence with the reprobate she was required to call 'father'. The risks to recover her would have been slight, especially for a woman so clever and devious.

"What else did you lie to me about? My husband is dead, isn't he?"

"I can't hold that against you, my dear, considering my own late-husband's fate. When the New Orleans authorities sent men after you, I shielded you. You owe me that."

"I am leaving here, leaving you, old woman. I don't believe you would have me arrested. Not because I am your daughter, but because of all that I know about you and your little family here." She lowered the pistol.

"Stay, child! Stay, please," Missus French pleaded. "I've put you in my will. Do you know what you will inherit? Daughter?"

Without a final glance, Antoinette turned and hurried away, pistol in hand.

Missus French slumped in her chair, the footsteps of her brightest hopes vanishing through the doorway and down the hall. Now only the weak one was left. The weak and mad one. Her life had come to a heap of ashes.

***

The men guarding Devereau French's door posed no greater obstacle than the ones guarding her mother's. She entered the room.

In the faint light, she detected a form scurrying furtively to and fro, like a threatened squirrel with no tree in sight. She soon made out French, wearing what appeared to be a lacy, almost transparent white nightgown. Not surprised, Antoinette looked over the French heir, unaffected by her adversary's shape and *couture*.

"It's time for some answers, *Mister* French. Your servants tell me you buried a child here."

French forced what she hoped would be a winning smile. "Now, don't get suspicious, Antoinette. Remember, in an ironic way, we're Louis Edward's parents, you and I."

"That is ironic," Antoinette answered, "because I've known about you since the day we met. I'm not sure how you did it all these years, but I can guess why. It isn't easy being a woman in this man's world."

"At least you've managed to live as a flesh and blood female," French rejoined, defiant and self-pitying. "Try living as I've been forced to."

"If the law comes after me, I will be quite vocal on the subject," Antoinette warned. "And I'm a desperate woman, as you must be."

French expelled her breath, impotent against the fury of this woman's obsessive quest. She slid a legal document across the desk.

"Louis Edward is yours as soon as he returns." Her voice caught.

Flourishing her pistol, Antoinette tossed the paper back.

"My recourse to the courts is somewhat limited, French. Your mother told me the truth about the black headstone. How did he die?"

"Please," French pleaded. "You know I wouldn't have harmed the boy. He was all I had."

Controlling her rage, Antoinette lowered her pistol and backed away, knowing no more could be found here.

"Antoinette, wait!" French cried as Antoinette reached the door. "In a different world we might have been friends!"

"Like sisters," Antoinette replied, staring at this sorry creature wearing the gauzy, pathetic nightgown. Then she hurried away.

Chapter Twenty-nine

She must have dozed beside the stove until Old Fredric rushed in to wake her. The two riders were close. Fredric took her hand to help her up.

He led her upstairs to an abandoned second-story room with a window that fronted the mansion, a well-placed view chosen from among the mass of empty rooms that made up the French house. From there, they overlooked the front portico which covered the verandah. To her delight, she discovered he'd set up two large armchairs and one of the house's brass spyglasses.

Sitting lightly, Fredric looked through the glass until he found the two silhouettes on horseback, then drew her to the eyepiece, pointing out where she would find them.

She took a moment to locate the intruders. Finally she saw them.

Three of the Frenches' riffraff waited at the front gate. Soundlessly, she turned the glass over to Fredric, and the two sat forward, craning their necks. Something bad was going to happen.

***

The storm's harsh savagery quieted to a lull. Only a steady drizzle fell, a dispensation from the pounding rain, for which the miserably wet and cold guards were grateful. One of the men pushed himself to his feet and announced he was going to get some hot coffee, but the other's hand stayed him.

Two dark riders headed their way in the distance. The men checked their muskets, frantic, frightened; they'd heard stories about Mister Dark Horse.

***

Isaac and Hurst drew rein, studying what lay ahead through the drizzle. Before them, the mansion stood like a fortress, forbidding and dark. They made out the main gate, and the armed men attending it.

Isaac wondered if Hurst had cooled enough to sensibly turn back, but one glance told the story. "I'll wait here," Isaac said.

Hurst spurred his horse and split off; his stomach tightened.

He wiped his wet face, a futile gesture. He could go forward, a deadly bet, or run—and running wasn't promising either. Even if he got his partners to the Union lines, he'd be trapped in a war with dangers beyond any he'd ever faced. Did he want to survive his misbegotten Turkle episode only to dig ditches for an alien army, the plaything of politicians he'd never met, until they left him dead in a ditch? If the North had the slightest chance to win, the gamble might be worth it. But from everything he'd heard and read…

He tried to control his terror. Perhaps Antoinette would prefer to remain under French protection rather than become a fugitive with him. He had little to offer her. For a moment he considered turning the roan and riding back to the hollow, or heading in some other direction to start fresh. If he didn't ask her, he could be comforted by the belief that she wouldn't have turned him down.

If he died by moving forward, at least he would die without facing her answer. There was peace in that thought.

Hurst decided, then urged the roan forward, pulling his wrap tightly against the now more insistent rain. Finally, he was within shouting distance of the gate.

"It's me, boys! Durk Hurst!"

At that very instant, a huge crack of lightning split the night, illuminating the sky in an eerie white glare. This dramatic flash was followed by a gargantuan explosion and then hollow thunder. Cringing in mortal fear, the riffraff recognized the figure on the approaching horse. "It's him, for sure! Dark Horse!"

"That's all I needs to know'd!"

One fired his musket aimlessly into the air. Then, terrified, the three dropped their weapons and scrambled away, slipping and falling in the mud.

They screamed "Dark Horse," beginning a general alarm that led to panic for everyone within earshot. Most of the men posted around the mansion, already demoralized by the rain, heard the screams and quickly abandoned their posts, heading straight for the stables or to the safety of the Big House, intent on making their run for it on the back of good French horseflesh.

The elderly groom slave who ran the stables, disturbed by the racket, rose from his straw pallet and lit a lantern. Everywhere he looked he saw riffraff throwing open stall doors and trying to control alarmed, wild-eyed horses. Seeing the general disorder and thievery taking place, the groom grabbed a musket from the nearest pair of hands and, with a shout, fired into the air. The shot only served to inflame the kicking and rearing horses and to further unnerve the fleeing men.

Panic-stricken, terrified men and crazed beasts rushed for the stable door. Of those sitting French horses, two made it to the door clinging bareback, but outside, they were quickly thrown into the mud-churned ground, their stolen mounts scattering in all directions. Others attempting to saddle the bucking beasts were knocked to the floor. Still others carried away saddles and halters embossed with golden French emblems.

The door offering escape was wide, but not wide enough. Frantic horses and men running at full speed hit the opening, only to collide with late-arriving riffraff heading for the stables. Many were knocked to the ground and trampled by both four- and two-legged creatures. Once into the cold air, those still able headed directly for the nearby cabin where their bedrolls waited to be hauled off to safer parts. The ones carrying rich French leatherwork or too terrified to think straight were already in flight, their backs to the mansion.

The groom was quick to close the stable doors. That done, he took control of the horses that hadn't escaped and, calming the snorting and screeching animals with gentle tones, guided them to their stalls. There was chasing to do, but he was too old for that.

***

She almost fell off her chair laughing, watching them riffraff run away in fright. Beside her, Fredric laughed so hard he couldn't catch his breath, slapping his knee and wheezing as if death was upon him. Finally, gasping for air, he managed to inhale, but the sight of the last riffraff's herky-jerky flight sent him into further hysterical spasms.

Finally, they gathered themselves enough to go downstairs where Fredric got a towel to hand to the approaching stranger, and she heated up coffee 'case he might need it to warm hisself.

***

Lightning flashed as Hurst threw open the front door, illuminating the spotless entrance foyer, empty but for the heroic bust of Devereau French's late-father sitting atop its marble column. Seeing a man's stern visage facing him in the sudden white glare, Hurst froze as if it were some omen, a warning that he was trespassing into a world reserved by wealthy planters exclusively for their own kind and for the ladies who were clever enough to work their way into their company. Overcoming his sense of foreboding, he hurried to the stairs, driven by his need to find her. A dark hand offered him a towel as he passed, breaking the spell. He dried his face and neck before handing it back with thanks and ascending the stairway.

A gale blew against the windows that fronted the staircase, rattling them with its force. When Hurst reached the second floor landing, he paused to get his bearings.

So this is where they live, he thought, feeling like a refugee who'd stumbled into a palace. *All the anger and jealousy torturing me these many years, and the wood merely smells like wood, the dust like dust. Why is this house more sacrosanct or desirable than the one we built? Because it's older? Because the people inhabiting it are accepted by folks I don't know and never will know, nor would I prize their company if I did? I've been a fool to let the thought of them waste so much of my life.*

Dark hallways seemed to lead off in all directions, each one lined with rows of closed doors. "Like searching for your soul," he said aloud.

He picked a direction and strode down a hall, stopping frequently to open doors and look in. The cavernous building was so empty he could hear the eerie echo of his own boots following him. He reached one four-way corner and, spying what could have been a faint light reflecting from a mirror hanging at its dead end, hurried double-speed toward it.

As he neared the place where the hallway teed, the faint glow of a lantern grew brighter to his left. He continued that way until he came upon two riffraff squatting on the floor. They rose when they saw him.

"Tell them Frenches Dark Horse is here," Hurst said as ominously as he could, gambling that these men would react the same way the others had. The pair nodded and backed off, leaving their muskets behind. When they were ten feet away, they turned and ran. Hurst breathed a sigh of relief, grinning; his reputation had held.

He turned the knob of the door they'd been guarding, finding it locked. Furious, he put his shoulder to it repeatedly until the wood split and he burst in, the door crashing against the wall.

A woman wearing a delicate, transparent white nightgown stood before a full-length mirror. Startled, she turned around. It was French's head, with French's short hair, sitting atop the lithe body of Charlotte, the French cousin Hurst had met at the county seat hotel.

Instantly, doubts he'd had about French fell into place. The two looked at each other, frozen.

A blast of wind blew open the room's large window and rain began to pour onto French's desk. Neither turned, but it broke the spell. "This is a lady's bedroom!" French remonstrated.

"French?"

With a sneer, French yanked open her gown, baring her breast, revealing the birthmark Hurst had touched that night. "Don't play the fool, Hurst!" she said. "You're not the only one playing at charades."

"Why?"

"Not by choice, I assure you."

Hurst moved to the center of the room, balling his fist. "Where is she?" he demanded.

"Gone. Run off."

"I don't believe you."

French opened a drawer beside the mirror and drew out a pistol she'd been keeping since the incident at the church. Holding it on the interloper, she circled until she stood between him and the door.

"You can live here with me, Durk!" French said, sticking her pistol into his ribs. "It'd be our secret."

"I don't need any more secrets," he replied, pushing her pistol aside.

"You weren't so cold toward me that night."

"That was my appetite, not my heart."

French laid the pistol on the table and sidled toward him, as if in a jaunty mood. "I've got a deal for you," she said. "I can guarantee her safety away from here. It's you and me that belong together." She was inches from him, glaring at him face-to-face.

"I want Antoinette."

"You'd give up all this to be true to a woman like her?"

"Imagine that," he answered, his voice malevolent.

French grabbed Hurst's wrist and placed his hand on her breast—but he pulled it away.

"You're not man enough, are you?" she challenged.

His eyes softened. This poor creature was damaged, something he understood. "I guess not, French."

"You can run Dark Horse, Durk" she offered. "We'll rebuild it together."

He pushed past her for the door.

"You can run both plantations!" she shouted at his back. "I'll make you rich!"

This perpetually unwanted man could barely resist someone who claimed to need him. He turned back to French one last time.

"Your outside is good enough for any man," he said. "But you need work on your heart, lady."

He slammed the door behind him.

"Anything you want," French shouted after him, "anything! Please! If you don't come back, I'll see she hangs. Both of you hang! Trash!"

***

She heard him in the hall, shouting for Antoinette. As his voice faded,

French rose, a repressed sobbing coming from her lips. Another impossible dream gone in a wisp of smoke like all the others.

As if in a trance, tears rolling down her cheeks, she picked up the pistol and drifted to her desk. Placing the pistol by her side, she sat in her padded leather chair, oblivious of the chilling rain blowing through the open window, soaking her through.

She reached far into the back of the right-hand drawer and removed a key. She then used the key to open the top left drawer. From there, she removed a large box, withdrew a mirror, and stood it on its turtle shell base. Examining her reflection, she brushed her rain-soaked hair from her forehead. Next, she withdrew from the box small earthen pots and fine brushes. Without a word, and heedless of the sheets of rain soaking her nightdress, she took a thin brush, dipped it in the pot and began to paint her lips. Slowly, carefully, she dipped the tip of the brush and applied the bright red a dab at a time, as if there was no time or existence outside her mirror. Done, she admired her lips' lush, ruby glow.

"An irresistible corpse," she said to herself in the mirror.

A violent rash of lightning crashed outside. All her life had been swamped in sorrow, and now she was descending into a bottomless, suffocating despair. Drowning. Now that she had won, had beaten Dark Horse, she had no escape from her own trap, no life, no air. She was condemned by lies she had promulgated to live a false, lonely life with no hope of companionship to warm her bed, to brighten her endlessly dreary life, no prospect of offspring to comfort her, to cuddle to her breast. The lowest slave in her kitchen had a man to warm her at night, to lay beside and tell her troubles to. The lowest cotton picker had children hanging around her neck, kissing her face, while she was as alone as a human being could possibly be.

Through her teary haze, she was transfixed by the red-rimmed eyes staring back at her from her mirror. She felt on the desk for the pistol. She slipped her finger around its trigger and raised it ever so deliberately to her mouth. Her red lips parted and, hand trembling, she inserted its barrel, tasting its cold steel with her tongue, closing her lips.

But try as she might, she could not squeeze the trigger. Wailing with despair, she struck the mirror with the pistol, sending it clattering across the floor. Then she rose and crossed to her full-length mirror, the pistol held limply at her side.

She brushed the sticky wet hair from her forehead. The soaked nightgown clung to her body, a body fully revealed—breasts, curves, secret places. She touched herself, in one place and then another, a bittersweet smile on her lips. A woman. Her mother could not take that from her.

***

Even the drawn curtains could not keep the flashes of lightning from penetrating her darkness, could not keep its crash and following thunder from disturbing her game. The Creator did not want her to concentrate tonight.

She studied the board intensely, but the glowing, multicolored lights flashing upon it diminished ever so subtly. Then they flickered off, and she could not will them to return. *So,* she thought bitterly, *I cannot even play a game of chess in peace.*

She heard a disturbance at her door, her daughter's footsteps light on the floor. The soft feet wound their way through the piled valuables to the board, then stopped. Missus French tried to break away from the game, but her eyes refused to leave it.

Without warning, her daughter's hand swiped a number of pieces over, breaking the ones that fell to the floor. Startled, Missus French raised her eyes to see her daughter wearing the soaked and revealing nightgown. The riffraff and servants must have seen her!

"What are you wearing, fool?" Missus French asked.

"Mother, I can't live this way any longer. I need my own life, my own children, somehow."

Why couldn't the weakling leave well enough alone? Missus French didn't know what made Devereau so madly, utterly consumed with this motherhood notion. But now this urge threatened to destroy them both.

"Are you insane? You're risking *French Acres.*"

"I'll take that chance."

Missus French looked at the scattered pieces, then raised her head.

"You'll never be free—and you'd best learn it. This house owns you, this plantation owns you. And I own you." Then, lowering her voice, she revealed, "She knows about Louis Edward. We cannot hold her."

Devereau stumbled back, weakened at the knees. "What did you tell her?" she asked, her eyes narrowing. No answer. "Does she know the boy would be alive if it wasn't for his grandmother?"

"He called out to me," Missus French said wistfully, as if from far away. "He was a good little man, a quiet boy, but not that time."

"What did you put in his milk to quiet him? And how much? It was your opiates!"

"Children were dying every day."

"He didn't die of his fever, Mother. The doctor knew the signs. He died of crying out for your help when you were consumed by this damned game. He died of violating your silence. If it wasn't for Annie, I would have died the same way."

"Stop it," Missus French pleaded. "You should have known not to leave a sick child with me. I know nothing about children."

"No, nothing, Mother. You never knew anything about me, except to keep me safely in a case, to take me out for display as it suited your purpose."

Devereau's hand shook as the pistol exploded, breaking the stillness; its ball hit her mother in the chest, throwing her back. The room fell eerily silent. Startled by the ear-shattering blast, Devereau looked at her pistol—astonished that she'd willed it to fire. Then she dropped it.

Missus French slumped forward onto the board, her shoulder knocking over the white king in woman's form and the pieces arranged to protect it. Blood spread beneath her, covering square after square in no discernible pattern.

"Now, it's God's move," her daughter said.

Missus French's lungs filled with blood. "He…" she spat out, coughing blood, struggling to get the words out. "cheats…women."

"Yes, He does, Mother," French agreed morosely.

Missus French raised her head to see her daughter's face for the last time. With difficulty, Missus French smiled gratefully—the child finally understood. Then she shuddered and slumped forward, stilled.

"He cheats *everyone*, fool," Devereau French said.

French faced the blood on the board, forcing herself not to turn away. She touched it with her finger, then brought it to her mouth and tasted it. At once she sunk both palms into the sticky fluid and smeared it on her face, the dead-deer ritual that had so revolted her on the Dark Horse hunt. The crimson, mixed with the sweat and rain on her face, ran down onto her white shoulders and pale nightgown.

Then she was off, running, past the pair of guards at her mother's door. Not slowing, she passed others, whose startled faces she saw in flashes. A cook and a butler, hearing the shot, scrambled from the kitchen and, seeing her predicament, politely averted their eyes.

She crossed the yard, nightgown flying behind her, the storm pouring on her full blast. Bloody rainwater ran down her back and breasts.

At long last, she was free.

Chapter Thirty

The shot spooked most of the riffraff stationed inside the house. They fled through the hallways and down the stairs, pushing and shoving out the kitchen door into the rain.

Others, brave or curious, attracted by the shot converged on Missus French's room in groups of two and three, muskets poised. Seeing the door ajar, they entered the room tentatively with their lanterns raised high. Once inside, they saw the pair who guarded Missus French's room leaning over her body, examining it for signs of life.

"French did it! He finally kill something," one man said.

"Well, he a man at last," another concluded.

Seeing no danger, the men swarmed into the room like hungry locusts. "The banker and the lawyer gonna kill each other splitting all this up!"

One grabbed a silver cake knife sitting atop a lowboy and worked it to pry open the locked wooden strongbox at the foot of Missus French's bed. The strongbox's existence seemed to confirm all the old tales people had heard.

"This is where she keep it!"

His companion, frustrated by the time this was taking, pushed him aside and repeatedly smashed his musket butt against the lock. Seeing this disregard for caution, the others, overcome by frenzy, ransacked the room. Discarding their lanterns and rifles, they pushed through, kicking aside the paintings, statues, chests, and metalworks piled and stacked in every conceivable manner. Tripping and stumbling through the treasures, a few reached the windows and yanked down the velvet draperies to carry off their booty. They took hold of nearby shiny objects and tossed them onto their curtains. Those that followed began to tug and tear at these same drapes for their own ends, while others pushed through the piles seeking any container large enough to hold reachable loot.

Within minutes, the room was a chaos of valuables, and moving from place to place became difficult. Items one man pushed aside blocked the movement of another, so that every man kicked and pushed aside anything between him and a gleaming prize that caught his eye. Soon pushing and shoving became punching and swinging. Raised voices, mixed with the clatter and crunch of items flying about, escalated into a horrific din. Burning lanterns smashed to the ground as piles they rested on were knocked over. In a chain reaction, obstacles shoved and tossed about merely created larger obstacles, adding to the confusion.

Finally the trunk shattered from the lock. The two men working it, pressed by many hungry faces, threw open the lid, their eyes blazing with the vision of piles of bonds and notes in denominations of hundreds and five hundreds. There it rested, the raw substance from Missus French's last planned financial coup.

"Confed'rit Bonds! A slew of 'em!" one shouted.

"We gone be rich after the war, boy! Rich!" his companion exulted.

With a wild yell, they began stuffing their pockets. Soon their pockets could hold no more and most of the bonds still sat in the box. Thinking fast, they grabbed a bed sheet from another looter, causing the man to spill his silver. The three came to blows. When others in the room heard of the negotiable treasure in the strongbox, they flocked to it, pressing forward with their awkward loads, while the original pair fought to defend it. The rush to the bonds turned into a wild brawl.

"Hey! I found it! I seen it first!"

Men reeling and sprawling from punches began throwing heavy statues and precious vases at each other, using priceless sculpture for clubs. They knocked over more lanterns, and drapes and furniture soon caught fire.

When the brawlers realized the room was burning, each desperately grabbed what he could. Shouting "Fire!" and fighting and clawing, they stumbled and climbed through flames and piles of debris toward the door.

Once they'd escaped Missus French's lair, they raced away clutching their loot. Through the halls and down the stairs and out the doors they ran into the now mild drizzle.

In a remarkably short time, the old French mansion was fully ablaze, burning just as the *DarkHorse* edifice—now a charred ruin on the opposite side of Turkle—had only hours before. The kitchen woman and the butler ran to the quarters and, with the rest of the French slaves, huddled in fear, waiting for events to guide them. Elsewhere throughout the French estate, riffraff scattered in every direction, some with only their fear to spur them on, others with their hands full.

No one was left to put out the flames that consumed the great monolith from which various Frenches had ruled like petty tyrants for more than fifty years. The French empire was no more.

***

The last of Turkle's Frenches ran to the stables through the steady drizzle, the streaked blood on her face thinned and runny. Her drenched nightdress was almost transparent, pressing and clinging against her body. Once inside the barn, she paused to appraise the situation. Two riffraff were absconding with gleaming halters. Nearby, the groom was shouting at them, to no avail. French was about to issue an order herself, but realized no one would know who she was.

She ran to the white stallion's stall, but someone had already gotten there before her. The gate hung open, her horse gone. Although no man could ride her steed, they'd spooked him to escape. She was surprised one of the hands wasn't killed by his hooves.

She looked to see which horses were left. One brown, already saddled, remained. She mounted it and rode away, her flimsy white dress flowing behind her.

Once outside, she drew rein, trying to decide where in the whole, empty world she could go dressed—or undressed—as she was, with no money or name, nothing but herself. She had only one place to go, and dug her heels into the brown. She only wondered, if she made it, would she survive?

***

The cloud-obscured moon supplied no illumination, but Antoinette knew the way to the French family graveyard. She'd often seen and wondered about the black tombstone. Now she stood before it, knowing its cryptic words meant her son. For once, a French had been truthful.

Holding the umbrella aloft against the drizzle, she felt her legs weaken. She staggered back and sat on one of the wet markers, covering her eyes. She had never really cried yet, never let herself go. She didn't know if that comforting act was still possible. Attempting to compose herself, she rose unsteadily, trembling.

Having been directed to this place by slaves from the big house, Hurst rode into the graveyard and found her. Then, seeing her face, he knew.

Hurst rode up to her and dismounted. "Antoinette, we've got to get away from here," he said, wrapping his arm around her to steady her. "This place is a hanging for us."

"I don't care. They've got to pay." Antoinette pulled away and took up her pistol, then faced the burning house. She had failed to protect her little boy, but she wasn't going to fail to avenge him. She'd already taken the first of Louis Edward's transgressors, her husband, in New Orleans. She must take two more before the boy's death would be satisfied. She would have justice no matter what.

Hurst held her back, afraid of losing her again, desperate to never again be parted. "It's too late for them now. Besides, living's their punishment." If she dismissed him now, he'd truly have nothing.

Hurst mounted the roan and looked questioningly at her, but she stared him down. For a long moment they searched each other's face. "You've got friends waiting for you," he said, offering his hand.

She hesitated, dazed, absently staring at him, as if not recognizing him. Trying to grasp some coherent thought, she turned to face the huge wall of flames the French mansion had become, but even its roar and heat didn't register. Her mind was far away, in a place with smiles and loving warmth, with a child who had lived and laughed—a place to which she would never return.

Flames poured out of every window and consumed the roof, yet she did not see the conflagration. She saw only memories of her mother, young again. With an unbearably heavy heart, she remembered the sweet-smelling woman holding and dressing her. And she saw, again, this woman give her hand over and depart, not to be seen again for so many, many years.

Antoinette was precipitously struck by the searing realization that the fire before her eyes spelled the end of her mother; the woman could never have escaped. She would have no other word from her, no understanding between them, no apology. Never even another lie.

All the feelings and wonderings she endured for so many years roared unrelentingly inside her mind; sharp spikes penetrated her heart.

Turning away, Antoinette pictured the tortured Devereau French, with the words "my sister" echoing in her head. Who had had the worst life? She, who wore the white, pressed pinafores and was forced to live a life of fear with the scurrilous old man or that of the lovesick fraud?

She thought back to the suitor from a family whose name was legend, a name painted on street signs and buildings in honor of his forbearers, a name read in the newspapers. The wedding. The great mansion on the broad, tree-lined avenue. The child she loved so dearly. The child...

Then she pictured Devereau, *my sister*, trapped in her loneliness with little chance to be free. She felt pity for French and herself, two hopelessly damaged peas from the same stunted pod.

She felt the pistol, cold in her palm, as she looked at the man on the horse. He had told the truth that night, was true to her without question. He would forsake everything he had for her, though there was little left to forsake. He cared about her more than his life; his coming here, knowing violent men lay waiting, proved that.

He continued to hold his hand out to her. Tossing away the pistol, she took his arm, and he pulled her up behind him onto the horse. She wrapped her arms tightly around his waist and rested her cheek on his back. For the first time in all these weary endless months, she allowed herself to cry.

***

The long, muddy road lay ahead in the night. The pair on the roan were hit by periodic gusts of rain, which ceased momentarily as they passed below overarching trees lining the road, only to be hit again as the conjunction of leaves and branches dissipated. They rounded a bend, and Hurst saw Isaac a quarter mile up the road, sitting his mount, waiting for them. Hurst felt unexpectedly warm inside, thinking to himself that Isaac had been a true friend to the last, in spite of his perpetual anger and suspicion. He waved, and the man waved back.

Hurst kneed the roan to a slow cantor, as fast as the weary horse could go, until they reached Isaac. Then he drew rein. Isaac turned with them and, together, the two horses plodded away.

Hurst forced himself to think about *DarkHorse*—lost. It didn't hurt as much as he expected it to hurt. Thinking back to before *DarkHorse*, he barely recognized the man who'd ridden into the Chickasaw forest alone, the man running from the consequences of his own unraveling divination.

He felt Antoinette's arms around him and glanced across at his friend, thinking maybe what happens next won't be as magnificent as *DarkHorse*, but what he might accomplish might be strong and true, even if it only lasted a short time.

He turned for one final look. The ancient French mansion was already greatly reduced to smolder and a thick cloud of smoke, a reflection of their own mansion, now little more than a deformed heap of wet ash and scorched chimney.

Antoinette turned back for a final glimpse as well. This was her legacy: the wind, the rain, the man she barely knew.

***

She knew it was coming. She didn't know how, but she knew why.

She applied Mister French's elegant signature, perfect to the loops in the *D* and the swirls in the *F*, to the last of the official Manumission Certification documents and set down her pen. The honor store had just five quills left when she started, and over the past three days she'd worn them all out. She was grateful the Lord had given her five and not four, so that she could complete her mission; although in the last twenty hours, a great deal of ingenuity and effort had been required. Her dress showed many stains and her fingers, covered in ink, hurt. Let no man stay in bondage for want of her effort.

She rose, stretching her lower back, stiff and painful from hunching over a table hours upon hours without sleep. Her body, pressed beyond its limits, was a mass of hurt. She tried to stretch her small white right arm, but her muscles were fixed and she could not. Her hand had grown progressively numb, while a relentless throbbing inside her palm added to her discomfort. She shook her hand to get feeling back and attempted to crack her finger joints and knuckles, but the strength and feeling in her fingertips were gone.

She gathered the last batch of the certificates and tapped them together, then placed them neatly into the box. It was very late on this second straight night of work. She went to the front window and pulled back the threadbare curtain to see if the storm had passed.

Even in the dark she could see it was still drizzling. She was ready to fall into bed when, outside, commotion, voices, movement, and light caught her eye. A neighbor shouted, followed by louder voices from across the street.

All at once, her neighbors poured into the street. At first there was a trickle of them, lanterns in hand, bedclothes partially covered by hastily thrown-on coats, trousers and robes. People's excited voices rose steadily in pitch, accompanied by wild gestures and pointing. They clotted together in one spot for a view through the houses and trees at some distant attraction. Something important was happening.

She stepped out onto the porch. Because of its missing shingles, the overhang only partly protected her from the raindrops. She asked a man rushing by what was going on, but the man, pulling his suspenders over his nightshirt, passed her like a ghost, not hearing her question.

She reached inside the door and took the only umbrella left from its stand. She'd had to nail an elegantly lettered "Not For Sale" sign above it to keep customers from commandeering her umbrellas on "honor store credit" every time it rained. Its three broken spokes supplied little more protection than the porous porch. Regardless, she followed the crowd to where others gathered, all staring off in the same direction.

"What is it?"

"See the fire, girl? It's the French place burning like a barn full of cotton!"

She turned toward the spot, lifting on her toes to see a huge glow in the distance.

"His purposes ever to His own time," she said to herself, grateful that the Lord had enabled her to finish the Mister French signings in time.

She looked about, the idea already formed in her head. Then she saw him, standing across the street in his house britches and work boots. A clean, freckle-faced, skinny young man with scarecrow straw hair, about her own age, who lived with his parents. She'd often seen him about the church. Grandfather had made her avoid the boy for the last two years because he worked at the big general store on the town square that gobbled up all the honor store's customers. But she knew him to be clever and industrious, not much in Bible class, always clowning with the other boys, but a good-hearted person nonetheless.

Not much interested in any kind of big ideas, he didn't join the army like all his excitable friends, but instead stayed on to help support his family. Over the last year he'd saved his wages and bought his own single, horse-drawn wagon. He used the wagon to earn extra money from the general store by bringing in shelf stock and making deliveries, in addition to his regular duties. This wagon seemed to the girl to be simply another in a long unbroken string of Signs from God.

She walked up to him and pulled on his sleeve, but he ignored her. Not to be denied, she repeated her tug with greater urgency until he turned his attention to her.

"What do you want?" he said.

"Hitch up. I'm going out there."

"Hit's past midnight. It'll be done burnt out 'fore we git to it," he said.

"I got papers to get there by daybreak," she answered. "The Lord done tole me to do it." She paused, thinking of how to explain. "He will not abide a bondsman."

The boy lifted the heavy box as if it was light as laundry and strapped it in the wagon bed. Then he covered it with a good tarp and efficiently tied it down.

Pleased at the way the boy had protected the papers, the granddaughter stepped into the muddy street and grabbed hold to climb up onto the wagon. The boy surprised her by taking her waist in his two strong hands and lifting her up, then climbed up beside her. He'd jerry-rigged a tarp over the seat to protect riders from the elements.

He whistled and flicked his mare, and they were on their way. Soon, they had left Turkle's outermost streets and were on the road west of town that led to the French place.

She was determined. With these signed papers she would stubbornly stand against every banker and lawyer who came at her.

"I been working for days on them papers, the last two straight through," she mumbled wearily, almost in delirium. "Something tole me this Sunday, and so it is. Each one of them papers, every single page of it, is one of God's creatures gonna be set free. Ain't that something?"

Then, in total exhaustion, she settled her head against his knotty shoulder and closed her eyes. Well, yes, she'd been a wanton woman twice over, first desiring Mister Dark Horse, even sharing intimacies—a kiss—with him back at the honor store that day. Then, wearing Lilith's gown, she'd traveled out to seduce Mister French. She was a wicked woman with evil thoughts, destined for an eternity of Hell, but this would redeem her. This would even-steven and overtop her case in the Lord's Big Book of Souls. Relieved at this accounting, as accurate as anything in her honor store ledgers, she let her breathing slow to a wagon crawl, in time with the creaking of the boy's conveyance.

Seeing how spent she was, her fingers covered in ink, the boy reached his arm around her shoulders, resting it on the seat back, letting her cuddle into his chest. There, at peace, she fell asleep, slumped on the jolting wagon seat.

He looked down at her, admiring her almost white, fine hair and small feet, feeling her warm breath through his shirt. He lightly flicked the reins so as not to wake the girl.

Unconsciously she slid down on the wagon seat and curled up, her head nestled in his lap. Smiling gently he looked down upon her pretty sleeping face, feeling her regular warm breath through his threadbare trousers.

Clearly, there were going to be things in his life that would overshadow his work in the general store.

He'd let her sleep till the French ruin came in sight, which at their pace would probably be near daybreak. Then, when he woke her, she could explain about the papers and freeing the French slaves. Now he simply enjoyed the ride, satisfied to be with her, this girl he'd watched ever so shyly over the years from the distance of his family porch.

***

The sun rose to her left, its rays petering through the smoky tangle of swamp trees and hanging Spanish moss. Sparkles glinted on a moving body of water ahead, a separated living precursor to the stagnant backwash on her right, which she passed so ploddingly upon her bone-weary mount.

French drew rein momentarily to make out where she was and to give the horse a blow. It had been a hard, all-night ride through the storm and confused tangle, and she'd often felt lost.

The faint promise of day spread gradually, its illuminating transmutation turning everything about her suddenly alive. Even the muggy dawn haze seemed merely a temporary guise, lifting. She shivered uncontrollably, chilled to the bone in her thin soaked nightgown and frozen bare feet. Then she saw it.

Through the mists of morning she made out smoke from new fires rising gently into the skies ahead.

She rode through the village, now coming to life with Chickasaws busy with their morning rituals. Women watched pots hung over small cooking fires. The men whittled arrows, flexed their bows, sharpened their knives. As she passed, each Chickasaw followed the progress of this apparition. What could a sane People make of a white woman appearing magically as if risen from the depths of the foggy swamp, naked beneath a drenched, blood-sotted sheer gown? But they let the mystery continue, returning their attention to their preparations for another glorious day on earth.

She drew rein before a wrinkled old Chickasaw woman, smoking her pipe before a modest fire.

"Where's that damn Wounded Wolf?"

The old woman looked up from the pot she was stirring, squinting her eyes at the vision. What was this creature? Was she a Sign? Why would the ancestors send a white woman to her? What was being foretold?

Then she knew who it was.

"Won't grind corn, won't chew leather."

She withdrew the stained pipe from her lips and spit, preparing a lie. But it was too late, the apparition spotted Wounded Wolf walking toward them from the council hut.

"You son-of-a-bitch!" French shouted, turning the brown and heeling it forward. Startled by the sudden cry of vengeance breaking the morning tranquility, Wounded Wolf saw her coming and ran toward his lodge— where he'd left his knife hanging from the main pole.

French rode him down. Once alongside him, she dove from the horse onto the Chief's back. The force of her plunge brought the pair tumbling into the mud where they wrestled, with French struggling to stay atop, as Wounded Wolf wriggled wild to get free.

Pulling his hair back, she bit Wounded Wolf's ear so her teeth penetrated the flesh, and he screamed with pain. Then, straddling his chest, she choked him with all her strength, twisting the dozen rawhide necklaces he wore.

Gagging for air, he managed to sputter out, "I—miss—you."

Suddenly, he could breathe; the hands released their hold. French stared into his eyes to see if he was lying, then fell upon him, kissing him hard on the mouth. And he returned her kiss.

Shaking her head, the old Chickasaw woman watched the proceedings with disdain. She remembered this white woman who had come to live with the People for a full season, a woman who had slept in the lodge of the mad Chief. She knew the two would never find peace. When not copulating noisily, they were fighting, raging and screaming, day and night. The old woman spit in disgust.

"The forest will not sleep at night again."

Chapter Thirty-one

Big Josh watched the cotton-puff cloud drift overhead through the blue sky. The afternoon sun was warm and rapidly growing hotter. Flicking the reins, he glanced at a weary Antoinette beside him on the wagon seat, her eyes closed. He thought it remarkable that they'd gotten so far on the wits of an unlikely pair like Durk and Antoinette. The ill-matched couple had portrayed themselves as everything from rich planters to Confederate agents, fast-talking the *DarkHorse* partners through towns, countryside, forests, Confederate army lines, past hunger, terror…

The mule-drawn wagon creaked loudly, holding miraculously together as it crept up the dusty, rutted road toward the stand of maple and overgrown scrub. Big Josh looked behind him. There, bedraggled and dirty, the women and his partners followed barefoot, shuffling through the dust, most carrying their store-bought shoes tied over their shoulders.

At his signal, they pulled off the road seeking a safe place to rest. A shaded flat near the river bend would suit their purpose just fine, offering a good place to soak blistered feet and make cooking fires. Vegetation blocked any view from the road.

Unexpectedly, Bammer ran toward him from his lookout position, warning, "A rider!"

Everyone stopped, then madly scrambled into the brush. The rider was almost past them, headed back the way they'd come, when Bammer saw it was Little Turby. Hurst stumbled through the thickets onto the road and cried after him, until Little Turby saw him and headed back for the campsite, all excited.

"A Union advance post!" he shouted as he reached the clearing.

The air filled with spontaneous cheering and celebratory hugging, as everyone filtered back from the woods. Big Josh hugged Ceeba hard, joyfully, and she returned his affection. He and his woman, and all their partners, were going to be free. Big Josh had got them there.

***

It wasn't much. In a clearing about fifty yards from a river bank surrounded by scrub and pine, a large, main tent faced a fire pit and two neat rows of smaller tents. The strong wind whipped the Union flag, bending its pole.

Two groups of strangers stood facing each other, stupefied, wary. Both bands had recently been uprooted from homes and familiar surroundings, destined through hazard and chance to intersect at this isolated spot. Both watched the other warily, their breaths coming in shortened, ragged draws. Both hoped hard violence and quick death weren't in this hand of cards.

The *DarkHorse* partners and the women formed a ragged line in the clearing between the tents, near the dead breakfast fire. Facing them were five Union soldiers, the rest of the company having been sent out at sunrise to forage and scout the countryside. A sergeant looked them over suspiciously, while one of the privates tried unsuccessfully to load his musket. The other three privates stood loosely, their muskets cradled in their arms, looking Antoinette over and whispering among themselves.

The *DarkHorse* partners hadn't made any plans for actually reaching their goal, the Union army. With so much else to worry about, they assumed the bluecoats would solve all their problems. Now the whole partnership stood staring at their feet, confused, not knowing what to do.

The sergeant barked an order, and one of his men began a search of the ragged group. Checking the white man first, he felt a bulge in Hurst's coat pocket. He reached in and pulled out a sack; opening it, he found gold coins. The captors whistled and whispered. The sergeant told his men to quiet and pile up all the captives' personal goods on a table outside the main tent.

The soldiers were amazed when they found that each man in the group, from the littlest to biggest slave, had a sack of gold like the white man's. As the pile grew higher, the soldiers' eyes grew bigger.

"Looks like they split up some kind of stolen gold," the sergeant surmised.

"I assure you, sergeant—" Hurst attempted to interject.

"Probably robbed their master," one soldier guessed.

Hearing this, the partners all began speaking at once, trying to come up with a story to get them out of this mess.

"He our master— We not his slaves, I mean—"

"W-w-we not s-slaves. We belong to him, I mean."

"I'm their—I mean, I was— I mean they ain't no slaves."

Big Josh could see this chorus of disparate half-truths was getting them nowhere. Raising his voice, he ordered everyone to be quiet. Then he reached into his pocket and pulled out his Manumission Certification that Hurst had acquired from the honor store. Careful not to make quick movements, he deliberately unfolded the wrinkled paper and offered it to the soldier.

"W-we's all free men, s-sir. We's come to help the Union army."

Instantly everyone else pulled their papers from their pockets. The sudden movement by the guests alarmed the soldiers, who leveled their muskets at them.

The sergeant instructed the three soldiers to confiscate the certificates double-time, while the first soldier finished gathering the gold. The sergeant turned to Hurst. "We'll show'em to the major when he gets back. If everything is in order, you'll get your property back."

"What 'bout us h-helping win this war?" Big Josh asked.

"Yes," Hurst said, trying a new gambit, "we're all free men who want to help save the Union."

"We ain't got no orders for that," the sergeant said, examining Hurst's companions with a puzzled expression. "This here is a white man's army."

Hurst and Big Josh exchanged glances. Both looked toward Antoinette, who shrugged, dumbfounded. *What now?*

***

The partners and their women were split up. The men were placed in one series of tents, Antoinette and the other women were seated by the river. Meanwhile, a query was sent forth by horseback to the major.

Dusk fell, and no orders came back. Hurst paced in the center tent.

"Will you sit down!" Isaac hissed. Hurst sat, but was soon on his feet again.

Suddenly, they heard the unmistakable sound of horses and mules thundering off. "What? Horses!" Little Turby exclaimed.

Everyone froze to listen, then rushed out of the tents. The Union sergeant lay on the ground, bleeding from the head, while the other soldiers were disappearing with the *DarkHorse* mounts and mules in a cloud of dust in the distance.

"Them soldiers! They' stealing our stock!" Little Turby exclaimed.

Then Hurst saw that the table was empty, devoid of the stack of bags filled with gold coins.

"Our gold!" Hurst cried. "They stole our gold!"

Then it became apparent to everyone that the treasured Manumission Certificates of freedom were scattered afar, at the mercy of the brisk wind. Some floated on the nearby river, some were stuck high in trees, some tumbled and fluttered till they were out of sight.

"Our papers!" Isaac shouted, his voice sinking. "We escaped slaves again!"

There ensued a panicked, breakneck chase of the flimsy papers, women and men, that went on for hours until they'd recovered every one.

***

As darkness fell, Ceeba saw to treating the groggy, barely conscious sergeant. He'd been struck a hard blow to the side of his head by a rifle butt. Meanwhile, Antoinette and the other women set to cooking up Union meal fried in bacon grease to be served with hardtack.

On the other side of camp, the men gathered under a large oak to plan the next move.

"The main U-union lines can't be too f-far off," Big Josh said.

But Hurst was having none of it. "You still thinking of…? They ain't going to let you fight in no Union army. The best y'all can get will be digging trenches."

"Then we d-dig trenches, or ditches either, if that's what they want us to do," Big Josh answered in a tone that brooked no debate.

Isaac sprang to his feet, inspired. "They have us digging ditches—'less we gots us *a white officer* to lead us into battle."

"If we k-keeps together," Big Josh said, "when they let black folks fight, we be ready. All we n-needs is a white man."

Every eye turned to Hurst. "Now, wait a minute, fellahs," he said, backing off. "I ain't fired a musket since—"

But Big Josh pressed on. "What 'b-bout all them things you say 'bout being p-partners?"

"And freeing our people?" Little Turby added.

"Ain't you said yourself there some things worth dying for?" Isaac added. Then an idea struck him.

Grinning slyly, Isaac placed his arm around Hurst's shoulders. "Lordy!" Isaac crowed. "Won't ole' Massur look good in blue and gold! Yes, sir. One of them officer uniforms, maybe with them gold frilly things on his shoulders, and his hat kind of cock' off to one side. See?"

Hurst studied his friends surrounding him, from familiar face to face, mortified, but contrite. Everyone grinned hopefully at him. Throughout the entire flight from Turkle, he'd wondered despairingly what was in store for him. Now he knew he would be digging ditches until the rules changed, at which time he would find himself dodging Minié balls and mortar shells. Yet, horrifying as that prospect seemed, he saw in it a kind of release. He examined the surrounding country, surely a fine place to live in better times, but now a hotbed of angry assassins skulking behind every tree. Nevertheless, however unforeseen, however willingly or unwillingly, he, like everyone else in this limitless land, was about to be swept up in the turbulent tides of history.

It was time to leave behind the half-formed, knotted dreams of a wounded boy and discover visions suitable for the complete man he had finally become.

"I don't care if I have to wear a private uniform," Durksen Hurst exclaimed. "We're going to win this war and free every slave in the country!"

The spontaneous uproar at this vow was so exuberant it startled the weary womenfolk working in the distance. Not even Isaac held back.

Deaf to the din, Hurst gazed lovingly at Antoinette, busy working the cook fire. Wearing a simple gingham dress, her skin sun-darkened through their perilous journey, she clearly hadn't stepped from any servant-driven carriage recently. Nonetheless, what he beheld was truly a vision, an absolute beauty.

His *DarkHorse* family had trudged many hard miles through the stygian labyrinth of yesterday. Along the way, Hurst saw the war tearing up the rich land, plowing the old tangled vines and wild brambles under to nurture abundant new harvests to sustain endless ages of greatness for people both white and black. Ahead he saw long stretches of violent downpour, of backwash flooding the landscape—its swift currents, nevertheless, accreting alluvial soil to nourish implacable roots. Fated also was bitter drought, yet the burning sunlight's radiant brilliance would succor hardy green buds.

His direction set, he took his first steps toward the new country. He, too, was free. Plantation-less, broke, a fugitive, yes, but at last he was worthy of her. He asked no more.

Acknowledgements

I would like to thank those who have elevated my life. First and foremost my wife, Janet, for her selfless, enduring encouragement over the years and for her remarkable insights. Thanks also to my friends and mentors Dick Friedrich and Angela Harris for their unwavering belief in my writing potential. And lastly, to my dedicated agent, Jeanie Loiacono at Loiacono Literary Agency, and my publisher, Sheri Williams at TouchPoint Press, for their belief in *The Lies That Bind*.

About the Author

Ed Protzel

The Lies That Bind is the first completed novel in Ed Protzel's *DarkHorse* trilogy. The story is based on his original screenplay, which was honored by the Missouri Playwrights Association. Ed has written five original screenplays for feature film and worked developing film scripts/projects for 20th Century Fox.

Ed's expertise is in the American tragicomedy movement, science fiction, and several historical periods.

He has bachelor's and master's degrees in English Literature/Creative Writing [University of Missouri-St. Louis, University of Hawaii].

Ed is married and lives in St. Louis, Missouri, where he writes and teaches college English.

Learn more about Ed at www.edprotzel.com.

Made in the USA
Charleston, SC
01 February 2016